PRAISE FOR JOEL C. ROSENBERG

"Joel Rosenberg has an uncanny talent for focusing his storytelling on real-world hot spots just as they are heating up. He has done it again in *The Kremlin Conspiracy*."

PORTER GOSS, *former director of the Central Intelligence Agency*

"Marcus Ryker rocks! Breakneck action, political brinksmanship, authentic scenarios, and sharply defined characters make Joel C. Rosenberg's *Kremlin Conspiracy* a full-throttle and frightening ride through tomorrow's headlines."

BRIGADIER GENERAL (U.S. ARMY, RETIRED) A. J. TATA, *national bestselling author of* Direct Fire

"Joel C. Rosenberg writes taut, intelligent thrillers that are as timely as they are well-written. Pairing a fast-paced plot with an impressive understanding of the inner workings in the corridors of power of the Russian government, *The Kremlin Conspiracy* is a stellar novel of riveting action and political intrigue."

MARK GREANEY, *#1* New York Times *bestselling author of* Agent in Place

"*The Kremlin Conspiracy* is my first Joel C. Rosenberg novel, and I am absolutely blown away by how good this guy is. The story moves at a blistering pace, it's crackling with tension, and you won't put it down until you reach the end. Guaranteed. Simply masterful."

SEAN PARNELL, New York Times *bestselling author of* Outlaw Platoon

"If there were a *Forbes* 400 list of great current novelists, Joel Rosenberg would be among the top ten. . . . One of the most entertaining and intriguing authors of international political thrillers in the country. . . . His novels are un-put-downable."

STEVE FORBES, *editor in chief,* Forbes *magazine*

"One of my favorite things: An incredible thriller—it's called *The Third Target* by Joel C. Rosenberg. . . . He's amazing. . . . He writes the greatest thrillers set in the Middle East, with so much knowledge of that part of the world. . . . Fabulous! I've read every book he's ever written!"

KATHIE LEE GIFFORD, *NBC's* Today

"Fascinating and compelling . . . way too close to reality for a novel."

MIKE HUCKABEE, *former Arkansas governor*

"[Joel Rosenberg] understands the grave dangers posed by Iran and Syria, and he's been a bold and courageous voice for true peace and security in the Middle East."

DANNY AYALON, *former Israeli deputy foreign minister*

"Joel has a particularly clear understanding of what is going on in today's Iran and Syria and the grave threat these two countries pose to the rest of the world."

REZA KAHLILI, *former CIA operative in Iran and bestselling author of* A Time to Betray: The Astonishing Double Life of a CIA Agent inside the Revolutionary Guards of Iran

"Joel Rosenberg is unsurpassed as the writer of fiction thrillers! Sometimes I have to remind myself to breathe as I read one of his novels because I find myself holding my breath in suspense as I turn the pages."

ANNE GRAHAM LOTZ, *author and speaker*

"Joel paints an eerie, terrifying, page-turning picture of a worst-case scenario coming to pass. You have to read [*Damascus Countdown*], and then pray it never happens."

RICK SANTORUM, *former U.S. senator*

THE PERSIAN GAMBLE

JOEL C. ROSENBERG

THE PERSIAN GAMBLE

Tyndale House Publishers, Inc.
Carol Stream, Illinois

Visit Tyndale online at www.tyndale.com.

Visit Joel C. Rosenberg's website at www.joelrosenberg.com.

TYNDALE and Tyndale's quill logo are registered trademarks of Tyndale House Publishers, Inc.

The Persian Gamble

Designed by Dean H. Renninger

Unless otherwise indicated, all Scripture quotations are taken from the New American Standard Bible,® copyright © 1960, 1962, 1963, 1968, 1971, 1972, 1973, 1975, 1977, 1995 by The Lockman Foundation. Used by permission.

John 14:6 in chapter 65 is taken from the New King James Version,® copyright © 1982 by Thomas Nelson, Inc. Used by permission. All rights reserved.

The Persian Gamble is a work of fiction. Where real people, events, establishments, organizations, or locales appear, they are used fictitiously. All other elements of the novel are drawn from the author's imagination.

For information about special discounts for bulk purchases, please contact Tyndale House Publishers at csresponse@tyndale.com or call 1-800-323-9400.

Library of Congress Cataloging-in-Publication Data
Names: Rosenberg, Joel C., date- author.
Title: The Persian gamble / Joel C. Rosenberg.
Description: Carol Stream, Illinois : Tyndale House Publishers, Inc., [2019]
Identifiers: LCCN 2018051043 | ISBN 9781496406187 (hc)
Subjects: LCSH: Terrorism—Prevention—Fiction. | GSAFD: Suspense fiction. | Christian
    fiction.
Classification: LCC PS3618.O832 P47 2019 | DDC 813/.6—dc23 LC record available at
    https://lccn.loc.gov/2018051043

ISBN 978-1-4964-0631-6 (International Trade Paper Edition)
ISBN 978-1-4964-0622-4 (Softcover)

Printed in the United States of America

25	24	23	22	21	20	19
7	6	5	4	3	2	1

To the noble, enslaved people of Persia, who have suffered four decades of cruel and bloodthirsty tyranny— may you soon breathe the sweet air of freedom.

CAST OF CHARACTERS

Americans

Marcus Ryker—*former U.S. Secret Service agent; former U.S. Marine*

Jennifer Morris—*CIA station chief, Moscow*

Nick Vinetti—*deputy chief of mission, U.S. Embassy, Moscow; former U.S. Marine*

William McDermott—*deputy national security advisor; former U.S. Marine*

Andrew Clarke—*president of the United States*

Robert Dayton—*U.S. senator (D-Iowa); member of the Senate Intelligence Committee*

Peter Hwang—*advisor to Senator Robert Dayton; former U.S. Marine*

Annie Stewart—*senior foreign policy advisor to Senator Robert Dayton*

Cal Foster—*U.S. secretary of defense*

Richard Stephens—*director of the Central Intelligence Agency*

Martha Dell—*deputy director of intelligence (DDI), Central Intelligence Agency*

Barry Evans—*U.S. national security advisor*

Tyler Reed—*ambassador, U.S. Embassy, Moscow*

Carter Emerson—*pastor, Lincoln Park Baptist Church, Washington, D.C.*

Marjorie Ryker—*Marcus's mother*
Curt Berenger—*commander of SEAL Team Six*
Héctor Sanchez—*Blue Team leader, SEAL Team Six*
Donny Callaghan—*Red Team leader, SEAL Team Six*

Russians

Oleg Stefanovich Kraskin—*senior aide and son-in-law to the late President Luganov*
Mikhail Borisovich Petrovsky—*minister of defense*
Maxim Grigarin—*prime minister*
Boris Zakharov—*former chief of staff to President Luganov*
Boris Yamirev—*deputy defense minister*
Nikolay Kropatkin—*deputy director of the FSB*
Marina Kraskin—*Oleg's wife; Luganov's daughter*

Iranians

Alireza al-Zanjani—*deputy commander of the Iranian Revolutionary Guard Corps*
Grand Ayatollah Hossein Ansari—*Supreme Leader of Iran*
Yadollah Afshar—*president of the Islamic Republic of Iran*
Mahmoud Entezam—*commander of the Iranian Revolutionary Guard Corps*
Haydar Abbasi—*director of Iran's missile program*

North Koreans

Hyong Ja Park—*Dear Leader of North Korea*
Yong-Jin Yoon—*deputy chief of military intelligence*

Others

Reuven Eitan—*prime minister of Israel*
Asher Gilad—*director of Mossad*

Abdulaziz bin Faisal—*minister of defense; heir to the throne of Saudi Arabia*

Abdullah bin Rashid—*director of Saudi Arabia's General Intelligence Directorate*

Khalid bin Ibrahim—*chief of intelligence for the United Arab Emirates*

Mohammed Yakub—*Pakistani nuclear physicist*

PART
ONE

Don't die, and don't get arrested.

Marcus Ryker hurtled through frigid darkness at terminal velocity as words from his childhood echoed through his head.

From the day he'd become a teenager, his mother had uttered these words to him more times than he could possibly remember. Every time he left for school. Every time he went out with friends. Every time he borrowed the car or hiked a fourteener or went white-water rafting. Marjorie Ryker knew her only son well. Marcus wasn't simply a kid who loved adventure and pushing all limits all the time. He was an adrenaline junkie, and she'd genuinely—and rightly—feared one misstep could prove catastrophic.

Now pushing forty, Marcus was free-falling through a thick band of cloud cover, somewhere over northwestern Russia. He could see nothing. Not the moon nor the stars. Not the twinkling lights of a single city or village or hamlet below. Nor could he hear a sound, save the steady hiss of the oxygen flowing into his helmet. He couldn't hear the air whipping past at 120 miles per hour. He couldn't even hear the scream of jet engines as six MiG fighters bore down on him from multiple angles at twice the speed of sound.

Only moments before, Marcus and his two colleagues had lunged out of the side of a Gulfstream IV at an altitude of eighteen thousand feet. Now they were quickly passing under ten thousand feet. But they had swerved far off their intended flight path before jumping. What actually lay below them now was anyone's guess.

To their left was the Gulf of Finland. Off to their right—*far* off, Marcus hoped—was Lake Ladoga. Were they to hit either body of water during the unseasonably early and intense blizzard engulfing the region, their fate would be sealed. They would freeze to death in minutes. Yet if his calculations were correct, they should more likely come down somewhere on a spit of land known as the Karelian Isthmus. That would still put them in Russian territory and thus in serious risk of being hunted down and found. Should that happen, he'd rather die than be arrested. But they could also land within striking distance of the Finnish border, giving them a shot at reaching safety.

In the early morning darkness, Marcus forced his mother's words from his thoughts and began mentally ticking through all the gear he'd asked the Agency to load onto the plane ahead of their escape. It would be all they'd have to keep them alive. There were a sniper rifle, an AK-47, and two pistols, all Russian-made. There was a box of ammunition, though certainly not enough to get them through more than limited contact with Russian forces. They had a handheld GPS unit and a satellite phone. They also had an all-weather tent, a hatchet, a hunting knife, ropes, three water bottles, a medical kit, matches, and—

A massive explosion erupted above them. The heat-seeking missiles had finally found their target. The dark sky was engulfed in a blinding fireball of searing orange and red. In moments, molten metal—remnants of the $40 million business jet—would begin raining down around them, and the icy earth was rushing up fast.

Plunging downward in a spread-eagle posture, Marcus wiped away the ice crystals forming on the altimeter strapped to his wrist. *Six thousand feet. Five thousand feet. Four thousand. Three thousand.* Had he been alone, he would have held out longer, until he was closer to the ground and far less likely to be spotted. But while Marcus had trained for HALO jumps during his stint in the Marines, the forty-six-year-old Russian at his side had not.

Oleg Kraskin—code-named the Raven—had served in the Red Army. He'd completed basic training but had gone on to work as a clerk in the office of military attorneys. He'd neither jumped out of a plane in his life nor imagined having to do so. Marcus had seen the terror in the man's eyes when he'd briefed him on the escape plan. But there was no other way. He needed the Raven alive, so the decision wasn't hard. Better they should pull their rip cords now than delay any further and risk a miscalculation that could prove fatal.

As they broke through the cloud cover around twenty-three hundred feet, Marcus spotted his Russian comrade thirty yards to his right and gave the signal that it was time.

There was no response.

Again Marcus signaled with a wave of his arms, but again Oleg neither acknowledged him nor opened his chute.

Something was wrong. Marcus had drilled into Oleg the few essential things he needed to remember to survive this jump. Why wasn't he responding?

Plunging beneath fifteen hundred feet, Marcus tried again to get the Russian's attention, to no avail. Now he had mere seconds to act. He could feel his heart rate spiking. A massive shot of adrenaline surged through his system. Pulling his arms to his sides and bringing his feet together, Marcus leaned right, cutting a path through the rushing wind and blowing snow. It was an awkward maneuver, made more so by the wounded woman slipping in and out of consciousness strapped to the front of his tandem jumpsuit, complicating his every move.

A moment later, Marcus slammed into Oleg's side. Still no response. The Raven had blacked out. Marcus forced himself to stay calm. Back in his earliest days in the Marines, during jump school at Parris Island, he had practiced helping a fellow diver in distress, though they'd never trained him to do so during a tandem jump. Marcus had no idea whether his canopy built for two could adequately slow the rate of descent for three jumpers without killing them all. But as he flipped on his night vision gear and got his bearings, he knew there was no other way.

They were coming down over land, not water. But below them were forests thick with snow-covered pines. Off to his left, Marcus could see a small clearing. He could steer to it if he deployed his own chute immediately. But if he pulled Oleg's rip cord first, he had no way to direct the Russian's descent. Oleg could easily get caught in trees sixty to eighty feet high, unreachable by Marcus from the ground. Or Oleg could simply become impaled on one of the soaring pines.

They were now passing below a thousand feet. Marcus maneuvered himself forward through the near-blinding snowfall, grabbed Oleg's harness with one gloved hand, and yanked the man toward him. Reaching into his vest with his other gloved hand, he drew out a carabiner and bound Oleg's harness to his own.

Eight hundred feet.

Seven hundred feet.

Now or never. Gripping Oleg with one hand as tightly as he could, Marcus pulled his own rip cord with the other. His chute instantly deployed. The metal fastener binding the two men held fast, so Marcus desperately tried to steer the three of them out of danger and toward the clearing he had spotted.

They didn't make it.

THREE MONTHS EARLIER

"You're not listening to me. I'm flying home tomorrow. I've done everything you've asked. But I'm not going to miss my daughter's wedding. Period. End of story."

The fifty-six-year-old physicist stood in the center of the corner suite on the fourth floor of the Electra Palace hotel. He was surrounded by banks of video monitors, recording devices, wireless receivers, and miles of electrical cords duct-taped to the plush carpet. He was surrounded, too, by nine men, each brandishing automatic weapons, all staring back at him.

His own eyes were bloodshot. His nerves were frayed. But his voice was defiant after months away from his lab and the sole remaining love of his life.

What he said was all true. Dr. Mohammed Yakub, one of the most important players in Pakistan's nuclear weapons program—a protégé of Abdul Qadeer Khan, whom he nearly worshiped as the "father of the Sunni Bomb"—had done everything they had asked of him. Actually, he had done quite a bit more.

He was being paid a small fortune for his efforts, and all of the funds were neatly stashed away in untraceable Swiss bank accounts. But Yakub had never been driven by money. He had put in eighteen- to twenty-hour days since his undergraduate life solely due to his pure love of science and his deep love of country. He'd helped Khan create a nuclear arsenal to protect Pakistan from India, from China, from the Soviets, from the Americans, and from anyone else who might seek to take advantage of them or even threaten their existence.

Now, however, he was a widower, and a recent one at that. He was the grieving father of an only child, a breathtakingly beautiful young woman who was not really a child any longer but who needed—and more importantly, *wanted*—her father at her side.

Yakub knew he was approaching his breaking point. He had not made any significant missteps in the negotiations thus far. But the more fatigued he became, the more anxious he became, the greater the risk he would lose focus and make not simply a mistake but one that could prove fatal.

"Mohammed, Mohammed," said the dark man sitting in the corner, holding a secure satellite phone in one hand. "You need to take a deep breath and trust me. I *am* listening to you, to every syllable, and I give you my word: I'm going to do everything in my power to ensure that you make it to your daughter's wedding. Indeed, I have booked reservations for you on six different flights over the next forty-eight hours. All first-class. Any one of them will get you there on time. So believe me when I tell you everything is going to work out just fine."

Slowly Yakub's irritation drained away, replaced by a profound sense of sadness. His shoulders sagged, and his eyes grew moist. "She's all I have left," he said, staring at his shoes.

The dark man stood and walked to the center of the room. "I

know, Mohammed, and I am sorry for your loss. We all are. Your wife was a remarkable woman. We were all fortunate to know her, however briefly."

"Thirty-seven years," Yakub said, shaking his head and taking a handkerchief from his pocket to dab his eyes. "Then one day you wake up, and she does not. You make all these plans for retirement, for your lives together when your child is grown and it's just the two of you. And then in a single, unspeakable moment . . ."

His voice, almost a whisper now, trailed off, and the room was silent.

"My daughter needs me," Yakub finally said, pocketing the cloth and composing himself.

"And come this time tomorrow," said the unit commander, a man half Yakub's age, "you'll be back in Islamabad, back in that lovely villa of yours, a rich man, hosting your new in-laws-to-be, and never having to think about any of . . . this . . . again."

Still, the man with three PhDs could not let it go. "What if he makes new demands?" Yakub pressed, looking up again, his eyes narrowing. "What if he quibbles over the changes we've already agreed to?"

"He won't."

"How can you be sure?"

"Because he wants this more than you do, Mohammed, and his superiors want this even more than he does," the commander said, stepping closer and grasping the physicist by his shoulders. "Trust me, sir. Tonight, you two are going to consummate this deal. You're going to shake hands. You're going to give him the bank codes. He's going to transfer the money. *Chick-chock.* Your part will be over, and my men will whisk you to the airport."

"You're certain of this?"

"Absolutely."

"Tonight?"

"No question."

Still the Pakistani was not completely convinced. "But you've made five other airline reservations," he said.

"Just in case," said the commander.

In case of what? Yakub thought, but he said no more.

Alireza al-Zanjani lit a fresh cigarette.

Dressed in a finely tailored Parisian suit, his jet-black hair slicked back with a touch of gel, he stared at the flame of the match for several seconds, then extinguished it with his thumb and forefinger. He glanced at his Rolex, then sat back and closed his eyes. It was nearly one in the morning. But there was no need to worry, he told himself. His guest would be on time, and it would all be over soon.

Though he had never been to Athens before, he refused to look out across the twinkling lights of the Greek capital from the rooftop restaurant on the fifth story of the five-star Electra Palace hotel. The stunning view of the Acropolis interested him not at all. The stars were out and the air was fresh. But he couldn't have cared less that the Parthenon stood before him, so close in the summer moonlight that he could nearly reach out and touch it. The "temple of the virgin goddess," built some five centuries before the birth of Christ, held no special fascination for him.

He was not a tourist. He had not come for the view. He was the newly appointed deputy commander of the Iranian Revolutionary Guard Corps, and he had come to finish the business his predecessor had not.

"Sir," one of his bodyguards whispered. "He's approaching."

Al-Zanjani opened his eyes, took another drag of his cigarette, then stood. He turned in time to see the diminutive Pakistani—wiry and habitually disheveled—stepping off the elevator, alone. The man was met by four IRGC operatives, all in suits far less expensive than that of their boss. They asked Yakub to show his ID. They instructed him to hand over his mobile phone and patted him down for weapons.

Satisfied, the head of the security team nodded and said in Farsi, "He's clean."

Finally, al-Zanjani thought. All of his painstaking work and exhaustive preparations had come down to this moment. He had the green light from his superiors back in Tehran. The time for talking was over. It was time to do business.

3

"Welcome, my friend," al-Zanjani said in heavily accented English.

His smile was wide, his open arms wider still. "Come, join me on the balcony."

He watched carefully as Dr. Mohammed Yakub crossed the restaurant. There were no patrons present, just an elderly manager and a lone waiter. Both stood off to the side, mute but ready to serve. The only other men in the large room were al-Zanjani's security detail, positioned at the two stairwells, by the door to the kitchen, and by the elevators.

As Yakub came closer, al-Zanjani saw the man's eyes riveted once again—as when they had first met months before—by the four-inch scar running down the left side of his face, only partially obscured by the thick beard. The Iranian no longer felt any physical discomfort from the scar but never failed to notice its effect on others.

When the Pakistani scientist reached the round table covered in a crisply starched white tablecloth and set for two, his smile seemed forced. He and al-Zanjani embraced and kissed each other on both cheeks.

"*Assalamu alaikum,*" said the Iranian, bidding his guest to take a seat.

"*Wa-alaikum assalam,*" Yakub replied, putting his hand to his heart and then taking his assigned chair.

Al-Zanjani wasted no time on small talk. "Let's be honest, my friend. There are only two ways for a nation to acquire atomic weapons," he said, almost in a whisper. "Build them or buy them."

"Well, maybe three," Yakub said softly. "One could always steal them."

The comment was clearly made in jest, but al-Zanjani neither laughed nor cracked a smile. He was not a lighthearted man to begin with, and in any case, this was not the night to indulge in humor. He ignored the remark and pressed on. His patience was thinning, and the hour was late. "The Western powers made us a very generous offer to persuade us to refrain from building nuclear weapons," he said. "Yet, remarkably, they never actually insisted that we refrain from purchasing them. They effectively gave us what amounts to $150 billion, and for what? To buy our assurances that we would stop enriching uranium for a decade? To rent our promise not to build any nuclear warheads? Why would we have said no? The whole thing was a farce. We were not even asked—how does the saying go?—to *sign on the dotted line.*"

"So, you took their money and came to me," the bespectacled Pakistani said.

"Of course we took the money—we're not fools, Mohammed," the Iranian replied, taking another drag on his cigarette. "Yet as I recall, you came to us."

"Well, that's true. I did."

"My question is this: Why did you choose to bestow upon my people such magnanimity?"

There was a long, awkward silence.

"Let's just say I saw an opportunity," the Pakistani finally replied. "Look, I've already told you, my retirement is fast approaching. My mentor, Dr. Khan, received all the glory for our work, and rightly so. I'm not looking for fame. I'm not looking to be heralded or even remembered. But after all I have given to my country, I deserve to live in comfort and provide my daughter and her husband a comfortable life. This is impossible on a government pension. So I asked for more. Khan said no. I went above him but was repeatedly told that I'd been paid handsomely and should be content. Well, I am not content. You can understand such a thing, can you not?"

"I can," al-Zanjani said.

"Of course you can. You're much younger than me, to be sure. But you're a husband. You're a father and a loyal government servant, too. You're not trying to get rich, or you would have chosen a different profession. But you like to dress nicely. You have an expensive watch. You clearly enjoy the finer things, as well you should."

The Iranian said nothing.

"But that's not all," Yakub added. "It's not just about the money. I find myself seething that no one has stood up to the Zionists. No one has really shown them their place. Maybe you can. And if I can play some small part, then all the better. So, my friend, enough talk. Let's get this thing done."

The Iranian nodded. "Let's."

"If you're ready to move the money, my colleagues and I are ready to move the merchandise immediately."

"The money is ready."

"Very good," Yakub said, reaching into his pocket to fetch a folded piece of paper, which he handed to al-Zanjani. "The banking details," he said. "It's all there."

"Fine," al-Zanjani said as he slipped the paper into his breast pocket without opening it. "And yet my superiors have some concerns."

Yakub looked confused. "Concerns?"

"Tehran wants ironclad guarantees."

"I told you before," Yakub said, "we can get you the first ten warheads within twenty-four hours of receipt of payment and the next ten within ten business days. I can't do any better than—"

"No," al-Zanjani interrupted, speaking more forcefully than he'd intended. "We need other assurances."

"Assurances?" Yakub's hands were now clasped together as if to keep them from shaking. "What about the assurance you gave me? You know I'm taking an enormous risk meeting you here. You insisted I come, yet you *assured* me that if we met in person, we could complete this deal once and for all tonight."

"And so we shall," al-Zanjani said. "I just need you to answer one simple question."

"What question is that?"

"Are you working for the Israelis?"

The blood suddenly drained from Yakub's face. "What are you talking about?" the Pakistani stammered.

"You heard me."

"I heard you. I just don't believe you."

"That's not exactly a denial, now is it, Mohammed?"

"Have you gone mad?"

"It's a simple question. Yet you haven't answered it."

"I'm not going to play any more games with you. Do you want my merchandise or not?"

For the first time in all the months they had been negotiating this deal, al-Zanjani smiled. He'd seen the Pakistani's photographs of twenty gleaming new nuclear warheads. He'd seen the blueprints of the bombs, the specifications, the schematics, the mountains of test results. He'd listened to Yakub explain how his people would sneak the weapons out of Pakistan, through the mountains of Afghanistan, and into Iran. He'd seen his previous boss salivate at it all, as had their superiors in Tehran. It had all seemed so promising, this offer to bypass years of expensive and exhausting technical development—and setbacks—in a single, seamless transaction.

Yet al-Zanjani had never believed any of it. He just hadn't been able to prove any of his suspicions. Until now.

He took a final drag on his cigarette, snuffed it out on the sole of one of his handcrafted Italian loafers, then stood. As he did, he unbuttoned his jacket, drew a silenced pistol, aimed it at the Pakistani's forehead, and squeezed the trigger. With a puff of pink mist, the man slumped to the ground.

"*Not*," al-Zanjani said, nearly under his breath.

He turned on the wide-eyed manager and waiter standing near the kitchen doorway. He double-tapped them both to the chest, then pulled a mobile phone from his pocket, speed-dialed a colleague, and said, "Now."

From the roof of a darkened office building adjacent to the Electra, six rocket-propelled grenades came sizzling through the night sky. One by one they smashed through the windows of the corner suite one floor below al-Zanjani and his men. The ensuing explosions made the hotel rock and sway, nearly knocking the Iranians off their feet. Moments later, al-Zanjani heard machine-gun fire erupt in the hallway below. He closed his eyes and imagined the survivors of the corner suite crawling through the smoke and debris, groping their way to safety, only to be cut down by his team, lying in wait.

Again he smiled. Then he glanced at his watch one last time and counted silently—*one, two, three, four*—and then another massive explosion split the night. The Iranian casually strode to the edge of the balcony and looked down to find a white rented van that had been parked across the street from the hotel, now a twisted pile of flaming metal.

The mobile phone in al-Zanjani's hand rang. He answered it immediately.

"It is finished," said the voice at the other end.

On the contrary, the Iranian said to himself. *It has only just begun.*

4

The Mi-8 transport helicopter touched down just before four in the afternoon.

Alireza al-Zanjani stepped out into the sunshine carrying a single overnight bag. He was glad to stretch his stiff legs and pleased to be back at the heavily guarded air base nestled in a densely wooded valley outside the city of Kusŏng, North Korea. Just over seven weeks had passed since his final encounter with Dr. Yakub in Athens. Now he was on the brink of completing his mission and fulfilling his nation's dreams at last.

Al-Zanjani was immediately welcomed and saluted by General Yong-Jin Yoon, a three-star who had served for the past three years as North Korea's deputy chief of military intelligence. The Iranian returned the salute and shook the man's hand. Having made this exact trip a dozen times over the past several years, there was no need to be introduced to the general's driver or young translator. Instead, the men climbed into the back of the general's sedan.

"I trust your trip was pleasant, Mr. Ali," the general said as they drove off the tarmac onto a service road.

Al-Zanjani smiled at the nickname chosen by Yoon upon their first meeting in the general's main suite of offices in Pyongyang. "To be honest with you, it was a nightmare."

Except he wasn't being honest. Al-Zanjani had started his journey more than a week earlier and had loved nearly every minute. To cover his tracks and elude any and all foreign intelligence agencies, he'd left Tehran alone, traveling without a security detail. He'd flown first to Venezuela. For that leg, he'd used the alias of a South African businessman, complete with a disguise and fake passport. After spending several lovely days lounging by the pool at the home of a dear childhood friend whose father was the Iranian ambassador in Caracas, he'd flown to Johannesburg, where he'd enjoyed several days at the sumptuous Four Seasons, dining at the finest restaurants and nightclubs, all at the IRGC's expense. The call girls and the liquor he'd happily paid for out of his own pocket.

From there, he had switched identities and begun using a separate set of forged passports, flying to Moscow and meeting with several of his counterparts in Russian intelligence, members of President Luganov's inner circle whom he liked very much and trusted implicitly. Then it was on to Beijing, where he'd spent twenty-four hours making certain no one was on his tail. That morning, he'd awoken early, gone for a long run before the heat and smog became unbearable, then showered, had a light breakfast, and enjoyed a massage before finally heading for the airport and boarding an aging Tupolev twin-engine jetliner that felt like it was being held together with bobby pins and duct tape. Upon deplaning in the North Korean capital, he'd been met by an air force colonel who had whisked him to a waiting chopper for the brief hop to Panghyon.

So why hadn't al-Zanjani simply said all that to his North Korean colleague? The general could certainly be trusted. They were working together on the most sensitive of secrets. Surely the Iranian's travel schedule was not something the general would leak or use against him. Yet even as he flat-out lied to a man he had come to consider a friend, he found himself asking this very question.

Al-Zanjani was a spy. He lied for a living. It ought never trouble him, even in the slightest—and yet it did now. He wasn't sure why. Perhaps it was as simple as common courtesy. Al-Zanjani knew full well the general was not just his elder. The man was far more intelligent than he, far more experienced, more clever, more shrewd. Yet the man had no hope of advancement. No ability to travel. No chance to line his own pockets or enjoy a bit of the good life at his government's expense. Yong-Jin Yoon was a good man, a loyal man, a patriot. But he was a North Korean. He didn't own a passport. He'd never set foot on foreign soil. He was forbidden from owning a satellite dish or even a shortwave radio. He was, indeed, trapped in the single most bizarre social and political system al-Zanjani had ever encountered in his global travels.

Soon they reached the launchpad in the northwest quadrant of the sprawling military base.

"There she is," said the general, beaming. "Meet the Hwasong-17."

Al-Zanjani was genuinely astonished. "She's massive."

Gleaming in the late afternoon sun stood the most advanced intercontinental ballistic missile the North had ever developed. It was nearly eighty feet tall, a good six feet taller than the previous model al-Zanjani had seen. Admittedly, he had hoped to see the liquid-fueled missile set up on a mobile launcher rather than mounted on a fixed launcher.

The general said they were still building nine-axle vehicles with both the grit and the horsepower to move such a beast. "As you'll recall, the last model proved unfit for the task. We believe we are close to a better design—perhaps a few months—but given your visit, we wanted to be fully ready for this latest test."

"You are most kind," al-Zanjani said.

"Not at all—it is your Supreme Leader who is the gracious one," the general demurred. "He never ceases to show us great honor and respect, paying for this test, as he has for so many others, supporting the work of our scientists and the most special projects on which they toil night and day. He is a great friend of our people, and his wish is our command."

The Iranian accepted the acknowledgment without comment, then asked to meet with the chief engineer and the commander of launch control. He'd been tasked with gathering and bringing back to Iranian Space Command and the minister of defense the minutest of details on Hwasong-17. There was speculation back in Tehran that this just might be the last test that would be needed. If that proved true, then those above him needed to know not only each and every technical improvement the North Koreans had made to the rocket and its guidance systems but every tweak they had made to the staging and launching of the rocket as well.

As with every missile test over the past several years, such precious data could not be safely transmitted by phone or over the Internet. The Americans and the Zionists were far too sophisticated at intercepting communications. There was too great a chance the data would wind up in their hands. Washington, in turn, would hand it over to the U.N., to the media. Or the Zionists would leak it. One way or another, Iran would be exposed. They would lose the moral high ground they'd achieved during the negotiations with the international community that had led to the Joint Comprehensive Plan of Action, or JCPOA. Worse, they would lose the element of surprise, and that would be the most egregious sin of all.

Thus, it had fallen to him, Alireza al-Zanjani, born the ninth of twelve children to a poor but deeply religious family in a small village in the Zanjan province of northwestern Iran, to be the courier responsible for bringing such precious jewels safely home to a high command counting the minutes until their arrival. He knew full well he was an unlikely choice for this critical assignment. Humanly speaking, he had no place serving the highest levels of the regime. There were others from prominent families in prominent cities who were far more qualified than he. Yet he also knew this was not the luck of the draw or a mere twist of fate. He had been chosen by Allah for this role and thus for every mission that came with the title of deputy commander of the Revolutionary Guard Corps. No other explanation for his meteoric rise could possibly suffice, al-Zanjani knew, and the knowledge gave him both a sense of calm when facing new and complex challenges and a conviction that he was destined for even greater things to come.

5

"How much time do we have?" al-Zanjani asked the launch director.

"A little under three hours," the director replied, his face impassive, as if he had all the time in the world.

Satisfied, al-Zanjani nodded and turned back to his host. "Perhaps we should let these men complete their tasks," he told the general. "We can return when the countdown is about to begin."

"Very well," said General Yoon. "Would you care to join me for dinner?"

"I'd love to."

While technicians scurried about making final preparations for the launch—and well-armed sentries with shoot-to-kill orders patrolled the grounds to keep everything secure—the two men retreated to the dusty sedan. They were driven the three kilometers back to head-quarters in silence as al-Zanjani scribbled notes in his small leather-bound notebook.

In the general's office, they took their seats at a small conference table, alone, save the North Korean's translator. The three men enjoyed a meal together of brown rice, spicy kimchi, and traditional bulgogi, which the chef who served them proudly explained was made of marinated strips of fresh beef. Al-Zanjani would have bet his entire year's salary the meat was, in fact, freshly slaughtered dog, but he said nothing. He simply ate what was set in front of him without comment. This visit was the most important and certainly the most sensitive of any he had made thus far.

"General, please forgive me for not saying this sooner," al-Zanjani said as they ate. "I bring you and your colleagues personal greetings from my colleagues in Tehran. They asked me to convey to you and the Dear Leader that they are most encouraged by the progress your missile program has achieved. We are deeply grateful for all the data you have provided us from these test launches. As we had hoped, your findings have been immensely valuable to us in improving the payload, range, and accuracy of our own missiles, and we have no doubt today's test will prove decisive."

The general smiled graciously but said nothing.

"That said," al-Zanjani continued, "I must confess that I am not here merely for tonight's launch, important as it is."

"No?" the North Korean replied, looking up from his food for the first time.

"In all candor, I have come with a shopping list," the Iranian said. "And a great deal of cash."

"But you brought only one suitcase off the plane."

"True enough. Perhaps it's more precise to say I came with a new credit card."

"What are you shopping for?"

Al-Zanjani took a sip of tea, then set the cup aside.

"It is a delicate subject but one that comes directly from the highest authority in my government," he began, knowing full well that everything he was saying was being recorded and that this conversation would almost certainly be listened to by the Dear Leader himself, likely within the next twenty-four hours.

"The Islamic Republic of Iran is our truest friend and brother. What is it that we can do for you?"

"Thank you, General. And rest assured that the DPRK is our most revered ally. We take deep pride that we have been able to invest so heavily in the development of your ICBM program as well as your research and development efforts to build atomic weapons."

"However . . . ?" the North Korean pressed.

Al-Zanjani nodded. "However . . . the deal we made with the Americans and the entire P5+1 now precludes us, as you know, from building nuclear weapons. Thus, while the information you have supplied has been most helpful, we have come to a crossroads."

He paused for a moment. He'd discussed this very speech with the head of the Revolutionary Guard Corps, with the president, even the Supreme Leader. What's more, he had rehearsed it for the past week, en route to the hermit kingdom. Yet now he hesitated, fearful lest he inadvertently discomfort or even insult his Asian allies whose cultural sensibilities were so different from his own.

"Please speak freely," the general said. "You are among friends."

"Very well. My government has sent me with a sensitive and confidential request. It must not become public. Not now. Not ever. This is for your ears only and as few people as necessary to relay the request directly to the Dear Leader."

"Of course. You have my full discretion and that of our most senior officials."

"Thank you," al-Zanjani said. "I have been tasked with requesting that the Islamic Republic of Iran be permitted to purchase from you some twenty nuclear warheads. We are prepared to be generous both in terms of cash, food commodities, and oil to compensate for these weapons. And we would like to take possession of them no later than the end of this year."

"Why the rush?" the general asked.

"To this question I have not been authorized to give a reply other than to say your understanding in this matter would not go unnoticed or unappreciated."

The general sat back in his seat. Then he said, "To tell you the truth, Ali, my government has been expecting this request ever since we read about what happened in Athens."

Al-Zanjani visibly tensed, but General Yoon immediately put him at ease.

"Relax. I am authorized to say we are not entirely unfavorable to the idea."

The Iranian brightened.

Two hours later, the deal could hardly be considered done, but it was certainly moving forward, and it was all al-Zanjani could do to mask his euphoria. More questions would be asked, and he would need to return home to get the appropriate answers. But for the first time, the contours of a deal were taking shape.

For now, however, there was other business at hand.

The two men were driven to the observation post, where they donned the appropriate goggles to protect their eyes from the fireball to come. At the appointed hour, they stood in awe as North Korea's most advanced ballistic missile surged into the air and arced over Japan, deep into the Pacific, without flaw, without malfunction. There it was, al-Zanjani thought. With much hardship, many mistakes, and boatloads of Iranian cash, Pyongyang had finally done it. They had not only built operational nuclear warheads. They had also built and successfully tested an ICBM that could now reach every American state and Washington, D.C. as well.

And soon enough, al-Zanjani realized, Tehran would have the same capability.

6

Asher Gilad landed at Heathrow just after six in the morning.

Arriving on a private, unmarked jet from Tel Aviv, the sixty-three-year-old head of Mossad and his four-man security detail were not met by anyone from the Israeli embassy for one simple reason: neither the Israeli ambassador to the U.K. nor any of his associates had been notified that Gilad was coming. The welcome committee consisted of a single advance man from the Israeli intelligence service, and he greeted them all with umbrellas as he whisked them into a black, bulletproof Mercedes van for the long drive into London.

Typical rush hour traffic would have been bad enough, but today thick fog and a cold, driving rain made the trip all the worse. It was nearly eight o'clock when they finally arrived at the Four Seasons at Park Lane, the posh five-star hotel located near Buckingham Palace and the Court of St. James's. The team entered discreetly through a side entrance. Gilad, walking with the aid of a beautifully carved cane, proceeded to the presidential suite on the fifth floor with its rosewood-paneled walls and typically stunning views of Hyde Park, though the mist was now obscuring most of it. There the security team swept the room for listening devices, switched on the gas fireplace, ordered room service, and set up their communications gear.

By eleven, Gilad had finished his preparations and his egg-white omelet with bangers and mash. He had completed a lengthy secure call with Prime Minister Reuven Eitan and the Security Cabinet, made sure their breakfast dishes had all been bussed away, ordered new pots of Earl Grey tea and Colombian coffee and fresh fruit, and was ready to greet his guests.

The first to arrive was Khalid bin Ibrahim. Known by his initials, KBI, the fifty-three-year-old was the chief of intelligence for the United Arab Emirates and a nephew of one of the UAE's most powerful sheikhs. The two greeted each other warmly with an embrace and a kiss on each cheek in a manner befitting the depth and breadth of their friendship. Though it was not known by the public—and certainly never reported in the press—the Israeli and Emirati spymasters had been working together in the shadows for almost two decades now, safeguarding their countries from common enemies despite the fact that their governments had still not formally recognized one another, much less signed a peace treaty. Unless and until the Israelis and Palestinians found a way to resolve their long-standing conflict, the leaders of the UAE felt they could not openly acknowledge the Jewish state. Nevertheless, over time the emirs had come to regard the Israelis as key allies against their most serious enemy—the mullahs of Iran—and no one had played a more critical role in building that once-unthinkable bridge of friendship and mutual trust than Asher Gilad and KBI.

Soon, Gilad's second guest arrived. At seventy-one, Prince Abdullah bin Rashid was not only the director of Saudi Arabia's General

Intelligence Directorate, he was also a member of the royal family and one of the most trusted advisors to Crown Prince Abdulaziz bin Faisal, the young heir to the throne. Dressed in a well-tailored charcoal-gray suit rather than the flowing white robes and red-checkered kaffiyeh he typically wore back in Riyadh, Prince Abdullah did not embrace Gilad, though he did shake his hand warmly. The two had, after all, only first met each other in person a few years earlier and had only begun to correspond with one another and speak by phone more frequently in the last eighteen months.

The decades-long cold war between Israel and the Saudis was finally thawing. Still, Gilad's relationship with Prince Abdullah was nowhere near as developed as with KBI, though he hoped it would be someday. Indeed, Gilad increasingly believed it was possible—perhaps even likely—that their countries could stun the world by officially making peace, opening embassies in each other's capitals, and linking their economies in a way that could transform the region. This was Gilad's private passion, and he believed the sooner it could happen, the better.

Peace, however, was not on the morning's agenda.

War—specifically war with Iran—was.

"Thank you, gentlemen, for agreeing to meet with me on such short notice," the Mossad chief began as they took their seats on the plush gray couches beside the roaring fire. "As you know, forty-eight hours ago, the North Koreans successfully tested their longest-range ballistic missile to date. They claim the launch was not a missile but merely a rocket designed to put communications satellites into orbit. But my government certainly does not believe that, and I suspect you do not either."

Both men nodded.

"What concerns us most," Gilad continued, "is not simply that North Korean ICBMs could now hit all of our cities and yours—not to mention London, Paris, New York, Washington, and Los Angeles. This would be serious enough. But that we have conclusive new evidence that Iran is funding *all* of Pyongyang's research and development for its missile program and nuclear weapons, all as a way of getting around the JCPOA."

As he spoke, Gilad handed out a thick stack of Farsi documents stapled to translations in Arabic and English. "I have been authorized to tell you both that we have a source in Tehran. In the last few days, the source was able to provide us with extraordinary and previously unknown details regarding the chilling degree to which the Iranians are cheating on the nuclear deal and feverishly trying to accelerate their race to the Bomb."

The men took the documents and began to read through them. As they did, the Israeli intelligence chief got up and served them tea and plates of fruit. Though he winced from the pain in his knees, he waved off his aides who offered to help him. This he was going to do himself.

"How exactly did you get these?" asked KBI, marveling at what he was looking at.

"You know I can't tell you that."

"But they're from inside the office of the Supreme Leader," KBI continued. "There can't be two dozen people in all of Iran who have access to this stuff."

"All the more reason I can't talk about it," Gilad said. "But as you can see, Tehran is using the North Koreans to completely bypass the JCPOA, and they are doing so with a level of urgency that we find of great concern."

"We're hearing rumors the Russians are pressuring Pyongyang to give up its entire nuclear program," KBI said. "If that really happens, the Persians won't be able to use North Korea as their test lab anymore."

"We're hearing that too," Gilad confirmed. "But these documents make clear that if Pyongyang stops testing warheads and missiles, Tehran will turn off the spigot of cash."

"It may not matter," said Prince Abdullah.

"Why not?" Gilad asked.

The Saudi spymaster reached into his briefcase, pulled out several eight-by-ten black-and-white photographs, and set them on the table. They were grainy and not entirely in focus, but there was no question who was in them. The first showed Alireza al-Zanjani shaking hands with General Yong-Jin Yoon. The second showed the deputy director of the Iranian Revolutionary Guard Corps and the deputy chief of North Korean military intelligence together in the backseat of a military vehicle of some kind. A third showed the two men exiting the vehicle.

"When were these taken?" Gilad asked.

"Two days ago," the prince replied.

"Where?"

"At a North Korean missile testing facility not far from Pyongyang."

"Which one?" KBI asked.

"Panghyon Air Base."

"How did you get these?" Gilad asked.

The Saudi stroked his gray beard and shrugged slightly. "You have your secrets; we have ours," he said. "The point, gentlemen, is that al-Zanjani just returned to Tehran with all the data from the latest missile test. This means the Persians now have everything they need to improve their own ICBMs to the point they can reach London, New York, and Washington. My staff estimates that if Ayatollah Ansari commits enough funding—and we have no reason to believe he will not—the Iranians could build and deploy fully operational long-range missiles by the end of this year. We know from the sting operation you were running in Athens, Asher—and again, I'm so sorry for the men that you lost—"

Gilad winced. The wounds were still fresh. But the prince continued.

"—as painful and costly as it was to learn it, we now know what we have long feared: the Persians have significantly ramped up their efforts to acquire off-the-shelf nuclear warheads and the missiles to deliver them. Rather than wait for the JCPOA to run its course and then restart their enrichment program when the sunset provisions kick in, they are racing for the finish line as we speak. The question is why. What's driving them to move so hard and so fast right now? Why take the risk of being caught and exposed by the international community? Who might they turn to next? And what are we going to do to stop them?"

7

Oleg Kraskin felt like a trapped animal.

Had the then-up-and-coming corporate lawyer known he would be marrying into a nation's leading crime family, he would never have proposed to the daughter of Aleksandr Ivanovich Luganov. But he had not known. Nor had he even suspected such a thing. He had met Marina Luganova in university. They had become acquaintances, then friends, and in time they had fallen madly in love.

From the very beginning, Oleg had known Marina's father was the head of the FSB, Russia's internal security services. But he had honestly given it little thought at the time, and how could he possibly have foreseen that the man would rise to become not only the next president of the Russian Federation but a crime boss and a modern czar? And how could he have known that his future father-in-law would draft him into government service the very day he asked the man for his daughter's hand in marriage? Or anticipated being recruited to serve at Luganov's right hand, giving Oleg a front-row seat to witness—and worse, to participate in—such terrible crimes almost from the moment he was ensconced in the vortex of Russian political power?

People didn't say no to Aleksandr Ivanovich Luganov. Not if they wanted to live. And for the better part of two decades, Oleg had wanted to live. So he had kept his head down and played the cards he'd been dealt. He wasn't proud of it. In fact, he had become deeply ashamed, and thus his calculus was rapidly changing.

Oleg was surprised to feel the landing gear engage. Checking his watch, he found it was approaching noon. Luganov's plane soon touched down at Heijo Field, an air force base along the Taedong River in the heart of the North Korean capital. Before long, they were taxiing toward a secure hangar surrounded by both Russian and DPRK Special Forces units on high alert. Inside the hangar, a nineteen-vehicle motorcade awaited their arrival, ready to whisk them to the palace of the Dear Leader for a press conference that Oleg knew would shock the world.

He turned and looked out the rain-streaked window. It was a gray, drizzly morning in Pyongyang. The temperature was in the midfifties and was only supposed to reach sixty-two that afternoon. A thick fog hovered ominously over the river and the cityscape beyond it. Just then a thought came to Oleg that had never before occurred to him. It was only a seed, really, a kernel of an idea. But as he processed it, the fog in his brain slowly began to lift. For the first time since entering the Luganov orbit, he thought he just might see a way out.

What if he simply defected?

Oleg had already made contact with the Americans. He had already given former Secret Service agent Marcus Ryker highly classified information, including the very war plan by which Luganov was preparing to invade three NATO countries within the next few days. Oleg had no doubt Ryker was passing the information on to the Central Intelligence Agency, who would surely share it with President Clarke and the National Security Council. He desperately hoped it would force their hand, deploying additional U.S. and NATO forces and matériel to Estonia, Latvia, and Lithuania in quantities sufficient to forestall Luganov's troops and force him to call off the war. But even if it did not, Oleg knew his father-in-law would realize someone had leaked the plans. A mole hunt would ensue. How could it not lead to him?

To stay in Moscow was to face discovery and certain death, Oleg now concluded. To flee, or attempt to, was risky beyond measure, but it appealed more to Oleg with each passing minute.

There was at its core, however, a complication, and it was not an insignificant one. If he asked Ryker to help him escape the borders of Russia before war came, he might save himself. But what of the motherland he loved? Was it not selfish to think solely of his own fate and not that of the 143 million countrymen he counted so precious? Not to mention his family. What if the Americans did not believe the intelligence he had just risked his life to give them? What if they dithered or outright refused to take action to deter Luganov from invasion? These were distinct possibilities. America was the world's only superpower, but her government was not exactly known for acting decisively. Was passing along such critical information enough? Did he not have an obligation to try to stop the madness his father-in-law was setting into motion? Almost certainly yes, he told himself. But how?

Such thoughts were tantamount to treason, he knew full well. Yet by the time he got into the armor-plated stretch limousine, directly across from the Russian leader who was making final notes on the text of his speech, Oleg could think of nothing else.

The motorcade roared away from the airport.

They raced through the rain-soaked streets—cleared of all rush-hour traffic—and arrived at the Ryongsong Residence. The opulent, sprawling palace served as both home and office for the reclusive and bizarre North Korean leader. Surrounded by massive concrete walls, soaring guard towers, and miles of barbed wire, along with swaths of minefields bordered by tanks and armored personnel carriers every-where, the complex was patrolled by thousands of heavily armed troops, an elite class of Praetorian guards. Yet as the motorcade approached, the gates swung open, and everyone Oleg could see was standing at attention for the first-ever state visit of the Russian president.

Back in the spring of 2009, Luganov had first met Hyong Ja Park, the newly installed and very young president of North Korea, a man who insisted upon being called "Dear Leader" or "Great Leader" or "the Savior" or "the Ever-Victorious, Iron-Willed Commander" or "the Guiding Star of the Twenty-First Century." Indeed, Oleg remembered being at his father-in-law's side as a young aide, taking notes and forging relationships with several North Korean officials, including a young colonel named Yong-Jin Yoon.

That had been a secret meeting, held on a Russian military base in Vladivostok. The "Highest Incarnation of the Revolutionary Comradely Love" had traveled by train because he was too paranoid to fly. This time was different.

For starters, the entire international press corps had been alerted, and most were broadcasting Luganov's arrival live around the globe. What's more, the last time, Luganov had been trying to quietly flip Pyongyang's allegiance from Beijing to Moscow, offering massive incentives—bribes, really, Oleg knew—to help tip the scales. The Dear Leader had said yes to it all, but the agreement had been kept under wraps, hidden from the international community.

This time, everything had changed. The two men were not only ready but eager to go public with the alliance they had been building for a decade. But first Luganov wanted to meet privately to discuss a matter he had not previously raised.

8

The security detail led them into Hyong Ja Park's immense office.

Looking left, Oleg was impressed by the floor-to-ceiling windows—no doubt bulletproof—overlooking a lush, apparently uninhabited forest. To the right, he couldn't help but notice the large and exquisitely painted portraits of Park's father and grandfather hanging on the wall over a roaring fireplace.

What intrigued Oleg most, however, was the contrast between the two principals as they embraced each other warmly before the pool of photographers, all of whom were ushered out of the room the moment the photo op was complete.

Neither of the principals was a tall man. Luganov, in his late sixties, stood only about five and a half feet tall yet was at least four inches taller and thirty years older than the North Korean. Luganov's taut, oval, clean-shaven face was hard and impassive. The man was in as impressive physical shape as when Oleg had met him nearly two decades earlier. His eyes were pale and milky blue, devoid of emotion. They were, Oleg had come to learn all too well, the eyes of a killer, and he longed for the day when he would never see them again.

The Dear Leader's eyes were chocolate brown. Behind his retro, horn-rimmed glasses, they seemed giddy, brimming with an almost-childlike joy as their owner firmly shook Oleg's hand and warmly welcomed him to Pyongyang. The man had an immense head, a round, flat face, a double chin, and thin, jet-black hair. He was a soft, pudgy man of wide girth and doughy hands, clad in a dark Mao suit and freshly polished black shoes, and he could hardly hide his enthusiasm in having the czar of Moscow in his home.

"President Luganov, you have bestowed upon me and my people a very great honor by making your first-ever state visit to Pyongyang and coming here to the Ryongsong Residence," he said when the two men had taken their places directly across from each other at a long and ornate mahogany conference table, surrounded by their foreign ministers, generals, and senior staff. "In your honor, I have declared this a national holiday. All of our factories are closed, as are our schools and universities, shops, restaurants, and other places of business."

"It is very special to be here, Dear Leader, for today you and I will make history," the Russian leader replied as a steward served tea. "This is an alliance we began working on a decade ago. We took our time. We built the appropriate infrastructure. We got to know each other over many calls and private meetings in places other than here and in Moscow. But now we have come to a critical moment. No longer will you or your people ever have to concern yourself with the prospect of an attack above the thirty-eighth parallel—not by the Americans or anyone else. When we sign this treaty in a few minutes, the DPRK will formally and officially become a strategic ally of the Russian Federation. Any attack on you will be regarded as an attack upon us. And should this ever happen, I assure you that the Russian people will respond with the full might and fury of the greatest nuclear arsenal the world has ever seen."

All the officials on the other side of the table burst into applause.

"I have the greatest confidence in you, my friend," the Dear Leader responded through a translator, his plump face beaming. "And you have my personal pledge that as of this day, the DPRK is wholly committed to serving as the Pacific partner of the expanding Russian Empire. The world does not see what is coming, but they will. In due time—indeed, not that long from now—they will, and what a glorious day that will be."

"We have come a long way from our first meeting," Luganov noted.

"We have," said the North Korean. "I want to especially thank you for all of the scientists and technical assistance you have provided since then. As you know, our most recent missile test of the Hwasong-17 was completely successful, making it effectively comparable to your SS-18 ICBM. This now gives us the capability of hitting any target in the United States, or anywhere else in the world, delivering a payload of far greater devastation than anything we've been able to do heretofore."

"Yes, I have been briefed on this, Dear Leader, and let me just say that I couldn't be more thrilled about this development. It is a testimony to how much we can accomplish when we work together, and you are correct when you say neither the Americans nor the rest of the world powers see what is coming."

"The day of reckoning is fast approaching," the Dear Leader said.

Luganov nodded. "It is indeed. Have I ever told you what nickname the Pentagon has given to our signature SS-18 long-range ballistic missile?"

"I don't believe you have."

"They call it the *Satan*—how appropriate, no?"

The North Korean roared with laughter. Actually, both men did. It was one of the few times Oleg had ever seen his father-in-law laugh, but as he took down every word in his notebook, he felt as if he was going to be violently ill.

"Have you seen the warheads I sent you?"

Luganov asked the question when they had both regained their composure.

"Not yet," said the North Korean. "But my generals assured me that they did all arrive last night, by train, intact. I want to say to you how profoundly grateful I am. This gesture speaks volumes about your illustrious character and the depths of our partnership that you would deliver all twenty state-of-the-art weapons even before we have signed the treaty."

"The treaty only codifies the trust we have already forged," Luganov demurred. "No one fully understands just how powerful your new missiles are—no one but our friends in Tehran, that is, because we will soon bring their missiles up to the same standard. More importantly, though, after today, the world will believe that you have given up your entire nuclear arsenal and your entire nuclear industry. They have no idea that we have secretly provided you with twenty warheads that are among our most powerful."

"Seven hundred and fifty kilotons each, I understand."

"Precisely," Luganov said, "more than two and a half times as powerful as the last warhead you tested."

"You honor us greatly with your tremendous generosity," the Dear Leader said. "Everything is about to change."

The Russian nodded. "How true. Which brings me to a favor I must ask for before we begin the press conference."

"Whatever you wish, my friend," the North Korean responded. "What is it that you would ask of me?"

Luganov paused and took a sip of tea, and Oleg took a moment to look around the room. Due to strict rules of protocol, neither he nor his father-in-law had been introduced to the Dear Leader's advisors. Indeed, they had all entered after the press pool had been escorted out. Now, however, Oleg studied each face, trying to match them to the names on the single-spaced, typed guest list resting on the plate before him. He recognized only a few from his previous trip.

But there was one face he recognized immediately—Yong-Jin Yoon. Once a colonel and a personal military aide to the Dear Leader, Yoon had been Oleg's chief point of contact with the regime during the past decade, and Oleg had watched as Yoon had been repeatedly promoted over the years. Today, he not only held the rank of three-star general, but he was also the DPRK's deputy director of military intelligence. Given the poor health of his boss, Yoon was effectively the acting director of his ministry.

On paper, Yoon was outranked by every other North Korean in the room. Thus, he was seated at the far end of the table. Officially, North Korea's prime minister, defense minister, foreign minister, and ambassador to Russia— all currently sitting to either side of the Dear Leader—jointly managed the DPRK's Moscow portfolio. Practically speaking, however, Oleg Kraskin and General Yoon were the conduit for the most sensitive messages between Luganov and the Dear Leader.

Oleg was glad to see his old friend. It was only the second time they had been in the same room. But they spoke frequently via a secure satellite phone channel and communicated regularly through a secure email system unknown and inaccessible to nearly everyone else in their respective governments. Indeed, the details of this very meeting had been arranged primarily by the two men, and Oleg hoped he and Yoon could exchange personal greetings on the sidelines of the press conference or before the lavish lunch planned after that.

Luganov set his teacup back on the conference table. As he did, Oleg returned his gaze to the two men at the heart of the discussion.

"Earlier this month, our friends in Tehran asked you to sell them twenty of the atomic warheads you have built," the Russian said softly. "Is this correct?"

"It is," the Dear Leader replied.

"But you have not yet given them an answer."

"How could I until I had met with you?" the Dear Leader asked. "Our agreement was that you would remove all of our warheads, and do so with a great flourish of publicity, so the world would think we were completely disarmed."

"Quite right," Luganov said. "But are you opposed to such a sale to the Iranians?"

"Not in principle, no, though I do have reservations, which you and I have discussed in the past."

"You don't believe the Iranians will prove loyal to us."

"I hesitate to speak so bluntly."

"You fear they have their own agenda."

"They certainly want to join us in neutralizing the Americans. I have no doubt about this. But given the opportunity, is there any question they will try to annihilate Israel first?"

Luganov took another sip of tea. "Your concerns are valid," he said at long last. "But leave that to me. For now, I would like you to sell Tehran fifteen warheads. The Supreme Leader has assured me he is willing to increase his price."

"To what?"

"He is ready to pay up to $100 billion of the money the Americans and Europeans gave Iran for agreeing to the JCPOA," he said.

"Why not the full $150 billion?"

"I asked him that," Luganov said. "He told me the missile upgrades will be costly, and of course there is the small matter that the people expect some tangible benefits from the deal. They have, after all, been asked to make sacrifices for far too long."

"What about my people? They have sacrificed for far longer."

"And you know that I have been and remain committed to improving the lives of your people," Luganov said, still outwardly pleasant, though Oleg could see the man's patience wearing thin. "Look, I know you are reluctant. Nevertheless, I would consider it a personal favor if you would not only agree to the sale but would expedite delivery of the warheads to Iran."

The North Korean thought about this for several moments. "How soon would you want the transfer made?" he finally asked.

"By the end of October—no later."

Again, the room was silent. Oleg looked up from his note taking. He tensed, expecting the volcano to blow. This wasn't in reality a request. It was an order. Luganov in no way considered the North Korean a coequal partner. The man was a subordinate, and Oleg braced himself, expecting Luganov to make this abundantly clear. But either sensing impending danger or simply stumbling to the appropriate conclusion, the Dear Leader finally set down his tea and gave his answer.

"Say no more, my friend," he said. "Your request will be granted."

10

A few minutes later, the principals broke to prepare for the press conference.

Their advisors, however, mingled for a while, congratulating each other on the achievement of this historic alliance and complimenting one another for how carefully they had guarded the great deception of Washington, Seoul, and the rest of the world.

Oleg felt a tap on his right shoulder. When he turned around, he found General Yoon waiting to greet him.

"General, my friend, you look well," Oleg said, grasping his hand and forcing himself to smile and look pleased with the horror of the morning's events.

"As do you, Oleg Stefanovich. It has been too long. How is Vasily?"

"He's well, and growing like a weed."

"What is he now, eight? Nine years old?"

"No, no, a very precocious eleven," Oleg corrected. "And arguing with his mother and me about everything from when he has to go to bed to the amount of his allowance to when he will be allowed to travel abroad by himself."

"He will grow up to be a lawyer, just like his father."

"Don't say that, General. The last thing the world needs is another lawyer."

The two men laughed.

"And Marina? Is she well?"

The question caused a stab of pain to shoot through Oleg's heart, though he was careful to mask it. The couple was not as close as they had once been. Not nearly so. The demands of his job, the long hours away, and the mounting geopolitical tensions had all taken their toll. Yet Oleg still loved his wife deeply. How had the great Russian poet Mikhail Lermontov put it? *Love, like fire, goes out without fuel.*

"A greater mother a man could not find," he told the general.

"How I would like to meet her one day," the general replied.

"I would like that very much. But how about you? How are you and Yuna Kim?"

"Better than we deserve," the general replied with a modesty Oleg found rare among military men. "Indeed, we have some good news. Yuna Kim is expecting, and if all goes well, she will give birth in December."

The smile Oleg felt spreading across his face was genuine. Oleg knew the couple had no children. He suspected the general's wife had had several miscarriages, though he had never asked. "I could not be more happy for you, my friend," he said. "This is very welcome news. Marina and I will be honored to send you a gift when I get back to Moscow."

The general shook his head. "There is no need, Oleg Stefanovich. Just to see you in person after so many years is more than enough."

The two men shook hands again just as President Luganov began heading out a side door. Oleg glanced at his watch. It was five minutes to noon. The press conference was about to begin. The international media were waiting, and they were hungry.

Hundreds of journalists crammed into the Mansudae Assembly Hall.

Two enormous chandeliers glistened in the klieg lights as Luganov and Hyong Ja Park entered the far end and strode down a wide, plush red carpet to the table where they would sign the treaty and the podiums positioned on either side.

In that moment, Oleg found himself crossing the Rubicon. No longer was he struggling with how to proceed. He knew what he must do. He couldn't say exactly how the fog in his thoughts had cleared or why he felt so certain. But it had, and he did.

Oleg would defect.

But not yet. He would defect to the West, specifically to the United States, at his first opportunity. But first, Oleg had come to the irrevocable conviction that he must do everything in his power to stop his father-in-law from launching a war to invade and seize the Baltic nations. He couldn't allow Luganov to put Russia at risk of nuclear war with NATO. Nor could he allow North Korea to transfer nuclear weapons to the lunatics running the Islamic Republic of Iran. He certainly couldn't stand silently by as Luganov authorized both North Korea and Iran to launch decapitating nuclear strikes against the United States—and, no doubt, Israel as well—with such speed and surprise that retaliatory strikes might not even be possible. He had to act. That much was clear. The question was, how?

"Today, it is my honor to join the Dear Leader in taking a bold move toward peace in the Pacific," Oleg heard his father-in-law say to the hundreds of reporters, cameramen, and producers who had assembled to record and disseminate all the lies that would flow forth that day. "I am pleased to announce that today the Russian Federation will create a political and military alliance with the Democratic People's Republic of Korea. I pledge to come to Pyongyang's defense if it should ever be attacked by the South or by the U.S. or by any other force. In return for coming under Russia's umbrella of protection, the Dear Leader has agreed to completely abandon its nuclear program and turn all nuclear weapons, uranium stockpiles, and nuclear materials over to me for immediate and permanent destruction."

A murmur of surprise swept across the room. Cameras began clicking and flashing furiously.

"What's more," Luganov continued, "the Dear Leader has agreed that all of his nuclear reactors, laboratories, and research facilities will be dismantled or destroyed. And he has agreed to invite international inspectors to observe and monitor the process, all of which will begin on or about October 15."

More photos. More flashes. Then the Dear Leader made news of his own.

"Everything President Luganov has just told you is true," he began. "And I welcome this strategic alliance with the Russian Federation and this great man of peace. And now, with the security of the DPRK assured, it is time to end the state of belligerency in our region. Therefore, I invite the president of South Korea to meet with me immediately to work out the terms of a full and comprehensive peace treaty and the denuclearization of the entire Korean Peninsula. To this end, I also invite the president of the United States, the premier of China, and of course my great friend President Luganov to attend a five-party summit to create a true partnership for world peace and prosperity."

Another wave of astonishment engulfed the press corps. Oleg even heard one reporter whisper to another that they should probably book their flights to Stockholm immediately, as Luganov and the Dear Leader were no doubt going to receive the Nobel Peace Prize.

Oleg could take it no longer. With every deception broadcast live around the world, his revulsion was growing. By the time the opening statements were completed, and the time for questions had commenced, he had resolved himself to the only course of action available to him that just might be able to prevent war in Europe, war in the Pacific, and war in the Middle East. He had no other choice. It was not just an option. This was his solemn duty.

Oleg Kraskin had to assassinate the president of the Russian Federation.

11

DOMODEDOVO INTERNATIONAL AIRPORT, MOSCOW, RUSSIA—29 SEPTEMBER
ONE HOUR AFTER THE RUSSIAN PRESIDENT'S ASSASSINATION

Marcus Ryker slammed on the brakes.

They skidded to a stop just in time. Grabbing his machine gun and kicking open the driver's-side door, he looked back at Oleg and told him to run to the idling Gulfstream IV. The drivers behind him tried to brake. One of the police cars slid right past them and smashed into the side of the terminal. The others stopped more successfully, within twenty yards of them, and officers emerged, guns drawn.

Marcus pivoted into the nearly blinding snowstorm and opened fire. Oleg burst out the other side of the car and bounded up the steps of the business jet as a hail of bullets erupted all around him. Marcus kept firing in short bursts as he moved around the hood of the car. He popped out a spent magazine and reloaded. Then he opened fire again—still in short bursts—as he crouched low and worked his way backward up the steps.

Rounds pinged off the metal stairs and the fuselage. Someone fired from just over his right shoulder. Marcus turned and saw Jenny Morris. The CIA's Moscow station chief was at the top of the stairs. She was holding a Russian-made sniper rifle and yelling for him to get in.

Marcus scrambled up the last few stairs. Jenny fired off several more rounds and hit the switch to pull up the stairs. Together, they shut and locked the door behind them and headed for the cockpit.

Marcus shouted to Oleg to buckle up, recline his seat all the way, and stay away from the windows as Jenny revved the engines. More rounds began hitting the side of the plane. From the copilot seat, Marcus couldn't see who was firing. He urged Jenny to push the engines harder and get moving, away from the terminal. As she did, Marcus saw her wince, then saw blood all over her jacket and shirt.

"You're hit."

"I'm fine, Ryker. We'll deal with it in the air."

But she wasn't merely wincing now. She could barely sit upright.

"You're not fine," he said.

"Never mind," she gasped. "Do . . . your job." She was now having trouble breathing, as well.

"You're not going to be able to get us off the ground."

Jenny tried to protest, but she couldn't get the words out. She began coughing up blood.

Marcus took the controls. Ground control was screaming at them from the tower, ordering them to stop. Marcus could see flashing lights converging from all directions. The G4 was approaching the first possible runway, but every light was red, indicating an aircraft was about to land.

Marcus looked right and saw lights in the sky at two o'clock. Oleg began shouting that the police cars heading toward them were being joined by armored personnel carriers with .50-caliber mounted machine guns.

Marcus couldn't wait any longer. He increased speed and eased the G4 out onto the runway, turning right, toward the approaching plane.

"No," Jenny whispered. "You can't."

Marcus didn't respond.

"You're insane. *Stop.*"

An Aeroflot jumbo jet was dead ahead of them, less than a mile out, landing gear extended, on approach for the very runway they were hurtling down.

Marcus didn't stop. He checked the flaps. They were at the zero position. Preparing for a short takeoff, he throttled forward to full power while pressing hard on the brakes. The high-pitched whine of the dual Rolls-Royce engines filled the cockpit. When he released the brakes, they all snapped back in their seats as the Gulfstream began hurtling down the runway.

Oleg, watching what was happening through the still-open cockpit door, was yelling at him to stop, that he was going to kill them all. Marcus didn't respond. He was trying desperately to keep the plane centered on the runway. Yet with only a private pilot's license and not a single hour in a business jet, he was having trouble. The plane veered to the right, then lurched left. They were picking up speed but were in danger of sliding off the icy runway.

Marcus could see the chain-link fence at the end of the ten-thousand-foot strip. It was covered in snow and ice, and it was coming up fast. Jenny ordered Marcus to increase flaps to takeoff position. The moment he did, they reached 150 miles an hour.

"*Now!*" she yelled.

Marcus yanked back on the yoke. The instant their wheels were off the ground, he pulled even harder, creating a far steeper angle for takeoff than normal. The ground controllers were cursing at him. Marcus refused to change course.

Alarms sounded in the G4 cockpit.

"*Caution, obstacle. Caution, obstacle.*"

The Russian plane—filled with hundreds of passengers—was coming directly at them. Despite the storm, Marcus could actually see the pilots in their cockpit, frantically waving them off. He could hear them yelling at him over the radio. Yet he kept increasing speed. They had to gain velocity and altitude if they had any chance of survival, even if that meant playing chicken with a jumbo jet.

12

At the last second, the Aeroflot banked hard to the right.

The G4 cleared the Russian plane by less than fifty yards. Jenny was ashen. Neither she nor Oleg said a word. Marcus retracted the landing gear and pulled into the clouds and the freak storm bearing down on Moscow.

"Where's the transponder?" Marcus asked as they passed two thousand feet.

"Why?" Morris asked, her voice thin and raspy.

"We've got to go dark."

Jenny looked at Marcus like he needed to be institutionalized as he turned off all the external lights and all the cabin and cockpit lights as well. Only the glow of the instrumentation remained. Relenting, Jenny pointed to the transponder switch in the lower right section of the center console, then used hand gestures to indicate he should turn it three clicks to the left.

Now they were nothing but an unidentified radar blip, heading into a storm and one of the most congested air corridors in Europe. Tracking or intercepting them wouldn't be impossible, but it would be difficult.

Marcus ordered Oleg to come up to the cockpit and take Jenny to one of the seats in the back. "They teach you any first aid in the army?" he asked.

"A little."

"Then take care of my friend."

Oleg nodded and was about to pick up Jenny when Marcus grabbed him by the arm and pulled him close so she couldn't overhear what he was about to say.

"She doesn't know what you just did," he whispered, "and she's in no shape to hear it now. Understood?"

Oleg simply nodded. There was no time for questions. He unbuckled Jenny and carried her to the back of the plane.

A few minutes later, they reached a cruising altitude of forty-three thousand feet. They were racing for international airspace at a speed of nearly five hundred knots—about 575 miles per hour. Marcus engaged the autopilot. According to the extraction plan he and Jenny had mapped out, they were headed for Helsinki. That was just 893 kilometers away. They'd already been in the air for twelve minutes. They had another fifty to go.

Marcus knew they'd never make it that far.

Mikhail Petrovsky was headed back to the war room when the call came.

The Russian defense minister had gotten only three hours of sleep. As his driver sped toward the center of the city, he took a secure call from Nikolay Kropatkin, deputy director of the FSB.

"Where are you?"

"Four minutes out," Petrovsky said in exasperation. "Can it wait?"

"No, it cannot," Kropatkin said. "Brace yourself, Mikhail Borisovich."

"Whatever for?"

"The president, sir."

"What about him?"

"He's dead."

Petrovsky sat bolt upright in the backseat of the bulletproof sedan, its flashing blue lights—and those of the security cars flanking them—illuminating his face in the stormy darkness. "When? How?"

"It was Oleg Stefanovich—he shot the president and Dmitri Dmitrovich at point-blank range," Kropatkin replied breathlessly. "They were alone in the president's study. It all happened so quickly. But it appears that he had help. He got to the airport, where someone was waiting with a private plane."

"Tell me the police stopped him."

"There was a shoot-out, but Oleg was able to get on board a jet and take off. We were tracking it, but they've turned off their transponder, and for the moment, we've lost it."

Petrovsky let fly a string of expletives.

"Scramble a dozen MiGs," he finally said. "Find that jet and take it down."

13

Marcus unbuckled his seat belt and headed back to the cabin.

Jenny had been hit in the right shoulder, Oleg explained. The wound was serious, but there was no evidence that either of her lungs had been punctured. Upon closer examination, he said, Morris had simply bitten her tongue at some point in all the chaos. She'd been spitting out blood, not coughing it up. It was a small bit of good news, but Marcus welcomed it. Oleg gave Jenny several shots of morphine to dull the pain, then covered her with a blanket.

There was nothing he could do for her at the moment, so Marcus excused himself and went into the lavatory. Shutting and locking the door behind him, he stared into the mirror at his unshaven face and the bloodstains all over his copilot's uniform. His blue eyes were now exhausted and bloodshot. He had scrapes and bruises all over his body—and for all his morning runs and evenings at the gym, he'd been surprised how quickly he'd been winded that night.

The mission had cost more than Marcus had wanted to pay. He wasn't morally opposed to killing bad guys. He would do whatever was necessary to protect the people and country he loved. But killing anyone took its toll.

Marcus washed the blood off his hands and face. Then he stepped out of the restroom, unlocked a storage bin in the back of the plane, and pulled out Nomex flight suits, parachutes, oxygen tanks, and related equipment.

"It's time to suit up," he said.

"What are you talking about?" Oleg asked.

"Don't worry; it's just a precaution," Marcus replied.

"Forget it—no."

"Put on the gear and get Morris into her gear—just in case."

"Absolutely not," Oleg protested, backing away. "I haven't jumped out of a plane in my life, and I'm not about to start now."

"Look, it may not come to that, but we need to be—"

Marcus never finished the sentence. The Gulfstream hit a massive patch of turbulence. He raced back to the cockpit as a series of alarms started sounding and lights began flashing. Marcus flicked a switch and a new radar display flickered to life. Gone were the weather data and the images of the massive snowstorm hitting the northwestern provinces of Russia. Now he was staring at a display showing two blips forty miles back and gaining fast.

"What's that?" Oleg demanded, appearing behind Marcus.

"*You need to get ready—now!*" Marcus yelled with such force that Oleg said nothing more and went to do what he was told.

The blips were Russian MiGs, and they were coming in white-hot. The Kremlin had just ordered fighter squadrons to shoot them down.

Marcus turned the yoke, banking the plane to the north, off the flight plan and away from St. Petersburg and beyond it Helsinki. There was no way he was going to let the Russians force them to land. Under no circumstances could they let themselves or this plane and its contents be taken intact.

The fighter jets were only thirty-two miles behind them. Yet no sooner had Marcus turned off and reset the alarms than they sounded again. Two more MiGs were coming up from a base just south of St. Petersburg. These were only twenty miles out. Again the alarms blared. This time, Marcus spotted two more MiGs on the radar, converging on them from the north, less than fifteen miles out.

So that was that. No fewer than six fighter jets were streaking toward them with orders to keep them from reaching international airspace at all costs. Marcus picked up the intercom and ordered Oleg and Jenny to finish putting on their jumpsuits and then cinch their seat belts as tight as they could. They had two minutes—no more.

Marcus tried to stay cool as the MiGs approached. After ninety-three seconds, he couldn't wait any longer. He pushed the yoke forward, commencing a brutally steep dive. It took mere seconds to plunge from forty-three thousand feet to only twenty thousand feet. Marcus found his stomach in his throat. The g-forces threatened to knock him out. But he hadn't shaken the MiGs. They were screaming in from every direction, and as he leveled out the G4—now around eighteen thousand feet—he knew they were going to be fired on at any moment.

Marcus decreased speed and once again turned on the autopilot. Then he unbuckled himself and bolted from the cockpit. He found Oleg sitting alone, his head in his hands. He hadn't put on his suit.

"We jump in twenty seconds," Marcus said. "Trust me, you'll be happier with a parachute than without one."

Morris, meanwhile, was bravely trying to put on her own gear, even as she struggled to stay conscious. Marcus rushed to her side, helped her finish, and donned his own gear.

Oleg still hadn't moved.

"What?" Marcus demanded.

"I can't do it. I can't jump."

"Fine," Marcus said, turning away and moving to strap Jenny to himself. She was in no condition to parachute on her own. Marcus was going to have to tandem jump with her. He clipped her harness to his vest, then moved to the door.

"Last chance, Oleg," he said, putting on his gloves and unlocking the door with one hand while steadying Morris with his other.

The moment the door released, it was ripped off its hinges and sucked away into the darkness. A gust of frigid air surged into the cabin.

Finally Oleg relented. Resistance morphed into terror. He was scrambling to don all the gear as fast as he could. Marcus tried to explain how to pull the rip cord, tried to show the Russian the backup chute and how to use it, and gave instructions on how to land. He was shouting at the top of his lungs over the screaming winds, but it wasn't clear Oleg was even listening. The Russian seemed fixated on the alarms that were once again sounding from the cockpit.

"*Jump—now,*" Marcus shouted as he turned on all three oxygen tanks.

Oleg's whole body was shaking. He was paralyzed with fear. But there was no more time to argue. So Marcus drove his balled fist into Oleg's stomach, doubling the man over, then grabbed the Russian and shoved him out the side of the plane.

14

Mikhail Petrovsky sat alone in his immense corner office.

He had only minutes. He picked up the secure phone on his desk and dialed a number from memory. "Is Grigori there?" he asked when a young woman came on the line.

"*Grigori?* I'm so sorry, but there is no one here by that name," the woman replied.

Message sent, message received. The defense minister hung up. Then, grabbing one of the remotes on his desk, he turned on a bank of television monitors on the far side of the room. He scanned through the Russian and international news channels but found no breaking news. His secrets were holding, but not for long. Petrovsky knew he had to seize the initiative.

Just then, three of his most senior aides rushed into the room and informed him the air force chief of staff was on line two.

"Tell me you have good news, General," Petrovsky demanded as he took the call.

"*We've got them,*" said the general, the jubilance in his voice restrained only by three decades of rigorous professionalism.

"You're certain?" Petrovsky demanded.

"My pilots picked up the G4 on radar south of St. Petersburg. No lights. No transponder."

"Did they issue a warning?"

"Yes, sir, multiple times."

"And?"

"There was no reply. The Gulfstream tried to take evasive action. It broke north, then dove for the deck from forty-three thousand feet. My men fired when they reached eighteen. The fireball, sir, was something to behold."

"Survivors?"

"Sir?"

"*You heard me, commander. Were there any survivors?*"

"Sir, with respect, that would be impossible. Our air-to-air missiles travel three times the speed of sound. There's no way that—"

"*No—that's not good enough, General,*" Petrovsky bellowed. "I want a massive search operation. I want every helicopter in the region in the air immediately. Deploy every police and army unit. And I want your best man heading up the search."

"Minister, with respect, the wreckage is strewn over dozens of square miles across the Karelian Isthmus. The same storm system battering Moscow is blanketing the entire region. It's not safe for helicopters. And as I say, it would have been impossible for—"

But Petrovsky, seething, cut him off again. "General, there were three people on board that aircraft," he snapped. "Each one of them is guilty of capital crimes against the Russian state. They are high-value targets, and I expect you to bring them—or their bodies—to me with all haste. That is an order. Do I make myself clear?"

There was a slight hesitation at the other end of the line, but only slight. "Yes, sir. You can count on me and my—"

Petrovsky didn't wait for the rest. His motorcade was ready. The cabinet was waiting at the Kremlin. He slammed down the phone and bolted out the door.

Deputy National Security Advisor Bill McDermott's secure phone rang.

He instantly recognized the number. It was Nick Vinetti, the deputy chief of mission of the U.S. Embassy in Moscow. McDermott answered in a hushed tone so as not to distract the president, who was tracking the unfolding events in Russia on the other side of the White House Situation Room.

"Are you with the president?" Vinetti asked.

"Yeah," McDermott confirmed. "You calling about Marcus?"

"No." Vinetti's tone was strained in a way McDermott had never heard in even their worst moments together in Afghanistan. "Listen, Bill—something's about to break here, and you need to let the president know before he hears it from anyone else."

"What's wrong?"

"It's President Luganov."

"What about him?"

"He's been assassinated."

"*What?*"

"And not just him—Dmitri Nimkov, too," Vinetti explained, referring to the head of the FSB, Russia's main intelligence service.

"That's not possible."

"It's true, and there's more. The guy you just put on that G4 to whisk out of Moscow—the Raven—that's the guy the Russians say pulled the trigger."

PART
TWO

15

Rushing just above the treetops, their feet could nearly brush the pines.

They were almost there—almost in the clear—when they were hit with a sudden downdraft. The back edge of the chute caught the top of one of the pines, puncturing it like a balloon. The three of them, bound together, dropped like a stone. Marcus braced for impact. But they never hit the ground. At the last moment, they were yanked back up, then dropped again, and found themselves dangling in the howling wind.

Marcus craned his neck to see what had just happened. His view was partially obstructed, but the answer was clear enough. While their canopy had been pierced, it had not been completely ripped in two. Instead, his chute and lines had gotten entangled in branches on the way down, cutting short their fall.

Now, hanging less than five feet off the ground, Marcus pulled a hunting knife from the pouch at his side and cut through the straps on his vest, freeing the carabiner supporting Oleg's weight. The Russian dropped to the ground, landing in the foot-high snow with a thud. Marcus cut away the chute lines. He, too, landed hard but absorbed Jenny's fall as best he could. Looking around, he realized they had another problem. They had not landed on the edge of an empty field or park. They had come down on the side of a two-lane road snaking through whatever forest this was. He saw no one coming from either direction. In fact, the road was covered in a fresh blanket of white powder, like everything else. It had not yet been plowed, nor might it be for hours—perhaps even days. But Marcus wasn't about to take a chance. An army patrol or a search helicopter could approach their position at any moment. They had to move.

At present, Marcus wasn't even certain that Oleg Kraskin and Jenny Morris were still alive. But checking on them or providing medical attention wasn't his highest priority. Not yet. Getting them off that road was. Marcus grabbed Jenny's harness first and dragged her a good thirty yards into the forest. Only then did he rip off his helmet, turn off his oxygen supply, and double back to do the same with Oleg before returning to the landing site again and making sure he hadn't left anything behind.

Satisfied, he backtracked to the woods, smoothing out the snow in hopes of covering their tracks. It wasn't perfect, but it would have to do. And if no one came driving through in the next twenty to thirty minutes, new snow would erase all evidence of their arrival—all, that is, except their ripped parachute whipping like a flag of surrender from the top of the pines.

Marcus next turned his attention to his two wounded colleagues. Jenny was still alive, still breathing, though her pulse was weak. Oleg was beginning to come to. Marcus removed Oleg's helmet and turned off his oxygen. He checked the man for broken bones and sprains but found nothing. Though somewhat dizzy, Oleg insisted he would be all right. Marcus nodded but said nothing, turning back to Jenny.

Unzipping her jumpsuit down to her waist, Marcus found the towels Oleg had used on the plane to apply pressure to her gunshot wounds. Both were soaked through with blood, as was her sweater. Removing the towels, he replaced them with the only thing he had—snow, and lots of it. He packed as much snow as he could on the entrance wound near the top of her right shoulder and more around the exit wound on her back.

Oleg looked confused by the tactic. He offered his sweatshirt and T-shirt as replacements for the towels. Marcus just shook his head. There was no time to explain. There was too much else to do. Saying nothing, he zipped up the jumpsuit again to keep the snow in place and not further expose her to the elements. He left Jenny's helmet in place and kept her oxygen flowing, though he dialed it down slightly to conserve what he could.

Next Marcus pulled the sniper rifle and the Kalashnikov out of his rucksack. He loaded a magazine into each, made sure the safeties were on, and set them aside. He did the same with both of the pistols. Then he handed the GPS unit to Oleg and told him to figure out where they were.

Marcus glanced at his watch. It was almost seven thirty. Sunrise was nearly an hour ago. Yet the storm was so intense, the cloud cover was so thick, it still felt like the dead of night. For now, the blizzard was working to their advantage, giving them the cover they needed and making it difficult for helicopters and other search aircraft to operate until the storm began to subside. Still, they had a severely wounded colleague, no transportation, and no plan of escape.

As Oleg fumbled in the darkness with the GPS unit, Marcus stripped off his own jumpsuit, exposing the black jeans, black fisherman knit sweater, and the combat boots he'd changed into on the plane. He rolled up the jumpsuit and stuffed it into the rucksack. Then he pulled out and donned a black leather jacket, balaclava, and a black knit wool cap.

Seeing Oleg wasn't having much success with the American-made electronic device he'd never used or even seen before, Marcus took back the GPS unit and motioned for Oleg to change his clothes. The balaclava was going to be especially critical for his Russian friend, Marcus knew. It would shield Oleg against the bitter winds and blowing snow. More importantly, it would mask his identity if and when they came across other Russians. Oleg's face, after all, was known by every man and woman in the country. He had been one of President Luganov's most senior advisors. What's more, he had married Luganov's only daughter. Their wedding had been televised across the country and around the world. Yet even if the nation had somehow forgotten what Oleg Kraskin looked like, Marcus suspected the man's picture would soon be on every screen in Russia with a label describing him as the criminal who had just murdered the country's godfather.

The GPS unit told a disturbing story. They had landed at sixty degrees, nine minutes, twenty seconds north; thirty degrees, thirty-one minutes, thirty seconds east. That put them a lot closer to Lake Ladoga than Marcus cared to be. They were now on the edge of a national park just outside Toksovo, a ski resort town of no more than six thousand residents. Under other circumstances, it might be an ideal place to find a dacha that wasn't yet being used for the season—it was only September, after all—and hunker down for a day or two until they could figure out their next move.

But as Marcus studied the digital map, he realized that Toksovo was less than fifteen miles north of St. Petersburg, Russia's second-largest city, home to five million inhabitants and a first-rate police force, and proximate to numerous elite military bases. The map showed that the snow-covered road to which they were now adjacent was the main thoroughfare connecting the people of St. Pete to their closest ski lifts. True, it was only Monday morning, not the start of a weekend. Most people would be heading to work or school, not the slopes. But given the intense search operation Marcus knew was coming their way, there was no question this road was going to be plowed. The only question was, how soon?

Marcus motioned to Oleg to sit tight and keep an eye on their wounded colleague. Grabbing the weapons and the hatchet from his rucksack, he returned to the edge of the forest. There he saw the shredded remains of his parachute whipping wildly in the frigid winds high in a Siberian pine. Given the storm, there was no way he was going to be able to climb the tree. His only option was to cut the tree down.

Nearly half an hour later, the crash brought Oleg running.

"Are you mad?" the Russian began to shout as he approached but caught himself and lowered his voice, glancing all around.

Marcus didn't answer him. Instead, he raced across the road, cut loose the remains of the parachute, gathered it in his arms, and dashed back to the cover of the forest's edge.

Oleg was beside himself. "Why in the world would you drop the tree into the road, rather than back into the forest?" he said as much in astonishment as in anger.

"Listen to me very carefully," Marcus said calmly. "You did your job. Now I'm doing mine. I promised to protect you and get you out of this country alive. But you need to understand one thing—we are in a race against time. So you need to do everything I say without question, without complaint, without delay. Understood?"

"Look," Oleg protested, "I appreciate everything you're doing for me, but I—"

"No, you're not getting it," Marcus interrupted. "We have one mission right now: survival. Period. Now, take this chute back to Jenny and wrap her up in it in a way that she'll be easy to pull through the snow when I give you the word. Got it?"

Oleg's eyes again flashed with defiance. But just then they heard the rumbling of a vehicle coming from the south. When headlights approached around the bend, Oleg nodded and moved quickly through the shadows.

16

It wasn't just one set of headlights approaching.

It was a convoy.

Marcus backtracked, moving deeper into the protective darkness of the forest. Slinging the Kalashnikov over his back, he hoisted the sniper rifle and peered through the scope. He counted four sets of headlights, then a fifth, and finally a sixth. It was not a column of military vehicles. Rather, these were heavyweight trucks, each painted orange, mounted with large plow blades on the front and industrial salt spreaders on the back. A bar of rotating yellowish-orange lights flashed from atop each cab, and the vehicles slowed to a halt as they approached the downed tree.

Marcus had been anticipating a single plow, not a half dozen moving as a team, and this complicated his plan. More drivers. More eyes. More chances to be spotted. Still, this might be their only chance, so he had to act fast.

Arcing farther into the forest to reduce the chance his movements could be spotted, he raced through the deepening snow until he'd reached the end of the convoy and the last of the trucks. Using the scope of the sniper rifle again, he could see the drivers exiting their cabs. Soon, six rather burly men had converged around the felled pine, no doubt discussing what they were going to do to clear it away and get moving again.

Fortunately, they hadn't thought to trudge over to the tree's stump. If they had, they'd have known immediately the tree had not been felled by the winds but had been chopped down, and recently. That would put them all on alert. Marcus was certain they each had two-way radios in their cabs and probably mobile phones as well. He had no way of knowing whether state workers or the general public had been alerted to Luganov's death and the hunt for his killers. But if these men grew suspicious and radioed back with news of something odd in the forest, how long would it take for the dispatcher to contact local authorities and for someone to make the connection?

Marcus peered at the men through his reticle, calculating range to target, wind speed, and air temperature, making minute adjustments to the rifle as he did. But just as his right index finger switched the safety lever to the single-shot position, Marcus caught himself. Blinking hard, he looked up, flipped the switch back to the no-fire position, and lowered the rifle to his side.

He had no right to kill these men and certainly no authority. This was not war. These were not enemy combatants. He was not a sworn officer of the law, and if anyone was guilty of a crime in the last few hours, it was him, not them.

"Mr. President, we have a problem," McDermott said, putting down his phone.

Andrew Clarke, deep in conversation at the other end of the Situation Room, turned and looked back at his deputy national advisor, annoyance in his eyes. "What is it?" the president asked.

"Could I request, sir, that we all retake our seats?" McDermott said, stalling slightly for time to process the information he'd just learned. "We have new information out of Russia, and it's . . ."

"It's what?" the president asked, taking his seat.

"Well, sir, our embassy in Moscow has intercepted encrypted radio traffic between several top Russian military and FSB officials indicating . . ."

McDermott could hardly finish the sentence. He felt light-headed, short of breath. He, too, had to sit down. As he did, the anger on the president's face faded.

Clarke glanced at Cal Foster, his secretary of defense, and then at Richard Stephens, director of the Central Intelligence Agency, to see if they knew what was coming. It was obvious neither of them did. "Indicating what?" Clarke asked McDermott.

"Mr. President," McDermott replied, "I need to inform you that Russian president Aleksandr Ivanovich Luganov . . . is dead."

Marcus watched as two men grabbed chain saws from compartments on the sides of their trucks and fired them up.

The piercing buzz of the two-stroke combustion engines suddenly made it impossible to hear anything else.

This was the break they needed. Marcus raced back to his colleagues and to his relief found that Oleg had done exactly what he'd asked of him and more. Not only was Jenny ready to be transported, but Oleg had packed up the rest of their supplies—including the two remaining bottles of oxygen—and was ready to move out.

Without saying a word, Marcus motioned for Oleg to follow him. Then he grabbed the lines connected to his parachute and began pulling Jenny through the snow.

They moved south, away from the men and their work, until they were parallel to the last snowplow in the line. This was the tricky part.

From this distance, and with the saws running, there was no way they could be heard by the drivers.

But if they were seen . . .

"*Dead?*" asked CIA director Stephens. "That's impossible."

"Apparently not, sir," McDermott said. "We don't know much at this point. There's a great deal of confusion. But our people say three facts are emerging."

"Go on," the president said.

"Well, sir, the first is that Luganov isn't simply dead. That is, he didn't simply die in his sleep. He was assassinated—shot in the head, to be more precise, multiple times, and at point-blank range."

A buzz filled the room. The president called the group back to order and told McDermott to continue.

"Apparently President Luganov was not the only target. Moscow station says Dmitri Nimkov was shot in similar fashion, and both men died instantly."

"That's preposterous," snapped Secretary of Defense Foster. "The president of the Russian Federation and the head of the FSB, gunned down inside the palace? By whom? Where were their bodyguards? How could anyone get near them? We're watching that palace by satellite twenty-four hours a day. The place is a fortress. There's no way someone could get inside there to . . ."

Foster stopped himself, and CIA director Stephens picked up the thought. "Unless it was an inside job."

"What do you mean?" Clarke asked. "A bodyguard? A disgruntled employee? How would that be possible? Wouldn't everyone with access to Luganov have been carefully screened and exhaustively vetted, especially on the eve of war?"

"Absolutely," Foster said. "Which means it would have to have been someone trusted by both men."

"But why?" the president asked. "And why now?"

"Maybe the goal wasn't simply to settle a grudge or some personal score but to stop the war," Stephens said. "Stop Luganov, stop the war."

"It could also be the beginning of a coup," the SecDef said to the president and the members of the National Security Council huddled around the table.

The room again grew quiet. Then people remembered that McDermott had a third fact to offer into evidence. All eyes turned to him.

McDermott's mouth went dry. He reached across the conference table for a tumbler embossed with the seal of the White House and a pitcher of cold water. He poured himself a glass, drank it down, and then poured himself another.

"Right, well, yes," McDermott began, forcing himself to continue. "From what we've learned so far, it was without question an inside job, carried out by someone very much in Luganov's inner circle—and this is where things get complicated."

"Why? Who did it?" Clarke pressed, leaning forward in his seat.

"It would appear that the shooter was the man we're calling the Raven."

The president gasped. "Our mole?"

McDermott nodded.

"You mean the guy our people were trying to smuggle out of the country?" the president clarified. "The guy the Russians just blew out of the sky?"

McDermott nodded again.

"That's ludicrous," Clarke blurted out, now leaning back in his chair. "Impossible—our guy was nowhere near Luganov or the FSB chief. Right?"

For several seconds, the deputy national security advisor said nothing.

"Am I missing something, Mr. McDermott?" Clarke asked. "We're in the clear on this. Aren't we?"

17

GORKI-9, THE PRIME MINISTER'S RESIDENCE, 18 KILOMETERS WEST OF MOSCOW

The scream could be heard from every corner of the compound.

So, it seemed, could the sound of chinaware and glass goblets smashing to pieces on the hardwood floor.

An instant later, the French doors to the opulent master suite burst open. Two bodyguards rushed in, followed an instant later by five more, all with guns drawn. They found the remains of two break-fast trays scattered everywhere, and the prime minister cradled in his shrieking wife's arms. The man's eyes were wide-open but unblinking and frozen with fear. Blood trickled down his chin.

The lead agent wrenched his protectee from the grip of the incon-solable woman. He searched for a pulse but found none. He ordered the man's personal physician be summoned at once, then began adminis-tering CPR and mouth-to-mouth resuscitation. Another agent grabbed a portable defibrillator. The team tried again and again to shock the PM's heart back into motion. But it was no use.

Maxim Grigarin, only fifty-six years old, was dead, and the bitter taste on the lead agent's lips left no doubt as to the cause of death.

The thirteenth prime minister of the Russian Federation had just been poisoned in his own home.

"Now," Marcus said.

He slapped Oleg on the back, and the Russian bolted across the clearing. When he reached the rear of the last truck, he pressed himself against the salt spreader. A safety light was flashing above his head. Marcus peered through the reticle of the sniper rifle at the men making quick work of the felled tree. None were looking in their direction. Those who weren't using the chain saws were passing around a bottle of vodka. One was trying to light a cigarette, though in the blowing and drifting snow, he was not having any luck.

Marcus signaled for Oleg to keep watch. Oleg complied, peering around the right side of the truck. When he nodded, Marcus shouldered the rifle, grabbed the lines of the parachute canopy, and sprinted to the rear of the truck, pulling Jenny behind him.

"All clear," Oleg said breathlessly when Marcus arrived.

"Good, now follow me," Marcus replied.

He glanced around the left side of the truck. The way the other trucks were angled, they created a barrier that prevented any of the drivers working up front to see them on this side. With their movements shielded from the men, Marcus easily advanced to the driver's-side door of the rear truck, pulling Jenny across the snow. Oleg was right behind, making sure no one surprised them by coming around the back.

At Marcus's signal, Oleg opened the door and climbed into the driver's seat. Marcus hoisted Jenny over his shoulder and handed her up to Oleg. The Russian carefully eased her onto the middle of the bench seat as he backed over to the passenger side, careful to remain crouched down and out of sight.

The truck's engine was running. So were the windshield wipers and the defroster. Marcus turned these off, wanting snow and ice to build up on the windows to further obscure their movements. Then he slid the rifle and AK-47 along the floor of the cab and stuffed their three rucksacks in a sliver of storage space behind the bench seat.

He was about to climb into the driver's seat when both of the chain saw motors stopped. A moment later, Marcus heard a nasty, phlegmy cough, and a pair of thick hands grabbed him hard from behind. Instinctively Marcus snapped around and head-butted his attacker. The husky, bearded driver slumped down in the snow, motionless.

Marcus drew a pistol and pivoted toward the front of the truck, ready to fire. But no one was there. He moved to the back edge of the truck. No one else was coming. He ducked under the salt spreader and came to another of the truck's corners. He took a quick peek. No one was approaching, but he could see that the tree had been cleared from the road and the rest of the drivers were returning to their cabs and preparing to roll.

By the time Marcus returned to the driver's-side door, Oleg was in a panic. "They keep calling for this guy Misha over the radio, asking him if he's ready," Oleg said. "What do we do?"

"Say yes," Marcus said calmly.

The Raven looked surprised but finally took the microphone of the CB radio, pressed the button, and said, *"Da"* in as gruff a tone as he could muster.

Next, to Oleg's visible shock, Marcus bent down, grabbed the unconscious driver, and hoisted him up. With some difficulty, he shoved the man onto the seat beside Jenny. He fished their medical kit from Jenny's pack, pulled out a syringe, loaded it up with a heavy narcotic, and jabbed the driver in the neck. He wouldn't be bothering them for several hours, at least.

Oleg said nothing. His face said it all.

The convoy began to move. Marcus pushed everyone over to the right—not that they had much room to spare—and climbed into the driver's seat and slammed the door. Then he flipped on the windshield wipers and the defroster again and handed his pistol to Oleg.

"Just in case," he said as he took the wheel and pressed the accelerator.

18

The Russian Defense Ministry was less than a mile from the Kremlin.

It took Petrovsky's motorcade just minutes to get there, but he received two calls during the ride. By the time he was finished with the second call, his driver was being waved through the main gates. The armor-plated SUV roared up to a pale-yellow eighteenth-century building shaped like an enormous isosceles triangle. The building had been known for centuries as the Senate, but in modern times these were the offices of the Russian president and his administration.

Petrovsky's security detail, triple its usual number given the events of the last two hours, rushed him through a side door and up a back elevator to the conference room on the third floor where nearly the entire cabinet had assembled. It was strange to see Luganov's chair at the head of the table unoccupied. But Petrovsky refused to show any emotion. He took his usual seat, to the right of the president's and across from three chairs also conspicuously empty that morning.

One belonged to Prime Minister Maxim Grigarin.

The second, to Dmitri Nimkov.

The third, to Oleg Kraskin.

Aside from these, the room was packed, not only with cabinet members but with their chief deputies, sitting behind their bosses in an outer ring of wooden chairs. But all eyes were on Petrovsky, in part because he was the last man to enter, and in part because they knew that it was he—not the president or the prime minister—who had called this emergency meeting.

The defense minister rose and called the meeting to order.

"Gentlemen, I'm afraid this is a tragic day, one that will become known in the annals of Russian history as Black Monday," he began.

No one made a sound, and as he scanned the eyes of the men gathered around the room, he suddenly realized how closely the secret had been held. No one in this room knew what he was about to say—not all of it, anyway. Not even Nikolay Kropatkin, the deputy director of the FSB, knew everything that had transpired. They all knew something terrible had happened. Many of them had heard rumors of a shoot-out at one of Moscow's international airports and the closure of all Russian airspace to traffic of any kind. But none of them knew the whole truth.

"There is no easy way to say this, so I will be direct," Petrovsky continued. "I regret to inform you that early this morning, our beloved president, Aleksandr Ivanovich Luganov, was assassinated, along with FSB chief Dmitri Nimkov."

There were audible gasps around the room, and Petrovsky paused before continuing.

"Adding to this tragedy is the fact that a foreign conspirator is not to blame. Both men were murdered in cold blood by one of our own— Oleg Stefanovich Kraskin."

More gasps, now accompanied by angry looks.

"They were shot at point-blank range by the president's son-in-law, in the president's private study, in the palace at the Novo-Ogaryovo estate. Kraskin used a handgun fitted with a silencer."

Several cabinet members stood as Russia's most senior leaders tried to process the magnitude of the crimes and their disbelief at who had committed them.

"There are many questions to which I have no answers at the moment. Why would Oleg Stefanovich perpetrate such a crime against the motherland? How did he get the weapon? How did he smuggle it into the palace? Why were no bodyguards in the room at the time? This was an unspeakable breach of security protocol, and we must get to the bottom of how it could have occurred. But as troubling as any other question is this: How did Oleg Stefanovich manage to slip away from the palace and get to the airport before his crimes were even noticed? We know this much—he had help. A driver was waiting for him on the tarmac when he arrived at the airport. A pilot was waiting with a plane, a Gulfstream IV business jet, fueled and ready for departure."

Near pandemonium broke out in the cabinet room. The rage and the bloodlust for revenge was palpable, but Petrovsky held up his hand to call for order. When that was not forthcoming, he rapped on the table, again demanding the ministers' attention.

"Who was helping Oleg Stefanovich?" he asked. "This we do not yet know, but I can inform you that less than thirty minutes ago, the Russian Air Force identified the plane he was using and upon my command shot the plane down outside of St. Petersburg. It is reasonable to believe Kraskin and the criminals assisting him were killed in the explosion, but we are not taking any chances. I have ordered a massive search of the area until the bodies are recovered and positively identified."

Petrovsky paused again to let his words sink in.

"Now, as incomprehensible as all of this is," he finally continued, "I'm afraid there is more bad news."

The room quieted.

"Just minutes ago, on my way here to meet with you, I was informed that our highly esteemed prime minister—indeed, one of my dearest comrades and colleagues—Maxim Grigarin, was found murdered in his bedroom."

The shock in the eyes of every man around the table was profound.

"We are working under the assumption that Oleg Stefanovich is responsible in some way for this crime, as well, but I assure you a full and intensive investigation is under way." Petrovsky took a sip of water from a glass on the table in front of him. "Gentlemen, I know you are all devastated at this horrific news. As am I. I know you are grieving, as one must when a nation loses such heroic and irreplaceable leaders— three in one day. But I don't need to remind you that this body has been entrusted with sober responsibilities by our constitution that we must carry out faithfully for the good of the people and the security of our state."

Heads around the table nodded in agreement.

"Our chief of state has been murdered, as has his immediate successor. And as we all know, the speaker of the Duma had a stroke several weeks ago and for now has been tragically incapacitated. So, amid our searing loss and wrenching pain, we face a constitutional crisis unparalleled in the history of the Russian Federation. The painful fact is that we have no leader and no clear process for choosing one, and we are just hours away from going to war with the United States and the NATO alliance."

19

McDermott cleared his throat and took yet another sip of water.

Then he laid out the chilling story for the president and his advisors.

The original plan was for Marcus Ryker and Jenny Morris, the thirty-two-year-old chief of the CIA's Moscow station, to link up with the Raven, retrieve the thumb drive containing all the intelligence the Raven had promised to give to the Americans in return for safe passage out of the country, and then get both the Raven and the thumb drive out of Russia as quickly as possible. But it seemed the operatives had gone rogue. Morris and Ryker had apparently conspired with the Raven to assassinate Luganov and Nimkov before taking the Gulfstream jet the CIA had positioned at the airport. A jet that had now been shot down by the Russian Air Force.

President Clarke's face and neck turned beet red. Turning to Director Stephens, he demanded an explanation. "Are you telling me that two officers of the Central Intelligence Agency executed a hit on two of the most senior leaders of the Russian Federation—an operation I never heard of, much less approved?"

"Absolutely not, Mr. President," Stephens replied. "Neither Morris nor Ryker was ever authorized to do such a thing. They certainly never discussed, mentioned, or even hinted that they were contemplating such actions, and I would never have allowed them to, either."

"Nevertheless, your people just committed an overtly hostile and provocative act on the eve of a war between the Russians and NATO that, as you've all advised me, could very well go nuclear," countered an enraged commander in chief.

"Mr. President, please," Stephens implored. "Let's back this thing up a moment. First of all, Ryker doesn't officially work for the CIA. And with respect, we don't know if any of this is true."

"What are you talking about? Did you hear what McDermott just told us?"

"Yes, sir, and I have no doubt our people in Moscow are picking up such reports from electronic and human sources in Moscow and beyond," Stephens replied. "My people are highly trained professionals and are faithfully passing along what they're hearing. I just caution that we don't know that any of it is accurate. Is Luganov really dead? Is Nimkov? Has it been confirmed? Has it been reported in the Russian news? Or is it possible this is a ploy to distract us as war is set into motion?"

The CIA director turned to his deputy, sitting in the row of chairs behind him, and ordered him to step out of the room and get all the up-to-the-minute information Langley had. Then he said, "Mr. President, what if this is all an elaborate disinformation campaign to set up the American government to look horrible—to make us out to be the bad guy in the eyes of the world—and give Luganov the pretext he wants to go to war? Can I tell you that's the case? No, sir, I cannot. But if that *were* the case—and I stress, *if*—then the Russian news media will very likely start reporting it soon. Such explosive reports would be immediately picked up by the international media and certainly by the American media. It might all be fake news, but it would give Luganov and his generals a serious edge."

"That would be quite a head fake," the SecDef said.

"It would indeed," said the president, suddenly not clear on what to believe.

"But let's take the other side," the Pentagon chief said. "What if it's true?"

"That's crazy," Stephens shot back. "None of my people would be engaged in anything like that."

"Then why did the Kremlin just order that G4 and our people be shot down?" Foster asked, careful not to raise his voice.

The director of Central Intelligence had no reply.

"Your pilots flew that Gulfstream in with an airtight cover, did they not?" Foster continued.

"I believe so," Stephens replied.

"Your people had no indication prior to takeoff that anything was wrong, did they?"

"Not that I'm aware of."

"Your station chief in Moscow had a solid alibi. The Russians had no idea that Marcus Ryker was back in the country. So far as the Russians knew, Ryker flew out with Senator Dayton and his delegation several days ago. We have no reason to believe the FSB or any other security service in Russia somehow knew that Ryker HALO-jumped back into Russia to link up with your station chief and the Raven, correct?"

"Correct."

"Then we have to ask, what went wrong?" Foster said. "Why did Moscow suddenly shut down Russian airspace minutes after your G4 lifted off? Why did they scramble all those MiGs and give them orders to blow any Gulfstream business jet they found to kingdom come?"

Again, the CIA director had no answers.

Secretary Foster turned back to Clarke. "Mr. President, I don't know what to believe yet. There simply isn't enough factual data in front of us to warrant a conclusion. I grant that a disinformation campaign is possible, especially if Luganov is still alive and determined to go through with this attack on our NATO allies in the Baltics. But we should consider the alternative as well."

"Which is?" the president asked.

"Assume Luganov really is dead," Foster replied. "Nimkov, too. How could it have happened? There is absolutely no way Jenny Morris or Marcus Ryker got into or anywhere near the presidential palace. That much I'd stake my life on. It's impossible. But what about the Raven? What do we really know about him? We don't even know his name."

"One hasn't been given to me," Stephens said.

"But we're told he's close to Luganov, right?" Foster asked.

"Yes."

"Close enough to give us the war plans Luganov has been developing with his senior leadership."

Director Stephens nodded.

"And close enough to give Ryker and Morris a treasure trove of other high-value intel, which they transmitted back to Langley several hours ago, well before they took off," Foster continued. "That suggests—at the minimum—that they made contact with the Raven and received the thumb drive he promised. That means it's also very likely he was on that plane when it took off."

"What are you saying, Cal?" the president asked.

"I'm just saying someone who's close enough to Luganov to get this kind of information is someone highly trusted by the president, his closest advisors, and very likely his security detail. We know the Raven, whoever he is, was horrified by what Luganov was doing. We know he told Ryker he was willing to lay down his life to stop Luganov from going to war with NATO. Clearly the Raven found a way to hand off the thumb drive to Ryker, the only handler he said he would work with. But what if he didn't head directly to the airport with Ryker as planned? What if he went back to the palace—alone—to take care of unfinished business?"

"Come on, Cal, you really think this Raven person walked up to Luganov and Nimkov and popped them like something out of a gangster movie?"

"Who else would have had better access?"

"How would he have gotten a gun into the palace?"

"There are hundreds of guns in the palace," the SecDef said. "He only needed one."

"And then he just waltzed out, took a cab to the airport, met Ryker and Morris, and tried to fly out?" Stephens asked, incredulous.

"It's not impossible. *Something* caused the Russians to shut down all civilian air traffic, scramble their fighters, hunt down this one plane, and shoot it out of the air. Now our G4 is gone, our people are dead, and we've got a hundred thousand Red Army troops poised to pour into the Baltics within the next few hours. I, for one, don't want to be caught off guard worrying about whether Luganov is dead or not if Moscow is about to take us to war."

"I don't either," the president said. "Mr. Secretary, take us to DEFCON 2."

20

They couldn't plow Russian back roads all day.

But Marcus hadn't yet found an exit strategy. If he peeled away from the convoy too soon, the other drivers would get suspicious. For the moment, they were stuck clearing snow. They had already reopened access to small towns from Toksovo in the center of the peninsula to Ozerki, a rural fishing village nestled on the northeastern shores of the Gulf of Finland. Now they were working their way northwest on the main thoroughfare that connected St. Petersburg with Vyborg, the second-largest city in the region with a population of some eighty thousand.

The driver Marcus had head-butted had still not come to. But Jenny was beginning to stir. The helmet and oxygen were no longer necessary. She was able to breathe on her own, and her pulse was steady. But she was groaning in pain and shivering. All the snow Marcus had packed around her wounds had melted, and she was soaked through. When he felt her forehead, it was hot. She was developing a fever. Marcus directed Oleg to give her another shot of morphine. Oleg gave her the shot, put his own coat around her, and turned up the heater another notch. After several minutes, she quieted and drifted back to sleep.

Via the CB and the AM radio, Marcus had been trying to track the latest developments. To their bewilderment, there had been no word about the assassination of Luganov, but Radio Moscow was reporting that a business jet had gotten caught in the storm and had exploded over the Karelian Isthmus. No survivors were reported. Emergency crews were dealing with multiple fires from burning wreckage that had fallen from the sky on private homes, shops, and even an elementary school.

In a separate story, Radio Moscow reported that three suspected bank robbers were believed to be on the loose in or near St. Petersburg. The anchor said an extensive manhunt was under way, adding that all three suspects were considered armed and dangerous. Citizens were advised to stay inside and call authorities if they spotted anything suspicious. The surprise blizzard dominated the rest of the coverage, with updates every ten minutes.

Neither Marcus nor Oleg understood why the authorities in Moscow were purposefully misleading the nation. Why weren't people being told of the assassination? Why wasn't Oleg's name and description being distributed in an all-points bulletin?

Oleg's theory could be summed up in one word: *pride*. The leaders of the FSB and other Russian security agencies had to be mortified by what they had allowed to happen. They had to be dealing with a firestorm of outrage from cabinet members and soon would face the fury of the Duma and the public. At some point they would have to acknowledge Luganov's death both to the nation and the world. But Oleg wasn't sure they could actually admit it had been done by an insider, a member of the First Family, no less.

Marcus, however, was sure the story would come out soon.

"Pride cuts both ways," he said as they kept driving. "I grant you the Kremlin doesn't want to admit they failed to protect the two highest leaders in the country. But I can tell you from experience, the only thing more humiliating than failing to stop an assassination is the failure to arrest or kill the person or persons responsible for the crime. We may have a few hours, but that's it. Once the Kremlin realizes we didn't die in the G4, believe me, they'll hunt us down with everything they have."

For now, however, Marcus had a more urgent matter. They had to find a way to ditch this snowplow and get away from the convoy. Finally the moment he'd been looking for came.

"Get on the radio—say we need to stop for fuel," he told Oleg, seeing a rest stop approaching and easing his foot off the accelerator.

When Oleg complied, the driver in the lead plow radioed back that they all had enough fuel to make it to Vyborg, a city still thirty minutes ahead. They would refuel there, he insisted. But Marcus told Oleg to inform his comrades he also needed a bathroom stop.

The second announcement worked like a charm. The five other trucks had just missed the exit, and none of them slowed or made a U-turn. Rather, they pressed northward while Marcus pulled off the main highway and into the parking lot of a petrol station and adjoining restaurant.

Pulling around to the back of the facility, Marcus came to a complete stop in front of a snow-covered SUV that had clearly been there for hours. He turned off the snowplow's wipers and lights and shut down the engine. Then, telling Oleg to wait, he pulled up the collar of his leather jacket to protect himself from the elements, opened the driver's-side door, and dropped to the ground.

21

Marcus strode across the parking lot to a service door located next to two large metal garbage bins.

The door was unlocked. Slipping inside, Marcus entered a well-lit hallway leading to the convenience mart attached to the petrol station. To his left was a restroom and a walk-in freezer. To his right was the manager's office. Marcus knocked on the office door. There was no answer. He tried the knob. It, too, was unlocked. There was little of value inside. A large steel drop-slot safe sat in one corner. At this time of day, it was probably full of cash. Yet Marcus doubted the manager even knew the combination, and he wasn't there to rob the place. Not exactly. He just needed a set of keys.

The rest of the cramped office contained two file cabinets, a desk strewn with piles of paperwork, a few pictures of the manager's husband and children, and a new bottle of Stolichnaya with a pink bow wrapped around it and what looked to be several hand-drawn birthday cards. Hearing no one approaching, Marcus checked the desk drawers. They were locked, as were the file cabinets. But next to a wall calendar, he finally found what he was looking for: a hook with keys to the 2009 Jeep Compass Sport parked out back.

Outside, Marcus brushed off the beat-up SUV and revved up the stone-cold engine. Oleg helped him move Jenny from the cab of the snowplow to the backseat of the Jeep. Marcus transferred the weapons and the rest of their gear, then gave the driver one more shot of sedatives and sat him in the driver's seat, slumped over the steering wheel. Marcus, Oleg, and Jenny were all still wearing the gloves they'd jumped with, so he didn't have to wipe the cab down for prints. But he did toss the keys to the plow onto the seat beside the driver. Then he opened the bottle of vodka he'd swiped from the office, poured some onto the man's face and his jacket, and set the open bottle on the seat next to the man. With that, he shut the door to the truck and slipped into the driver's side of the Jeep.

"I know where we can go to lay low for a while, just until we can figure out our next move," Oleg said as he cranked up the Jeep's heater, desperate to get warm and keep Jenny warm as well.

"Where?" Marcus asked.

"Marina's mother lives in St. Petersburg."

"Yulia?"

"Right—I sent Marina and Vasily to stay there. I know they'd—"

Oleg wasn't finished, but Marcus shook his head. "No. No family. No friends. We can't take the risk."

Oleg tried to protest, but Marcus cut him off.

"Keep thinking," he said as he put the Jeep in gear and pulled away from the petrol station and back onto the highway. Rather than continuing north, however, he headed south on the E18. Police cars with sirens blaring were streaming southward, passing them often. Army vehicles too. Marcus and Oleg tensed each time, but so far no civilian cars were being pulled over, certainly none heading *toward* the site of the plane crash. Nor had they encountered any of the roadblocks or checkpoints that the radio was reporting had been set up closer to St. Petersburg.

Marcus didn't have a plan. Not yet. He just didn't want to be a sitting duck at the petrol station. Better to be moving. Better to be taking the initiative. But suddenly he saw Oleg pull out his phone and begin scrolling through his contacts.

"What are you doing?" Marcus asked, an edge in his voice. "You shouldn't have your phone on; it can be tracked."

"I put it on airplane mode," the Russian replied. "Isn't that enough?"

Marcus had no idea, but before he could say anything further, Oleg found what he had been searching for.

"I've got it," he said. "Does the name Boris Igorovich Zakharov mean anything to you?"

"Sure—Luganov's former chief of staff, right?"

"Right. Now he's in a prison in Siberia somewhere, serving a life sentence."

"What'd he do?"

"It's a long story. The point is, his brother has a dacha here on the isthmus. It's not thirty minutes from here."

"You have the address?"

"Better than that, I've actually been there. He took me there once before he was arrested. We went fishing. It's right on the Gulf of Finland."

"How do you know his brother won't be there?"

"No one's ever there this time of year. Boris's brother always spends autumn on the Black Sea. That's why Boris and I were able to use his place. I could call if you'd like, just to make sure he's not there."

Marcus shook his head. "No calls. We'll check it out. And turn your phone off all the way. We don't want the FSB tracking you, airplane mode or no airplane mode."

At Oleg's direction, Marcus exited on a side road labeled *Roshchinskoye Shosse*. They were soon heading south, then southwest. It was slow going, as the roads they'd helped plow were being covered with fresh snow. Eventually, however, they made it to the coastal road. There they took a right, heading west toward the village of Ozerki.

It was then that the news about the assassinations of Luganov and Nimkov finally broke on Radio Moscow. The anchor, her voice thick with emotion, read a statement that had just been issued by the presidential spokesman. The report had few specifics, but two items hit Marcus and Oleg like a double-barreled shotgun blast.

The first was that Prime Minister Grigarin was dead as well.

The second was that Oleg was being accused of the murders of all three.

22

This was the first they'd heard of Grigarin's death.

Neither Marcus nor Oleg had been anywhere near the prime minister's residence, nor had Jenny. So who had killed him? How had it been done? And why? And why were the authorities pointing the finger at Oleg?

As they drove, the questions kept coming. The answers did not. Soon they were approaching the outskirts of the fishing village. Lights were on in every home along the way. Fires blazed in every fireplace; they could see smoke pouring out of every chimney. Businesses and schools were closed due to the freakish weather. Marcus could picture families huddled around their televisions or radios, listening to the horrifying news out of the Kremlin.

He was starting to feel guilty for having left an open bottle of vodka at the snowplow driver's side. It was clever but unkind. The man would be found soon enough. If his fellow drivers or the police found him "blacked out" in the cab, he'd protest his innocence and insist that someone had jumped him, framed him. But would anyone believe him? Marcus had noticed the driver was wearing a wedding band. What if he also had kids? What if he were fired? How would he support his family?

Marcus wasn't used to lying and deceiving people. He wasn't cut out for it. He didn't work for the CIA. He wasn't a spy. He'd never dreamed of being a NOC, a "nonofficial cover" officer. He'd never been drawn to the black ops side of the intelligence community.

He'd grown up on the Front Range of Colorado with a simple dream of being a police officer. He wanted to enforce the law, not break it. He wanted to protect people, not kill or frame them. His decision to enlist in the Marines had been spontaneous. He'd seen the al Qaeda attacks on TV on 9/11. He'd watched the Twin Towers collapse and the Pentagon burn, and he'd been enraged. He couldn't abide the thought of sitting on the sidelines while his country was savaged by radical Islamists. So he'd signed up and headed for Afghanistan and Iraq. Later he'd joined the Secret Service for pretty much the same reason. He knew the Islamists were going to come after his nation's leaders. He had the skills to protect the president, the vice president, and other dignitaries and felt the responsibility to do so. It wasn't more complicated than that.

Now, however, he was in uncharted waters. He wasn't acting on orders from Langley or the White House. In fact, for the first time in his adult life, he was not acting under any legal authority, and it unsettled him. What exactly were the rules he was playing by? And how was he going to get the three of them out of Russia without further injury or needless violence? At the moment, Marcus had no idea. So he uttered a silent prayer—of gratitude that they'd survived this long and for the wisdom to know what to do next.

It was well past midnight on the Front Range when Marjorie Ryker got home.

It was rare that she stayed up this late, rarer still that she went out to a movie with the ladies from her Bible study. It wasn't simply that she couldn't afford many extras, living on her monthly Social Security check and a modest Air Force pension after the death of her first husband. She also had no desire to fork over a single dime to the movie moguls who kept pumping toxic sewage into the country she both loved and feared for, even if her senior discount did entitle her to free popcorn and a soda.

She fumbled with her keys for a moment upon arriving back at her modest two-story home on the north side of Monument and wished she had remembered to change the lightbulb on the porch before she'd left for the multiplex. The moment she finally got in the door, the phone was ringing off the hook. It was her eldest daughter, calling from Fort Collins. The tone in her voice put Marjorie instantly on edge.

"Mom, where've you been? I've been calling you all night."

"I went to the movies with Helen and Pam."

"Have you seen the news?"

"No, why? What's going on?"

"There's been a shooting in Moscow."

"Where?" Marjorie asked, not immediately grasping the import.

"*Moscow*, Mom—isn't that where Marcus is?"

"Uh, well, he was, but—"

"Someone has killed the Russian president and the prime minister and some other guy. Wasn't Marcus going to meet the Russian president?"

"Yes, yes, he was, but relax, honey; he left there several days ago. He should be back in Washington by now. I'm sure he's fine."

"That's what I thought. But I called him, Mom—six times in the last hour. He's not answering his phone."

"Okay, I'll call him myself," she told her daughter. "I'm sure he's fine, but I'll get back to you the moment I hear anything."

The two women reluctantly said good-bye and hung up. Marjorie Ryker steadied herself against the wall with one hand and a kitchen chair with the other. She'd had to fight back her worries for her son for as long as she could remember. Her defense mechanism was to tell herself that everything was fine until she knew otherwise. She'd been the wife of a fighter pilot, after all. She knew all about the men in her life taking risks. She would never get herself out of bed in the morning if she let herself constantly dwell on her fears. It wasn't denial, she told herself. It was faith. God was real and he was big and he was sovereign, and she'd better trust him every moment of every day or she'd be a paralyzed wreck.

Her dependence on God had driven her out of her bed and down to her knees in prayer on countless nights when those men didn't come home. It had driven her to her knees the night she'd learned her daughter-in-law and grandson had been murdered. And she knew it would drive her to her knees tonight as well.

23

About a half kilometer east of the tiny fishing hamlet of Ozerki, Oleg pointed to the dacha owned by Boris Zakharov's brother. Marcus slowed and studied it carefully. It was dark and shuttered. No light emanated from any of the first- or second-floor windows. No smoke curled from the chimney. The driveway hadn't been shoveled or plowed since the storm first hit. It was covered in nearly a foot and a half of freshly fallen snow.

"Empty," said Oleg. "Just like I said."

Marcus stopped but didn't pull in.

"What's the matter?" the Russian asked. "That's the place, and we need to get Jenny inside."

"An unplowed driveway doesn't tell us anything," Marcus said. "How do we know the brother isn't there but just sleeping? Or what if he's away, like you said, but someone else is visiting or house-sitting? How many brothers and sisters does Boris have?"

"Just the one brother."

Marcus was still wary. To pull in and enter the house without any idea what was happening inside was a risk. With the news breaking out of Moscow, they could not afford to be seen by anyone, and any miscalculation could prove fatal.

But finally he decided Oleg was right. They needed a base camp, at least for a day or two, for Jenny's sake as well as their own, some place safe to sleep and cook and figure out their next moves, and the Zakharov dacha was as good as any. The chance that anyone was home was minimal. And where else were they going to go on the Karelian Isthmus in a blizzard in their second stolen vehicle of the day?

Marcus switched on the four-wheel drive and backed down the driveway. If they needed to get away quickly, this ought to give them a bit of an edge. Putting the Jeep in park, Marcus double-checked the silencer-equipped, Russian-made pistol in his pocket. Then, leaving the engine running, he stepped out into the drifting snow, partially closed the driver's door behind him, and moved around to the rear of the house.

Peering through the back windows, he saw no signs of human activity nor evidence of a pet. He spotted a boathouse down by the water's edge, already boarded up for the winter. There wasn't another dacha for at least a half kilometer on either side. For the moment, he was satisfied. There was no one around.

He tried to open the back door. It was locked. He tried several windows, but they were either locked or frozen. He unsheathed the hunting knife from his belt and used it to pop out a small pane of glass from the frame of the back door. He expected to hear the glass clatter on the floor, but when there was very little sound, he concluded the floor must be carpeted. He paused for at least a full minute, straining to hear any sound indicating someone stirring inside, but it was difficult to hear much of anything over the roar of the storm. Finally he reached his gloved hand inside the window and turned the lock to the right. Then he pulled his hand back out, put away the knife, and turned the handle.

When the door creaked open, Marcus stepped inside and shut the door behind him. There were white utility curtains on all the windows, and they were drawn. He realized he'd forgotten to bring a flashlight. He stood motionless for a moment, letting his eyes adjust to the shadows and listening for movement.

He had entered a small dining room. There was an antique mahogany table in the center of the room, surrounded by five matching upholstered chairs, two on either side and one at the far end. Across the room was an antique hutch containing fine china—plates, goblets, and serving dishes of various kinds. The floor was covered by a thick carpet that looked Persian or perhaps Afghan. Through an archway, Marcus could see into a darkened living room. He spotted an overstuffed chair and the edge of a coffee table, and he could hear the rhythmic *ticktock, ticktock, ticktock* of what sounded like a grandfather clock around the corner.

The kitchen was to his immediate right. It was sparse and spotless. Marcus saw no dishes piled up in the sink, no pots on the stove. A refrigerator hummed against one wall. There was a coffeemaker plugged in on the counter. It was empty and off. The room was cold, as was the entire house, though not cold enough to see his breath. That meant the heating system was on but left on a low setting, perhaps simply to keep the water pipes from freezing and bursting.

The house had all the signs of being owned by an older man—a pensioner, in all likelihood. Comfortable but not wealthy. The place seemed empty, yet something bothered Marcus. For a moment, he couldn't place it. He scanned both rooms again, and then a third time, before it struck him. There was no dust on the kitchen counters or the dining room table. He could not see a fireplace from this vantage point, but the longer he stood there, he began to smell the slightest trace of woodsmoke. It was not fresh, but it was not old. And where was the sixth chair at the table? The carpet was worn down where the four legs of the chair usually sat. So where was it?

Marcus's pulse quickened. His fists tensed. Someone *was* living here, and they had been here recently.

Slowly he moved toward the living room, measuring each step, his senses on full alert. His right hand moved toward the pistol in his pocket. But it was too late. As he came around the corner into the living room, he found himself smashed over the head with the missing dining room chair. Stumbling back, he saw a figure charging at him. The man drove into Marcus's gut and sent him sprawling back over the table and into the hutch, which toppled onto him, sending dishes crashing. His assailant shoved the table aside and grabbed another chair, raising it over his head and bringing it down with all his might.

Marcus rolled right just in time. The chair shattered in a hundred pieces. Splinters went flying everywhere. Marcus held his hands over his head in a defensive posture, protecting his eyes and face. The man kicked Marcus in the back and then in the stomach as he tried to roll away. Then he reached down, seized Marcus by his jacket, yanked him to his feet, and began landing one blow after another into Marcus's stomach and ribs.

The man was enormous, well over six feet tall, and immensely powerful. Caught almost completely off guard by the attack, Marcus was having trouble fending off the blows. Then the man landed a direct strike to Marcus's face.

He heard the cartilage in his nose crack.

24

The force of the blow sent Marcus staggering across the kitchen.

He slammed into the fridge and collapsed to the floor. Blood was gushing from his nose. But when his assailant moved in to finish him off, Marcus counterattacked. Surging with adrenaline, he lunged, driving his head into the man's midsection. They smashed into the back door, and Marcus began returning blows.

Suddenly the man drove his knee deep into Marcus's stomach, then shifted his weight and achieved a reversal. Marcus was now on his back. His attacker was on top of him, pinning his legs to the floor and driving his meaty fists into Marcus's bleeding head.

Face-to-face now, Marcus was stunned. He had expected to see a young man. Instead, the figure raining blows down on him had to be in his mid to late sixties. He was completely bald and had a thick graying beard, yet his body was rock hard. He was not only a skilled fighter, he had the eyes of a killer.

Marcus feverishly tried to maneuver, to alter the dynamic, but he was being overpowered and beaten to a pulp. No one could hear them struggling, and no one was coming to help him. He'd given Oleg strict orders to stay in the car and keep Jenny safe. Marcus's mind reeled, searching for options.

He'd been foolish in taking Oleg's advice and coming to this house. He had failed to listen to the warning bells going off in his own head. In so doing, he'd put their lives and mission in mortal jeopardy. But there was no room for hesitation now. It was kill or be killed. So Marcus stopped second-guessing himself and let his training take over.

The first thing he did was stun his attacker by no longer protecting his face with both arms. The man's eyes flashed with fury and delight, assuming his victim was giving up. But as the blows came down even harder now, Marcus reached for the hunting knife attached to his belt. He quickly unsheathed it, and before the man saw what was coming, Marcus plunged the blade into his stomach—the only organ he could reach—and ripped it laterally with all his strength.

The killer's eyes turned to shock and then to horror. The punches stopped coming. Blood began to pour from his mouth. Marcus felt his weight shift and seized the moment. He pulled the knife out of the man's midsection, grabbed the handle with both hands, and drove it into his chest. Simultaneously he kicked his legs free and flipped the man onto his back, where he thought he could finish him off.

But he refused to die. Instead, he kneed Marcus in the groin and shoved him away. Marcus lost his grip on the knife and scrambled backward. The man rose to his feet and brought both hands to his chest as though he was going to remove the knife but then seemed to think better of the idea. Instead he stumbled to the kitchen, ripped open a drawer, and pulled out two butcher knives.

A twisted smile spread across the man's face. His teeth were dripping with blood. This was no mere pensioner. He had to be a former Special Forces operator, perhaps even a Spetsnaz commando. Without question, this was a man who had seen far more combat than Marcus had, a man who had killed for a living and loved what he did. Even though he now knew he was going to die, he clearly had no intention of dying alone.

Marcus sprang to his feet and backed away. His opponent was moving toward him, raising both knives as he approached. Marcus knew what was coming. He was going to hurl them, one after the other, and when Marcus was down—and he would surely go down—his attacker was going to gut him like a deer.

Marcus suddenly backed into something. The grandfather clock. He glanced left, looked right, but there was no place to run, no chance to flee. The front door was locked. The back door was blocked. He was out of options, save one. He, too, was a trained professional, with reflexes honed after years in the Marines and the United States Secret Service.

His eyes locked with the killer's, Marcus slipped his right hand into his jacket pocket, careful not to make any sudden moves to shift the man's gaze. Finding the pistol, he gripped it hard. There wasn't time to draw it out, and there was no need to. Marcus simply squeezed the trigger once, then again, and then a third time. Shock came across the man's eyes. Then those same eyes rolled up in the man's head. The knives fell from his hands, and he collapsed to the floor.

Marcus didn't dare go near him to check his pulse or see if he was still breathing. Even if he was, what then? He hadn't the skills to put this guy back together, and he certainly couldn't take him to a hospital or call an ambulance. So Marcus finally drew the pistol from the smoking pocket of his leather jacket, aimed, and put two more bullets in the man's chest, just to be sure.

Only then did he go to the lavatory, crack his nose back into place—wincing in pain—and stuff his nostrils with toilet paper. Only then did he wash the blood off his face and proceed to thoroughly search the house. Only then did he pick up the knives and take them back to the kitchen. And only then did he head for the garage.

Oleg gasped when he saw Marcus's battered, swollen face.

"What in the world . . . ?"

But Marcus said nothing. Instead, he got in the driver's seat and slammed the door behind him. Then he backed the Jeep into the garage and parked next to a gleaming new Mercedes C 300 sedan. He shut off the engine, got out, pulled the garage door down, and locked it.

"Help me get her up to one of the bedrooms," Marcus said quietly. "Then I'm going to need a little help cleaning up."

Oleg nodded but said nothing more. Instead, he got out of the passenger side and came around the Jeep to the rear door that Marcus had just opened. He took Jenny's legs as Marcus slipped his arms under hers and lifted her out.

It was not difficult work. Jenny was slender, lean, and by no means heavy. Oleg pegged her weight at about fifty-five or sixty kilos, give or take—maybe 130 pounds. Probably in her early thirties. She was of medium height—about Oleg's height, in fact—with a runner's build.

He still had no idea who this brunette really was. He didn't even know her full name. All Oleg could really say about this woman was that she was fluent in Russian, an accomplished pilot, an expert shot, and as brave as anyone he'd ever met. She had taken a bullet to save their lives and hadn't cried, hadn't whimpered, hadn't complained, had barely seemed bothered by it at all. Given the circumstances and her skill set, he had to assume she worked for the CIA.

As they entered the house, Oleg was completely unprepared for what he saw. There was blood everywhere. Broken furniture. Shattered dishes. Shell casings. The acrid stench of gunpowder hung thick in the air. Then he saw the bullet-ridden body lying on a blood-soaked carpet, half in the living room, half in the dining room, the handle of a six-inch blade protruding from his chest.

Oleg swore when he recognized the face. "You've killed Zakharov's brother!"

"Was he Spetsnaz?"

"Yes, he was."

"You might have mentioned that," Marcus said without emotion. "Give me a hand."

Oleg was too stunned to say anything more. He wished he had been more forthright about the home they were breaking into. He had owed Marcus Ryker the whole truth. Ryker had, after all, repeatedly saved his life in the last twelve hours. Indeed, Ryker had saved countless lives by keeping their two countries from going to war. The American had shown astonishing courage under fire, and Oleg owed him a great debt. He'd been intrigued with Ryker ever since he'd first seen him on TV, receiving a medal in the East Room of the White House a week after the Secret Service agent and his colleagues had saved the lives of the American president and the First Family during a terrorist attack on the White House. After that, Oleg had done a good deal of research on the man. The more he learned, the deeper his respect grew.

So Oleg kept quiet and remained focused on the task at hand, though he promised himself he would not hold out on Marcus again in the future.

The two men carried Jenny to the second floor and laid her on a bed in a corner room.

"Grab our gear from the Jeep—all of it," Marcus said, propping up Jenny's head with several pillows. "Put it in the master bedroom, and bring me the medical kit. Don't turn on any lights."

Oleg did as he was asked. He returned a few minutes later with all three rucksacks, the sniper rifle, and the AK-47. When he entered the master bedroom, he found Marcus already there, staring at the walls. As Oleg set the gear on the king-size bed, he followed Marcus's gaze. The walls were covered with framed photos, letters of citation signed by some of the highest-ranking officers in the Russian military, and a half-burnt Afghan flag shot through with multiple bullet holes. Marcus said nothing as Oleg handed him the medical kit. Instead, he headed back to Jenny's room, removed her boots and socks, and then unzipped and removed her jumpsuit. Now she was lying there in faded blue jeans, a black T-shirt, and a navy-blue sweater, all of which were completely soaked through with melted snow.

"Boris Zakharov's brother was not just Spetsnaz," Oleg finally admitted, standing in the doorway. "He was the commander of Directorate C."

"*Spetsgruppa Smerch,*" said Marcus, clearly familiar with the unit.

"*Da,*" Oleg said. "The man was a legend. Served with distinction in Afghanistan, Chechnya, the Northern Caucasus. You name a hellhole Russian Special Forces were sent to, and he was there. During my brief stint in the army, the mere mention that he was coming to your base was enough to give you nightmares."

"Then you ought to sleep peacefully tonight, knowing he is gone," said Marcus, his voice flat but tinged with an edge of reproach. "The guy was dirty."

"The Mercedes in the garage?" Oleg asked.

Marcus nodded as he stripped off his leather gloves and donned medical ones. "Wanna guess how much that car retails for in the States?"

"I have no idea."

"Forty thousand dollars, easy," Marcus said, examining Jenny's wounds.

"That's a bit steep for a retired general living on a pension."

"I'd say," Marcus agreed, asking for a flashlight and a pair of rubber gloves.

"You think he was selling drugs or running prostitutes?" Oleg asked, fishing both out of the kit.

"Probably both. When we're done, you might want to go through his papers. I doubt you'll need to dig too deep. All right—here, hold the flashlight."

Marcus asked for a pair of scissors, which he used to cut away Jenny's sweater and T-shirt, revealing an entrance wound on the front of her right shoulder and a much larger exit wound on her back. "Hand me that blanket."

Oleg reached for a hand-knit wool blanket lying on a wooden rocking chair and gave it to Marcus, who draped it over Jenny, covering her for modesty as well as warmth, leaving only her wounded shoulder exposed. Then he stepped into the bathroom, filled a glass with water, and returned to the bedroom, where he dabbed and peeled away a few remaining shreds of cloth around the wound. The swelling was beginning to go down.

"How'd you know all that snow would stop the bleeding?" Oleg asked, scooping up scraps of T-shirt and throwing them into a waste bin in the corner of the room.

"Something I picked up in the Corps," Marcus replied as he examined the wound more closely. "The freezing temperature of the snow slows the flow of blood until it coagulates and seals up the hole. That's the theory, anyway. I'd never actually tried it till today. Not much snow in Kabul or Baghdad. But she was lucky. The bullet went right through the flesh. It came out the other side and didn't shatter any bones. If it had . . ."

"She would have needed more than snow."

Marcus nodded. "So far there's no infection, so that's something."

Marcus grabbed a tube of antibiotic ointment from the kit, applied it to two gauze pads, and taped one over the entrance wound and the other over the exit wound. He gave Jenny several shots—an antibiotic, another dose of painkillers, and a sedative. Then he hooked up a makeshift IV to get some fluids and a bit of nutrition back into her system and asked Oleg to go back into the master bedroom and find a clean T-shirt and sweater.

"Be sure to keep your gloves on," he warned.

"You're worried about fingerprints?" Oleg asked.

Marcus nodded. Oleg was incredulous but held his tongue. *The American couldn't be serious,* he told himself. *The man's blood—and thus DNA—was all over the living room, dining room, and kitchen.* Oleg seriously doubted fingerprints would be the thing that gave them away.

26

Oleg brought back the items Marcus had asked for.

Then he stepped into the hallway. His hands were shaking. He desperately needed a cigarette. But he didn't want to smoke anywhere near Jenny, so he crossed the hallway into the master bedroom, lit a match, and took a long drag. The warm smoke filled his mouth and nostrils and lungs. The familiar sensation was soothing, but it did nothing to calm his nerves.

The body count resulting from his decision to take out Luganov was mounting, but Oleg didn't regret what he'd done. He'd acted in defense of his nation, he told himself, to prevent a needless and likely apocalyptic war with NATO. On this, his conscience was clear. He'd never intended to kill Dmitri Nimkov, however. He'd expected President Luganov to be alone. The FSB chief wasn't supposed to be at the presidential palace, much less joining the president in his private study. But once Nimkov had entered the picture, Oleg had had no choice. Taking out Nimkov was unfortunate but essential. But then who had assassinated Maxim Grigarin? He certainly hadn't. Nor had Marcus. They'd been nowhere near the Russian prime minister. Nor did they have any motive to kill the man. But someone did, and it was clear they'd used the assassination of Luganov and Nimkov as cover to make their own move.

Oleg ran through various suspects in his mind, but for the moment he couldn't see a front-runner. Whoever it was, Oleg knew they were likely coming after him next. Marcus was right. It wouldn't take long for Moscow to discover that Oleg, Marcus, and Jenny hadn't been killed in the downed G4. They'd been lucky. Extremely lucky. They'd cheated death far too many times that day. How long would it be, he wondered, until their luck ran out?

Peter Hwang raced through the rain-swept streets of Washington.

He knew he was driving too fast. He knew he risked a ticket and a hefty fine. But it couldn't be helped. He was late.

Turning off Massachusetts Avenue onto Second Street, he nearly sideswiped a pedestrian, then screeched into a lot next to the Hart Senate Office Building and pulled his Saab into one of the last available parking spaces. He didn't waste time wondering why the place was so crowded in the middle of the night. He'd been summoned by the senator, so here he was. Grabbing his umbrella and briefcase, he made a dash to the Staff Only entrance. There, he showed the Capitol police officers his ID, put his things through the X-ray machine, and cleared through the magnetometer. Sixty seconds later, he bounded up the marble staircase, sprinted down the hall, and burst into the senator's office, soaked and breathless.

Robert Dayton sat behind his large oak desk, his feet perched on a credenza. The senior senator from Iowa sported a brown linen suit, a light-blue silk tie with matching pocket square, and blue suspenders. At seventy-one, Dayton was not only a lifelong member of the Democrat Party. He was also widely considered one of the nattiest dressers on

Capitol Hill. And he was the ranking minority member of the Senate Select Committee on Intelligence and now actively exploring a run for the Democratic nomination for president.

The only other person in the room was Annie Stewart. A sharp, articulate, and quite attractive blonde with big green eyes, Stewart was the senator's foreign policy advisor and longest-serving aide. She'd worked with Dayton since earning her bachelor's in history from American University and a master's degree from Georgetown's School of Foreign Service some fifteen years earlier. Privately, Hwang was smitten with her, but while she was friendly and professional, she had not shown him any particular interest, and Hwang hadn't yet mustered the courage to ask her out.

Neither the senator nor Stewart acknowledged Hwang as he entered the room. Both were glued to the bank of four TV screens mounted on the far wall. One was transmitting live images from the Senate floor. The other three were turned to CNN, MSNBC, and Fox News, though only audio from MSNBC could be heard.

"What's going on?" Hwang asked, trying to catch his breath. "Where's everyone else? What happened to the meeting?"

When neither answered him, Hwang turned to the monitors and suddenly realized why. For the better part of the last twenty-four hours, he had been tied up in a health care policy conference in Los Angeles and thus in a news and social media blackout. He'd taken the red-eye from LAX and upon landing at Dulles International Airport headed straight for the parking garage and sped into D.C. Now every muscle in his body tensed as he saw the wall-to-wall coverage of the triple assassination in Moscow.

How was this possible? He and Stewart and the senator had just been in Moscow. They'd just met with Luganov in his office, inside the Kremlin. They'd seen the security. It was airtight. There was no way someone could have penetrated it. And then a single terrifying thought flashed across his brain.

Where was Marcus?

27

As Oleg lit his second cigarette, Marcus entered the master bedroom.

He had found a laptop in Zakharov's study. It was not password protected, and since Zakharov had clearly been living here and had no doubt been online recently, there was no risk in using it to connect to the Internet via the dacha's Wi-Fi. Oleg peered over Marcus's shoulder as the American pulled up various news websites and scrolled through them, looking for stories out of Moscow and St. Petersburg.

More details were beginning to leak out about the three assassinations and the manhunt for those responsible. Some two hundred Muscovites had been arrested and hauled in for questioning, and a forty-eight-hour curfew had been imposed on the capital city. Prime Minister Grigarin had not been shot, as Oleg had assumed. Rather, the preliminary assessment of the bodyguards and FSB agents on the scene at the prime minister's residence was that he was poisoned by something slipped into his tea. Acting FSB chief Nikolay Kropatkin was scheduled to give a press conference in a few hours and was expected to reveal damning evidence that Oleg Kraskin was not only to blame but had been working with at least two collaborators.

Then Marcus came across a story that hit Oleg harder than he'd have expected.

"Katya Slatsky, the acclaimed figure skater who competed in three Olympic Games, winning a gold medal and two silver medals, was found dead in her Moscow apartment this morning," reported Reuters. "Moscow police have ruled the death a suicide. They say she suffered a single gunshot to the right temple. A handgun registered in her name was found at her feet and there was gunpowder residue on her right hand. The skater, widely rumored to be a longtime paramour of the late President Luganov, was thirty-three years old."

"They killed her," Oleg said, half under his breath.

"Not necessarily," said Marcus, as a picture of the stunning blonde appeared on the screen. "She had to have been distraught."

"No," Oleg insisted. "They killed her. There was no reason to, but they just did it anyway."

"How can you be sure?" asked Marcus.

"She was left-handed," Oleg said, smoke curling about his head.

They finished the story, but there were scant details.

"Look, I need you to search all the Russian news sites for any mention of my name or Jenny's," Marcus said, shifting gears. "They're saying you had two accomplices. We need to know if they're specifically linking us to you."

"All right," said Oleg, still in a daze. "What's her last name? I never thought to ask."

"It's Morris," Marcus replied, "but it doesn't matter. I don't think it's her real name anyway. Just search for Jenny or Jennifer and let me know what you find."

"Okay, but where are you going?"

"I need to shower and give myself a bit of first aid. Then we have to clean up the downstairs and figure out some food. Keep an eye on

Jenny, and don't do anything stupid like turn on your mobile phone or send an email. Got it?"

Oleg nodded, a bit offended for not being trusted but grateful for a few moments to himself. Everything was moving so fast. In some ways he was at the center of it all. Yet in other ways he was a million miles removed. Never had he felt so alone.

As Marcus headed to the bathroom, Oleg sat down on the bed and began searching every Russian news site he could find. But his thoughts soon turned to Marina and Vasily. How were his wife and only son? Where were they? Were they safe? Did they know what he had done? Would they ever forgive him?

Oleg couldn't imagine how. What he could imagine was FSB thugs bursting into his mother-in-law's home on the southern edge of St. Petersburg in the wee hours of the morning, arresting them all, and interrogating them for hours. Surely the authorities would suspect Marina knew all about the plot. They might even believe that Yulia Luganova had hatched the plot herself and persuaded her son-in-law to implement it, not to stop her ex-husband from launching a suicidal war with NATO but to take revenge for the cold, even savage way the president had divorced her, banished her from Moscow, and then taken up with Katya Slatsky.

Neither Marina nor Yulia were involved, of course. Oleg hadn't told them a word of what he'd been planning. For all the strains in this twisted family, and there were many, Oleg loved these women and his son. Above all, he had done what he had done for them. But he shuddered at the thought they might come to harm because of his actions.

Then the TASS news service out of Moscow broke a major new story.

CABINET NAMES PETROVSKY ACTING PRESIDENT
(TASS NEWS SERVICE — MOSCOW)

In an emergency vote following the assassination of President Aleksandr Ivanovich Luganov, the Russian cabinet named Mikhail

Borisovich Petrovsky as acting president of the Russian Federation, effective immediately.

Petrovsky will speak to the country in a live televised address at 9 p.m. Moscow time. He is expected to brief the nation on the events of the last few hours and the manhunt under way to bring the perpetrators to justice.

The 64-year-old native of Volgograd previously served as the nation's defense minister.

His appointment as president was approved on a voice vote of 29 to 0, according to a Kremlin spokesman.

The cabinet further voted to name Boris Yamirev, 53, as acting defense minister. The three-star general, who commanded the army's successful 2008 invasion and reacquisition of the eastern provinces of the Republic of Georgia, previously served as deputy defense minister.

Nikolay Kropatkin, the 42-year-old deputy director of the FSB, was named the security agency's acting director.

Each man will serve for sixty days, at which point the cabinet is required to reauthorize their appointments.

No successor has yet been named to the post of prime minister, but two senior Kremlin officials said an announcement would likely come in the next few days.

So Petrovsky was taking over, Oleg mused. That hadn't taken long. And it had been unanimous. But what did that mean for the war? Was the Kremlin going to back down from a head-to-head confrontation with NATO? Or were they already too deeply committed?

28

"Please tell me it's not possible," Senator Dayton said.

Pete Hwang started to answer, then realized the senator wasn't talk-ing to him.

"What exactly isn't possible?" Annie Stewart asked.

"Tell me Marcus Ryker isn't involved in this thing."

"Of course not, sir," Stewart said, clicking a pen open and closed again and again and shaking her head.

"You're absolutely certain?" Dayton pressed.

"Sir, he saved your life and mine," Stewart said. "How can you even think that?"

"That was a long time ago."

"You think he's changed?"

"People do."

"Not Marcus. He saved the president's life and the lives of so many others just a few years ago. You yourself hired him to keep us all safe on our trip to Europe. That was just last week."

"I know all that, Annie, but I—"

"Sir, please, you know Marcus Ryker. We both do. We've known him for years. He's not an assassin. He's a patriot, sir. What's more, he's a committed Christian. I'm not sure I've ever met someone who loves this country more or is more committed to protecting her and her leaders. But don't ask me. Ask Pete. He knows him best."

The senator turned to his new domestic policy advisor. A physician by training—and one of the most sought-after cardiologists in the country—Peter Hwang had only been on the team for a few months. Technically, he worked for Dayton's political action committee, not the government. But he had known both the senator and Annie Stewart a long time. They'd first met in Afghanistan years before, when Hwang and Ryker were part of a security detail that had come to the rescue after the military helicopters transporting the senator and his entourage were shot down near Kandahar and came under withering fire by Taliban jihadists. Since then, Dayton had made a point of staying in touch with the Marines in that unit, calling or writing each man every year on the anniversary of the rescue to say thank you and catch up on their lives and families.

When the senator had started planning his presidential run and needed an expert to come on board to help him develop a new health care plan, Stewart had suggested Hwang. The senator had loved the idea. So had Hwang. He was going through a nasty divorce and practically jumped at the chance to get out of his routine and change everything else about his life, even for a significant pay cut. In the short time they'd all worked together, Hwang knew, both the senator and Stewart had come to appreciate his counsel, his judgment, and his wit. It was Hwang who had brought Marcus Ryker back into their orbit, an idea Dayton had thought inspired days before.

Now the senator took his feet off the credenza and leaned forward in his chair. His face was pale. Hwang had never seen him like this. The man looked like he was about to have a stroke.

"Annie's right, Pete. You've known him the best and the longest. Could the Marcus you know be involved in taking out not just one but three Russian leaders?"

Hwang could see the anxiety in the senator's eyes. He knew what the man hoped he would say. But as much as Hwang wanted to say it was impossible, he found himself hesitating.

Marcus was not a cold-blooded murderer. That was for certain. And Annie Stewart was right when she said Marcus was a man of deep faith and strong convictions. Yes, he was willing to kill, but only to protect lives. Even after the murders of his wife and son, Marcus had let the police do their job. He'd never set out on his own to hunt down and arrest, much less kill, those responsible. Marcus Ryker was a law-and-order man, pure and simple.

Still, Hwang couldn't discount the bizarre chain of events that had unfolded in Moscow. It was, after all, Marcus who had suddenly made an unscheduled visit back to the U.S. Embassy early in the morning after they had met with Luganov and his son-in-law, Oleg Kraskin. In the hours that followed, Dayton, Stewart, and Hwang had learned that a senior-level Russian official had made contact with Marcus in the middle of the night. Apparently the mole had passed him highly classified information, including detailed war plans for Russia to invade the Baltics. Why Marcus? That still wasn't clear to Hwang, but the intel had been cabled back to the CIA and the White House and had proven both accurate and timely.

From there, Hwang remembered, things got stranger still. Senator Dayton had been asked by the U.S. ambassador to Russia to race back to D.C. to brief President Clarke on his meeting with Luganov. Marcus and the entire security detail he had assembled had been with them on the private jet as they'd flown out of Moscow. But rather than fly directly to Washington, they had made an unscheduled stop in Berlin. Why? Because Marcus said he had to get off there. Hwang had pressed his friend to explain. They didn't need to refuel. They were racing against the clock for the meeting at the White House. Yet Marcus had been evasive. He'd apologized to the team and explained that he needed to get off and attend to urgent business in the German capital. Hwang had even asked if Marcus wanted him to stay in Germany with him, but Marcus had brushed him off, saying it was something he had to take care of alone. Twenty minutes later, they had taken off without him.

Hwang remembered Stewart coming to sit next to him once they were over the Atlantic. She'd asked him what kind of business Marcus had in Germany. Hwang hadn't been able to give her an answer. Why wasn't Marcus flying back to Washington to brief CIA director Stephens, the president, and the National Security Council himself? she'd pressed. Wouldn't they want to talk to him, of all people, directly? How else could they adequately assess the reliability of the source?

Again, Hwang had no answers.

29

Hwang didn't want to believe it.

Every fiber of his being tried to resist the notion that Marcus could somehow be mixed up in this whole affair in Moscow. It went against everything Hwang thought he knew about his friend. Nevertheless, the idea was difficult to dismiss. He could imagine himself under oath before a federal grand jury or testifying before a congressional hearing.

Did Marcus Ryker have the capacity to sneak back into Russia and make his way to Moscow? he might be asked. Unless he planned to perjure himself, Hwang would have to answer yes. The two of them had trained together and served side by side in the Marines. The man was well acquainted with infiltration, escape, and evasion.

Did Marcus Ryker have the skills to kill President Luganov, Prime Minister Grigarin, and FSB chief Nimkov, or the skills to advise an accomplice to do so? Again, if Hwang were honest, the answer was yes. He had seen Marcus's skills under fire in Afghanistan. None of the guys in their unit had been a more accurate shot, not even Nick Vinetti, their sniper.

Did Marcus Ryker have an expert working knowledge of the security protocols of foreign governments—including the Russian government—that might enable him to obtain access to a world leader for the purpose of assassinating him? Yet again, if Hwang were under oath, he'd have to say yes. He knew how high Marcus had risen in the ranks of the Secret Service. The man hadn't just busted counterfeiters in Atlanta. He'd served on the Presidential Protective Detail, the most elite VIP protection unit on the planet. In Hwang's eyes, there was no one in the American government who was better trained than Ryker in the art and science of countering the threat of an assassin. Didn't that mean, by definition, that Ryker also knew as well as anyone in the world how best to circumvent such countermeasures?

The last question would be the most difficult of all, and perhaps the most damning. *In your expert opinion, Dr. Hwang, and from close observation of Mr. Ryker after the murders of his wife and son in a convenience store robbery in southeast D.C., did the defendant ever exhibit signs of clinical depression or other psychological or mental ailments that could have caused him to engage in behavior—including violent behavior—outside his typical character and usual behavior?*

How, Hwang thought, could he answer anything other than yes? The very night of the murders, Marcus's supervisor had required him to surrender both his service weapon and personal weapon. Hwang and Vinetti had personally stayed with Marcus in his apartment for weeks to make sure he didn't harm himself or others. Hwang had been there when his friend had to resign from the Secret Service, a job he loved, because he had fallen so deeply into depression.

Had things improved over time? To be sure, and a big part of that Hwang attributed to Marcus's faith. The man was in church every Sunday morning and every Wednesday night. He volunteered at the church, doing all kinds of odd jobs, even helping put on a new roof. Along the way Marcus had developed quite a friendship with the pastor,

Carter Emerson, an African American fellow in his seventies who'd battled his own demons from years in Vietnam. It was a friendship Hwang couldn't help but notice and admire and perhaps even envy.

Still, Hwang had also seen firsthand the tremendous loneliness and the lack of purpose that had continued to dog his Marine buddy. Aside from the pastor, Marcus wasn't making new friends. He wasn't keeping up with old friends. He wasn't dating. He wasn't even in regular contact with his mother or his sisters.

Hwang had talked to his friend about his depression repeatedly and encouraged him to get professional help. They'd talked about it as recently as two weeks ago. It was one of the reasons he'd urged Ryker to lead Senator Dayton's security detail on their trip to Estonia, Latvia, Lithuania, and Russia—he was worried about him, wanted to get him out of the house and doing something with purpose. Was it possible the pressure had been too much, that Ryker had simply snapped? Hwang couldn't say. He didn't have enough evidence one way or the other. As a friend, he wanted to say, "No, absolutely not." But as a medical professional—even though not a psychiatrist or psychologist—he couldn't rule it out.

The whole situation was horrifying on many levels, but clearly the one that worried the senator most was the possibility, however remote, that he could be directly linked to the man who had murdered or con- spired to murder Russia's top three leaders. The implications were dev- astating. If the press caught wind of the story, there would be a media firestorm. The pressure for the Ethics Committee to hold hearings would be enormous, and the scandal could very well crash and burn the senator's fledgling bid to take down Andrew Clarke and replace him as the next president of the United States.

Though it felt much longer, Hwang's entire analysis took just a mat- ter of seconds. But in the end, all he could manage to say was "I don't know, sir. But I'll find out."

30

Oleg decided he could wait to tell Marcus about Petrovsky's appointment as acting president.

With Marcus still in the shower, Oleg continued scanning the Russian news sites. Condolences were starting to pour in from Russian allies around the world. The president of Cuba was the first to put out a statement. This was followed by press releases from the leaders of Iran, Venezuela, China, and Syria. When Oleg saw a statement from the Dear Leader in Pyongyang, he couldn't help but think of his friend and comrade General Yoon.

Wondering whether Yoon had been trying to contact him in the three days since they'd seen each other in Pyongyang, Oleg logged in to Google mail, then kept typing until he entered a back door into a secure account used only by his North Korean counterpart. Marcus had warned him not to send an email, but he thought it was okay to check his secure account.

Waiting for him were more than a dozen urgent messages.

Complications with the Iranians, read the first. **Need to discuss immediately.**

My friend—Dear Leader is committed to keeping his word to President Luganov, but Tehran doesn't want our warheads, read the second. **They want yours, the new ones you just delivered to us. Not sure how they even know we have them, but they are putting heavy pressure on us to sell them at least five. We are not comfortable with this for reasons discussed during your recent visit. Please contact me immediately.**

Then, a few hours later, the tone and content of the next message was entirely different.

Hearing disturbing rumors out of Moscow—please advise, read one.

Reports of a coup—what can you tell me? read another.

Each message grew more frantic than the one before.

Is His Excellency the president safe? Are you? We are hearing terrible reports. Please contact me immediately.

Six minutes later: **Our ambassador in Moscow has been told President Luganov has been attacked. Foreign Ministry won't comment. Nor will our contacts in the FSB. Are you safe?**

Twenty minutes later: **Now we're hearing FSB chief Nimkov has been shot, severely wounded. Is this true?**

Sixteen minutes later: **Radio Moscow reporting Nimkov dead. They say President Luganov has been injured, but no other details. My wife is sobbing. We are all in shock. Where are you?**

Forty-three minutes later: **Dear Leader just called me personally, asking for the latest information. I told him I have four sources who confirm President Luganov is dead. Radio Moscow silent. All other Russian media refusing to confirm. DL does not want to issue statement until he is 100 percent convinced. Has ordered all our forces on high alert.**

Several hours later had come a new burst of messages from the general that made the hair on the back of Oleg's neck stand erect.

Just spoke to Nikolay Kropatkin—he says you were the shooter. They

haven't told the media yet, but a manhunt is under way for you. Please, my friend, tell me you had nothing to do with this.

Nine minutes later: Minister Petrovsky just called me, wanting to set up a call with DL. Says the evidence is conclusive that you shot both President Luganov and Nimkov. I don't know what to say. Why would you have done such a thing?

Four minutes later: Now hearing you stole a plane and are trying to escape out of Moscow to the West. What in the world is going on?

Thirty-one minutes later: Just spoke to a source in your Defense Ministry who says they found your plane and shot it out of the sky. My head is spinning. Don't know what to believe.

The final message read, I know you are not dead. I must speak with you immediately. Much to discuss, too much to convey in this format. Call me.

Thinking hard, Oleg logged off and slowly backed away from the screen. He wondered why Yoon seemed so certain he was still alive. Was it just a hunch? Wishful thinking? Or did he somehow have actual evidence? Oleg couldn't be sure. And what was it Yoon needed to tell him so urgently? One thing was certain: he had to alert Marcus to this new development. He stepped out into the hallway.

Marcus was checking on Jenny. Oleg told him about Petrovsky's appointment and Yoon's messages, then went into the steam-filled bathroom and locked the door behind him. He removed his gloves, stripped down, and stepped into the shower. As hot water streamed down his face, he tried to regain his bearings. He wondered again why Yoon was so desperate to contact him. If he had intel about the Russian nukes, Oleg and Marcus needed to craft a response right away.

A few minutes later, Oleg turned off the water, toweled off, and got dressed again. As he reemerged from the bathroom, Marcus read him the latest breaking news story from the Associated Press. First responders sifting through the wreckage of the Gulfstream business jet had recovered the remains of three bodies.

Oleg stepped into the master bedroom as Marcus kept reading.

Each body was burned beyond recognition, the AP reported. A

high-ranking Russian police source said that one of the bodies had been decapitated in the crash. Another was merely a torso. The third was missing both arms and a leg. It would take several days to do DNA analysis to identify the remains, the source said, speaking on condition of anonymity. But, the AP noted, "investigators feel they are making progress more quickly than they had expected, given the extent of the wreckage."

Oleg leaned over Marcus's shoulder and read the story silently for himself.

"I don't understand," he said. "All of us are present and accounted for in this house. What three bodies have they found?"

31

CIA HEADQUARTERS, LANGLEY, VIRGINIA

The director was furious.

Richard Stephens arrived back at Langley from his disastrous meeting at the White House and unleashed on his senior staff, who had gathered in the secure conference room adjacent to his seventh-floor office suite.

"How is it possible that a mere staffer on the National Security Council—a deputy, mind you—has more up-to-the-minute intelligence for the president of the United States than the director of the Central Intelligence Agency?" Stephens fumed. "Then, as if this weren't bad enough, on the drive back here to Langley I learn from NPR—not from any of you—that not only have Luganov and Nimkov been knocked off, so has the Russian prime minister. This is amateur hour, people. We look like fools—uninformed and unprepared. It stops now. You either start acting like the world's premier intelligence agency, or heads are going to roll. Now, tell me something I don't already know."

Martha Dell, the agency's fifty-six-year-old deputy director of intelligence—fluent in Russian, Mandarin, and Arabic with a master's degree from Oxford and two PhDs from Stanford—had anticipated both the emotion and the question, and she was ready with her reply. "Sir, we do have several new developments for you," Dell began.

"Let me hear them."

"Well, sir, first off, Mikhail Petrovsky has been named acting president, at least for the next two months until the Russian cabinet can assess his performance."

"Petrovsky? Interesting. What do you make of that?"

"Historically, we've seen him as a hard-liner. But my team and I are beginning to consider the possibility that Petrovsky is actually more moderate than Luganov."

"Why?" Stephens asked.

"Two reasons," said the DDI. "First, you'll recall what the Raven told us about Petrovsky's confrontation with Luganov in a recent cabinet meeting, warning Luganov that a move against NATO would be a mistake."

"Maybe," Stephens said. "But at this point, can we trust anything the Raven has told us? Maybe he's in league with Petrovsky in engineering a coup."

"It's possible," the DDI admitted. "But Petrovsky was elected unanimously by the cabinet, which means he's the consensus candidate in that room. And get this: we're just getting new reports in the last fifteen minutes that all Russian forces massing near the borders of Ukraine, Lithuania, Latvia, and Estonia have received new orders from the Kremlin. They're being told to withdraw immediately to positions at least one hundred miles from the border. NSA confirms what our HUMINT sources are telling us. They've intercepted messages from Russian central command to their generals in the field, ordering them to pull back."

"Petrovsky is moving to de-escalate," Stephens said.

"With the full support of the cabinet."

"So maybe he *is* more of a moderate. Okay, what else?"

"Sir, Russian media just started reporting that Oleg Kraskin was, in fact, the assassin responsible for the murders of all three leaders."

"Confirming what we've been hearing from Moscow station."

"Yes, sir."

"Does that also confirm that Oleg Kraskin is the Raven?" Stephens asked.

"It would appear that way, sir. And it's consistent with everything Marcus Ryker has told us and all the intel Ryker has passed on to us so far."

"How so?"

"Ryker was insistent from the beginning that he was not authorized to tell us the name of the mole. But Oleg Kraskin certainly had knowledge of the most up-to-date war planning. As the president's son-in-law and senior advisor, he had access to Luganov's personal correspondence and directives and the classified private phone numbers and email addresses of the highest-ranking officials in the Russian government, military, and intelligence networks. The analysts here have only just begun processing the tens of thousands of pages of documents—classified top secret or higher—that the Raven turned over to us. It's going to take a long while to get through it all. But again, it's all consistent with coming from Oleg Kraskin—with one exception."

"Which is?"

"Kraskin somehow found a way to meet up with Ryker to hand over the thumb drive. After that, it's possible Ryker allowed Kraskin to go back and meet with Luganov to get more intel, not knowing that Kraskin was going to assassinate the president and FSB chief. However, it's more likely that Ryker advised Kraskin on exactly how to pull off the hit and escape cleanly. He probably collaborated with Kraskin every step of the way. Indeed, the consensus here is on the latter scenario. Kraskin had access to the president, but he had no prior training for pulling off something of this magnitude. It strikes us as nearly impossible that Ryker didn't design the hit and walk Kraskin through the entire scenario, move by move."

"But . . . ?"

"But that doesn't explain the assassination of Prime Minister Grigarin," the DDI continued. "There was simply no time after taking out Luganov and Nimkov for Kraskin to get to Grigarin's home before heading to the airport to link up with Ryker and Jenny Morris. The distances, the traffic—none of it adds up. And what would Kraskin's motive have been for killing Grigarin, much less taking the risk of doing it? His motive for killing Luganov is fairly straightforward. Kraskin knows Luganov better than anyone. He concludes the man is not only evil but unstable and single-handedly dragging Russia into what could well become a nuclear confrontation with the West. Such an event could spell the end of the Russian Federation and the deaths of millions—possibly tens of millions—of Russian citizens. Kraskin considers himself a patriot. He becomes sickened by the ghoulish realization that he has married into a crime family, and he feels it's his duty to take action that no one else could or would."

"And his motive for taking out Nimkov?"

"That's not clear," the DDI conceded. "Certainly Nimkov was close to Luganov and shared the same aims. Maybe Kraskin feared Nimkov would carry on the Kremlin conspiracy against NATO and needed to be taken out as well. But it's equally plausible that Nimkov was simply in the same room with Luganov when Kraskin chose to strike, and Kraskin felt he had no choice but to take them both out in order to have any chance of escaping cleanly."

"Perhaps," said Stephens, maintaining a poker face but finally pleased with the work his staff was now producing. "Anything else?"

Dell nodded and smiled.

"Well?" Stephens prompted.

"They're alive."

The Raven might have been a mole, but he was not a spy.

Not a professional one, anyway.

Oleg Stefanovich Kraskin was an attorney by training, Marcus knew. But apart from a year working at one of Moscow's most prestigious law firms, the rest of his career had been spent at the vortex of the Kremlin. He had not only married into the First Family, he had served at the right hand of the former head of Russia's spy services. Yet Oleg had had little direct involvement in any matters of espionage. That is, until he had become the highest-ranking mole in the history of the Russian Federation.

Oleg's military experience had been brief. His parents were involved in international finance, not the intelligence services. Nor did Oleg have friends in the great game. While Luganov had brought his son-in-law slowly but surely into some of the most sensitive state secrets and given him the highest possible security clearance, the president had also shielded Oleg from many matters he considered his "private business."

Thus, the more Marcus explained the elaborate scheme that had been employed to get Oleg out of the country, the more intrigued Oleg became.

"Jenny and I concluded from the beginning that a private aircraft was a safer bet than flying commercial," Marcus explained, shutting down the laptop. "We knew we wouldn't have time for fake passports and disguises. And we couldn't take the risk of walking you through one of Moscow's major airports. What we needed most was privacy, secrecy, flexibility, and speed. Jenny has her commercial pilot's license with instrument ratings, so we decided on the Gulfstream. But like all missions, from the beginning you have to plan for everything that could possibly go wrong. What if the plane malfunctions in midair? What if Russian airspace is suddenly shut down? What if we're found out and chased by MiGs? And so forth. That led us to insist that there be parachutes, jumpsuits, and oxygen tanks on board, along with all the supplies we'd need to survive for a time on the run."

Oleg was listening intently, even as Marcus kept glancing out the window of the master bedroom to keep an eye on the driveway and the front walk.

"So we asked ourselves, *What if we have to bail, and the plane goes down for whatever reason?* That's when Jenny recalled a trick one of her mentors taught her. She requested that the Gulfstream be loaded with three bodies—people recently deceased in Germany, from which the flight was going to originate—two men and one woman, dressed like a pilot, copilot, and navigator. The bodies were to be loaded into the cargo hold but specifically positioned directly under the cockpit, or as close to it as possible, so that if the plane were shot down after we'd all jumped out, the three bodies would eventually be found and the FSB would think we were all dead."

"Whom exactly did she ask for the bodies?" Oleg asked.

"Not relevant for this conversation."

"You don't think I've earned your trust at this point?"

"Of course you have; that's why I'm telling you this," Marcus said. "But there are certain things you don't need to know—not now, perhaps not ever."

Oleg was clearly not satisfied with that answer. But Marcus didn't care and continued with his explanation.

"The Russian authorities found the bodies a lot faster than I would have guessed. I'm sure they're conducting DNA tests as we speak. We may have thrown them off the scent, but not for long."

"How much time do you think we have before they realize none of the bodies is mine?" Oleg asked, anxiety in his eyes.

"Maybe twenty-four hours—I doubt much more."

"Who's alive?" asked Director Stephens.

"One of them, at least—possibly more," said the DDI.

"What are you talking about?"

"Sir, we believe that either Jennifer Morris or Marcus Ryker is alive—possibly both of them—and Oleg Kraskin as well."

"Why? How?" Stephens asked, blindsided by the notion.

Dell explained that an NSA satellite had picked up a signal earlier that morning from the satellite phone the Agency had put onto the Gulfstream. The phone could only be operated by entering a nine-digit passcode, and only Morris and Ryker knew those codes by heart. While they couldn't be certain whose hands the phone was in, it had to be either Morris or Ryker.

"You think they jumped from the plane before it went down?" Stephens asked. "And lived?"

"One of them, at least. The phone was only turned on for a few seconds. We were able to pinpoint the location to a forest in the Karelian Isthmus, about twelve miles north of the largest amount of debris from the crashed Gulfstream."

"And then the signal went dead?"

"Someone turned the phone off, yes."

"So if it's Morris or Ryker, why haven't they called us and asked for an extraction team to come get them?"

"That, sir, is the $64 million question, the one we were discussing while we waited for you to arrive."

"And?"

"The consensus in the room is that Ryker is the one in control of the phone."

"Why is that?"

"If Morris had the phone—well, sir, she's a highly trained and disciplined officer, one of the Agency's best operatives and a station chief, at that. We have no doubt she would have made contact immediately upon getting to a secure location, out of immediate danger from the Russians."

"All right, I'm with you," said the director. "Go on."

"We know there was a shoot-out on the tarmac in Moscow just before the Gulfstream took off. We also know Morris was shot and wounded—severely enough that Ryker had to fly the plane. Marcus told the watch commander in the Global Ops Center as much when they spoke briefly after their chaotic departure from Moscow. At this point, several scenarios are possible. One, Morris died on the plane, and Ryker and Kraskin jumped without her. Two, they all jumped, but Morris didn't make it. Three, Morris did make it, but her injuries are preventing her from taking the lead among the three of them."

"Which leaves Ryker because Kraskin didn't know the passcode."

"Correct."

"Then why hasn't Ryker called in?"

The question was followed by silence. Stephens looked at the DDI, then around the room at his top Russia analysts. He turned to one, a twenty-nine-year-old woman with a PhD in Russian studies from Georgetown.

"Why hasn't Ryker called in?" he asked again.

"Would you?" the analyst asked.

"What do you mean?"

"Sir, Marcus Ryker was the Raven's handler. He had one job—get the guy's intel and get him safely out of the country. Instead, after getting the thumb drive, Ryker allows the Raven to leave his custody— a direct violation of his orders. The Raven goes straight to the presidential palace and pops Luganov in cold blood. Then he pops the FSB chief. Now, as Dr. Dell has noted, Kraskin has no experience in such matters. Ryker had to have helped him. Yet Ryker knows full well that this is all in blatant violation of U.S. law, international law, the Agency's code of conduct, basic morality—the list goes on. Sir, there's a lot we don't know right now. We're operating in the fog of war. But two things we do know: First, the Raven is an assassin. Second, Ryker is an accomplice. Would you call in under those circumstances?"

"Probably not," said the director. "But then why turn on the phone at all? Why let us know you're alive if you've gone rogue and are on the run?"

"Right now we don't know, sir," the analyst said. "Maybe Ryker wasn't carefully briefed by Morris in how to use the phone, though I doubt it. I know Jenny Morris. As the DDI said, she's an outstanding officer. I don't see her making a mistake like that."

"Then what?"

"Maybe in all the chaos and confusion of the last twenty-four hours, Ryker forgot that the code doesn't simply power up the phone but also sends us a flash confirmation that the person using it is alive."

"But you don't buy that," Stephens said.

"No, sir, I don't. Ryker's too smart. He's not one of us. He wasn't trained by the Agency. He doesn't know our tradecraft. But he's sharp. He's not just a Marine but a highly decorated combat veteran from Afghanistan and Iraq. He's a former special agent with the Secret Service, also highly decorated for bravery under fire. His file indicates he's got a near-photographic memory. Believe me, sir, he didn't forget."

"So he wants us to know he's alive, but not exactly where he is."

"That's what we're thinking, sir."

"Why?"

When the analyst hesitated, Martha Dell spoke up again. "I think he wants to make a trade, sir."

That took Stephens by surprise. "A trade? What kind of trade?"

"I think he's going to offer us the Raven."

"In return for what?"

"If it were me?" the DDI said. "I'd be asking for a full presidential pardon and entrance into the Witness Protection Program."

33

The call from Pete Hwang could not have come at a worse moment.

"I can't talk right now," Nick Vinetti said from behind his desk at the U.S. Embassy in Moscow with the ambassador holding on line one and deputy CIA director Martha Dell expected to call at any moment.

"Why not?" Hwang asked.

"Because I can't. My hands are a little full around here right now, Pete."

"But you'll call me the minute you hear something?"

"If I can."

"What does that mean?"

"Just what it sounds like, Pete. I'm sorry—I've got to go."

Vinetti had known Peter Hwang all their adult lives. Almost twenty years after boot camp, it still astonished Vinetti how high they and their two buddies from the Corps had risen. Hwang was a senior advisor to a U.S. senator that a growing number of columnists and TV pundits believed could be the next president of the United States. Their onetime sergeant, Bill McDermott, was now working at the White House as the second-highest-ranking official on the National Security Council. Vinetti himself was now the second-highest-ranking American diplomat in Moscow, while his beautiful and brilliant wife, Claire, was also in the Foreign Service, serving as the embassy's cultural attaché.

And then there was Ryker.

Over the years, the four men had done everything together. They'd fought together. Killed together. Chased girls together in their bachelor days. They'd also stood as groomsmen in each other's weddings, occasionally vacationed together as families, and gone to more funerals together for more fallen friends than any of them cared to remember.

Now one of them was wanted for murder and crimes against the Russian state. Vinetti hadn't seen it coming, and the dread he felt for what was surely ahead was growing.

He hung up the phone and shut his eyes. He wasn't being coy with Hwang. He simply had no answers. But this was a capital offense. As every hour passed, Vinetti's fear grew. As the ambassador's second-in-command, he would be the one ordered to oversee an operation to hunt down and take out the best friend he'd ever had.

"I apologize, Mr. Ambassador," he said, finally taking his boss off hold. "What can I do for you?"

"We'd better clean up downstairs," Marcus said.

Oleg nodded. "Of course. But first, I found something."

"What's that?"

"You really need to see it for yourself."

Oleg led him to a bedroom across from the master, not the room where Jenny was sleeping but another one next to it. Marcus followed him, and when Oleg flipped on the light and opened one of the dresser drawers, he saw dozens of large clear plastic sandwich bags filled with white powder. Oleg opened another drawer, revealing dozens more. He opened the closet to reveal still hundreds more, plus a large wall safe and several padlocked file cabinets.

Marcus opened one of the bags. One whiff and it was clear the elder Zakharov was running quite a drug operation, and a lucrative one at that. Marcus wasn't up on the latest street prices of cocaine in St. Petersburg and Moscow, but he had to figure this cache was worth at least several million dollars.

"I saw some tools in the garage," Marcus said. "See if you can find a bolt cutter."

Oleg hurried to it, and while Marcus waited for him to return, he scanned the framed photos on the walls, wondering where in Siberia the former Kremlin chief of staff was serving his prison term. The pictures saddened him. They had all been taken when Boris' brother was much younger. There was nothing more recent than high school except for one presumably taken the day Boris's brother had been inducted into the Red Army and had had all of his hair shaved off. Most were from his teen years—on a wrestling team, in a boxing ring, cliff diving with friends, standing on top of a mountain with his arm around a pretty blonde.

The faded photos reminded Marcus of his own youth, growing up in Colorado. It made him wonder. Why had this man taken the trail he had? Had he always been corrupt, even in his days in Spetsnaz? And what about Boris? Perhaps one brother had corrupted the other. The higher Boris had risen in Luganov's sphere, had he felt invulnerable? Had he pulled his brother into his criminal world to taste the fruits of what he felt were "just rewards"?

"Don't die, and don't get arrested," Marcus whispered aloud. But for the prayers of a godly mother, Marcus knew he might very well have gone down the same road.

Oleg returned with a pair of hedge clippers—not bolt cutters, but they would do. Marcus took them, fixed the blades against the first padlock, and pressed the handles together with all his might. The lock snapped apart and fell to the floor. Marcus did the same for each of the four other cabinet drawers. Inside the file cabinets was a gold mine of intelligence on a network of drug dealers, couriers, and middlemen throughout much of the northern Russian provinces. Then again, they weren't looking to bust a drug ring, and they hardly needed more evidence the elder Zakharov was dirty. What Marcus did need was hard, cold Russian cash. They had some that the CIA had included in their rucksacks, just in case. But if Marcus couldn't find a way to persuade the Agency to bring them back in, they were going to need to run, and that would take more rubles than they had. A lot more.

Marcus searched carefully through the cabinets. Finally, taped to the back wall of the last drawer, Marcus found what he was looking for—the override key for the safe. Fifteen seconds later, the tumblers had been bypassed. The safe door swung open, and both men smiled. They weren't going to need to worry about money anymore. And there was more in the safe than just stacks of cash. There were passports and driver's licenses of all kinds. There were diamond necklaces and bracelets and earrings. There were Rolex watches, a half-dozen boxes of Cuban cigars, two unopened boxes of brand-new satellite phones, and a dozen handguns with plenty of ammunition.

Maya Emerson was surprised at the name displayed on her caller ID.

She had just gotten home from an early choir practice and warmed up some of her homemade oatmeal. It was an unusually chilly and windy morning in Washington, and she and Carter, her husband of fifty-odd years, lived in a drafty town house in southeast D.C., just a few blocks from the Capitol in one direction and Lincoln Park Baptist Church in another. Carter was still there in a men's Bible study, and Maya didn't expect him home until afternoon. So, after finishing her oatmeal and washing her dishes, she'd begun ironing some of Carter's shirts and watching coverage of the crisis in Moscow when her cell phone rang.

"Hello?"

"Mrs. Emerson, this is Marjorie Ryker—Marcus's mother," came the familiar voice. "I do hope I'm not bothering you."

"Not at all, Marge. And how many times must I insist you call me Maya?"

"Well, I appreciate that. I saw that you'd called and I'm so sorry I missed you."

"That's all right, dear. Yes, I tried to reach you, kept getting your voice mail. Just wanted to see how you are and whether you'd heard from Marcus. Carter keeps calling but can't get ahold of him. We hoped you'd heard something."

There was a long silence before Marjorie answered.

"I'm in the valley of the shadow, Maya." Her voice began to crack.

"I'm sure you are, honey, but fear no evil," Maya replied. "Fear no evil—none whatsoever. Just keep calling on Jesus—your sweet, strong Jesus. You hear?"

"I'm trying."

"I know, and don't you give up now. He is with you, sweetheart. His rod and his staff will comfort you."

Maya heard no reply, just the sounds of a woman who had already suffered so much losing her battle to fight back another avalanche of tears.

"You've heard nothing from him?" Maya finally asked.

"Not yet, no," Marjorie managed to say, her voice trembling.

"Then come on, honey, let's pray right now—you and me. Let's kneel before the throne of grace."

34

By nightfall, Marcus and Oleg had cleaned up most of the downstairs.

They found nothing indicating why Boris Zakharov's brother had broken his normal pattern and remained at the dacha this late in the season. Marcus suspected he'd been conducting illegal business deals, but it didn't really matter now. The point was the neighbors had to know he had stayed behind and had likely seen him coming and going from time to time. Marcus concluded that anyone who passed by would expect lights to be on and smoke to be coming from the fireplace, and given that everyone on the isthmus was still being warned by authorities to stay inside due to the blizzard, they likely didn't have to worry about guests stopping by unexpectedly.

Thus, the broken furniture became firewood, and the blood-soaked Persian rugs turned out to be flammable as well. Indeed, anything that would burn and could not be meticulously scrubbed and cleansed of all DNA evidence was tossed into the roaring fire. When all the evidence was consumed, Marcus and Oleg brought in a few stacks of firewood from the garage.

Zakharov's body was another matter. They couldn't burn it. They couldn't dig a grave amid so much ice and snow. But they didn't want it in the dacha with them. So they wrapped it in the shower curtain from the upstairs bathroom, then buried him in the snow in the backyard. Almost two feet had fallen, and more was coming down every hour. Oleg was a dutiful worker. He did everything Marcus asked of him without pushing back. But when they'd finished covering the body, Oleg vomited until there was nothing left in his system.

The conversation between the two men during all those hours had little to do with cleaning and everything to do with evaluating their situation and plotting a solution. Oleg had not found any mentions of either Marcus or Jenny in any Russian media reports or in any international news stories. But they had kept the TV in the living room on at all times. Acting FSB director Nikolay Kropatkin had held a news conference in Moscow that was broadcast live. He'd spent a good deal of time on the manhunt under way, not just for Oleg but for "two additional accomplices," both of whom he considered "armed and extremely dangerous." When a reporter asked why authorities were not satisfied that the three bodies already found proved Oleg and his coconspirators were dead, the answer was both cryptic and ominous.

"I'm afraid I cannot get into the details at this hour. Suffice it to say we have reason to believe the conspirators may still be at large, and until we can prove otherwise, the manhunt—the largest in our nation's history, involving some five thousand soldiers and police officers—will continue."

At a few minutes after 9 p.m., Petrovsky, the acting president, addressed the nation. He began by taking a moment of silence for the three murdered leaders and vowed both to care for their families and to bring their killers to justice. Petrovsky announced that the Kremlin was offering a reward of one billion rubles—equivalent to roughly sixteen million American dollars—to any Russian citizen who could provide information leading to the arrests and convictions of the con-spirators. He also provided a phone number the public could use to call in tips to the police.

He then announced that he was ending Russia's military exercises along NATO's border, claiming he was doing exactly what President Luganov had promised to do. It was a bald-faced lie. Before his death, Luganov had publicly promised to pull Russian forces away from the borders but in reality had intended just the opposite—to order the sur-prise invasion of the Baltic states. Petrovsky knew it. The cabinet knew it too. Oleg had been there for the discussion, heated as it was. Still, Petrovsky made it sound like he was simply carrying out Luganov's final wishes and blamed the Americans and Europeans—not Luganov—for the soaring tensions between East and West.

Petrovsky prattled on for another few minutes about the need for global peace. He praised Luganov for the "historic agreement" he had recently signed with Pyongyang to denuclearize the Korean Peninsula. That, too, was a lie. Luganov had no intention of disarming the Dear Leader. Once again, Oleg knew, the opposite was true. He wondered if Petrovsky knew about the deal Luganov had actually cut with the Dear Leader.

The biggest takeaway for the two fugitives was that the stakes had just gone up significantly. Talk of a reward would deputize every Russian in the northwest of the country to be on the alert for anything suspicious.

Oleg was growing antsy. "We can't stay here," he insisted. "We have to get to Finland. Every hour that goes by increases the chances of us getting caught. So tell me—what's your plan?"

"Well, for one thing, we're not going to Finland," said Marcus, on his hands and knees and wearing rubber gloves as he scrubbed blood off the dining room walls.

"Why not?" Oleg asked. "We're less than two hours from the Finnish border."

"A border now guarded by thousands of soldiers on hair-trigger alert, ready to shoot us on sight," Marcus retorted. "No one in Moscow plans to 'arrest and convict' us, much less pay out such a big reward. If they find us, they'll kill us. Period. End of story."

"Then tell me we can fly out," Oleg pressed, the tension thick in his voice.

"In what?" Marcus asked. "We have no access to a plane or helicopter, and even if we did, anyone trying to penetrate Finnish airspace without a flight plan would be shot down either by the Russians or the Finns."

"Then by sea," Oleg said as he scrubbed a few drops of blood off the kitchen floor. "You saw the boathouse. We're on the Gulf of Finland. Surely we can find plenty of fuel, life preservers, everything we would need."

"You want to outrun the Russian fleet in a fishing boat?" Marcus asked, not bothering to look up. "Forget it. Your navy has dozens of combat ships and planes moving in and out of the gulf every day. The Finns have their own coast guard patrolling their waters with heightened vigilance. We'd never make it."

"Then what?" Oleg demanded, getting to his feet. "We can't just hunker down here. We have to move—and not just for our sake, but for Jenny's."

"I agree," Marcus said, stopping his work and looking into Oleg's eyes. "Look, I told you I'd get you out of Russia safely, and I will. But you've got to trust me."

"Trust you?" Oleg erupted. "What am I doing if not trusting you? I eluded my own security detail to come to you in the dead of night, at the risk of my life, to warn you of my father-in-law's plot against your country and all of NATO. I gave you our war plans. I gave you thousands of my country's most highly classified secrets. I left my wife and son to save my country. I even jumped out of a plane—all right, you pushed me out, but still—because you said it was the only way. Don't talk to me about trust unless you're willing to show me some by telling me your plan to get me out of this country before it's all too late."

Marcus was taken aback by the outburst. He stood slowly.

"All right, Oleg, calm down. I got it—and I'm sorry," Marcus said. "I'll tell you what I can, but you have to promise me you'll keep it together."

Oleg was trembling. His bloodshot eyes were watering. But he nodded as Marcus got him a glass of water from the tap. Oleg gulped it down, trying to catch his breath.

"Have a seat," Marcus said calmly. "I'll tell you what I know."

Oleg peeled off the medical gloves he was using to avoid contact with all the blood. He set them in the sink, went into the living room, and sat on the couch. Marcus also removed his gloves, then followed Oleg and took a seat in the overstuffed chair directly across from his Russian friend.

"The first thing you have to understand is this," Marcus began. "We're not only being hunted by the Russians. The Americans are hunting for us too."

35

Oleg, apoplectic, was back on his feet.

"Sit down," Marcus ordered.

"No," the Russian said, pacing the living room. "I don't understand. I did everything you asked, and now—"

"*Sit,*" Marcus repeated, more firmly this time.

Oleg hesitated, staring at Marcus, but finally retook his seat.

"Let's be honest with each other, Oleg," Marcus began. "The United States government did not ask you to kill President Luganov. Nor did they ask you to kill Dmitri Nimkov. You did that on your own."

"With your help," Oleg protested. "I wanted to, but you gave me the gun. You told me how to do it. You're as much in on this as I am."

"All true," Marcus said. "I believed you to be a patriot, not a traitor to your country, and I believed this was the only way to stop the war. But start looking at things from Washington's perspective. This isn't what they signed up for, is it?"

Oleg said nothing, but his right knee bobbed up and down with nervous energy.

"You offered the CIA information—good information, extraordinary information—and they said yes because they couldn't say no," Marcus continued. "In exchange, they offered you a boatload of money, safe passage out of your country, a new identity, and a new life, a safe life, far from the reach of the FSB, correct?"

"It was never about the money," Oleg insisted.

"Nevertheless," Marcus said. "They offered. You accepted. And they transferred $10 million into a Swiss bank in a numbered account—no name, just a number—and there it waits for you to come claim it or transfer it. Am I wrong?"

Oleg said nothing.

"Now, it's important for you to know that I never told Washington what you were going to do," Marcus continued. "For that matter, I never told Jenny, either."

Oleg's face betrayed how taken aback he was.

"I told no one," Marcus repeated. "I helped you because you asked me to. I helped you because I believed taking out Luganov was, in fact, the only way to stop Russia from invading the Baltics and taking NATO and the rest of the world to the brink of nuclear war. And frankly, I helped you because I could. I spent the best years of my life protecting my president. That gave me a little insight into taking out yours. But I never told Jenny, and I never told the higher-ups in D.C. They would have said no and cut us off completely. No plane. No supplies. We would have been cut loose to survive—or not—on our own. Love it, hate it, I don't really care—that's the choice I made. But now Washington is making their own choices. They cannot afford to be implicated in the assassination of two, much less three, Russian leaders."

"You know full well I had nothing to do with Grigarin's murder," Oleg shot back.

"It doesn't matter what I think," Marcus responded. "It only matters what the senior officers at the CIA think, what the folks on the

National Security Council think, what the president of the United States thinks—and right now, they think you're an assassin and that Jenny and I are your accomplices. Worse, they know it's going to look like the U.S. government just paid a Russian national $10 million not simply to spy for them but to kill for them. And they're right. That's exactly how it looks. Let's just say the chances of them helping us are pretty much zero. Follow?"

Oleg contemplated the gravity of that thought. "But just because Washington knows we weren't in the crash, that doesn't necessarily mean they know we survived, right?" Oleg asked, his desperation growing more evident.

Marcus shook his head.

"Why?" Oleg demanded. "It's possible we all could have died from the jump, right? I mean, they already know Jenny was seriously wounded back at the airport."

"They know we're alive," Marcus said calmly.

"How do you know?"

"Because I signaled them," Marcus said.

"*When?*" Oleg demanded.

"Earlier today, back in the forest. They know we're alive. They don't know where. But you can be sure they're looking—hard."

"But why would you do that?"

"Two reasons. First, Jenny needs professional medical attention. We've stabilized her. She's improving. But she still needs a doctor and probably surgery. We're certainly not taking her to a Russian hospital, which means we need to put her in the hands of the American government."

Oleg was quiet.

"Second, we need to get you out of Russia, or the FSB is going to find you and kill you, though they will probably torture you first. You're the most wanted man in this country. The longer we stay on Russian soil, the greater the chance we have of being tracked down. Our best chance—frankly, our *only* chance—is to persuade Langley to help us."

"But you just said—"

"I know what I said," Marcus replied. "You needed to hear it, because that's exactly how the Agency sees us. But we're going to change that."

"What do you mean?"

"We're going to get them to look at you and me as assets, not liabilities."

"How?"

"We're going to make them an offer they can't refuse."

THREE

36

Alireza al-Zanjani was late.

Bolting out of the armor-plated sedan that had whisked him from his office across the Iranian capital, the deputy commander of the Iranian Revolutionary Guard Corps and his senior intelligence advisor cleared through security and rushed up the marble staircase. They were greeted at the top by the chief of protocol and led down multiple corridors and through numerous checkpoints until they reached the private office of Iran's octogenarian spiritual guide.

"Principals only," the protocol czar whispered.

The intel officer didn't object. He knew his place. He had never entered the office before, nor would he today. He handed his boss a briefing book and took a seat in a lounge area where a half-dozen other aides were already milling about, drinking coffee, and talking in hushed tones about the political earthquake under way in Moscow.

Al-Zanjani was no longer wearing one of his expensive European suits. Rather, he was dressed in his standard attire of green combat fatigues and combat boots. He took a deep breath, then nodded to the security guards, who proceeded to open a massive vault door. Stepping forward into a spacious vestibule, he waited for the door to shut and lock behind him. Two well-built bodyguards—part of the ayatollah's personal detail—double-checked his credentials, though they both knew him well. A moment later, they unlocked and opened a steel door vaguely reminiscent of a submarine hatch and signaled for their guest to enter.

While al-Zanjani had met or briefed the Supreme Leader a number of times in his career, this was his first time to the cleric's inner sanctum. It was not a traditional office by any Western sensibility. There were no desks or chairs, nor any radios or televisions. Rather, the concave walls were lined with exquisite blue-and-green tile work. The floor was covered with a thick Persian carpet. A few small lamps provided only dim light. There were several lit candles on a low wooden table in the center of the room and a swirling fan hanging from the ceiling.

As al-Zanjani stepped over the threshold into what could be better described as a small prayer room than an office, he found the hastily called meeting already under way. Sitting to his left against the wall on a pile of large cushions was Grand Ayatollah Hossein Ansari, Iran's eighty-four-year-old Supreme Leader. He was dressed in a thick, flowing brown robe and black turban. He sported wire-rimmed glasses whose lenses seemed smudged with fingerprints and needed a good cleaning, and he stroked his neatly trimmed gray beard as he listened intently to the briefing. He was covered with a blanket and had a sizable stack of ancient religious texts beside him.

To the Supreme Leader's left, directly in front of al-Zanjani, was Yadollah Afshar. The sixty-one-year-old president of the Islamic Republic of Iran was also sitting on a pile of cushions, though he was not covered with a blanket. He wore a modest three-piece gray suit, more likely purchased in Moscow or one of the former Soviet republics than anywhere in Iran, and was taking frequent sips from a large water bottle due to the chronic problems he had with his one functional kidney.

To the Supreme Leader's right was one of his young personal aides. Al-Zanjani could not immediately remember his name. Ansari's aides were all typically recent graduates of the Shia seminary in Qom, and none of them seemed to last more than a few months. This was a tall and rather gangly fellow with a mop of thick black hair offset by small, round wire-rimmed glasses, sitting cross-legged on a cushion on the floor and taking notes on everything that was being said.

Directly across from the Supreme Leader, to al-Zanjani's right, was Mahmoud Entezam, the commander of the Iranian Revolutionary Guard Corps. Only fifty-three, Entezam was al-Zanjani's immediate boss. He was the youngest of the generals ever to rise through the ranks to lead the IRGC, in part because of his cunning and peerless leadership in helping Tehran effectively seize control of four Arab capitals—Baghdad, Beirut, Damascus, and Yemen's Sana'a—over the past decade, and in part because he had married a favored and quite lovely young niece of the ayatollah.

At present, Entezam was wrapping up his explanation of what was known so far about the triple assassinations in Moscow, drawing on firsthand reporting from Iran's ambassador to Russia and their many sources in Russia's security establishment. Al-Zanjani bowed to the Supreme Leader, ignored the leader's aide, and nodded to the other principals in the room. Then he took his seat on a cushion next to his boss. He wondered why neither the defense nor foreign minister was present until he remembered both were traveling abroad.

"So what you're saying, General, is that our three closest allies in Moscow are dead, and Petrovsky is now running the country," President Afshar said. Al-Zanjani was not surprised that it was the president, rather than the Supreme Leader, who spoke. Ansari rarely uttered a word in such meetings unless it was to pray or discuss a theological or spiritual matter.

"I'm afraid that is correct," the general replied.

"Was this a coup?"

"No, the evidence does not support such a conclusion," Entezam replied. "By all indications, it was the work of a tiny group led by the president's son-in-law."

"Tell me about this Petrovsky," President Afshar said.

"Until today, he was Russia's defense minister," the general said. "I've met with him a number of times. He has sold us a great deal of advanced weaponry and certainly sees us as an important ally of Moscow. But I must emphasize that we have not developed nearly as close a working relationship with Petrovsky—and certainly not the warm personal chemistry—as we had with His Excellency President Luganov."

"Is it true that Petrovsky has already blinked in the face of NATO and American threats?"

"He is withdrawing Russian forces from close proximity to NATO borders, if that is what you mean, Mr. President. But I wouldn't characterize him as a moderate by any means. Indeed, I believe he could not only be useful to us, but . . ."

"But what?"

"He might be easier for us to work with than Luganov."

"How so?"

"President Luganov rarely countenanced discussions over strategy, particularly in the Middle East," Entezam said. "He told us what he wanted, and given our unique relationship, we did our best to accommodate him."

"And with Petrovsky?"

"We might find we have a freer hand."

37

The president turned to al-Zanjani.

"Commander, I understand you have news from Pyongyang."

"Yes, Your Excellency. I just got off the phone with my counterpart there," al-Zanjani answered. "He informs me that after several days of consideration, the Dear Leader is prepared to sell us five of the newest Russian nuclear warheads in their arsenal."

"Only five? You were supposed to request fifteen."

"And I did, Your Excellency."

"I was under the impression that President Luganov had personally intervened with the Dear Leader on our behalf and specifically for fifteen warheads."

"That was my understanding, as well, sir."

"Then what went wrong?"

Al-Zanjani paused for a moment.

"Permission to speak freely, Your Excellency?"

"Of course."

"President Luganov is gone. My assessment is that the Dear Leader has concluded he is free from any specific obligation he may have made to the late president. Still, he is ready to sell us five Russian nuclear warheads. And I would remind this august body that these are far more powerful than the weapons we were previously negotiating for with Pakistan—each has a yield of 750 kilotons."

There were nods around the room, except for the Supreme Leader, who kept his counsel to himself.

"And have our friends agreed to the price we discussed?" President Afshar asked.

"Not exactly," al-Zanjani said, glancing at the cleric for whom he held such reverence and then back to President Afshar. "I assure you that I did everything I could to get the North Koreans to agree to our price, but I'm afraid the final deal took more."

"How much more?" the president finally asked.

Al-Zanjani reached into his briefing book. He pulled out copies of the deal for everyone present. It took several minutes for each man to read and internalize both the price and the terms, but one by one they looked back to the IRGC's deputy commander.

No one looked happy. It wasn't that they didn't have the money. They did. The Americans and Europeans had given it to them on a silver platter. But even $150 billion only went so far. They couldn't spend it all on buying operational nuclear warheads, even ones as large and powerful as these. They needed to reserve part of the JCPOA funds to improve and finalize their long-range missile program. They had to be able to use North Korea's test data to significantly improve their range and accuracy. The Supreme Leader's mandate had been clear. Their missiles had to be able to reach far beyond Tel Aviv, Paris, and London. They had to reach Washington and New York.

What's more, they had to have ICBMs fully online and ready to launch in less than a year. This was imperative. And it was possible, al-Zanjani believed. All of Tehran's top scientists assured him of this.

But it wasn't going to be easy, and it wasn't going to be cheap. At the same time, the regime was rapidly burning through their cash reserves running proxy wars in Syria and Yemen, financing their operations to consolidate Shia control in Iraq, and rearming Hezbollah in southern Lebanon and Hamas in Gaza for the coming war with the Zionists.

Al-Zanjani had been certain he could drive the price down, especially with Moscow's full support for the deal. Indeed, he had assured this group not a week earlier that this would, in fact, be the case. Now, in a matter of hours, the dynamics of the deal had changed entirely.

For the moment, President Afshar chose to sidestep the issue of cost. "Assuming the Supreme Leader agrees to this deal you have negotiated, Commander, how soon can Pyongyang be ready to transfer the warheads?"

"Ten days to two weeks, Your Excellency," al-Zanjani replied. "I'm still working with them on some of the technical details as well as how best to conceal the transfer from the Americans and of course the Zionists. But in the absence of any unexpected complications, I would say we could have the warheads here by the middle of October, at the latest."

For the first time since the briefing had commenced, the Supreme Leader appeared to relax. A slight smile even emerged at the corners of his mouth. He finally looked pleased. They all did, and al-Zanjani was grateful to Allah that he could bring his leaders some positive news on an otherwise painful and traumatic day. No one had been a closer friend or more faithful ally to the Islamic Republic of Iran than Aleksandr Luganov. His death was a terrible blow to them, though al-Zanjani believed it also opened up new opportunities.

"Why the change of heart?" the Grand Ayatollah asked unexpectedly.

Al-Zanjani, who had just begun to close his briefing book, looked up, as surprised as the others to hear the cleric speak.

"Pardon, Your Holiness?" he asked, unsure he'd understood what his leader was really asking.

"For many days, I was under the impression that our friend in Pyongyang was resisting this sale," the ayatollah said in a voice so frail and soft that al-Zanjani had to lean forward to hear him. "Now, suddenly, he says yes. My question is why?"

38

All eyes turned back to al-Zanjani.

The deputy commander swallowed hard and gathered his thoughts. "It is a shrewd question, Your Holiness," he began, flattering the man but also buying precious time. "I've considered this for the past several hours."

Al-Zanjani shifted himself on the cushion.

"There is no question the money was a critical factor," he continued. "If you choose to approve and authenticate my offer, then we will have given the Dear Leader his asking price. But the timing of the flurry of communications I've had with my counterpart in Pyongyang today—"

"The estimable General Yoon?" the Supreme Leader asked.

"Yes, General Yoon," al-Zanjani confirmed, a bit surprised but still pleased that the old man was conversant in such minor details. "I have known him for many years. As you all know, we have worked closely on many sensitive projects. But in all honesty, I must say I was caught off guard by his messages today, agreeing to our terms and pressing me to conclude the deal by the end of the day."

"So in your opinion, why did he agree today?"

Al-Zanjani paused. He had only been to such a high-level meeting a handful of times in his life. If he thought carefully, he could probably list them all, and the number could be counted on two hands. But never once had he been asked his opinion. He had only ever been asked for hard, verifiable facts. Analysis was the province of his boss and the others in the room, not him. And yet the Supreme Leader was asking. What choice did he have but to answer?

"If . . . well, sir . . . if you are asking me to guess . . . ," he stammered.

The Supreme Leader raised his hand to stop him in midsentence. "It is not a guess, my child," he said in a tone al-Zanjani assumed he typically reserved for his nineteen grandchildren, not junior subordinates. "Commander al-Zanjani, you are an experienced, thrice-decorated military leader and intelligence officer, one of the Islamic Republic's finest. You have earned the trust and the appreciation of everyone in this room. If your exploits could be known to the nation, you would be regarded as one of the heroes of the revolution. Hence, I am not asking for conjecture. I am asking for your professional assessment. Why today?"

Al-Zanjani was touched by the incomprehensible, rare vote of confidence. "Well, Your Excellency, I think it has entirely to do with the death of President Luganov," he said, his voice quiet but more confident now. "As I said, I believe the Dear Leader suddenly feels liberated to make the deal he wants to make, at the price he wants to charge, without oversight—much less interference—from Moscow.

"Furthermore, it could not have been lost on the Dear Leader that the Russian president never brought his defense minister into the loop on the transfer of the twenty powerful warheads to the Korean Peninsula. So far as I know, Mikhail Petrovsky has absolutely no idea Pyongyang has such warheads.

"Moreover, my sources inform me that Luganov was preparing to sack Petrovsky and replace him with FSB chief Dmitri Nimkov. Nimkov, of course, not only knew about the transfer, but it was he whom Luganov had put in charge of coordinating both the transfer and the joint Russian–North Korean preparations to launch a preemptive strike against the United States sometime next year, once our missiles have been adapted and are fully operational.

"In sum, Your Excellency, it is possible that the Dear Leader believes Petrovsky may in some way be behind the murders of Luganov, Nimkov, and Prime Minister Grigarin. Certainly Petrovsky has benefited from the deaths of these three men. As president, he will likely soon become aware of the transfer of the warheads to Pyongyang. He may then try to rescind the deal and get the warheads back onto Russian soil."

Al-Zanjani stopped to take a breath and let his words have their intended effect.

"You believe the Dear Leader is seizing a window of opportunity, then?" the ayatollah asked. "You think he is moving with all haste to sell these five warheads to us and get our cash—for which he is so desperate to keep his regime afloat—before Mikhail Petrovsky figures out what is going on and walks the deal back?"

"Yes, sir," al-Zanjani said. "That is what I believe."

The Supreme Leader looked around the room. "Does anyone have a different assessment?" he asked.

No one did.

"Do we all agree that we must move quickly to secure these five warheads—more powerful than anything we've been able to develop thus far—even at this price?"

It took several moments in which each man looked to every other. But in the end, they all nodded. A tremendous amount of precious time had already been squandered in trying to make a deal with the Pakistanis. Al-Zanjani had tried to warn the group at the time that they were walking into a trap, most likely of the Mossad's or the CIA's making. He hadn't had proof, and so he had not convinced his superiors not to pursue the deal. But he'd been right. It had been the Israelis. He'd cleaned up the situation by ambushing the Mossad operatives in Athens, catching them completely off guard and killing every last one of them. In so doing, he had finally beaten the Zionists at their own game. He had also bought himself a seat in this room. His stock was soaring. These men were listening to him. They trusted him. And they were rewarding him and his family in ways beyond anything he could have imagined.

Al-Zanjani knew he'd have to be extra careful from this point forward. Managing the country's nuclear portfolio put a target on his back. Both the Americans and the Israelis would be gunning for him now. But he wasn't worried. To the contrary, he was ecstatic. For the first time since the Islamic Revolution had been set into motion in 1979, the Persian Bomb was within their reach. Total regional domination was within their grasp. Best of all, every step they took now was bringing them closer to the actual, literal, physical return of the Mahdi and the establishment of the Caliphate, not just in the Middle East, but around the entire globe.

"Very well," said the Supreme Leader, looking back at the deputy commander with a renewed fire in his dimming eyes. "We must not waste another minute. Make the deal."

"Hey, you're awake," Marcus said. "How're you feeling?"

He entered Jenny's room and set a tray on the nightstand next to the bed. On it was a pot of tea and a bowl of broth.

"Never mind me," Jenny said, her voice a bit scratchy. "How are *you*?"

"What are you talking about?"

"Are you kidding? Have you looked in the mirror lately?"

"Oh yeah, well, I guess I broke my nose."

"I guess so."

"It's nothing. I'm fine."

"You don't look fine. What happened?"

Marcus brought her up to speed on all that had happened since they'd jumped out of the G4 up to and including the brawl with Zakharov's brother. As he did, he helped her sit up, and she began sipping the broth while the tea steeped. Feeling her forehead, Marcus was encouraged that her fever was subsiding. He gave her a cool washcloth for her face, then set in her hand a decorative brass bell he'd found on a shelf downstairs.

"Now, get some rest and ring if you need something," he said, getting up to leave.

"Oh no, you don't," Jenny said with an icy tone that caught Marcus off guard. "You're not going anywhere."

"What do you mean?"

"We need to talk."

"About what? I just told you everything."

"Since we jumped," she snapped. "What about before?"

Marcus said nothing.

"You got Oleg to assassinate Luganov, after I told you not to."

"That's not how it happened."

"But Luganov is dead, right?"

"He is."

"And Oleg killed him?"

"Yeah."

"So tell me."

"I didn't *get* him to do it," Marcus protested, lowering his voice to a whisper so Oleg wouldn't overhear. "He asked me for help."

"And you helped him."

"I did, and I'd do it again."

The look on Jenny's face was one of disgust. She folded her arms, wincing in pain, then whispered back, "I thought you were a Christian."

"What does that have to do with anything?"

"I can't seem to recall Jesus or the apostle Paul encouraging the flock to assassinate Caesar."

"Maybe not. But your hands aren't entirely clean here either."

"What's that supposed to mean?"

"You're in this as much as we are."

"Wrong. I didn't conspire to kill the president of Russia."

"But you lay out in a forest with a sniper rifle and popped a slew of FSB agents at Oleg's parents' estate without so much as batting an eyelash."

"That's not the same."

"Of course it is—you were taking out enemies of the state, and so were we."

"Forget it, Ryker. I was on a state-sanctioned mission to extract a high-value asset who was trying to help us stop a nuclear war. You two are freelancing. You're private citizens in violation of about a dozen federal laws, possibly including treason."

"Think about it, Morris. Oleg realized there was only one way to stop the war and that was to stop Luganov. He didn't come to that conclusion lightly, nor did I. We didn't tell you—*I* didn't tell you—because I knew what you'd say."

"Because I'd already said it. What you did was not just illegal, it was wrong, Ryker."

"Saving tens of thousands of lives—ours and theirs—that was wrong? Forgive me, but I don't see it that way. Look, we made our decision, and—"

"No, you didn't just make *your* decision. You made *mine*."

"What's done is done, Morris. I didn't ask for your permission, and I'm not asking you to like what we did. But all that's irrelevant now. The only question left is how we turn you back over to the Agency. That's what Oleg and I are working on."

40

"What a fine weather today. Can't choose whether to drink tea or to hang myself."

Marcus, in a freshly foul mood, reentered the kitchen. Oleg was clearing dishes from the meal of pasta and vodka sauce he'd made for them.

"Chekhov?" he said. "Must not have gone well."

"It didn't." Marcus sighed as he poured them both piping-hot mugs of chai.

"Good choice," Oleg quipped.

Marcus recounted his conversation with Jenny. Oleg asked a few questions. In the end they concluded they'd better both go upstairs and take their lumps. They didn't expect Jenny to be happy with the situation they'd put her in. She certainly had every right to be angry with them. But they had to deal with it now. They would need her help to get her home, and the sooner the better.

"Go away," Jenny snapped.

But the knocking continued.

"Fine, come in," she said, relenting. "Make yourself at home. Anything else I can do for you two international fugitives?"

Marcus and Oleg opened the door cautiously as if prepared for her to throw something at them. When they saw the coast was clear, they entered and pulled a couple of chairs into the room. Then Marcus began explaining to the CIA's Moscow station chief more thoroughly exactly what Oleg had done, exactly how Marcus had helped, and the events that had been set into motion as a result. Though she remained furious, her pain and fatigue somewhat dampened her capacity, and perhaps her desire, to unleash on them. She fired question after question at them but eventually concluded—however reluctantly—that Marcus was right. They couldn't un-ring the bell.

Next Marcus opened a laptop and began to pore over the contents of the thumb drive Oleg had smuggled out of the Kremlin. He pressed Oleg for any scrap of intelligence they could use as leverage over Langley and the White House to regain their freedom.

Jenny listened but refused to participate. She wasn't exactly in a position to stand in their way, but she wasn't going to join the conspiracy.

On the drive from Oleg's parents' home to the airport, Jenny had transmitted the entire contents of the thumb drive to the analysts at the Global Operations Center back in Virginia via a secure satphone connection. That was well before the gun battle on the tarmac in Moscow and their dramatic takeoff in the Gulfstream. In that sense, Marcus and Oleg were playing at a disadvantage. They had already handed over every trump card in their possession. Still, the thumb drive contained an enormous amount of information. It included detailed notes Oleg had taken from every meeting he had ever been in with President Luganov, his cabinet, his generals, and other world leaders for twenty years. It included every transcript of every phone call

Oleg had ever participated in with Luganov and even voice recordings of some calls, provided by Russia's equivalent of the National Security Agency. There were thousands of memos sent to and from the Office of the President, including copies of Luganov's daily intelligence briefing, along with notes on his comments, the questions he had asked, and the answers he had received. There were detailed and highly classified personnel files of nearly every person who had ever worked on the president's staff, plus their FSB vetting and clearance reports. Oleg had also saved spreadsheets providing unprecedented access to Russian military spending—line by line, department by department—as well as travel and administrative budgets for the president's office. The list went on and on.

It would take weeks, if not months, for the Russian speakers at the CIA to simply read through everything, much less make sense of it all and turn it into actionable intelligence. Besides, most of it was interesting but no longer relevant. Luganov was dead. So was Nimkov, his most trusted deputy. What they'd done, what they'd thought, and whom they'd talked to and why would give officials in Washington a much richer understanding of how the Kremlin worked. But everything was changing—fast. With Petrovsky, there was a new sheriff in town. What did he believe? What would he want to accomplish? Who were his most trusted friends and advisors? Would any of Oleg's intel answer those questions? Jenny had no idea.

Yet with every hour that passed, the value Oleg could provide was diminishing.

It was just after 5 a.m. when Nick Vinetti was jarred out of sleep by a call.

When he finally managed to find his mobile phone and pick up, to his astonishment it was the unexpected voice of an old friend on the other end.

It wasn't exactly in Vinetti's written job description as a senior

State Department official to be involved in highly classified missions to extract high-level Russian moles out of the country. His job was not even primarily diplomatic in the classic sense—meeting with foreign leaders, attending black-tie dinners and glitzy diplomatic galas, and the like. Most of his days were spent managing the sprawling bureaucracy of hundreds of U.S. Foreign Service officers and other American government liaisons operating at the embassy compound and in various consulates and other diplomatic facilities spread across Russia's vast territory and eleven time zones.

But it was Vinetti to whom Marcus had come first to say he had made contact with a senior Russian official—a source, a mole—who was offering explosive inside information they needed to get to Langley and the president immediately. It was Vinetti who had instantly grasped the quality and implications of the intel Marcus had received from his source. It was Vinetti who had immediately brought the CIA's Moscow station chief Jenny Morris—and later, Tyler Reed, the American ambassador to Russia—into the loop. So perhaps he should not have been surprised that Marcus was reaching out to him now. But he was. The thought of Marcus being a coconspirator with the likes of Oleg Kraskin was more than Vinetti could bear.

"Nick, it's me. Can you talk?"

"Marcus, is that really you? I thought—"

"Are you alone?" Marcus pressed. "Can we talk safely?"

"Yeah, of course. Yes," Vinetti said, now wide-awake and scrambling out of bed and into the kitchen so as not to disturb his wife, Claire. "What in the world happened? Where are you?"

"We bailed just before the missiles hit. We're safe, but I don't have much time."

"And Jenny? How is she?"

"She was hit, but she's improving."

"Thank God," Vinetti said. "I really thought—"

"I know, but look—I'm serious; we need to move quickly, and I need you to do something for me," said Marcus, his voice calm but insistent.

"Marcus, man, you're completely radioactive—you know that, right?"

Marcus ignored the comment and plunged ahead. "You need to set up a call with me and the DCI," he said.

"Director Stephens? Have you lost your mind?"

"Just call Langley and set it up. I'm going to call you back in two hours—midnight Washington time, 7 a.m. Moscow time. And let me be crystal clear, Nick. When I call, I need you to patch me straight through to the director, or I'm gone—in the wind—with Oleg Kraskin and everything he knows."

"Oleg Kraskin—you mean the Raven? Marcus, what you're asking is impossible," Vinetti said. "Stephens can't talk to you, and you know it. He can't come within a million miles of you right now. You're about to be charged with being an accessory to murder. Perhaps with treason. And as your friend, I'm telling you, the best thing you, Jenny, and the Raven can do is turn yourselves in. Let us pick you up immediately so no one else gets hurt."

The line was silent for a moment.

Then Vinetti asked, "He is with you, right—the Raven?"

"He is," Marcus said, "and he's talking."

"What do you mean he's talking?"

"He has critical intelligence that Stephens and the president need to see—but it's time sensitive, and we need to move fast."

And with that, the line went dead.

41

They had only two hours to wait.

But Marcus suggested Oleg go upstairs and crash.

Oleg, visibly spent, agreed. Marcus heard the water in the shower turn on, but for only a few minutes. Soon, he heard the bathroom door open and Oleg trudge to the only other unused bedroom, the one with the now-open safe. He could hear the springs of an old bed creak as Oleg flopped down on it. Then all was quiet.

Marcus powered down the computer and tucked his own pistol into his belt at the small of his back. He washed their coffee mugs and the plates and pots they'd used for their modest pasta dinner. He double-checked the doors and windows to make sure they were still locked, then went upstairs to check on Jenny again. She was breathing peacefully. Color was returning to her face. Her pulse was steady, almost normal. And there was no sign of an infection. She still needed to gain strength, but she was definitely on the mend. It was a miracle, and Marcus said a silent prayer of thanks.

Stepping into the bathroom, he locked the door and brushed his teeth. Staring at himself in the mirror, he finally realized just how much of a beating he'd taken. His arms, chest, and neck were turning black-and-blue. His left eye had quite a shiner, too, but his mangled nose looked worse. Wincing, he removed the blood-soaked tissues from each nostril, tossed them into the toilet, and flushed. Then he replaced them with fresh wadding and scrubbed his hands with hot water and lots of soap. He was grateful his mother couldn't see him just now, but so far at least, he hadn't died or been arrested, and given all that had happened, that was a win.

Vinetti immediately called Langley.

He explained to the watch commander in the Global Operations Center that he'd just received a call and a demand from Marcus Ryker.

"Did the NSA trace the call?" Vinetti asked when he was finished. "Can they locate him?"

"I'll check," the commander said. "Call you back."

Marcus stepped into the master bedroom.

He dug through his rucksack, fished out a fresh pair of jeans, a clean white T-shirt, and an old black crew-neck sweater, and put them all on. Then he grabbed the AK-47, turned off the hallway lights, and headed back down to the living room.

The house was all dark now, and Marcus used his night vision goggles to peer out the curtains into the backyard. He saw nothing moving but the icy waves lapping onto a snow-packed shoreline. He moved to the window on the north side of the dacha, next to the damaged hutch that no longer contained any china. He lingered there, peering out for several minutes, but saw nothing except another darkened beach house a half kilometer away.

When he moved to the front windows, he scanned the front yard and the main road, his trigger finger stroking the wooden stock on the automatic weapon. He smiled slightly as a convoy of five snowplows drove by. He was sure the driver of the sixth had been found by now and prayed the man was okay.

There was now well over two feet of snow on the ground, and even more piled up at the end of the driveway due to the repeated plowing. The storm was subsiding. Very little more precipitation was accumulating, and even the harsh winds were slowing down. Yet Marcus knew their biggest test was coming. He couldn't abide the idea that the snow could block them in or at least slow down their getaway when they were ready to move. So he went to the garage, found a shovel, and headed outside before the sun rose.

Thirty minutes later, the group converged on the Oval Office.

"It's an enormous risk," the president said after hearing the summary of the call. "I don't like it—any of it."

CIA director Stephens sat directly across the *Resolute* desk. Joining them were retired Lieutenant General Barry Evans, the president's national security advisor—fresh back from Seoul, South Korea—and Bill McDermott, the deputy NSA.

"I don't disagree with that, sir," Stephens replied. "But in the current environment, can we really take the risk that Mr. Kraskin does *not* actually possess critical intelligence we need?"

"Secretary Foster tells me Russian forces on the borders of the Baltics and Ukraine are beginning to stand down," the president said.

"Our information indicates those forces have been ordered to retreat from the borders, but we have no confirmation that they have actually begun to do it, Mr. President," Stephens clarified. "Nor does the Pentagon. They're relying on intel we provided."

"You're saying this could be a head fake, that the Russians might still attack?"

"I'm afraid it's too early to draw any conclusions as of yet, sir. We're watching the situation closely. But as uncomfortable as I am with talking to Mr. Ryker at all, no one has given us more accurate or important intelligence on Russian motives or plans than Kraskin and Ryker."

"Richard, come on—they're stone-cold assassins," the president countered. "If it leaks out that you actually took a call from one of them, it would look to the Kremlin and the rest of the world like we knew what they were going to do, or even authorized it, which we most certainly did not."

"That's part of the risk; I readily concede that, Mr. President. But we'll record the entire conversation. I'll make our position crystal clear. If Ryker or Kraskin go to the press, so will we, and release the tape. What's more, we need to get my officer—Jennifer Morris—out of harm's way."

The president turned to his national security advisor. "Barry, how do you see it?"

"I don't like it either, Mr. President," said Evans, a thirty-two-year Army veteran who had at one time served as the supreme allied commander of NATO forces in Europe. "Still, I'd have to concur with Director Stephens. Let's hear Ryker out and tape it all. I suggest you authorize the director to make almost any deal necessary to get Morris back along with whatever intel they're dangling. But I also respectfully recommend that you be prepared to renege the moment we have what we want."

"And what about this Kraskin guy, the so-called Raven?" the president asked. "What do we do with him?"

"We certainly can't take the risk of bringing him onto American soil," the national security advisor insisted. "I'm not sure we can let Ryker back into the country either, unless it's to put him in a supermax prison. Personally, I'd recommend stripping him of his American citizenship and treating him as an enemy combatant. But obviously that's your call, not mine."

"Noted," said the president, giving no evidence he necessarily disagreed. "What about the call? Did the NSA trace it? Do we know where these guys are?"

"I'm afraid not," said Director Stephens.

"Why not?" Clarke demanded.

"Sir, Ryker wasn't using the satphone we provided him," Stephens explained. "We can guess why—he doesn't want to be found. What we don't know is how he got another satphone up there in the tundra wastelands of northern Russia. Either way, he was also smart enough not to call in to the embassy. He waited until the wee hours and called his friend Nicholas Vinetti—his old Marine buddy—on Vinetti's private cell phone. No one was expecting that. The NSA wasn't monitoring Vinetti's private calls. But don't worry, Mr. President. We won't make the same mistake twice."

The look on Clarke's face said it all. But despite his fury, he held his tongue for the moment and turned to Bill McDermott. "Bill, you've known Ryker the longest and best. What say you?"

"Mr. President, I say you tell Ryker and Kraskin whatever you have to to bring them in. Then immediately arrest them both. Turn the Raven over to the Russians, and try Ryker for murder and treason."

The president was taken aback.

"You'd do that to a friend?" he asked.

"He's not my friend anymore, sir. He crossed the line. Now he needs to pay."

42

Marcus suddenly sat bolt upright in the overstuffed chair.

He clenched the rifle and listened intently. In the end, he heard nothing but the grandfather clock. It was now 5:52 in the morning. He had a little more than an hour before his call to Langley.

He berated himself for falling asleep. On his lap sat his personal Bible, open to Proverbs. His habit since college had been to read a chapter of this particular book of wisdom—which happened to have thirty-one chapters—every day of each month, adjusting when needed for the months that had fewer than thirty-one days. The tactic obviously hadn't worked this month, though; he hadn't cracked the Good Book for several weeks, and he could barely remember finding, much less opening, his Bible before conking out cold.

Blinking hard, Marcus set the book aside and headed to the kitchen. As he started some coffee brewing, he peered out the windows and scanned the backyard. Seeing nothing unusual, he moved to the side window in the dining room and finally to the bay windows in the living room, looking out into the front yard and into the street. He saw nothing but snow and ice. The winds had died down. So what had woken him up?

He headed upstairs. Oleg was sound asleep. But to Marcus's surprise, Jenny was up. She'd already disconnected herself from the IV, changed into jeans and a sweatshirt, and was just coming out of the bedroom. And she had a 9mm pistol in one hand and two magazines in the other.

"Hey," Marcus said warily.

"Hey yourself," she replied.

"Trouble?" he asked.

"Habit."

Marcus nodded, wondering just how angry she was at him and Oleg at the moment and what she was capable of in that state of mind.

"Sorry I kept drifting off on you guys last night," Jenny said.

"No problem. How're you feeling now?"

"I've been better."

"Honestly, you're doing a lot better than I'd expected."

"I don't know. I just had my first look at my shoulder. It's pretty bad."

"You were lucky."

"Maybe." She sighed. "Hey, you got any coffee down there? I'm craving something stronger than tea."

"Yeah, just made a fresh pot," Marcus said. "But I've got something else, too."

Jenny raised an eyebrow as she loaded a magazine, shoved the pistol in her waistband, and stuffed the second mag into her pocket.

"What are you up to, Ryker? You've got a mischievous look in your eye."

"I'll tell you on the way."

"The way to where?"

He smiled. "Trust me."

"You've got to be kidding."

Marcus pounded on Oleg's door. A moment later, they heard the Russian stumbling out of bed. When the door opened, Oleg's eyes were so bloodshot it was clear he had barely slept at all.

"You need to pack," Marcus said. "Jenny and I are going to make the call. If we're not back in two hours, assume we're dead—just take the money and run."

Without waiting for a reply, Marcus returned to the kitchen. Jenny followed, a little slower. He poured them each a mug of coffee. Then they went to the garage, fired up the Mercedes C 300, and headed out.

As he pulled out of the driveway, Marcus handed Jenny his rucksack. "Open it," he said.

She did and found their laptop, the satphone they'd been given by Langley together with two unopened satphones Marcus had found in the safe, and a toolbox he'd found in the garage.

"And?" Jenny asked.

"I need you to do something for me," he said. "You're not going to be happy about it. But I don't have time to argue."

"What exactly did you have in mind?"

"I need you to use a little of your black magic to save our lives."

Forty minutes later, they pulled into the petrol station where he'd stolen the Jeep.

Marcus grinned as he pulled around back and found five snowplows parked there, engines off, lights out, not a driver in sight. He hadn't expected to find them. How could he have? Any car would have done for what he had in mind. But one of the snowplows would do better.

Making sure no one was watching, Marcus got out of the Mercedes, leaving it running, and walked over to the adjacent restaurant. Peering in the window, he saw four drivers sitting at a table. Their meals had just arrived. But there was food for five. Where was the fifth driver? Marcus scanned the other diners but didn't see him. He walked to another window to get a clearer view. Just then, a burly man wearing coveralls stepped out of the men's room and joined the others. A waitress came by and topped off their coffees. They were going to be a while.

Retracing his steps, Marcus returned to the Mercedes, opened the driver's-side door, and leaned in. Jenny handed him the satellite phone they had gotten from Langley. Checking his watch, he powered it up and punched in the security code. Then he used it to smash in the driver's-side window of the nearest snowplow—the one farthest from the restaurant—tossed the phone inside, got back in the Mercedes, and drove away.

The two sped north along the highway in silence. As Marcus drove, Jenny fiddled with the laptop and one of the Russian satphones, wiring them together somehow. Marcus got off at the next exit, crossed the overpass, and got back on the highway, heading south. A minute later, he pulled onto the shoulder, just a bit past the petrol station and all-night diner. From there, they had a direct view of the parking lot. He pulled the reticle from his sniper rifle out of his rucksack and looked across the highway. The five snowplows were still there. Their lights were still off. Their engines were still cold. Their drivers were still laughing and talking together and sipping their coffee.

Jenny powered up the laptop and connected satphone and handed the phone to Marcus, who immediately dialed the U.S. Embassy in Moscow. "You know you're out of your mind," she said.

"We'll know soon enough."

The call did not go directly through to Nick Vinetti. Rather, at Marcus's request, Jenny had reprogrammed the phone to bounce the call off a nearby cell tower, then route through the American satphone in the cab of the plow. It was one of the little items in her bag of tricks she'd learned at the Farm, the CIA's training facility in southern Virginia.

Vinetti answered on the first ring but asked Marcus to wait.

"Standard procedure," Jenny whispered. "They're tracing the call."

Ninety seconds later, Vinetti patched the most wanted American in the world through to the Global Operations Center, deep beneath CIA headquarters back in northern Virginia.

"You're late," said Director Stephens into Marcus's ear.

Washington was seven hours behind Moscow in the fall, making it now 12:27 in the morning.

"Nevertheless," Marcus replied, "you took the call."

"You said it was urgent."

"It is."

"It had better be," said Stephens. "Whom exactly am I speaking with?"

"Marcus Ryker."

"How do I know it's really you?"

"Who else knew the passcode to the phone?"

"Any technology can be hacked."

"Let's hope not."

"You understand we're recording this call?"

"As am I," Marcus replied as Jenny double-checked the levels on the laptop to make sure everything was working properly.

There was a slight pause. Then Stephens said, "I need you to verify your identity."

"Ask me whatever you'd like," Marcus said. "I've got nothing to hide."

"Very well," came the reply. "What was your father's full name?"

"Lars Pieter Ryker."

"When was he born?"

"July 9, 1952."

"When did he die?"

"January 16, 1991."

"How?"

"He was a fighter pilot in the U.S. Air Force. He was shot down by a surface-to-air missile while flying a combat mission in southern Iraq during Operation Desert Storm."

"What kind of plane was he flying?"

"An F-16C."

"What's its nickname?"

"The Fighting Falcon."

"How old were you when he died?"

"Eleven."

"And your mother's name?"

"Marjorie Ryker."

"Maiden name?"

"Carnes."

"When was she born?"

"March 5, 1957."

"Whom did she marry after your father died?"

There was a long pause.

"Would you like me to repeat the question?" Stephens asked.

"That won't be necessary," Marcus said, steadying his nerves. "She married Roger DuHaime."

"When was he born?"

"I have no idea."

"You don't know?"

"I never cared."

"Very well," the director said. "What day did he die?"

"May 19, 2001."

"How did he die?"

Again Marcus paused.

"How exactly did Roger DuHaime die?" Stephens pressed.

"I shot him."

43

"Anything yet on Marcus?"

Pete Hwang opened his eyes and found Annie Stewart ducking her head in his door. He realized he had drifted off and suddenly felt embarrassed. His tie was askew. His hair was a bit ruffled. A few slices of now-cold pizza lay in their box on his desk beside a half-finished Styrofoam cup of Coke Zero in which all the ice had melted.

"Sorry, no," he said, trying to rub the sleep from his eyes. "I've been making calls all night. No one has heard a thing, or if they have, they're not telling me."

"Nothing even from Nick?"

Hwang shook his head, surprised to see the sadness in her eyes. The senator's concerns he understood. Dayton was afraid his connection to Ryker—a connection Hwang had personally helped reestablish in recent weeks—could scuttle his bid for the Democratic nomination and ultimately the presidency. But Annie Stewart? Why was she taking this so hard?

"How about McDermott?" she asked.

"Bill's furious," Hwang said. "I spoke to him about an hour ago. I've seen him mad before, plenty of times. But wow, nothing like this."

"He thinks Marcus is guilty."

"*Treasonous* is the word he used."

"I don't buy it, Pete. Do you?"

Hwang hesitated and then said, "I honestly don't know."

"Pete, come on, Marcus isn't a murderer."

"No, of course not," Hwang said. "But it's not that simple, Annie."

"Meaning what?"

"Meaning Marcus is a man driven by what he believes is right and wrong."

"How exactly would assassinating two world leaders be right?"

"Well, let's change the names. Forget Luganov and Nimkov. If you lived in the forties and thought there was an opportunity to prevent or stop the Holocaust by taking out Hitler and Himmler, or Eichmann or Mengele, would you have taken it?"

Stewart thought about that for a moment.

"I don't know," she said. "I don't think I could kill anyone."

"Even Hitler?"

"I'm just saying, I wouldn't know the first thing about how to do it."

"But Marcus does," Hwang said. "Last summer, I invited myself down from Manhattan to stay with him for the weekend. I flew in late Friday night. We went out running on Saturday morning, then hiking Old Rag. Then I wanted to take him to a Nationals game, but he wanted to rent *Valkyrie* instead. Ever see it?"

"The Tom Cruise movie? No."

"It's about a group of German military officers who plot the assassination of the Führer to end World War II."

Annie Stewart was quiet.

"And guess what was sitting on his coffee table," Hwang said.

Stewart shrugged.

"A half-read biography of Dietrich Bonhoeffer."

"The German pastor who was executed for being involved in a plot to kill Hitler. So what are you saying, that Marcus was planning this for a year?"

"No, no, of course not." Hwang stood. "Marcus didn't even want to go on the trip, and he wouldn't have if I hadn't goaded him into it. He didn't have a plan to take out Luganov or anyone else. But the senator asked me if I thought Marcus was *capable* of doing it. And I'm telling you yes, if he thought it was the morally right thing to do, he'd absolutely be capable of it."

Stewart looked away for a moment, then asked, "So what do we do now?"

"It's simple," he said. "We've got to find him before . . ."

"Before what?"

"Before they find him first and kill him."

For almost a minute, Richard Stephens didn't seem to know what to say.

Marcus briefly wondered if the connection had been cut. But then the CIA director cleared his throat and asked, "How did it come to that?"

"Look, you have my file; you know what I did and why," Marcus replied, fighting to maintain his cool. "It was self-defense. The DA cleared me of all charges. So did the Marine Corps and the U.S. Secret Service. So let's get on with it. We're wasting time."

There was another long pause.

"Fine," Stephens finally said. "Just one more question: there was something your mother used to say to you—often, I understand—while you were growing up. What was it?"

Marcus resented Stephens's prying into his family's private affairs, but he answered anyway.

"Don't die, and don't get arrested."

"Very well. I'm satisfied you are Marcus Johannes Ryker," Stephens said, no doubt reading from a script prepared for him by his senior staff, all of whom were surely listening in along with most if not all of the National Security Council.

Marcus was grateful Stephens hadn't asked him anything about his wife or his son, how they had lived, or how they had died. The memories of Elena and little Lars were with him constantly. Not a day went by when he didn't think of them or mourn their loss. But he had no interest in discussing such personal matters with anyone in Washington, certainly not the director of Central Intelligence.

"Ryker? Mr. Ryker, are you still on the line?"

Jenny elbowed him, and Marcus suddenly realized that he had zoned out.

"I'm here."

"Is Jennifer Morris with you?"

Marcus turned to Jenny. They'd discussed this on the drive. She nodded.

"Yes," he said.

"And her condition?"

"Wounded but improving." Marcus decided it was time to seize control of the conversation. "Oleg Kraskin is with me as well. I have no doubt it's clear to you and your team by now that Mr. Kraskin is the mole who came to me at the Hotel National. Kraskin is the one Ms. Morris code-named the Raven. It is he who turned over some of the most sensitive and valuable secrets in the Russian government, including the plan to invade the Baltics. And yes, it is he who killed Aleksandr Luganov, the president of Russia, and Dmitri Nimkov, the head of the FSB."

Stephens again fell silent.

"Mr. Kraskin carried out these assassinations of his own accord," Marcus continued. "He did so to prevent President Luganov from ordering the invasion of NATO countries and triggering a nuclear war.

He did so, in my professional assessment, in his right mind and with a clear conscience. He did not, however, kill Prime Minister Grigarin, nor to my knowledge did he ask anyone to do so or assist in any way. I was with him when he heard the news, and he was as stunned as I was."

Marcus paused for a moment, but Stephens still said nothing. He pressed forward.

"As for my own involvement, I learned of Mr. Kraskin's plans to take out President Luganov less than six hours before the hit took place. At his request, I provided Mr. Kraskin with the weapon and a detailed strategy to be successful. I did it with a sound mind and a clear conscience, and I would do it again. Mr. Kraskin's actions—and by extension, my own—have thus far proven effective. The latest reports indicate that Russian forces have been ordered back from the borders of Estonia, Latvia, and Lithuania—and away from the Ukrainian border."

Marcus checked his side and rearview mirrors. Jenny scanned the sky through the sunroof, but there was nothing yet.

"To be clear, no one—not a single person employed by the American government—knew what Mr. Kraskin was planning to do, because I chose not to tell any of you," he continued. "I did not inform Ms. Morris of the plan. She had no idea whatsoever what we were planning. Nor did I inform DCM Vinetti or Ambassador Reed at the U.S. Embassy in Moscow of the plan. From the time I was informed by Mr. Kraskin of his intentions, I communicated these plans with no one. It was an act Mr. Kraskin and I engaged in by ourselves. Period."

Marcus looked through the reticle. The drivers were talking to the waitress again—ordering more coffee, he hoped.

"That said, I not only gave Mr. Kraskin counsel on how best to carry out his plan, I also gave him instructions on how best to escape. As you know, Ms. Morris and I worked out in great detail a plan to extract Mr. Kraskin out of Russia and get him to a secure location. The purpose of the plan was to safely extract a high-level Russian mole who had given the United States invaluable intelligence on plans by President

Luganov to attack, invade, and seize control of three NATO countries. At no time did anyone employed by the American government know that this mole had taken the lives of Mr. Luganov and Mr. Nimkov. I knew you'd never let him get on the plane if you had any inkling of what he and I had done. I knew Ms. Morris especially would go ballistic if she found out. So I kept her and you in the dark. This is my statement, on the record, and I'm willing to sign an affidavit with a precise transcript of what I have just told you."

And then Marcus added the kicker.

"However . . ."

"I think I've heard quite enough," the director interrupted.

"Actually, you haven't," Marcus shot back.

"Mr. Ryker, you have just admitted to me on the record—and to all my colleagues listening in—that you and Mr. Kraskin are murderers. You've confirmed that the two of you concocted and executed this plan entirely on your own, without either the knowledge or assistance of the American government or any of our employees. I should not have to remind a former federal law enforcement officer that in so doing, you have confessed to violating multiple U.S. and international laws. Your actions are tantamount to treason. It is therefore my duty to recommend that you surrender yourself to U.S. authorities immediately. You will be taken into custody and given a fair and speedy trial. Failure to give us your precise location and to surrender peaceably will require us to hunt you and Mr. Kraskin down, or turn the entire matter over to Russian authorities. Either option would put you both in danger of the gravest kind. I don't recommend running, Mr. Ryker. We will find you. I guarantee you that. Whether you live or die in the process—well, that is another matter altogether."

"Are you finished?" Marcus asked.

"Quite," Stephens said.

"Good—now, listen carefully, because I'm only going to say this once," Marcus continued. "I have a recommendation for you."

"And what's that?"

"Destroy the recording of this conversation—or at the very least, tuck it away in a vault in the bowels of Langley, never to see the light of day."

"Why on earth would I do that?"

"You and I and everyone else listening in know that what Oleg Kraskin and I did stopped a Russian invasion of NATO dead in its tracks. You know full well that our actions have prevented the most serious nuclear showdown between Washington and Moscow since the Cuban Missile Crisis. You're really going to prosecute me for stopping a war? You're really going to hand Mr. Kraskin over to be brutally tortured and executed by the Russian government because he single-handedly stopped the Kremlin from starting World War III? I don't think so."

Again Marcus checked his mirrors. Nothing. He glanced at Jenny.

She shook her head. It was still quiet, but he doubted it would be for long.

Marcus picked up the pace. "What you are going to do instead, Mr. Stephens, is extract the three of us out of Russia immediately. You're going to get Ms. Morris the medical care she needs. You're going to give Mr. Kraskin an entirely new identity and new life in the Witness Protection Program, having him sign a nondisclosure agreement that he will never reveal his identity or what he did as the most effective and important Russian mole in the history of the Agency. And you're going to give me a full presidential pardon and complete immunity from prosecution for any and all of my actions in assisting Mr. Kraskin and preventing the deaths of thousands, if not millions. And you're going to do all that in the next twenty-four hours."

"You've got quite an imagination, Mr. Ryker," Stephens said.

"Is that a yes?" Marcus asked.

"You have *got* to be kidding," Stephens shot back. "Why in the world would the American government ever do such a thing for the likes of you two?"

"Two words, sir—North Korea."

"What is that supposed to mean?"

"Oleg Kraskin possesses information about North Korea that is crucial for you and the rest of the U.S. government to know," Marcus explained calmly, though he was talking a bit faster now. "All the talk in recent days about Pyongyang agreeing to denuclearize and sign a peace treaty with Seoul is nothing but an elaborate disinformation plot. The fact is, the leaders in Pyongyang now have in their possession some of the most sophisticated nuclear warheads ever built. These are not warheads they built themselves. They're warheads built by the Russian government and transferred to North Korea in recent days. Each has a yield of 750 kilotons and is capable of taking out an entire American city. In a very short period of time, these warheads will be fitted atop intercontinental ballistic missiles scattered around the North Korean countryside, each of which has a far greater range than any current U.S. intel analysis suggests. Each can hit not only Los Angeles but Washington, D.C., as well."

"That's ridiculous," Stephens sniffed. "You're being sold a bill of goods. I won't be."

"Think about it, sir. Everything Oleg Kraskin told us about Luganov's plans and intentions proved correct. You know his intel is good."

Marcus didn't wait for a reply.

"And at my own risk I've just told you the truth about Oleg's and my involvement in the deaths of Luganov and Nimkov. We're not liars, Director Stephens. Oleg has critical information. You need to bring us in and let us help you."

"You're telling me the treaty Luganov signed with North Korea just days ago—a treaty in which Pyongyang publicly agreed to give up all of their nuclear weapons in return for a formal defensive alliance with Moscow—is meaningless?"

"Worse than meaningless. It's a ruse—a smoke screen—designed to cover up a far more dangerous plot."

"Which is?"

"Making Americans feel more relaxed about North Korea while actually giving Pyongyang greater capacity to inflict far more devastation on the American homeland than we previously thought was possible," Marcus said. "Some of this Oleg told me in my first meeting with him. I passed on everything he said at the time. Look back at the report I filed, and you'll see. I noted that the Russians have been working for years on an EMP bomb to fry our entire electrical grid and send us back to the Stone Age. According to the information Oleg provided us, the technology has been perfected, and the missiles are ready for launch. Luganov was fully prepared to detonate an EMP bomb over Chicago or somewhere in the Midwest if we fought him in the Baltics. But Oleg says the missile would have been launched out of North Korea, not Russia, seriously complicating our response. That was then. This is now. Oleg has told me more—far more than I'm telling you now. We'll tell you everything if you make this deal. But I'll tell you three more things for free."

"And what's that?" Stephens asked.

"First, Oleg knows every senior official in the North Korean nuclear and ballistic missile program. He knows their private mobile phone numbers, their emails, their code names, and even where they live. He's been in the room with Hyong Ja Park and Pyongyang's top generals. What's more, he knows where all the missiles are located—today, at least. He says some of them are on mobile launchers, which are moved every thirty days. The next rotation is scheduled for six days from now."

"And the second freebie?" Stephens pressed, his tone growing more cynical.

"Oleg says the secret deal Luganov negotiated with Pyongyang was predicated on a single safeguard," Marcus explained. "North Korea couldn't launch any of the missiles at the United States or any other target without the express permission of Luganov himself. Luganov created his own passcode that only he knew. If North Korea felt for any reason they needed to launch one or more missiles, Luganov would have to enter that precise code into an electronic relay system via a secure, direct fiber-optic link to Pyongyang. But with Luganov's death, everything has changed. Oleg has reason to believe that even as we speak, the North Koreans—free from any arrangement with a Russian leader who is no longer living—are rewiring the system so that the Dear Leader can launch the missiles himself. Based on this and other information, we believe the American homeland now faces grave peril at the hands of a vicious and unstable leader who has publicly vowed to annihilate the American people and our way of life."

"And the third?"

"Pyongyang has just agreed to sell five of those new Russian warheads to Iran, and we understand they will be transferred soon."

There was another pause.

"I need to talk to the president and the attorney general," Stephens finally said. "Give me a few hours."

Marcus's reply came back curt and fast.

"You have precisely one hour to get whatever authorization you need. Twenty-four hours after that, we disappear."

Marcus hung up, took a hammer out of his rucksack, and smashed the satphone into pieces that he promptly tossed out the window onto the snow-covered highway. Rolling up his window, he checked his watch and his mirrors again. They couldn't afford to wait much longer. Maybe he'd been wrong about Stephens.

But then it happened. Two enormous explosions in rapid succession shook the ground like an earthquake and shattered every window in the diner. The resulting fireball nearly blinded both Marcus and Jenny. Even from this distance, they could feel the searing heat. And when the smoke finally began to clear, Marcus could see nothing left of the snowplows but a flaming crater.

NORTHWESTERN RUSSIA

They drove most of the way back to the dacha in silence.

A few miles away, however, Jenny spoke. "When you said Langley might try to kill you, I thought you were nuts."

"At least now we know what we're up against."

"You mean we don't just have one government hunting you down, we have two."

Marcus held his tongue and just kept driving.

"You guys have put me in a terrible situation, Ryker," Jenny continued. "You've made me a traitor to my own country without me even knowing it."

"They don't consider you a traitor."

"They will when they figure out what I just did to help you."

"They'll never find out," said Marcus. "Right now they think all three of us are dead, but as far as they know, you're innocent."

"For now, maybe," Jenny said. "But soon enough they're going to find out we're very much alive. How long until their calculus changes? No witnesses. No loose ends. That's the way Langley likes it."

"They're not going to hunt down and kill a station chief."

"They just tried to take me out with a drone strike!"

"That was different. That was to get to me and Oleg. You were collateral damage. Once they find out you're alive, you'll be protected."

Jenny winced. The painkillers were wearing off. "Look, I don't agree with what you guys did, and I sure don't agree with how you did it," she said. "But I'll give you credit for one thing, Ryker: you owned up to it—to me and to Stephens. I don't know many people who'd do that. It took guts."

"Thanks."

"Don't start thinking I'm not mad at you. I am. I'm furious. And you owe me an apology."

"That's true. I'm sorry. Really, for everything."

"Nice try, Ryker. Talk is cheap. Get us out of this thing alive, and maybe I'll consider forgiving you. Until then . . ."

Her voice trailed off. It was just as well. They were back at the dacha.

Inside, they found that Oleg had packed up all their things. They quickly loaded it all into the trunk of the Mercedes. Then, at Jenny's suggestion, the three of them ransacked the place. First, they took all the drugs, loaded them into the trunk of the Jeep, and pushed the Jeep down the slope in the backyard until it rolled into the Gulf of Finland and sank to the bottom. Then they returned to the house, cleared out the safe, and ripped out the drawers of the file cabinets, making sure all of Zakharov's most incriminating correspondence and financial records were strewn across the third bedroom on the chance—slim though it was—that an honest cop might piece together the clues and vacuum up the rest of the drug network. They overturned tables and lamps. They ripped out bookshelves and emptied the kitchen cabinets of dishes. Finally, determined not to leave a trail, they wiped down the entire place to make sure they hadn't inadvertently left any fingerprints.

To whoever entered the house next, they hoped, it would look like Zakharov had been killed by rival members of the Russian mafia.

Soon they were back on the road, heading south.

"So how did it go?" Oleg asked from the backseat after a few kilometers.

Marcus knew the question was coming, but he and Jenny had decided not to tell Oleg about the drone strikes. There was no point terrifying Oleg even more. He had already taken enormous risks, and more lay ahead. They needed him calm, focused, and optimistic about their chances, even if their odds of getting out of this thing alive were fading fast.

"About as well as I expected," Marcus replied.

"What does that mean?" Oleg pressed. "Are they going to make the deal or not?"

"I'm not sure. Not yet. I made our case. They asked a lot of questions. There's a lot for them to consider, and they'll need to discuss everything with the president and, I suspect, the entire NSC. But let's just say, in the end, I'm hopeful."

Jenny, sitting in the front passenger seat, shot Marcus a look. But it wasn't a lie. Not for Marcus. And it seemed to calm Oleg, who stretched out across the backseat and closed his eyes. Jenny leaned her seat back and followed suit.

Marcus was grateful for some time effectively to himself. He'd been more shaken by the morning's events than he had let on. A mixture of rage and bitter betrayal roiled just under the surface. His own country—a nation he had served since he was twenty-two years old—had just tried to kill him. How was one supposed to respond to such a thing? And what exactly was he supposed to do now?

Two police cars—lights flashing, sirens wailing—raced past them, going in the opposite direction. A moment later, a pair of military helicopters roared by, flying low in a northeasterly direction. This helped snap Marcus back to reality. He couldn't afford to wallow in anger or self-pity. They were being hunted. He had to stay sharp.

He started by checking his speed. He was driving well over the speed limit, and there were more cars on the freshly plowed roads than there had been the previous day. Easing back on the pedal, he hit cruise control at the legal limit. The last thing they could afford was getting pulled over.

Using the car's onboard navigation system, Marcus plotted a course around St. Petersburg. He didn't want the fastest route. There would likely be roadblocks and checkpoints. He needed back roads, side roads, anything less traveled and less patrolled. That done, Marcus reviewed every action he'd taken before leaving the dacha, trying to think if he'd missed anything or made any mistakes. Short of setting the place on fire and burning it to the ground, he couldn't think of anything more they could have done.

The black Mercedes sedan raced east on the Primorskoye Shosse, the coastal road along the gulf. The storm had lifted. It was still cloudy, but the sun was beginning to peek through. As they got closer to St. Petersburg, Marcus saw police and army personnel everywhere, but civilian traffic was growing quite heavy as well. For now at least, they could blend in.

In the silence, Marcus's thoughts kept coming back to the drone strike. He tried to think about how his mother was doing, what his sisters and their husbands and his nieces were up to, how the Colorado Rockies had blown yet another season and would probably never win a pennant much less make it to the World Series.

None of it worked. The explosions were all he could think about.

46

The only good news about the drone strikes was that no one had been killed.

For this, Marcus said a silent prayer of thanks, something he should have done earlier as he was speeding away from the scene and back to the dacha.

Everything else about the call to Director Stephens and its aftermath had been a disaster, and the magnitude of it all weighed heavily. One question particularly nagged at Marcus. How could the CIA have gotten a Predator drone into Russia and over his location so quickly? It didn't make sense.

Marcus had wanted to see if Stephens was going to set him up. He'd hoped not, but he certainly hadn't been surprised when the attack came. He had not, however, expected a drone strike. Rather, he'd expected a crack unit of Spetsnaz operators to swoop in on the snowplows from every direction or to fast-rope from helicopters. He'd assumed Stephens wanted the Russians to arrest Oleg and give him a big show trial while quietly handing the two Americans back to the CIA. That's why he'd been monitoring his side and rearview mirrors so often and Jenny had been repeatedly checking the sky through the sunroof.

A drone strike wasn't even something he'd contemplated. He'd been certain he'd considered every angle. Clearly fatigue was clouding his judgment. He desperately needed sleep, but even more desperately he needed a plan. He'd offered the director of the Central Intelligence Agency actionable intelligence about a plot to put some of the world's most dangerous thermonuclear warheads in the hands of not one but two of America's worst enemies. But Stephens hadn't taken it. Why not? And now what?

They drove for another few minutes before the picture came into focus. Killing the three of them with a drone would have been simpler for the administration—a quick, satisfying resolution to a messy ordeal with no loose ends. Still, there was no way Langley had sent a drone into Russia. It was far too risky even in peacetime, and Moscow and Washington were already on the verge of war. The only other possibility was that Stephens had called Nikolay Kropatkin at the FSB. But what exactly would he have said?

Nikolay, my old friend, I'm so sorry for all that you and your country have been through in the last twenty-four hours, but I'm not calling with condolences. The NSA has just picked up a satellite call from Oleg Kraskin. We have the precise coordinates of his current location. We have no eyes on the target, but as an act of good faith—to show you we pose no threat to the Russian Federation—we want to offer you this information. You'll have to act fast. Any chance you have an armed drone flying over the Karelian Isthmus just now?

It would have been a lie, of course. The NSA hadn't intercepted a call from Oleg. The director of the CIA had been on a satellite call with an American. But Stephens couldn't say that. It would raise too many questions. Indeed, it would implicate the Agency in the assassinations, and that was the last thing Stephens wanted. So he would have had to fib a little. Would Kropatkin have taken the bait? Why not? The acting director of the FSB would be a hero to his government and nation. Stephens would have taken a big step in restoring détente between the U.S. and the Russian Federation. Two Americans would be killed in the process. But at least there wouldn't be any messy congressional hearings.

Stephens had had two hours to formulate his plan. That was more than enough to consider all the alternatives, discuss them with the National Security Council, and rule them all out. Why go through all the hassle of bringing Marcus and Jenny in and risk exposing them to the Russians when he could simply pass along their location to the FSB and have them taken out with one drone strike?

Did this explain why Stephens hadn't accepted his offer? Marcus couldn't be sure. Suddenly, though, he was distracted by two MiG fighter jets streaking across the sky. Thirty seconds later, another pair followed, flying low and fast. A shudder rippled through Marcus's body, but he kept driving, kept processing this question. Why wouldn't Stephens have wanted the information he and Oleg were offering?

Marcus had told Nick Vinetti that he had critical intelligence to pass along to Stephens and the president. He had no doubt Vinetti had conveyed his full message to Stephens. But perhaps the CIA director and the rest of the NSC had dismissed talk of a deal compared to the value of taking out the three of them in one clean operation, especially without the Russians even realizing they were obliterating the Clarke administration's exposure on the assassination. Perhaps, too, the NSC had assumed that the intelligence Oleg was offering had to do with the Kremlin threat to the Baltics, a threat that was steadily receding now that Russian forces were pulling back from NATO borders.

Stephens had certainly sounded skeptical about the North Koreans receiving new Russian nukes. He'd sounded even more skeptical that Pyongyang was in the process of selling several of those nukes to Iran. Could such skepticism, combined with a plan the NSC had already set in motion, have made the drone strike a fait accompli from the moment Marcus had dialed the phone? Might Stephens and his team have made a different decision if they'd had more time to process the full implications of what Marcus was offering?

Marcus could not be sure. But one thing was now certain. He and Oleg would have to run, but he had to clear Jenny's name and get her out of Russia and back to the U.S. alive and well. Could he trust the Agency to bring her in safely if he sweetened the pot and raised the stakes, giving them more information about the Persian gamble to buy Russian warheads from the North Koreans after agreeing never to have or use nuclear weapons? Or by signaling that he and Oleg were still alive, would he make Stephens even more determined to eliminate them after failing the first time?

47

"Pull over somewhere," Oleg said. "I need a restroom."

"Hold it," Marcus replied.

"I can't."

"We can't take the chance of someone seeing you—not here, in your country's second-largest city."

"Then where are we going?"

"Valdai National Park. There are cabins there. We'll hunker down there till we figure out our next move."

"Valdai? That's the middle of nowhere."

"That's why it's perfect."

"But it's five hours away. I can't wait that long."

"You should have gone back at the house."

"What are you, my mother?"

"Fine, I'll find a place—but not here in the city."

The snow had stopped falling, and the temperature was beginning to rise. The roads were becoming a bit slushy though still manageable. They soon saw signs for Pushkin, a municipal town about twenty-five kilometers south of St. Petersburg. There, Marcus exited the E105 highway and wound his way through quiet neighborhoods until he found a park on the edge of town, not closed but certainly secluded. Oleg stepped out to do his business.

Jenny, meanwhile, was sound asleep. The painkillers had kicked in. He felt her forehead. Her fever had come down significantly, but it was still there. Marcus began to rethink taking her to a remote cabin. As soon as night came, the unseasonably frigid temperatures would return, and having her in such a secluded place was probably a mistake. He switched on the car's GPS navigation system and searched for nearby hotels. By the time Oleg opened the back door—bringing a gust of cold air—Marcus had made his choice.

"Oh, sure, now you tell me," Oleg said, more pleased than annoyed when Marcus started driving and told him of the change of plans.

Ten minutes later, they pulled into the parking garage of the Tsar Palace on Sofiyskiy Boulevard.

For the moment, Marcus kept the engine—and thus the heat—running. "Stay here with her," he instructed Oleg. "Try not to wander off."

He headed into the hotel's basement alone. When he came back a few minutes later, he held up a set of brass keys and explained they were for a suite on the fifth floor.

"You checked in looking like that?" Oleg asked.

"Of course not. I lifted the keys when the clerk stepped away from the front desk."

At that, he tapped Jenny to wake her up. Bleary-eyed, she asked where they were. Marcus told her and explained what he'd just done. Then he asked if she knew how to hack into the hotel's reservations system.

"Probably," she said, sitting up straight and trying to get her bearings. "But why would I if you already have keys?"

"I want you to list our room as occupied—you know, fake name, fake passport number, credit card, home address, the works. We certainly don't want them giving the room to anyone else. So can you do it?"

"I told you I could."

"Good. It's a nice place, nicer than I'd expected so far from the city. And it's got lousy security. I didn't see any surveillance cameras either in the garage or near the stairwell entrance in the basement."

Jenny pulled out the laptop and used a remote administration tool to hack into the hotel's Wi-Fi system. Four minutes later, the reservation was set. The three of them moved quickly, gathering their rucksacks and heading into the basement entrance. They took the stairs and avoided running into staff or guests. The moment they reached their suite, they put a Do Not Disturb sign on the door and closed the drapes.

The mood on the seventh floor was despondent.

They had failed. The evidence was conclusive, and the Russians were furious.

Richard Stephens glanced at his watch. It was now 7:03 a.m. in Washington—2:03 p.m. in Moscow—and Stephens huddled with Martha Dell, his deputy for intelligence. He explained he'd just gotten off the phone with Kropatkin. The FSD director had been irate, screaming about being misled by the Americans and demanding to know what kind of game Washington was playing.

"I assured him our lead was solid," Stephens told his staff. "I said the Russians either entered the wrong coordinates or got there too late. Needless to say, he wasn't buying it, nor was President Petrovsky. In fact, President Clarke can expect a call from Petrovsky within the hour, and neither one of them is going to be happy."

"You don't really believe the Russians used the wrong coordinates, do you, sir?" asked Deputy Director Martha Dell.

"No, probably not."

"Then what happened? How'd they miss him—them?"

"You tell me," said Stephens, back on his feet and pacing. "I had Ryker on the phone for a good long time. We had a clear signal. It was definitely coming from the satellite phone we gave him, which means the coordinates were real. I don't get it."

"Could he have manipulated the signal somehow?" the DDI asked.

"Who, Kropatkin?"

"No, Ryker."

"How?"

"Well, in theory, Ryker could have been calling from a different location using another phone and routed his call through the satphone we gave him."

"Is that even possible?" Stephens asked.

"It's not easy, but yes, it's possible."

"Would Ryker know how to do that?"

"I don't know. He received all kinds of training in the Marines and the Secret Service. I doubt he'd have been trained for that. But Morris would know how. I mean, we taught her."

"But she's severely wounded and likely on heavy medication. And if she's actively helping Ryker, that would suggest she's now an accomplice. Does anyone buy that?"

"Probably not, but you said it yourself. She's injured. She's lost a lot of blood and fluids. She needs painkillers. And she's in the custody of two admitted assassins. Maybe they're compelling her to act. Or maybe she just snapped."

"Okay," Stephens said. "Maybe. But even if that's the case, why would they do it? Why relay the call?"

Dell hesitated to respond but only for a moment.

"To see if you could be trusted."

"You think Ryker *expected* us to give his location to the Russians so they could take him out?" Stephens asked.

"I can't say if he expected it. But it's one logical explanation for why he wasn't calling from the phone we gave him and why the strike didn't work."

"So what do we do now?" Stephens demanded. "And what do I tell the president?"

"Sir, we don't have a choice. We have to make the deal and bring them in."

"First we try killing them, and then we give them presidential pardons?"

"We don't have to admit we gave the Russians their coordinates," the DDI said. "We can tell them the Russians must have intercepted the call. We're sorry about that, but we're glad they're all alive, and now we want them back safely before anything else goes wrong."

"You think they'll believe us?"

"Morris might. Ryker won't. But that's why you shouldn't be the one to deliver the message."

"Then who?"

"Nick Vinetti," the DDI answered. "They've been friends forever. Even if Ryker doesn't believe the Russians intercepted the call—even if he thinks we tipped them off—he'll never believe Vinetti was in on it. And he's right. Vinetti had no idea because we never told him. That makes him the perfect emissary."

Stephens paced about his office, unsure what to do.

"Look, sir, I believe Marcus Ryker is a traitor to our country. Oleg Kraskln is certainly a traitor to his. As for Jenny Morris, I've known her ever since I trained her at the Farm. At this moment I honestly don't know what her role in all this is, so I'm withholding judgment until I know more. But either way, we don't have a choice. If it's really true that the North Koreans have obtained state-of-the-art Russian nuclear warheads, and if there's even a shred of possibility that the Iranians are angling to buy them, then we've got a serious problem on our hands. That's why you need to persuade the president to make this deal and make it fast. And we need to start working with the Pentagon to spin up options to find those nukes and take them out before it's too late."

Pete Hwang had taken an Uber from his apartment before sunrise.

Grabbing his carry-on bag, he raced into the terminal and headed for the Delta counter. There he purchased a business-class ticket on the next flight to London. What he really wanted was a nonstop flight to Berlin, but there simply were no such flights until late that afternoon. Better to spend the day in motion, he decided, getting himself across the Atlantic at least, than spin his wheels in D.C.

"That'll be $5,618," said the Delta rep. "I'll need a credit card and passport."

Normally Hwang wouldn't have flinched at such a steep price. He had been a much-sought-after cardiologist and had always had money to burn. But the divorce had taken a toll in more ways than one. His wife—or more accurately, his wife's attorney—was bleeding him dry. Plus, he'd given up his practice to get into politics and was no longer raking in an income in the mid-six figures. "You know what, let's make that economy instead."

The round-trip fare was still over $2,000, but Hwang handed over his American Express card anyway. Marcus Ryker was his friend, and he was in trouble. No one in this city seemed willing or able to help. But Hwang had spent quite a bit of time in Germany over the years. He had a lot of friends there, in government and out. Maybe he could get a lead on where Ryker was. Maybe he could find a way to help.

Stephens reviled the notion of making a deal with Ryker.

But he saw no other way.

Dell was right. For all his many sins, Ryker had never lied to the CIA director, at least not to Stephens's knowledge. Even if Ryker and Morris had manipulated the satphone signal to mask their true location, that wasn't lying. It was just good tradecraft.

The fact was, Ryker had been inexplicably candid. To Stephens's utter shock, Ryker had readily admitted his participation in the plot against Luganov and Nimkov. He had also taken full responsibility for his actions. Was there now any reason to believe he was lying about the North Koreans and the Iranians? The CIA director was skeptical about the nuclear deal Ryker had described. But if he was telling the truth, the Agency needed not just Ryker and Morris but Kraskin as well, and they needed to find them before the Russians did.

There was just one problem. Aside from the near impossibility of finding and establishing communication with Ryker, Stephens first needed to talk to the president. He needed an approval. He needed signed pardons. And he needed them quickly. But Clarke wasn't at the White House. At the moment, he was speaking on his administration's new immigration bill to a working breakfast of the National Governors Association at the Washington Hilton.

Stephens called the White House chief of staff and said he needed to talk to POTUS right away. To no avail. She refused to pull the president off the stage, arguing that the highly anticipated and highly controversial speech was being televised live on C-SPAN and most of the major cable news networks and was scheduled to run thirty minutes, followed by another fifteen to twenty minutes of Q&A. After that, he was meeting with the leaders of six Latin American nations, who would then hold an event announcing a new trade deal later that morning, followed by lunch. She could slot Stephens in around three thirty that afternoon, but unless the nation was about to go to war—and they were not—that was the best she could do.

Stephens was going to have to improvise. The hotel was on Connecticut Avenue, some ten miles from CIA headquarters. Depending on traffic, it should take him no more than thirty minutes to get there. Stephens ordered his legal staff to draft the necessary paperwork and send it by secure fax to the Secret Service's makeshift operations center at the hotel.

Five minutes later, the motorcade consisting of three black bullet-proof Lincoln Navigators was racing down the George Washington Memorial Parkway as autumn leaves and the Potomac River blurred by at speeds upwards of eighty miles per hour.

Acting President Mikhail Borisovich Petrovsky did not stand when his FSB director arrived.

Rather he sat behind the desk from which Luganov had ruled Russia with an iron fist since the first day of the first month of the first year of the new millennium.

Kropatkin knew the new president's first call had been to Pyongyang to get the Dear Leader's pledge of allegiance to him and his new regime, which had come instantly. Kropatkin also knew no mention had been made of the nuclear warheads about which Petrovsky still knew nothing. The next call had been to Tehran. The Grand Ayatollah's loyalty to the Kremlin was also immediately forthcoming, though he, too, avoided any mention of the deal with Pyongyang. The next call would be to the president of the United States, and Petrovsky was seething.

"Why did your people not intercept this call Oleg Stefanovich was making?"

"My people find no evidence of such a call, Your Excellency," Nikolay Kropatkin replied.

"Then why did the Americans give us these coordinates?" Petrovsky demanded. "Why would they intervene in this situation at all?"

"I wish I had a conclusive answer to that, Mikhail Borisovich, but I'm afraid at the moment I have only a theory."

"Which is what?"

"Perhaps Oleg Stefanovich was speaking on a secure satellite phone—one built by the Americans."

"With whom?"

"Perhaps with the man we suspect he was in collusion with, an American by the name of Marcus Ryker."

"And who is he?"

The FSB chief realized Petrovsky hadn't been read in on the details of the FSB's investigation. Luganov and Nimkov were the only ones outside of a handful of FSB agents and investigators who had known about Ryker, and no sooner had they been briefed than Oleg had shot them both in cold blood.

"Ryker is a former Marine, a combat veteran who later served in the U.S. Secret Service."

"Why would you believe this Ryker has any connection?"

Kropatkin gave a quick summary of the case. Kraskin had first met Ryker in Berlin years earlier. Ryker had come to Moscow as the head of Senator Robert Dayton's security detail and had participated in the meeting with Luganov. Nothing seemed amiss at the time, but then Kraskin mysteriously checked into the Hotel National in the wee hours after the meeting. He claimed to be having a rendezvous with his wife, Marina, who confirmed the story. But Kraskin had asked for a specific room, directly next to Ryker's room. By sunup, Ryker was making an unscheduled visit to the U.S. Embassy. By that afternoon, Dayton and his delegation were flying back to Washington. And within hours of their arrival, President Clarke had ordered a massive reinforcement of U.S. and other NATO military forces into Poland and the Baltics.

"President Luganov was convinced there was a mole operating at the highest levels inside his government," Kropatkin finished.

"How could I forget?" Petrovsky said. "I received the brunt of his fury."

"You did, sir. Some in his cabinet—not you, perhaps, but several ministers—were dismissive of the concern. Several expressed to me in private that Clarke didn't need a mole to be concerned for the Baltics."

"But there was a mole," Petrovsky said. "Luganov was right."

"He was, sir, and it cost him his life."

"And you think Ryker was complicit."

"Thus far the evidence is unclear," Kropatkin hedged. "We are certain he left the country on Senator Dayton's plane, but we have no evidence that he ever got to Washington."

"Get to your point, Nikolay Vladimirovich. I have urgent business to attend to."

"Yes, Your Excellency. I'm simply saying this: Oleg Stefanovich had help from at least two people, a man and a woman. This much we know for a fact. We found three bodies in the wreckage of the Gulfstream, but DNA testing was conclusive—Oleg Stefanovich was not among them. The identities of the other bodies have not yet been determined. But my people are operating under the premise that Oleg Stefanovich is still alive, as are his two associates. This is why we have issued bulletins to that effect to the entire country. This is why our manhunt continues unabated. We have growing confidence that Marcus Ryker is one of the people involved in this conspiracy. We believe he may very well be on Russian soil as we speak and may even be the person trying to get Kraskin out of the country."

"Then find him," Petrovsky demanded, "and kill him."

49

It was known by some as the "Hinckley Hilton."

The reason was painful for anyone in the U.S. government charged with protecting the nation and her leaders. The hotel had been the scene of one of the worst failures in the history of the Secret Service. On March 30, 1981, John W. Hinckley Jr. fired six shots at President Ronald Reagan as he was exiting the building after giving a speech to union members. Hinckley had hoped to kill the American leader to impress the actress Jodie Foster, with whom he'd become obsessed by repeatedly watching her in the movie *Taxi Driver*. His plot had been thwarted, but narrowly.

As they pulled into the hotel's protected side entrance on T Street, CIA director Richard Stephens couldn't help but note the irony. He had come to the Hinckley Hilton, of all places, to ask the current president of the United States to pardon two men who had successfully conspired to assassinate at least two and possibly three other world leaders. What had the world come to?

Rushed inside by his protective detail, Stephens met with the Secret Service's special agent in charge. The SAIC gave him the documents Langley had faxed ahead and then led the team through the bowels of the building to the holding room just off the main stage. Stephens checked his watch. It was 8:47 a.m. The president—well off-script but bringing the house down with a series of impromptu anecdotes and one-liners—was still speaking.

When he finally finished and entered the holding room, Clarke was in a buoyant mood, high-fiving hotel staffers and agreeing to selfies.

"Richard, my friend, that was a barn burner, eh?" The president beamed, slapping his CIA director on the back and asking an aide for a Diet Coke.

"I'm afraid I just got here, Mr. President," Stephens demurred. "But I need your full attention, sir. We have a situation developing."

"Of course, of course—just give me a minute to nosh a bit," said Clarke, heading over to a light breakfast buffet set up against the far wall. "I'm starved. Was talking to so many people at the breakfast, I never actually got to eat."

"Mr. President, with respect, this is time sensitive, sir."

"Just give me a moment. These cinnamon rolls are amazing. Here, have one."

"Sir, we have an urgent situation in Russia," Stephens replied, waving off the plastic plate the president was dishing up for him. "I need a few minutes, sir. Could we clear the room of everyone but our security details?"

This got Clarke's attention. "It's that serious?" he said, straightening up while taking a sip of soda.

"Yes, sir, I'm afraid it is."

"Very well," the president said.

He didn't clear the room. Instead, Clarke led Stephens out the door, down several hallways, and outside to his waiting motorcade.

"Ride with me back to the White House," he said as a Secret Service agent opened the back door of the armor-plated limousine known as the Beast.

The two men climbed in together. Sixty seconds later, the motorcade began to roll. The president took a bite of a Danish and nodded for the CIA director to proceed.

Stephens lowered his voice and gave as concise a summary of the situation as he could.

"A pardon?" the president asked. "This is a joke, right?"

"I'm afraid not, sir. At the moment, the U.S. intelligence community has only a handful of informants inside the North Korean and Iranian governments, none of them higher than mid-level bureaucrats. Whatever else you think of him, Oleg Kraskin has been to Pyongyang and Tehran with his father-in-law. He knows all the players on a first-name basis. He knows exactly what Luganov said to the Dear Leader and to the ayatollah and what those men said in return. He's been briefed on the Russian intelligence profiles of every single person he ever met with in Iran and North Korea, and we can assume he has close working ties with senior aides to both leaders. The way we assess it, Ryker may very well be telling us the truth. Kraskin may know things vital to U.S. national security, things very few people know. I'm not thrilled about this idea. But I believe it's our only course at the moment, and if we're going to do it, we need to do it fast."

"Richard, Oleg Kraskin shot two Russian leaders in the face," the president said. "Marcus Ryker helped him."

"Sir, with respect, Oleg Kraskin saved us from potentially going to nuclear war with the Russian Federation, and Marcus Ryker helped him."

"You do understand the political risk this exposes me to if this thing comes out in the press," the president whispered, almost inaudibly.

"I concede it's a risk, sir."

"An enormous risk."

"But consider the flip side, Mr. President."

"Meaning what?"

"Consider the scandal that will engulf your administration if what Ryker and Kraskin are telling us is true—that Pyongyang has an arsenal of advanced Russian nuclear warheads sitting atop ICBMs capable of reaching every American city *and* are planning to transfer some of them to Iran, whose leader openly makes threats to wipe us off the planet. What do you think would happen if people found out you turned down the best lead on understanding and neutralizing the situation we've ever had?"

The president was silent.

"And don't worry, sir," the director added. "It won't leak. I'll see to that."

"Don't make promises you can't keep, Richard," the president said. "This is Washington. Everything leaks."

Six minutes later, the motorcade pulled through the steel gates and onto the White House grounds.

"Mr. President, I need an answer. I've got all the paperwork right here," Stephens said, handing Clarke a black folder marked *TOP SECRET* in large, red block letters. "It just needs your John Hancock."

But Clarke refused to even look at the folder.

"Forget it," he said, stepping out of the limo. "My answer is no."

50

A new message was waiting for Oleg Kraskin.

"Look," he told the others. "General Yoon just wrote me again."

Marcus and Jenny moved quickly to the desk where Oleg was hunched over the laptop, which Jenny had wired to their remaining satphone in order to stay off the hotel's obviously insecure Wi-Fi. It was the fourth communication from the general in the last several hours, and it presented a grave setback to their strategy.

Back at the dacha, Oleg had cautiously made contact with the general, assuring him he was alive but giving no further details. But it seemed the North Korean had finally confirmed Oleg's involvement in Luganov's death. In his next message, Yoon had expressed his admiration for Oleg's stand on principle. He said he didn't approve of the methods but felt he knew Oleg well enough to know the man was "doing what was necessary to save the lives of millions." He went on to say that Oleg's courageous actions, however dangerous, had both shamed and inspired him.

To date, I have been a coward, he'd written. **I have been abetting evil that could lead to war on the most horrific scale ever seen in human history, and I have done nothing to stop it. But now I know I must try, and I need your help. I can provide you vital information, but I cannot stay here. You must guarantee me you can get me and my family out to safety, to freedom. Then I will tell you everything I know. Can you do this?**

The prospect of facilitating the defection of such a highly placed and well-informed North Korean military official was intoxicating—and fraught with danger.

With input from Marcus and Jenny, Oleg had written back. It was possible Yoon was being used by North Korean intelligence—working hand in glove with the FSB—to lay a trap. Moscow desperately wanted to find out precisely where Oleg was and take him out. If they were using Yoon's messages to track Oleg's computer IP address, finding him would not be difficult. But they'd decided they had to take the risk. Marcus and Oleg needed the information Yoon could provide, not just for the security of the U.S. and her allies, but to seal their deal with Washington and secure their own freedom.

Ready to help you, if I can, Oleg had replied. **But can't do it alone. Will need to call on friends to help me. Only way to get such help is to know exactly what kind of information you are willing to provide. How specific can you be?**

Nineteen minutes later, Yoon had responded.

Sickened at what has transpired since Dear Leader learned of events in Moscow. Leadership here feels liberated. Moving fast to enact changes before new Russian president is up to speed. DL has ordered generals to rewire command and control system so that they alone can launch warheads at a time of DL's choosing. Will no longer need authorization—either written or electronic—from the Kremlin, as had been the arrangement with Luganov. Also: deal to sell five of most powerful Russian warheads to Iran has been approved by DL. Iran will transfer one hundred billion U.S. dollars in two disbursements. Should happen this week. Transfer of warheads set for next week. I'm in charge of managing transfer.

It was on the basis of this—plus all that Oleg had learned in his personal meetings with the North Korean and Iranian leadership—that Marcus had formulated their offer to Washington. So far as Oleg knew, the deal was being discussed by the NSC, and they'd have a positive answer within the next few hours. So far as General Yoon knew from Oleg's next message, however, the Americans were going to need a lot more.

But in the third exchange, the general had called their bluff.

Nothing more unless I get a detailed plan from you to extract my family and me. I should not have to remind you of the risk I am taking or that time is of the essence.

Amid a flurry of ideas from his colleagues, Oleg furiously typed a list of questions they needed answers to before proceeding.

1. What exact kind of warheads do you have?

2. How is the transfer to Iran supposed to take place?

3. What day?

4. From where?

5. Who on the Iranian side will be orchestrating the transfer?

6. Where will the warheads enter Iran?

7. Where will they be stored?

8. How many people in NK know about the deal?

9. Who in Russia knows about the arrangement?

10. Will you be traveling with the warheads all the way to Iran to ensure their safe delivery?

Now, hours later, here in the Tsar Palace on the outskirts of St. Petersburg, they had their reply, simple and to the point.

Where is your plan?

General Yoon was done giving freebies. He was playing hardball and figured he had all the leverage.

"What do we do now?" Oleg asked, ready to type.

Marcus wasn't sure. Jenny was.

"Nothing," she said.

"What do you mean, nothing?"

"He made us wait. Now we make him wait."

"What if he goes dark?"

"Then we're no worse off than we are now."

"Are you kidding?" Oleg asked. "We'll be far worse off. If we have no specifics to give the White House, why should the president agree to make the deal with us?"

"Because Yoon isn't going to go dark. His greatest fear right now is that *we* might go dark."

"What do you mean?"

"Just what I said. What happens if we stop responding to him?"

"We lose our chance at freedom."

"But Yoon doesn't know that. Remember, he's not doing this to help us. He's doing it to save himself and his family. If we don't make a deal with him—assuming this whole thing is legit—then from his perspective you have your freedom, and he's trapped behind enemy lines, never knowing when the day might come that you decide to show a copy of his messages to his superiors. Then he's finished."

Oleg was aghast. "But I'd never do that. The general is my friend."

"Maybe so. But look at it from his perspective."

"What do you mean?"

"Luganov was your boss, your wife's father, the grandfather of your only son . . ."

"And?"

"And you shot and killed him in his very own home."

Bill McDermott was waiting on the steps of the North Portico.

As the president headed inside to prepare for his meeting with the Latin American leaders, the deputy national security advisor pulled Stephens inside the vestibule and off to a corner.

"Don't you ever try an end run around Barry and me again," McDermott whispered, referring to his boss, National Security Advisor Barry Evans.

"It wasn't an end run," Stephens protested.

"It was, and it better not happen again."

"We're talking about Russian nukes in the hands of two rogue powers."

"It's a bluff by two admitted traitors."

"One of whom is your friend."

"No friend of mine would betray his country."

"What if he's not trying to betray us but protect us?" Stephens shot back, keeping his voice down so as not to be overheard by staffers and reporters walking by.

"Come on, Richard—you *really* think the Russians gave Pyongyang 750-kiloton nukes and then gave their permission to sell them to the crazies in Tehran?"

"Look, I don't know, and neither do you. But if this intel is good, we're talking about the worst threat to U.S. national security in my lifetime or yours. And in case you'd forgotten, Bill, it's my job to steal secrets. It's what I swore an oath to do—to make sure the president has the best intelligence we can obtain from whatever source we can find at nearly any price. Do you really want it to come out on the nightly news or before a Senate investigatory panel that we had access to actionable intelligence regarding nuclear weapons in the hands of two of our worst enemies and we did nothing?"

Stephens had taken his best shot, but McDermott was unmovable.

"You're getting conned by two con men," he sniffed as he turned and walked away. "You need the president's authorization to move forward, and you're never going to get it."

51

Pete Hwang scanned through the movie options but found nothing worthwhile.

So he pulled out his laptop, connected to Wi-Fi, and found dozens of new messages. All of them could wait except one. Annie Stewart had written to him. But the moment he read it, a gloom settled over him. She wasn't asking how he was doing. She was asking about Marcus.

Had Hwang contacted his various sources?

Had he heard back from anyone?

Did anyone have any leads on where Marcus might be?

What was his next move?

Stewart was quick to note that she was wasn't writing on Senator Dayton's behalf. These were personal inquiries, written from her own Yahoo! account, not from her government email address. Hwang knew she was emphasizing the distinction for legal reasons, lest a federal investigation ensue and the senator and his staff and all their records and correspondence with and regarding Marcus J. Ryker be subpoenaed. But it was also true—she *was* asking for personal reasons. That just made it worse.

Hwang cursed himself for being so touchy. He flagged down a flight attendant and ordered himself a stiff drink. Two, actually. When they came, he stared at the clouds a good ten thousand feet below him and sipped them slowly.

As he did, he flashed back to the day he and Ryker had met this stunning woman. He remembered it precisely. It was the fifth of May. It had been hot as all blazes in Kabul—one of the worst heat waves in Afghanistan's history—and he and his fellow Marines had been assigned to serve as a protection detail for Senator Dayton, a big cheese on the Intel Committee. Annie Stewart had been a press assistant on the senator's delegation, fresh out of graduate school, in her midtwenties. Hwang had been mesmerized from the moment she'd scrambled on board the chopper for the flight over Taliban country.

Born and raised on the outskirts of Houston, Hwang hadn't grown up in a military family. Nor had he ever dreamed of becoming a Marine. His parents had come to the States from Seoul in the 1950s. They'd tried to raise him and his four older sisters in the ways of the old country, but he had turned out all American and nearly all Texan as well. He'd picked up his parents' language because he'd had to. They'd never learned much English, having secluded themselves in Koreatown in the Spring Branch community on the northwest side of Houston. He'd certainly inherited his parents' work ethic. But that and their name was about it.

Owning and managing a string of dry cleaners was not his idea of a future. So Hwang had joined the Marines for one simple reason: to get the government to pay for medical school. He'd wanted to be a doctor since he was ten years old, and by the age of twenty he found himself a combat medic, assigned to the Twenty-Second Marine Expeditionary Unit, serving in a battalion landing team known as the One-Six—First Battalion, Sixth Marines.

When he'd met Ryker and Vinetti in boot camp, they'd immediately become the best of friends. Their sergeant, Bill "Big Mac" McDermott, drove them hard, yet despite the brutal heat, Operation Enduring Freedom had been going reasonably well for them all.

Hwang vividly recalled boarding the Sikorsky CH-53E Super Stallion with his colleagues and the civilians who suddenly jumped aboard as the rotors were spooling up. Annie Stewart had caught his eye immediately. Hwang had never seen a more beautiful woman. Her big green eyes and short shag haircut nearly made his heart stop. He loved her enthusiasm, her sense of fascination about everything she was learning in country. He was charmed by her infectious smile and South Carolina accent. He loved that she was wearing almost no makeup at all and that her nails were short and unpainted. He'd never been attracted to girls who got themselves all painted and dolled up, preferring a simpler, more modest look.

After they came under fire by the Taliban, Hwang became even more impressed by Stewart. She saw friends die that day. Shot to death. Burned alive. Yet rather than panic, she proved surprisingly cool under fire. She'd immediately volunteered to help and had gotten right to work. She cleaned wounds and set up IVs and gave her wounded colleagues shots of morphine and even performed mouth-to-mouth on one woman who sadly didn't make it. When it was all over, her face and hands and clothes had been covered with mud and blood, and Hwang had been attracted to her all the more.

Unfortunately, she'd shipped out with the senator, back to Washington, twenty-four hours later. But not before coming to the field hospital to meet with each member of the One-Six. With tears streaming down her cheeks, she'd expressed her appreciation for what they'd all done to save her life and that of her boss and her friends. Hwang was about to ask for her number, but then he'd watched her become especially emotional at the foot of Marcus's bed. It was true that Marcus had probably done the most to fend off the Taliban attack. He'd killed nearly two dozen jihadists that day, and he'd paid a heavy price. Shot multiple times, he'd very nearly bled to death. Now he was lying there unconscious with this beautiful woman crying over him. Hwang had put his arm around Stewart, handed her some tissues, and gently eased her away and walked her to a waiting Humvee. But the moment had been lost. Hwang never asked her out but simply said good-bye.

Perhaps it was just as well. He couldn't quite imagine coming home to Houston with a blonde on his arm and expecting to get his parents' blessing. Then again, marrying a Korean hadn't exactly worked out for him, had it? Jane, the girl next door—the brown-eyed, black-haired beauty his parents had picked out for him because her family originally hailed from the Korean city of Busan—had not only divorced him, she'd soaked him for everything he had, taken his kids, and walked away with everything including the kitchen sink.

In the financial and emotional wreckage that had become Hwang's life, a blonde now seemed pretty good—especially one he'd had a crush on so many years before. And then, completely out of the blue, Annie Stewart had called him a few months earlier. *Could he come down to D.C. for lunch? Would he be willing to talk to the senator? Did he have any interest in coming to work on a presidential campaign?* He had jumped at the chance. Nothing had transpired between them, but at least they were working together. They were talking often, emailing even more.

Hwang felt ashamed of himself for his flash of jealousy. Could he really fault the woman for showing as much interest in Marcus's situation as he was? At least she was turning to Hwang for answers. If he kept his head about him, the whole thing could actually draw them closer.

Hwang glanced at his watch. He still had four and a half hours until he got to London. He'd better get some rest, he told himself. He turned off his phone and closed the window blind. Then he leaned back his seat, put on an eye mask, and tried to drift off to an image of Annie Stewart in his mind's eye.

It wasn't working. The unshakable image that haunted him now was Ryker's Gulfstream jet being blown out of the sky, over and over again.

52

Lieutenant General Barry Evans stepped into the Oval Office.

Clarke had just come from the luncheon in the East Room and was surprised to see his national security advisor.

"Good afternoon, General—I wasn't aware you and I had a meeting," he said as he shook the man's hand and accepted a cup of coffee from a steward.

"Sir, I just received official word that President Petrovsky wants to speak with you immediately. The Kremlin says he wants to establish a friendly dialogue and accept your congratulations on being named Russia's new leader. And given the dramatic developments of the past few days, he would also like to brief you on the retreat of Russian forces from NATO borders."

"You buy any of that?" Clarke asked as he sat down behind the *Resolute* desk and checked his schedule for the rest of the afternoon.

"No, sir," said the NSA. "He's fuming about the erroneous information the CIA fed him, and he's going to give you an earful."

"Can't wait," Clarke said. "Make the call."

Jenny was still running a fever.

Marcus figured there must be an infection somewhere after all. He
gave her the last shot of antibiotics they had. He also gave her another
shot of morphine, but that was running low.

"You need a doctor."

"I'll be fine," she said.

"Don't be an idiot."

"What's that supposed to mean?"

"You're tough—I get it," Marcus said. "You're lucky you're not dead
or in a coma. But let's not kid ourselves. We need to get you professional medical care, and soon."

"What exactly do you have in mind?"

"I don't know," Marcus admitted. "And that's what bothers me."

Jenny excused herself to use the washroom, and Marcus began to
pace. It was clear he had to get Jenny back to the States for her own
protection. He also knew he and Oleg couldn't go with her. The problem was, he no longer had a direct connection to the American government, yet he needed someone to turn to, a back channel who could get
a message to Stephens that Ryker was ready to hand over the Agency's
Moscow station chief immediately and without preconditions.

But who?

Nick Vinetti was the obvious choice, but he'd already tried that
approach, and it had gone badly. There was McDermott, but he was
too close to the center. And then there was the touchy matter that
McDermott—one of his oldest friends in the world—must have
known and approved of the president's decision to order drone strikes
against him. So that was out. There was Pete Hwang. Marcus was certainly closer to the good doctor than to McDermott. Yet how could he

be sure Hwang hadn't sided with Vinetti and McDermott in working against him?

Marcus immediately ruled out involving his mom or sisters. The less they knew, the better. Nor did he feel comfortable reaching out to Carter or Maya Emerson to intervene on his behalf. Emerson would do it, of course. He wasn't just a pastor. He had become a trusted friend, someone Marcus felt he could talk to about anything. Well, almost anything. He certainly wouldn't want to involve him in any of what he was dealing with now.

Senator Dayton came to mind, but Marcus doubted the man would even take his call, radioactive as he had become. What about Annie Stewart? he wondered. He and Annie didn't actually know each other that well. He wouldn't exactly characterize her as a friend. They'd never done anything social together, yet they were more than acquaintances. He'd known her for over a decade, and he sensed that she held him in some esteem. He certainly admired her. She was incredibly sharp. A clear thinker. Articulate. And discreet. Working on the professional staff of the Senate Intelligence Committee as a senior advisor to the ranking minority member, she was as well-placed as anyone else he knew. What's more, she was the one who had reached out to him to get him involved in Dayton's delegation to Moscow in the first place.

And yet . . .

The more he mulled the idea, the less comfortable Marcus felt reaching out to her, though he couldn't place his finger on exactly why. Might being mixed up with him compromise her security clearance? Might it jeopardize her work for the senator? A wave of other doubts flooded his thoughts. It just didn't feel right.

Marcus was quickly running out of people to ask. After several minutes, he doubled back to Pete Hwang. Had he ruled him out too quickly? Of course Hwang was friends with McDermott and Vinetti, but that didn't necessarily mean he was in league with them. He didn't work for them, and he was nothing if not an independent thinker. Technically Hwang didn't work for the government at all. He was paid by Senator

Dayton's political action committee. That gave him proximity to the center and thus the ability to pass on a message to those at the highest levels in Washington, yet he also had just enough distance that no one could use his involvement to accuse the U.S. government of engaging in any further direct communication with men accused of treason.

Marcus glanced at his watch, then powered up the laptop and connected to the Internet via the remaining satphone. He didn't want to use his own Gmail account, certain it was being monitored by Langley and perhaps by the Russians as well. So he created a new AOL account and dashed off the following note.

Pete, this is Marcus. You there? Got a question for you. And it's time sensitive.

53

The call started well but rapidly disintegrated.

Following the recommendation of his national security advisor, who was listening in on speaker, Clarke began by offering his personal condolences—and that of his nation—for the tragic events in Moscow. He wished Petrovsky well in his new role as Russia's president and said it was important they set U.S.-Russian relations back on a positive trajectory.

The president then listened politely, even took some notes, as Petrovsky described how he was pulling back Russian forces in Europe. And when Petrovsky asked his American counterpart to reciprocate by removing U.S. forces from the Baltics—something Clarke had no intention of doing—he followed Evans's counsel and told the Russian he would "take his recommendation seriously and discuss it with his advisors."

But that was five minutes ago. Now Petrovsky was screaming so loudly and speaking so rapidly that both the Russian and American translators were struggling to keep up. As anticipated, Petrovsky was accusing the Americans of putting innocent civilians at risk by providing coordinates that had proved inaccurate. He demanded to know what role the Central Intelligence Agency had played in the murders of Russian leaders and the destabilization of Russian society. It was a serious charge, and it was all Clarke could do not to respond in kind.

"Mr. President—Mikhail—please; you're angry and I understand why, but listen to me when I tell you categorically that the United States government had absolutely no role whatsoever in any of these events," Clarke said in as restrained a manner as he could manage. "We were blindsided by these assassinations. I have denounced them. My secretary of state has denounced them. We have done so in the strongest possible language. And we are trying to help you hunt down the killers."

"You deny having any role in these three murders?" Petrovsky bellowed.

"Absolutely—100 percent—we were not involved in any way," Clarke replied. "Mikhail, please, take a breath. For the sake of world peace and security, you and I must endeavor to get along better—"

He almost said, "better than your predecessor" but stopped himself when he saw Evans's hand shoot up. Instead he changed course awkwardly.

"—better, that is to say, for all of us, for the peoples in both of our nations who depend on us for peace and prosperity, that we should begin our new relationship on friendly, or at least civil, terms." Clarke looked at Evans and got an approving nod. "We will not agree on every issue. But we do not need to be disagreeable. Can we agree, at least, on this?"

"Do not test me, Mr. President," Petrovsky growled. "I am demonstrating my goodwill by pulling our forces back from NATO's borders. But I expect a tangible measure of good faith on your part."

"I already told you, Mikhail—your request that we remove our forces, or at least decrease our presence, in the Baltics will be given the utmost consideration."

"This is not all I am seeking," said Petrovsky, quieter now but clearly still furious.

"What, then?"

"Tell me: Where is Marcus Ryker?"

Clarke blanched, as did Evans.

"Who?" Clarke replied while scribbling on a White House notepad, *Where's he going with this?*

Evans shrugged.

"You know exactly whom I speak of," said Petrovsky. "Marcus Ryker. Former Marine. Former Secret Service agent. Saved your life. Now working for Senator Dayton."

"Okay, fine, I know Mr. Ryker, but what does he have to do with any of this?"

Clarke could see the anxiety in Evans's eyes.

"My security services have a growing pile of evidence that he collaborated with Oleg Kraskin, the man responsible for murdering all three of our leaders."

"That's impossible."

"Impossible, you say? Then where is he? He took part in Senator Dayton's meeting with President Luganov. Then, in the middle of the night, he had a meeting with Mr. Kraskin in his room in the Hotel National—don't deny it, Mr. President; we have it all on tape. He helped Mr. Kraskin pass classified information to your government. And now, in the aftermath of Mr. Kraskin's wicked work, Marcus Ryker is missing. He flew out of Moscow on the senator's plane. But no one has seen him since. He's not in his apartment. He hasn't shown up for his volunteer work at Lincoln Park Baptist Church. Nor has he met with Senator Dayton or the senator's staff since supposedly returning to Washington."

Clarke was speechless.

"This has my security services very puzzled," Petrovsky continued. "They are suggesting to me that Mr. Ryker was on the Gulfstream jet that Mr. Kraskin used to escape Moscow. They are suggesting to me that Ryker and Kraskin and another conspirator may have actually jumped out of the plane just before my air force shot it down. And if they are proven correct, then there is no way Mr. Ryker was working alone. Twenty-something years serving in the U.S. military and government? He has to still be working for you. I keep telling my generals, 'Don't jump to any rash conclusions, gentlemen. Do you understand what you're suggesting? You're suggesting the American government has just committed not just one but three acts of war against our nation. We had better have solid proof before we consider our retaliatory options.' But I must tell you, Mr. President, they are very convincing."

Retaliatory options? The Russian president was saying he was de-escalating the conflict his predecessor had set into motion while simultaneously threatening war anyway. Clarke wiped his brow and reached for a glass of water.

"So I ask again, Mr. President," Petrovsky continued, "in as patient a manner as I can muster under the circumstances: Where is Marcus Ryker?"

"I have no idea, Mikhail," Clarke replied. "He doesn't work for me. He's a private citizen and—"

"That is not the answer I'm looking for, Mr. President. If you cannot produce Ryker for my ambassador in Washington, I may be persuaded by my security advisors that he is, in fact, on Russian soil. That he is, in fact, responsible for the murders of our leaders. And that he just may, in fact, still be working for you."

Clarke was no longer sitting behind the *Resolute* desk. He was on his feet now, pacing, improvising. "That's a very serious charge, Mikhail. Don't go there. Look, Marcus Ryker is a good man—a patriot—completely incapable of doing what you're saying. And just because I don't know where he is at the moment doesn't mean I can't find him.

I have no doubt he came home with Senator Dayton. I'm sure he's in Washington or nearby—wait, one of my staffers is handing me a note—"

Evans froze, clearly unhappy with this turn of events and clueless about what the president of the United States was going to say next.

"Hold on; let me see here. Okay, yes," Clarke continued. "My staff says Mr. Ryker became very ill on the flight back home. Upon landing in Washington, he was rushed to Walter Reed medical center. That's a military hospital in Bethesda, Maryland. He's in the ICU there, undergoing aggressive treatment. I don't know what the ailment is, but apparently the doctors expect him to make a full recovery."

54

IranAir flight 319 from Tehran landed just before 9:30 p.m. local time.

When every other passenger had disembarked, the deputy director of the Iranian Revolutionary Guard Corps finally did as well. He had not flown in uniform, nor in first class. He'd been told to keep a low profile, and he was. No one was waiting for him at baggage claim or in the arrival hall. There was no government car waiting or even a friend there to welcome him, and there was a reason for that. No one knew he was coming.

It was unusually humid for the end of September. There was no breeze coming off the water, and the air was like an oven. As Alireza al-Zanjani emerged from the air-conditioned terminal, he saw a digital time and temperature display at a bank across the street. It was 46 degrees Celsius, nearly 115 Fahrenheit, and he was instantly drenched in perspiration. He found it hard to breathe, and he remembered why it had been years since he'd come down to the Gulf.

Wiping his brow and adjusting his sunglasses, al-Zanjani hailed a taxi and gave the wizened old driver the name of a café on the south side of this city of some two hundred thousand souls. The cab had no air-conditioning, and the dust swirling into the vehicle's interior from the four open windows nearly made al-Zanjani choke. But the traffic at this hour was mercifully light, and by a quarter to ten he had arrived at his destination. He tossed a wad of rials into the front seat—a good deal more than the fare—grabbed his leather satchel, and walked into the café.

The place was packed with teenagers, mostly girls in headscarves and abayas, but al-Zanjani passed them by without a glance. The young barista asked what he wanted to drink, but he ignored the kid and headed for a back room.

The door was locked. He knocked three times and whispered a password. He could hear a good deal of muffled discussion but could not quite make out the words. Eventually, however, the door opened, and two burly bodyguards stood there with suspicion in their eyes. They patted al-Zanjani down and removed his sidearm. Then the older of the two asked for his papers and studied them carefully while the younger kept his hand on his own sidearm and never took his eyes off al-Zanjani's. Finally satisfied, the older guard returned the papers and stepped aside. The moment al-Zanjani stepped in, the door was closed and locked behind him.

The IRGC commander now found himself looking at a thin, wiry, balding man in his late fifties with thick wire-rimmed glasses and a trim salt-and-pepper beard. He'd been sitting, reading the local daily paper and smoking a cigarette. But as al-Zanjani entered, the man stood. He wore a wrinkled white dress shirt that had been tucked into loose brown trousers and a belt that seemed to be fighting a losing battle to keep the trousers on the man's gaunt frame.

"Dr. Abbasi, I presume?"

"Yes, that's me," said the man, snuffing out his cigarette and brushing away a few crumbs from his shirt. "How can I help you, General? We weren't expecting you."

"How could you have?" al-Zanjani asked. "I didn't make an appointment. I didn't want anyone to know I was coming."

Abbasi nodded and looked down at the floor.

"Do you know how I found you, Doctor?" al-Zanjani asked.

Abbasi looked up and shook his head.

"You come here every night. My people say you come and drink—and not just coffee, I might add—and play poker and welcome the company of woman who are not, apparently, any relation to you. . . ."

Al-Zanjani's voice trailed off. Abbasi said nothing, but his eyes returned to the floor.

"Do you see where I'm going with this, Doctor?"

Still, Abbasi made no comment, much less a defense.

"You're getting tired—lazy—because you're bored."

"No, General," Abbasi suddenly said, looking directly in the commander's eyes. "I love my work. It's just been slow—and since the agreement with the Americans, slower still. But I—"

Al-Zanjani held up his hand, and Abbasi stopped.

"It's okay," al-Zanjani said. "I'm not going to report you. After all, whom would I report you to but myself? No, Dr. Abbasi, I have a new assignment for you."

"Sir?"

"You're a rocket scientist, Haydar, the best in all of the Republic. But some genius thought it valuable to have you babysitting a program that is going nowhere."

"It's not their fault, sir. I volunteered for the assignment. I can do the work. Please, give me another chance."

"No, Haydar, you're missing my point," al-Zanjani replied. "You're wasting your talents here, and we've been wasting your time. But I've come to change that. Can you keep a secret, all of you?"

Al-Zanjani looked at each man, waiting for each to see the seriousness in his eyes and nod his consent.

"Very well, then," he continued. "I have negotiated the purchase of five nuclear warheads from North Korea. The Supreme Leader approved the purchase himself. I briefed him and President Afshar earlier. But the warheads were not built in Pyongyang. They're Russian-made, 750 kilotons, and could annihilate the entire island of Manhattan—or the entire cities of Washington, Chicago, Dallas, or Los Angeles—in a matter of milliseconds. Can and will. That will be your job—fitting these warheads on five of our most powerful missiles. Tomorrow I leave for Pyongyang to coordinate the transportation of these warheads. They should be here by the fourteenth or fifteenth of October. You have until Nowruz to make them operational. The Supreme Leader was very clear on this point. You will have all the money you need and any personnel that you request. But you must have all five fully ready to launch, able to reach those five U.S. cities by the Persian New Year."

"Nowruz? That's March 20."

"Yes. A Friday, as it happens."

"A holy day."

"For a holy war."

55

"Mr. President, how could you say all that?"

The call had ended, and Evans was aghast.

"You saw what was happening," the president said, still on his feet. "Petrovsky was boxing me into a corner, and a dangerous one at that. I had to say something."

The national security advisor now stood as well, trying to make sense of what had just taken place and figure out how to contain the damage.

"But, sir, you flat-out lied to the president of Russia."

"So what? The man himself is a liar," Clarke shot back. "You heard what he was accusing me of—what was I supposed to do?"

Evans had no idea how to respond.

"Look," Clarke said, "get Director Stephens back on the horn. Tell him to make the deal with Ryker immediately and get him on a plane back to Washington."

This stunned Evans all the more. "But, sir, you told Stephens—"

"I know what I told him, but the situation has changed," he snapped. "Petrovsky is accusing me of acts of war. What's more, he's making Ryker the central issue in the whole thing. Well, I'm going to show that son of a—"

"Sir, please—this is a mistake," Evans said, knowing the risk of cutting the man off but hoping to calm the president and get him to focus on how to undo the mistake. "I know you're angry, but—"

The president was in no mood to be second-guessed. "Enough," he said. "I've heard all I care to hear. Whatever you guys have to promise Ryker, make the deal. Get him on a plane back to Washington immediately. I can stall the Russian ambassador for the rest of the day. But I need Ryker in a bed at Walter Reed—preferably comatose—first thing tomorrow morning or heads are going to roll, starting with yours. Am I clear?"

"Yes, Mr. President," Evans said quietly, whiplashed by the sudden turn of events, though not entirely convinced Clarke was wrong. "Anything else, sir?"

He hoped like crazy the answer was no.

"Yeah," Clarke said, walking around the desk and getting in Evans's face. "You tell Ryker he works for the Agency now."

"Sir?"

"You heard me. I'm not going to tolerate him going rogue for one second more. The moment he sets foot on American soil, he agrees to work for the Central Intelligence Agency, or there'll be no pardon and I'll simply hunt him down and hand him over to the Russians."

"Sir, Marcus Ryker left government service after the deaths of his wife and son. Even if he did want to come back, bringing him into the CIA creates a liability you neither want nor need."

"Perhaps I'm not making myself clear, Barry," Clarke replied. "Ryker joins the CIA, or we cut him loose."

"Mr. President, with all due respect, Ryker is never going to accept that."

"I couldn't care less," Clarke shot back. "He can take it or leave it, but it's not open for negotiation."

Night had fallen in Russia.

Oleg slept on the couch in the living room of the large suite. Having grabbed a spare pillow and blanket from a closet, he'd passed out shortly after nine. He had eaten little all day and insisted all the tension was wreaking havoc with his appetite.

Jenny had the master bedroom to herself. She'd agreed to let Marcus check on her every few hours. Her fever had risen several degrees since their arrival at the hotel, and she had vomited twice. Marcus found her curled up on the king-size bed in a fetal position. She was wrapped in the cotton bathrobe that had been hanging in the bathroom. The sheets and blankets were all rumpled and askew, suggesting she'd been tossing and turning, unable to get comfortable. At least she was asleep now and breathing peacefully, and Marcus felt a small measure of relief.

For his part, Marcus had tried sleeping on the floor of the living room, a few feet from Oleg. Yet rest would not come. For one thing, he was starving. He couldn't risk going out to eat, much less order room service, so he ripped open one of the rucksacks and sorted through the provisions they'd taken from the dacha. There were several cans of tuna fish, a few sleeves of crackers, two jars of pickled herring, and six fresh oranges. Though he easily could have eaten it all by himself in one sitting, he knew they were going to need to make it stretch. He just had no idea for how long.

After scarfing down a snack, Marcus brewed a cup of black coffee in some Russian version of a Keurig machine. Then he settled into a large overstuffed chair and put his feet on the coffee table. Oleg was snoring, but Marcus didn't care. He pulled his Bible out of his rucksack and opened to the first chapter of Proverbs, intending to get a head start on the coming month. If he had ever needed wisdom, it was now.

One passage almost jumped off the page. He'd read it a million times before, yet never had it resonated like it did that night.

My son, if sinners entice you,
Do not consent.
If they say, "Come with us,
Let us lie in wait for blood,
Let us ambush the innocent without cause;
Let us swallow them alive like Sheol,
Even whole, as those who go down to the pit;
We will find all kinds of precious wealth,
We will fill our houses with spoil;
Throw in your lot with us,
We shall all have one purse,"
My son, do not walk in the way with them.
Keep your feet from their path,
For their feet run to evil. . . .
But they lie in wait for their own blood;
They ambush their own lives.
So are the ways of everyone who gains by violence;
It takes away the life of its possessors.

Setting the book down, he leaned back in the chair and stared at Oleg. The poor man had been lured by Luganov into a wicked, brutish world. The would-be czar and his inner circle had run continuously toward evil. He had lain in wait, ambushing the unsuspecting. They had filled their homes with spoil. And it had cost them everything.

Marcus felt himself gaining a second wind. A plan began to form in his mind. He would leave Jenny in the room, take Oleg, and start driving southeast, headed for the Valdai forest after all. After several hours on the road, he would pull over and find a place with Wi-Fi. Marcus was certain he would have heard back from Hwang by then. At that point, he would tell Hwang exactly where Jenny was. He would ask him to alert Nick and get whoever was stationed near St. Petersburg to pick her up and get her immediate medical attention. He had no doubt his friend would do exactly what he asked. If he hadn't heard back from Hwang by that point, or if Hwang refused to help, Marcus decided he would simply email Vinetti directly. Either way, there were risks. Making contact would confirm to the Agency that Marcus was still alive and give them a lot of clues as to where he and Oleg had just been. Yet these were risks he was willing to take to make certain that Jenny was going to be okay.

From there on out, he and Oleg would be on the run. They'd ditch the last remaining satphone. They'd have no one left to talk to at that point anyway, and Marcus didn't dare take the risk that either the NSA or the FSB could get a bead on them electronically. They'd also ditch the Mercedes and steal another car—a 4×4 probably, something better suited to the winter conditions—and keep moving. They had cash. A lot of cash. They could buy fuel and food along the way. The farther they distanced themselves from urban areas, the less likely they were to be spotted or recognized. Russia spanned eleven time zones. That gave them a lot of room to maneuver.

Marcus sat in the darkness considering his plan from every angle. There were holes and thus risks. But the administration had cut them loose. He had to unload Jenny and go dark. He checked his watch again. It was 10:12 p.m. He began packing their things and wiping down the room. Oleg didn't know it yet, but they were leaving in an hour.

56

"What in the world are you talking about, Bill? You guys tried to kill him!"

Nick Vinetti had ordered everyone out of the SCIF—the Sensitive Compartmented Information Facility—located in the bowels of the embassy's basement. Alone and on a secure line back to the White House Situation Room, he couldn't believe what McDermott was asking of him, and he was livid.

"Get ahold of yourself, Nick," McDermott insisted. "The Russians must have intercepted the call. They tried to kill Marcus. We had nothing to do with it."

"Don't give me that crap, Bill. You told me yourself you'd decided Marcus was as much a traitor as Kraskin and the jury was still out on Morris. You as much as told me you guys were going to hunt Marcus down. But you guys blew it, thank God. And now you want me to fix it?"

"Just calm down, Nick, and listen to me. I'm not going to waste my time getting into an argument over things you're not cleared for. But let me be direct. The president is not asking you to reach out to Marcus. Your commander in chief is giving you a direct order. Now, are you going to follow your orders or not?"

Vinetti ran his hands through his jet-black hair. The whole thing was preposterous. There was no way to find Marcus now. He was in the wind. But what choice did he have?

Delta flight 4383 landed at London Heathrow twelve minutes early.

The Airbus A330 wide-body jet was held up on the tarmac for some time until the ground crew could get to the gate, so whatever time had been gained in the air had now been squandered. Nevertheless, it was still only 9:06 p.m. as Pete Hwang disembarked, cleared passport control, and found a restaurant named Giraffe.

A plump young waitress in her midtwenties with a shock of pink hair and dressed all in black led him to a table for two in the back and handed him a menu.

"Don't need one," he said, having been there countless times in the past.

Hwang was famished. He'd slept though the meal service and only woken up upon landing. His body clock had no idea what time it was, so he played it safe and ordered a pot of black coffee with a plate of scrambled eggs, sausages, beans in tomato sauce, hash browns, and a scone, then turned his phone back on and connected to the airport Wi-Fi.

Emails began pouring into his in-box faster than he could process them. Several were from Annie Stewart. None were from the senator. Marjorie Ryker had written several times from Colorado, asking him to call her immediately. Carter Emerson from D.C. had written too, the first time he'd heard from the pastor since the funeral for Ryker's wife and son. He, too, asked Hwang to call him immediately. He didn't say why, but Hwang hardly had to guess.

Waiting at the bottom of the pile, however, was the message that most caught his attention. It wasn't from an address Hwang recognized. It was from an AOL account, not Gmail. But he read it, hoping, and was rewarded. The message contained two useful facts. First, Marcus Ryker was indeed still alive. And second, he was making contact.

"Mr. Vinetti, you have a call from London."

It was his secretary on the intercom.

"Who is it?" he replied, his voice strained and impatient.

"It's a gentleman—won't give his name, sir—but he says he has an early Christmas present for you."

That was odd, Vinetti thought.

"Are you running a trace?" he asked.

"Already did, sir—Heathrow."

Vinetti knew immediately who it was. "Put him through and hold the rest of my calls."

A moment later, Hwang's voice came on the line. "Nick, it's me. I'm in London."

"Pete—what've you got?"

"It's Marcus. I've been emailing with him for the last few minutes. He's ready to turn over Jennifer Morris and says he wants nothing in return."

"Is he still online?"

"I assume so. His last email was moments ago. What do you want to do?"

"Tell him POTUS is ready."

"What do you mean?"

"Just type it out and send it before he logs off."

"Okay, done. Now what?"

"Tell him I'm standing by with the details, but there's a time factor. If he's going to say yes, he needs to call me now."

Vinetti could hear Hwang typing on his laptop. "Sent it."

"Good. What's his response?"

"Hold on."

There was a long pause—so long Vinetti thought the call had been dropped. "Pete, you still there?"

"Yeah, I'm here."

"What's Marcus saying?"

"I'm getting nothing."

Vinetti cursed under his breath. He was on his feet now. He'd switched to a headset, wireless but secure. He walked over to the windows and looked out at the snow-covered Russian capital, and then he heard his secretary again on the intercom.

"Sir, I have a call I think you'll want to take."

"I told you I need you to hold all—" Vinetti stopped himself. The irritation drained from his voice. "Which line?" he asked.

"Line four."

"Thanks—Pete, can you wait a sec?"

"Of course."

"I think it's him on the other line."

"Take it," Hwang said. "Call me back when you can."

"Will do." Vinetti let Hwang's call go and punched line four.

"Marcus, it's me. You okay?"

He was greeted with silence.

"Hey, man, it's Nick. Can you hear me? Hello? Marcus, are you there?"

57

Asher Gilad sat in the prime minister's living room.

He could see that his old friend Reuven "Ruvi" Eitan was not simply disappointed. The PM was becoming angry.

"*I don't know? I don't know?* What does this mean, *I don't know?* These are not words I want to hear from my Mossad director."

"I realize that, Ruvi," Gilad replied. "I'm just being honest with you."

"*Honest?*" Eitan said, mulling the notion as he got up from his chair to pour himself a brandy. "Well, you've certainly been honest with me today, Asher. You readily admit that you don't know where Alireza al-Zanjani is. You can't find the team that killed your men in Athens. You can't say for certain if the Iranians are still looking to buy nuclear warheads, though your working assumption is that they are. You don't know why Tehran took such a big gamble to try to buy warheads on the black market. Nor can you say for certain why Ayatollah Ansari hasn't been seen in public in recent weeks and hasn't delivered his Friday sermon in over a month. Have I missed anything that Israel's notorious chief spy does not know and thus cannot tell his prime minister?"

Gilad held his tongue. Three and a half weeks earlier, he and his team had delivered damning information about the extent of Iran's complicity in North Korea's nuclear and missile programs. Eitan had been so electrified by this that he'd ordered Gilad to share it immediately with the intelligence chiefs from Saudi Arabia and the UAE, both as a way to reinforce to two key Arab regimes the prowess of Israeli capabilities and to set into motion new and more urgent conversations about how the three governments—together with the Egyptians and Jordanians—should work to counter the Persian threat. Now Eitan was acting like Gilad was a bumbling moron who added no value to his national defense architecture.

It wasn't the first time. It would not be the last. Gilad was under no illusions. He'd known the prime minister since they were young boys growing up together in Rishon Leziyyon, a suburb on the south side of Tel Aviv. They'd graduated from high school together. They'd been drafted into the IDF together and had both been recruited into Shayetet Shalosh-esray, the Israeli version of the Navy SEALs and one of the country's most elite commando units. But that's where their paths, and their friendship, had diverged.

Eitan had become a Shayetet commander, and a decorated one at that. Then he'd left the IDF to go into business, where he'd helped launch a high-tech startup that he and his partner had sold a decade later for a cool $400 million. It was then that Eitan had been recruited into the center-right Likud Party and risen through the ranks, finally becoming prime minister.

Gilad, by contrast, had been recruited from Shayetet into the Mossad. The firstborn son of two linguistics professors, he was fluent in six languages—Arabic, Farsi, Russian, French, and English, in addition to Hebrew—and had operated as a field agent, often deep behind enemy lines, first in Syria and later in Lebanon and then Iran. After being severely wounded in his right leg during a mission in Sudan, Gilad had been restricted to desk duty. At first, he'd become deeply discouraged and had contemplated an early retirement. In the end, he chose to view the injury as an opportunity and rose to become one of the intelligence agency's most decorated analysts and later one of its most respected managers.

Somewhere along the way, the bonds of their once-tight brotherhood had frayed. Their wives didn't like each other. Their kids barely knew each other. They never socialized anymore. Gilad had not even voted for the man. Not once. And yet when it came time to appoint a new Mossad director, Eitan had surprised his old friend by calling him first.

"Ruvi, look, we have more than two hundred men and women working exclusively on the Iran matter," Gilad said quietly, gripping the brass crown of his cane with his right hand. "We are doing everything we possibly can. Trust me. When I have more, I assure you that you will be the first to know."

They'd ditched the Mercedes in a river and stolen an Audi SUV.

Now Marcus and Oleg were fueling up at a petrol station along the E95 highway, near Gatchina, a small city about thirty minutes south of the Tsar Palace. Marcus was routing the satphone call through the hotel's switchboard, something Jenny had taught him before they'd left her. He was not, therefore, worried that Vinetti—or any of the folks at the NSA and NSC who were undoubtedly listening to the call—were going to track him down through the phone's signal. He was far more worried about what his old friend was about to say.

"Marcus, are you there?" Vinetti asked.

"I'm here. We're gonna make this fast, Nick. I hear the drones approaching."

"We had nothing to do with that."

"Sure you didn't. You've got sixty seconds—ticktock."

It worked. Vinetti abandoned any thought of small talk and got right to the point. The presidential pardon was signed, he said. All was forgiven. Oleg would be put into the Witness Protection Program and allowed to keep the money that had been wired to his numbered account in Zurich. Jenny would not only be exonerated of all suspicion but get a promotion. For now, she needed to be secretly transported back to Moscow. She would be given first-class medical treatment by embassy doctors, but it was essential that she maintain her cover as an economic attaché and continue her life there for several months. It was critical to projecting an image of "business as usual." After the New Year, she would be transferred back to Washington.

So far, so good, thought Marcus. Then came three conditions.

First, Director Stephens was insisting that Marcus and Oleg be completely forthcoming about everything they knew regarding the nuclear weapons in North Korea and those heading for Iran. If they were caught in a single lie, the deal would be off. They would both be sent to maximum-security federal prisons for the rest of their lives. The pardons would only cover past crimes—or alleged crimes—they had committed. Any laws they broke after accepting the pardons they would be fully liable for.

Second, Vinetti explained that Petrovsky had insisted the Russian ambassador in D.C. be allowed to see Marcus immediately. He said they were under a time crunch. He didn't explain why.

"And third?" Marcus asked.

"You're not going to like this one, Marcus."

"Ticktock, my friend, ticktock."

"Fine," Vinetti said. "The president insists that you formally join the Central Intelligence Agency and that I leave the State Department and join the Agency too. You'll be Oleg Kraskin's handler. I'll be yours. I'll report directly to Stephens and the president. No one else can know you work for Langley. No one can know Kraskin is still alive, much less working for us. You can still volunteer at your church. That'll be pretty good cover, actually. But the president demands you be accountable to the Agency and to him. He says he can't afford to have you going rogue for another minute."

Marcus said nothing. Oleg now caught his eye. The Audi was fueled. It was time to move.

"I know this isn't what you wanted," Vinetti added. "The president was told repeatedly that you have no interest in coming back to work for the government, but—"

Marcus cut him off. "Done."

"How's that?"

"You heard me," Marcus said. "I accept."

58

Everyone stood at attention as President Yadollah Afshar strode into the war room.

The defense minister had gotten there only minutes before, just back from meetings in Caracas. The chiefs of the Iranian army, air force, and navy were there as well, along with Mahmoud Entezam, the commander of the Iranian Revolutionary Guard Corps. Now, following the direction of the president, they all got down on their hands and knees and bowed their foreheads toward Mecca for *Qiyam*—nighttime prayer.

When they were finished, Afshar asked for a situation report.

"My men are on their way to Pyongyang as we speak, Your Excellency," General Entezam began. "Per our standard tradecraft, their route is circuitous, this time more than usual, as we have indications that both the Zionists and the Americans are watching the airports extra closely."

"Which airports?"

"Any one that has direct flights to Pyongyang, Your Excellency."

"They suspect something?"

"We can't say for certain," Entezam replied. "But a close look at open-source media analyses following President Luganov's high-profile state visit there—prior to his tragic demise, of course—shows a significant degree of cynicism regarding whether Hyong Ja Park is truly ready to give up his entire nuclear program."

"Then why have I been informed that Western media coverage about the announcement has been glowing, that many columnists, not a few academics, and even some prominent left-wing lawmakers are saying Luganov and the Dear Leader should be awarded the Nobel Prize, even though it would be posthumous in the Russian's case?"

"That is all true, Your Excellency," Entezam said. "I refer instead to the intelligence and policy communities."

"They are more cynical?"

"I'm afraid so, Your Excellency. Polls show that the Europeans—at least those in Western Europe—are far more willing to believe the deal is legitimate. But a majority of Americans say they are skeptical. Our friends in Moscow are telling us the number of American spy satellite passes over the peninsula have doubled. Our sources in Beijing add that the number of known Western intelligence officers monitoring flights in and out of Pyongyang has quadrupled. I'm confident we can get our men in there. They're well trained. Their disguises are impeccable, and their documents weren't forged. They were stolen. So they're legitimate. They'll hold up."

"But it will take more time than you had planned."

"Yes, sir."

"Your Excellency, may I interject?" the defense minister asked. Afshar nodded.

"We may want to consider delaying the transfer of the warheads."

"Until when?"

"A few weeks, perhaps a few months—just until things quiet down and the eyes of the world turn somewhere else."

"No," Afshar said. "There will be no delay." The president turned back to the IRGC commander. "General, your man Alireza is heading up your team, correct?"

"Yes, Your Excellency."

"When will he and his colleagues arrive in Pyongyang?"

"Well, sir, it is now Wednesday. They are scheduled to arrive a week from today."

"And how soon after that can the ship be loaded and ready to leave the harbor?"

"Within twenty-four hours of their arrival."

"Fine," said the president. "The Supreme Leader has been clear. Taking possession of these five warheads is our highest national priority. Every hour they remain in the possession of the North Koreans, the higher the risk our mercurial friend in Pyongyang will change his mind and cancel the deal. There must be no changes, no delays, and I want updates on my desk every six hours."

Jenny was stepping out of the shower when she heard pounding on the door.

She ignored it at first. She hadn't ordered room service. She knew no one in the city. She didn't want the room to be cleaned just then. And there was, after all, a Do Not Disturb sign hanging on the door handle in the hall. Yet the pounding continued.

Putting her robe back on, she picked up her pistol, removed the safety, and moved slowly and quietly to the door. Had the FSB found her? If so, how? And what chance did she have with a 9mm against the firepower they were likely bringing to bear? Then again, if it really was the FSB, why hadn't they just kicked the door in and burst through the windows?

She exhaled when she saw the faces of Marcus and Oleg through the peephole. She quickly let them in and shut and locked the door behind them. "What in the world are you guys doing here?" she asked.

Marcus explained the call with Vinetti and outlined the deal he had just accepted.

"You?" she said, taking a seat in the living room along with Oleg. "You're joining the Agency?"

"I know it doesn't pay well, but I hear the benefits are quite something," Marcus quipped, opening a bottle of mineral water he'd just taken from the minibar.

"No comment," Jenny said, her hair dripping on her shoulders. "So how long do we have?"

"Nick is personally bringing a team to get us. They should be here within the hour."

Jenny excused herself and went to get dressed and pack up her things. Marcus asked Oleg to help him wipe down every surface to make sure they left no prints behind. When the three of them were finished, they regathered in the living room.

"Well, it's been a real pleasure doing business with you," Jenny said, looking first at Marcus, then at Oleg. "With you both."

"I'm very grateful for all your help, though you must believe me when I say how sorry I am that I got you into all of this, Miss Jenny," Oleg said. "I hope you will forgive me."

"It's fine. Don't mention it."

"No, it's not fine. You didn't sign up for this, and look how much it's cost you."

"I forgive you, Oleg Stefanovich—on one condition."

"Name it. Anything."

"Forget you've ever heard of me."

"How could I ever forget you, Miss Jenny, when you have saved my life and my country?"

"Okay, don't forget me—just never mention me to anyone—*ever*."

"So long as you never mention me either."

"My lips are sealed," she said softly. "Oleg who?"

"*Spasibo*—truly—for everything," Oleg said, thanking her in Russian and becoming unexpectedly emotional in so doing. He walked over and gave her a hug, careful not to touch her wound.

"*Pazhalstah,*" she demurred, touched by his genuine gratitude.

His eyes red and moist, Oleg abruptly excused himself, then headed through the master bedroom to the bathroom, shutting and locking the door behind him.

Jenny turned back to Marcus. "He's really kinda sweet, isn't he?"

"For an assassin, yes, I guess."

"So I'm heading back to Moscow?"

"Only for a few months."

"A few months more in the Russian capital—what could possibly go wrong?"

"I'm not worried about you, Morris. You really are one tough cookie."

"Very funny. Actually, I'm not sure I'm up for another Moscow winter."

"I'm not sure it's the snow and bone-chilling temperatures that'll be the problem," he said. "I'd be more concerned about Petrovsky's manhunt for anyone and everyone involved in the events of the last few days."

"My point exactly."

"Don't worry—there's nothing that links you to any of this. Lay low for a bit, and you'll be in the clear. I'm the one in the Kremlin's crosshairs. They've already taken a shot at me—two, actually—and I doubt that'll be the end of it. Most likely I'll spend the rest of my life looking over my shoulder. Then again . . ." He paused.

"What?" Jenny asked.

Marcus stared at his bottle of mineral water for a bit, then took a sip. "I got to meet you."

The comment caught Jenny by surprise and embarrassed her as well.

"It's been an honor to work with you, Jenny Morris," he added. "Or whatever your name is." Marcus smiled.

"And it's been a real pain in the—well, whatever—to work with you, Marcus Ryker. Or is that an alias?"

"No, that's my real name."

"Okay, well, good luck with everything."

"Thanks."

With that, there was a sharp knock at the door. Their rides had come.

59

Pete Hwang was on a plane again, this time bound for Tokyo.

Marcus had accepted the president's conditions, but in so doing he had insisted Hwang be drafted onto the team. Vinetti had immediately agreed. They were going to need a doctor on this little espionage team, one they could implicitly trust. Vinetti could think of no one better than his old friend—and pulling Hwang out of the nascent Dayton presidential campaign would be an added benefit.

For his part, Hwang hadn't hesitated. He didn't agree with Iowa's senior senator on every issue, but he had been enjoying his work. And he would miss interacting with Annie Stewart. On the other hand, she was showing no real interest in him, and Hwang couldn't think of any-thing he'd rather do more than team up with two old war buddies on a mission so critical to the security of two countries he loved so dearly, the United States and the Republic of South Korea.

Hwang was flying commercial and under his own name, but for the moment, that couldn't be helped. Once he touched down, Vinetti had assured him, someone would meet him at the airport and get him to a safe house. There he'd be formally sworn into the Agency, thoroughly briefed on what he was expected to do, and then forward-deployed to Okinawa to await the others.

As he sat in business class on board British Airways flight 4600, Hwang tried to make himself comfortable for the eleven-hour-and-forty-five-minute journey. It wasn't working. No amount of movies or free alcohol or melatonin or chatting with the flight attendants could calm his swirling emotions. In a single day, his entire life's path had taken the most radical turn.

A little more than twenty-four hours earlier, his best friend was on Russian soil, cut loose by the Americans and being hunted by the FSB. Now Marcus Ryker was likely in Washington, about to meet with a senior Russian official face-to-face at the request of the American president. If that weren't enough to make his head spin, when Hwang departed Washington Dulles yesterday, he was domestic policy advisor for a U.S. senator who had a reasonable shot at becoming the next president of the United States. By the time he'd lifted off from London Heathrow, he'd emailed his resignation to Senator Dayton, whom he had not told what he was doing; nor could he. He'd hardly processed the magnitude of it all for himself.

Peter Hwang had just agreed to become a clandestine officer for the CIA.

It was nearly midnight when Dr. Haydar Abbasi departed IRGC headquarters.

Even this late, the parking complex underneath the massive and heavily guarded compound was nearly full. The overnight shift of operatives and analysts had just arrived, and lights throughout the building were humming. The Supreme Leader had put the regime's elite agency on a war footing. All leaves had been canceled. Reservists had been called up. They were fast approaching one of the most dramatic inflection points in the history of the Islamic Republic, and everyone was working sixteen- to eighteen-hour shifts. Some were even sleeping on their office floors to handle the massive preparations that had to be made on so many fronts.

Abbasi wasn't going home to stay, of course. If any of his superiors or the guards at the gate asked him, he would tell them he was simply going back to get a pillow, a blanket, and his toiletries. He, too, would be making his new office his home for the next few months. But on this particular night he had a phone call to make, and it was urgent.

Pulling up to his newly rented efficiency flat on the north side of the city, closer to the mountains, Abbasi shut down the engine of his aging Volkswagen Passat, got out, locked the doors, entered the lobby, and took the elevator to the ninth floor. Upon entering his flat, he locked the door behind him and headed straight for the walk-through closet that connected the main room with a tiny bathroom. Glancing at his watch, he quickly pushed aside several boxes and lifted up a loose floorboard. There he found the satellite phone his Saudi handler had provided him. He powered it up and dialed from memory the number he'd been given.

The voice he recognized came on the line after the third ring.

"Code in," said the Saudi in flawless Farsi.

Abbasi entered a fourteen-digit code, also from memory, then recited his authentication phrase.

"I was not expecting your call tonight, *Kabutar*," the handler said, using Abbasi's code name, which in Farsi meant "pigeon." "Is everything all right?"

"No," Abbasi said. "We have a very serious development, and events are suddenly moving far faster than I had indicated in my last communiqué."

60

Abdullah bin Rashid's plane finally landed at an air force base outside the capital.

With lights flashing and siren blaring, his driver raced the armored Bentley the thirty-five kilometers to the royal palace in near-record time. The director of the Saudi Arabia General Intelligence Directorate had been summoned back from Seoul for an emergency meeting slated to begin at precisely noon.

When they pulled up to a covered entrance in the rear of the palace, it was 11:57 a.m. The security detail rushed Rashid inside to what he assumed would be a meeting with a wide range of generals and military advisors. Instead, to his surprise, he met alone with Crown Prince Abdulaziz bin Faisal.

"Good day, Your Royal Highness," he said with a bow.

The thirty-six-year-old son of the king nodded and bade him come and take a seat next to him. Rashid was still in the suit he'd worn on his private jet. The direct heir to the throne was wearing his trademark white robe, though his kaffiyeh was removed, revealing his prematurely balding head.

"You bring me news," the crown prince said with an air of assurance.

"I do indeed."

"His Majesty is in bed. He cannot seem to shake this bout with pneumonia. But he told me I may wake him if the situation warrants."

"Let him sleep," said Rashid. "The news I bring you is grave, but no decision he could make today will change that."

"Very well; proceed."

"Your Highness, we have two sources who have just contacted us to say that before his death, Russian president Luganov secretly gave a number of Russian nuclear warheads to the North Koreans to be attached to long-range ICBMs that could be launched only at Moscow's directive."

"That's . . . terrifying."

"Unfortunately, it gets worse."

"How so?"

"With Luganov's death, my sources indicate the Persians have persuaded the Dear Leader to sell them five of the Russian warheads. Alireza al-Zanjani is heading to Pyongyang as we speak to oversee the transfer of these weapons to Iran."

"How trustworthy are these sources of yours?"

"Very."

"Based in Pyongyang?"

"I wish—we are still working on that. But we do have two in Iran."

"Persian nationals or foreigners?"

"Persian nationals, Your Highness."

"Working in the government?"

"Your Majesty, please, I hesitate to say more."

"Why have I never been told about this before?"

"When your father appointed me to this position, he told me

not to brief him on sources and methods," Rashid said. "Since your father appointed you his heir as well as defense minister, you have not directed me otherwise. Thus I've continued under the instructions His Majesty gave me."

"And yet you are telling me now."

"Not names or titles."

"But you're telling me we have two sources in Tehran that have access to highly classified information."

"Yes, sir."

"How did you find them?"

Again, Rashid hesitated. But the crown prince insisted he be told more.

"One of them—the more junior—reached out to us," Rashid conceded. "The other, well . . . Remember when your father asked us several years ago why the Israelis assassinate every Iranian nuclear expert they find rather than trying to buy them off?"

"Yes."

"To be blunt, we bought one off."

"Do these two sources know each other?" the crown prince asked.

"No, sir, they do not."

"They serve in different parts of the government?"

"All I can say is I am absolutely confident they do not know each other and do not communicate with each other. Thus, the fact they have both transmitted urgent warnings to us in the last twelve hours tells me this is real and very, very dangerous."

"Have you told the Americans?"

"No, sir."

"The Emiratis? KBI?"

"No."

"What about the Israelis?"

"I've told no one but you, Your Highness," Rashid said. "Only two other people on my staff know it—the agents' handler and my chief of staff. When they learned of it, they called me on a secure line in Seoul and told me to make up an excuse and get home immediately. They didn't say why, but they didn't have to. They used a code word during our call that alerted me immediately that we had heard from not just one but both of our sources. That's why I asked for the emergency meeting with the king and you and the national security team."

The crown prince exhaled, stood, and paced about his spacious private office. "You know what this means, don't you?" he asked. "If those warheads reach Iranian soil, we will have no choice but to go to war. The Emiratis will join us. The Israelis, too." He paused and looked out the bulletproof window at the fountain in the palace courtyard, awash in multicolored spotlights. "But that's not all," he continued. "We will have to have atomic weapons of our own. Indeed, I fear we may have reached that point either way. His Majesty has asked me to fly to Islamabad next week. He has authorized me to begin negotiations immediately, and it goes without saying that price will be no object."

"The Pakistanis certainly have all that we would need," Rashid noted.

"The Persians were fools to think the Pakistanis would ever sell the Bomb to them. Absolute fools." Prince Abdulaziz turned and walked directly to Rashid and lowered his voice. "You will come with me, of course," he said. "But first you must stop this madness. I don't care what it takes. I don't care what it costs. I don't care whom you use. But on behalf of the throne, I'm ordering you to make absolutely certain those warheads never make it to Iran."

61

Much of the past week had been a blur.

Marcus knew he'd been to Washington, but he had no memory of what he had done there. Now he was in another Gulfstream business jet, about two hundred miles off the coast of Midway, sitting in a window seat next to Nick Vinetti and trying to make sense of what had just happened to him.

"Marcus, I love you like a brother; you know that," Vinetti said. "But let's face it; sometimes you can be a real . . ."

Marcus said nothing, just waited for the punchline.

"Look," Vinetti continued, "I didn't have a choice. We slipped a heavy narcotic into your coffee on the way to Washington, and you went out like a light. We kept you drugged the entire time you were at Walter Reed. And don't look so shocked. There was no way I was going to take a chance on you demanding to talk to the ambassador.

I certainly wasn't going to let you demand to meet with President Clarke and give him a piece of your mind. And you can't honestly think I was going to answer your incessant questions on where we were keeping your friend the Raven or how hard we were interrogating him. There wasn't time. The stakes were too high. So, yes, I ordered my team to incapacitate you. And that's that. End of story. Let's move on."

"You drugged me and kept me out of it for a week, just to make things look good for Ambassador Molotov Cocktail, or whatever his name is? On what authority?"

"Whose do you think?"

"No, really. On what authority exactly did you hijack my life?"

"Yours," Vinetti said. "You remember back in the hotel outside of St. Petersburg, when you signed all those government papers?"

Marcus nodded.

"Didn't you read them?"

"Forty-odd pages of fine print? How could I?" Marcus said.

"Then why did you sign them?"

"I needed a disguise and a new passport to get out of Russia, and that was the only way you'd give them to me."

"Well, if you had bothered to read them, you'd have seen that you were giving the Agency unlimited authority to take any measures deemed necessary to protect national interests, with or without your future consent."

"Nick, you've been in the CIA for fifteen minutes longer than me. So where do you get off acting like some Double-O agent with a license to drug?"

"It wasn't my call, if that makes you feel any better. The order came straight from Director Stephens."

"But you carried it out."

"Yes. And it was for your own good. So can we drop it? We've got work to do."

Vinetti tried to shift the conversation to the work ahead of them.

He started to explain the plan that U.S. Special Ops commanders were cooking up for them in Japan, but Marcus cut him off.

"We'll get to that soon enough," he said. "Tell me what happened in Washington."

Vinetti was about to protest but seemed to think better of it. He must have known his fellow Marine wasn't going to let it go until he had answers.

"Fine," he began. "We had an ambulance pick you up at Andrews when we landed early on Wednesday morning and take you directly to Walter Reed. We'd already worked with the senior staff at the hospital to create a trail of paperwork and electronic medical files documenting that you'd been there for days. The paper trail indicated that you had come back from Berlin with Senator Dayton's delegation but collapsed from some mysterious illness."

"And you kept me unconscious the whole time?"

"The whole time."

"Where?"

"The Infectious Diseases Unit."

"Oh, great, so I might really come down with Ebola or something after all."

"Relax—we had you in an isolation ward. There was no danger," Vinetti said. "And it kept you from being seen by other patients. Of course, it took a fair bit of makeup to cover up all the bruises and cuts on your face, and your broken nose—a real beauty, by the way. How did that happen?"

"Another time," Marcus said. "Keep going."

"That's about it. The secretary of state brought the Russian ambassador by the hospital later that day. We brought him to the isolation ward. He looked at you through the glass. We showed him all your paperwork. We let him talk to your presiding physician and the head of the unit. He chatted with some of the nurses for a bit. Then we sent him on his way."

"The doctors and nurses were all CIA personnel, I assume?"

"Every single one," Vinetti confirmed.

"And it worked?"

"Apparently. Petrovsky called Clarke a few hours later to apologize. I can't say Moscow really believes us. But they'd bet big on us not being able to produce you, and the ambassador seemed pretty stunned to see you lying there. So there you go. Mission accomplished."

"What about my mom? Did anyone call her?"

"Of course, and your sisters, too. In fact, the day after the ambassador dropped by, we flew your whole family to D.C. to see you. All expenses paid. Put them up at the Willard overnight, brought them to Reed the next morning. Then put them on a plane home. Oh, and Senator Dayton and Annie Stewart took them to dinner—them and that pastor friend of yours and his wife."

"The Emersons?"

"That's them. The senator told them all about your time together in Moscow and the Baltics, really talked you up as an asset to the team. It went quite well. I'm told they were all very grateful."

"And you say Annie was there?"

"Yeah." Vinetti smiled. "Why?"

"No reason." Marcus changed the subject. "So how's Jenny?"

"She's fine."

"Did she need surgery?"

"She did, and it went very well."

"Have you talked with her?"

"No, but I'm told she's back at her apartment in Moscow, recovering nicely."

"And the Russians haven't shown any suspicion?"

"Come on, Marcus, it's Moscow. The Russians are suspicious of everything. But officially Jenny is the economic attaché. She's got an MBA from Wharton, so that's a pretty convincing cover, and she plays her part well. Her deputy has covered for all her meetings and is telling everyone she's got a nasty case of the flu. The medical attaché performed the surgery himself with his own team inside the embassy.

It was all very discreet. Now she's back at her own place, like I said. Everyone is sending her flowers and cards. So far the story seems to be holding up."

"I'm glad," Marcus said. "When you get a moment, please pass along my greetings to Jenny."

"That's not going to happen."

"Why not?"

"Marcus, forget it. We need to build a firewall between you and this woman. Get this in your head and don't forget it: You've never met Jenny Morris. You've never even heard of Jenny Morris. You've certainly not spent any time last week with Jenny Morris. And if you want to maintain your cover story, you're never going to be in touch with her again."

It was dark when Yong-Jin Yoon arrived home to his flat.

The elevator was still broken. It had been for months, and there was no hope of it being repaired in his lifetime. So the general climbed the stairs to the fourteenth floor as he always did, pulled out his keys, and quietly unlocked the front door, then entered and closed and locked the door behind him immediately. He didn't want to turn on the lights. He knew his wife had been waiting for him. She always did. Sure enough, there in the moonlight, he found her asleep on the couch, seven months pregnant and as beautiful as when they had first met. She'd set a bowl of rice and steamed vegetables out on the counter beside the sink. It was cold, of course, but he was famished. Still, there were more important things to attend to just now.

"Yuna," he whispered. "Yuna Kim, I'm home."

Her eyes opened immediately, and the fear he saw in them was palpable. She was terrified of what lay ahead. It had not been her idea. She was a simple girl from a farming cooperative on the other side of the country, south of Tanch'ŏn.

"What time is it?" she whispered back.

"Did you pack?" the general asked, ignoring her question.

"I did everything just as you asked." With his help, she pulled herself to her feet.

"Good girl," he said. "It's time, and you must hurry."

"Tell me again—why can't you take me?"

"You know why," he replied. "It's too dangerous. But I should be there by this time tomorrow."

"But I need you, Yong-Jin. I cannot do this without—"

The general put his finger over her lips, then kissed her softly. "You're strong, Yuna Kim, and you'll do fine. Now, gather your things and go. I will join you as soon as I can."

A tear rolled down her cheek, but she nodded.

"Oh yes—there is just one more thing you must do for me," he said, holding her in his arms. "I have sewn something into the lining of your coat. I cannot bring it with me, but it is very important. Keep your coat with you at all times. It cannot leave your sight, for I will need it when I reach you."

Again she nodded. "What is it, Yong-Jin?"

"Our ticket out."

FOUR

62

"Gentlemen, we're facing a serious time crunch."

Captain Curt Berenger, commander of SEAL Team Six, began the briefing precisely at 9 a.m. It had been less than thirty minutes since Ryker, Vinetti, and Oleg Kraskin had landed and linked up with Pete Hwang. They'd had no time to unpack, eat, or catch their breath. Nor would they.

"I want to welcome you to the U.S. Navy's jewel in Asia," Berenger continued. "This is our main base and center of operations in this theater, and you'll have to take it from me—it is a sight to behold. Unfortunately, we're not going to be able to give you boys a proper tour of our fine facilities or Tokyo Bay, much less Japan's most populated city and national capital, breathtaking all. Instead, in a few minutes, you all and I and two of my platoons are going to board a group of choppers and head to Sado Island. That's on the other side of this main island, just offshore from the city of Niigata. There, we're going to link up with the USS *Michigan* and get under way."

The commander explained that from Sado it was a 531-mile journey to their intended destination, the city of Tanch'ŏn, North Korea. Marcus quickly did the math. Given that the *Michigan*'s top speed was about twenty-five knots—about twenty-nine miles per hour—it was going to take them no fewer than eighteen hours to get to the North Korean coastline. Factoring in the rest of this briefing and their flight to Sado, they'd be lucky to get to Tanch'ŏn by four the following morning, and possibly not even until five. Sunrise in early October was just before 6:30 a.m., and Marcus now understood why the SEAL commander was so eager to get moving.

"Before we leave, however, we need to finalize our intel package," Berenger said. "That means I need to ask you a few more questions, Mr. Kraskin."

"Whatever you need, Captain."

"When was your last communication with General Yoon?"

"About two and a half hours ago."

"In flight?"

"Yes, sir."

"Using the secure communications package Mr. Vinetti showed you?"

"Correct."

"Was General Yoon en route to Tanch'ŏn?"

"At that point, no—not yet."

"Why not?"

"He said he had sent his wife by bus and that she should be arriving at her mother's by early afternoon."

"But why not him?"

"He said there were complications."

"What kind of complications?"

"He said a team of Iranian officials is arriving by 9 a.m. tomorrow morning to help with the transfer of the weapons. General Yoon was not expecting them for several more days. But they changed their plans and decided to come early."

"So what changed?"

"He did not say."

"When will the general leave Pyongyang?"

"The moment his wife arrives in Tanch'ŏn, she will call him. The plan is that she will tell him her mother is dying and may not make it through the night. She will beg him to come help her. The general will then procure a military plane to take him to Tanch'ŏn, promising his superiors that he will be back well before the Iranians are set to arrive. But he indicated there are many variables that could change before then."

Berenger noted it was less than five hundred kilometers from Pyongyang to Tanch'ŏn. Depending on what kind of aircraft the general used, it would take him an hour or possibly less to reach Tanch'ŏn. This even further compounded their time crunch.

"Okay, look, gentlemen—we can't get to Tanch'ŏn until at least 0500 to 0530 tomorrow morning," Berenger said. That was even later than Marcus had figured. "Assuming the general needs to be back in Pyongyang no later than 0800, he'll need to be wheels up no later than 0630. That means he'll need to be leaving for the airfield by 0530— 0600 at the latest. That's an awfully narrow window of time to find him and get him and his wife and mother-in-law out of the city. At this point, we are running the risk of missing them entirely."

The commander turned back to Oleg. "Will the general be traveling with a security detail?"

"He said it should be just him and his driver," Oleg said.

"Will they be armed?"

"Yes. They will both have their personal sidearms."

"And he'll have the documents with him?"

"No."

"Why not?"

"Too dangerous. But he said he's created a thumb drive of everything he thinks we should see. He's sending it with his wife, sewn into the lining of her jacket. Even if he's delayed or somehow prevented from coming, so long as we find her, we'll have what we need. But if his wife is stopped or questioned by anyone, she won't be able to say anything because she doesn't know what she has."

"She knows they're about to flee the country, right?"

"Of course."

"Fine. When will you be in contact with him next?"

"At this point, he said he will only contact me again if he cannot leave Pyongyang. Otherwise, he will not have access to our secure channel while he's traveling or when he gets to Tanch'ŏn."

"Does he have a mobile phone?"

"Yes."

"You have the number?"

"Yes, but he begged me not to use it." Oleg wrote the number down on a piece of paper and handed it to Berenger.

"Good," said the commander. "Anything else from the general?"

"No, sir. That's it."

"All right—thank you, Mr. Kraskin. This is incredibly valuable. That's it. Any final questions?"

Hwang had several, from what kind of vehicles they would use to get to the apartment building and where they would secure them, to the layout of the apartment complex itself and what kind of security they could expect. Berenger promised he'd provide them all a detailed tactical briefing on the operation once they were on board the *Michigan* and under way.

Then the commander dropped a bomb.

"Mr. Kraskin, I'm going to need to ask you to stay here on base."

"What for?" Oleg asked.

"I need you to monitor your communications channel so you can provide us with any updates or changes, and you can't do that effectively from two hundred meters beneath the Sea of Japan."

"But General Yoon expects to see me when he arrives in Tanch'ŏn," Oleg protested. "That was part of the deal."

"And you'll do everything necessary to convince him that's still going to be the case," said the commander.

"But it's not."

"No, it's not. Look, Mr. Kraskin, aside from your year and a half in the Russian army, you have no military training," Berenger said. "That's not going to be sufficient for this mission. What's more, you're not an American citizen, and you're not cleared to be on board an Ohio-class nuclear-powered ballistic missile submarine. But don't you worry. My staff will take care of you. They'll see to it that you're billeted in officers' quarters, that you're fed well, and that you have access to the best and most secure communications system the U.S. government can provide to a senior advisor to a Russian czar."

"Former advisor," Oleg said.

"Whatever."

Then Marcus intervened. "I'm sorry, sir, but that's unacceptable."

"Say again?"

"The scenario you just laid out won't work for us," Marcus said. "Mr. Kraskin gave General Yoon his word that he would be there to take possession of all the intel the general will be bringing and personally escort him and his family to freedom. And my friend here is the only one of us who has ever met the general."

"Don't worry," Berenger said. "We know what he looks like. We have pictures."

"That's not the point, commander."

"Look, Mr. Ryker, this isn't a Socratic dialogue. I'm already taking a serious risk having you, Mr. Vinetti, and Dr. Hwang on this mission. You're not SEALs. But at least you're former Marines, and you've all been in combat. Mr. Kraskin isn't and hasn't, and he's not coming on the mission, and that's final."

"Says who?" said Marcus, on his feet now and bristling.

Berenger smiled and nearly laughed. "Says the commander in chief of the United States. That's who."

63

Marcus had never set foot on a nuclear-powered submarine.

He found the sheer enormity of the *Michigan*, combined with its devastating firepower, simultaneously terrifying and reassuring.

Some 560 feet long and weighing more than 18,000 metric tons when fully submerged, the Ohio-class boomer had been commissioned on September 11, 1982, more than two years after first departing the shipyard in Groton, Connecticut. It was built to carry and launch ballistic missiles with nuclear warheads capable of annihilating entire enemy cities. When the Cold War ended and tensions with Russia cooled for a time, the *Michigan*'s nuclear arsenal was removed. The sub was retrofitted to be able to launch Tomahawk cruise missiles equipped with 1,000-pound nonnuclear warheads and capable of reaching enemy targets at subsonic but still devastating speeds.

As Marcus followed his colleagues through the narrow corridors past crew members at their posts, the irony wasn't lost on him. In its first three decades in service, during some of the most tension-filled years of the Cold War, not a single missile had ever been fired from the *Michigan*. In the last decade, however, hundreds of Tomahawks had been fired at dozens of targets in Afghanistan, Iraq, Syria, and elsewhere, and he knew full well that if this mission failed, the chance of war breaking out between the U.S. and North Korea or Iran or Russia or all three would be sky-high.

Eventually they reached the crew's mess. Though hardly spacious, it was nevertheless the largest room on the ship. There were six metal tables and straight-back metal chairs to seat thirty-six men. There was no ceiling. Instead, large pipes and miles of thick electrical cords could be seen overhead, snaking between several rows of fluorescent lights hung from steel beams. There were a few microwave ovens, a large clock on one wall, various plaques and awards mounted on others, and a bulletin board with all kinds of notices tacked to it. On the front wall was a large flat-screen television next to a popcorn machine —for movie nights, Marcus assumed.

The captain of the *Michigan* welcomed them aboard and introduced his XO, who promised to make their brief stay as comfortable as possible. They answered a few questions about the location of various facilities, then headed back to the control room. At that point, Berenger began his own briefing by introducing the three Marines to his men. Two immediately stood out to Marcus.

Donny Callaghan, a huge man with closely cropped red hair and a bushy red beard, was from south Boston. His father had been a three-star Army general and West Point grad, but Donny—the rebel—had opted for the Navy and had been a SEAL for nine years. Callaghan would serve as Red Team leader—the team to which Marcus had been assigned—responsible for securing the apartment complex in Tanch'ŏn, making contact with the general and his family, and getting them securely back to the *Michigan*.

Héctor Sanchez hailed from San Diego. He did not come from a military family. His father had been a migrant worker of Mexican heritage who had insisted all eight of his children become hard workers and proud of their new country. Unable to afford college, the youngest son—though at six feet four inches by far the tallest and most physically fit among the siblings—had joined the Navy. Sanchez had just celebrated his seventh year in the SEALs. One of the best snipers in any branch of the military, Sanchez would serve as leader of Blue Team, which would be divided in two parts. One would hold and secure their landing site in Tanch'ŏn. The other, consisting of more snipers, would take up positions on the roofs of apartment complexes adjacent to the target building and provide both surveillance of the entire area and covering fire upon Red Team's egress, should that become necessary.

While there were three Asians on Red Team and two on Blue, Marcus was surprised that none of them were Korean. Three were Chinese Americans. One was Filipino. The other was Vietnamese. None of them spoke Korean. That made Peter Hwang the only team member who looked the part and could speak the language.

Once the introductions were complete, Berenger sketched out the plan—the exact location where they'd be landing, the routes they'd be taking from their landing site to the apartment complex, and how they'd obtain the vehicles they needed. He also described every piece of equipment they'd be using and the precise location where each man would be positioned. Then he walked them all through a slew of "known unknowns." It was this last part that most consumed Marcus's attention—all of theirs, really—as Berenger conceded that he couldn't remember a mission with less concrete intelligence going in than this one.

He showed them satellite photos of the coast of Tanch'ŏn, the Dongdae River flowing along the south side of the city, the city itself, and several shots of the apartment complex and the neighborhood around it. There were no HUMINT assets on the ground. Nor could they fly drones over the city. The only Korean Americans the analysts at the CIA and DIA had been able to find who had ever been to Tanch'ŏn were eighty years or older and hadn't been there since childhood.

After two and a half hours, the briefing finally ended.

For the next fifteen hours or so, they were on their own.

A few of the guys found bunks to get some shut-eye. Most stayed in the mess to fire up the popcorn machine and watch a Jason Bourne movie marathon. Vinetti and Hwang joined them. Marcus did not.

After hitting the head, Marcus changed into shorts and a T-shirt and went for a run. The XO had told them that seventeen laps around the upper level of the missile compartment equaled a mile. Marcus did five miles, then moved to the sub's makeshift gym to lift weights and do a few hundred sit-ups and pull-ups. He'd been off his routine for weeks, and despite the cramped quarters, it felt good to be back at it.

When finished, he took a brief shower, changed into sweats, and found an empty bunk near the back of the sub where he closed the curtain to give himself a bit of privacy and pulled out his Bible. It had been more than a week since he read it last. Nevertheless, it being the ninth of the month, he opened to Proverbs chapter 7. He didn't get past verse 1.

My son, keep my words
And treasure my commandments within you.

Marcus desperately wanted to be a man who kept and treasured God's Word. He wanted not just to serve God but to please him. He longed for the favor of God, especially now. But he was deeply frustrated with himself of late. He wasn't spending much time in prayer and spending even less in the Word. And what of Oleg? Had he even talked to this man about what it meant to know God personally, to really be forgiven by Christ of his sins? He could see the immense burden Oleg was carrying for the life he'd led before and for the decisions he'd made in recent days. Yet Marcus hadn't once told him what he knew, that there was a way to be free of every sin he would ever commit—past, present, or future. Why not?

And what of Nick and Pete? They certainly knew about Marcus's faith. They knew how central it was to his life. The three of them had discussed the gospel many times over many years. They also knew how imperfect he really was. Marcus had never tried to hide his flaws from them. But he'd also tried to convince them that everyone was a sinner and that everyone needed a Savior. Yet he'd gotten nowhere. Hwang had once been a devout Catholic but had lapsed in recent years. Vinetti had never expressed any interest in spiritual things. Didn't Marcus need to try to engage them again? They were, after all, just hours from going into harm's way.

What kind of Christian was he? What kind of friend?

64

"Allahu akbar."

The haunting call to prayer sounded from the minaret and wafted over the city of Tehran. The armored car carrying Grand Ayatollah Hossein Ansari pulled up under a portico and came to a complete stop. Flanked by bodyguards, Ansari slowly emerged from the backseat and quietly entered the mosque.

The facility had been cleared of everyone but his security detail, one of the many perks of being the Supreme Leader of the Islamic Republic of Iran. Ansari padded over to the right side of the vestibule, where he found a row of basins and faucets. There he began his ritual cleansings, washing first his right hand and arm three times, then repeating the procedure for his left hand and arm. Then he washed his mouth three times, followed by his nose and the rest of his face, neck, and beard, three times each. When this was complete, he removed his turban and ran his dripping hands over what was left of his thin gray hair, turning then to wash behind and inside his ears. Finally he removed his sandals and washed his right foot three times, then the left, and then dried himself with a small cotton towel.

Putting his turban back on but leaving his sandals off, the aging cleric made his way into the domed sanctuary and knelt on the thick and ornate carpet. His body was racked with pain. This was plain to anyone who knew or saw him. What wasn't known to anyone but his wife, his chief of staff, his personal physician, and the country's chief oncologist was that Ansari had recently been diagnosed with stage-four pancreatic cancer. The prognosis was not good. If he continued to refuse surgery and chemotherapy, which he had steadfastly done so far, he would be dead in as little as two months, and no longer than six.

He was ready to leave this earth. Ansari had little doubt paradise awaited him. No Muslim had lived a more exemplary life, he reassured himself. He just didn't want to enter eternity alone. And thus, facedown on the carpet, his regular prayers completed, Ansari now beseeched his god with the deepest longing of his heart.

"In the name of Allah, the gracious, the merciful," he whispered in Arabic, the holy language of the Prophet. "I seek refuge with Allah from Satan, the accursed. O Lord, increase my knowledge. Glory to Allah. All praise belongs to Allah. Allah is the greatest. Glory to my Lord, the Most High. My spirit and heart are prostrate for you."

A sharp pain shot through his abdomen. He winced and gritted his teeth, determined not to let his bodyguards hear him groan.

"O Lord, you have commanded me to fight those who do not believe in you or in the Last Day, those who do not consider unlawful what Allah and his messenger have made unlawful and who do not adopt the religion of truth from those who were given the Scripture," he continued. "You commanded me to fight against the disbelievers and the hypocrites and to be harsh toward them. You have declared in the Holy Qur'an that the only refuge of such infidels is the damnable fires of hell."

This time burning pains gripped his lower back. Ansari pressed on.

"O Lord, you know the number of my days, so in your mercy grant me the strength—and the courage—to bring your enemies to justice," the cleric pleaded. "Grant me the tools and the time to make your enemies burn in the atomic fires. My aides assure me that if I am prepared to spend the necessary resources, they can have these incoming Russian warheads mounted on vastly improved missiles—able to reach Tel Aviv, Washington, and New York—in just six to seven months. Five if you help us. They assure me neither the wicked Americans nor the filthy Zionists have the ability to shoot these missiles down, not if we launch them simultaneously with 200,000 Hezbollah missiles from southern Lebanon. O Allah, the great and awesome one, in your loving-kindness grant me this dying wish. And in so doing, I pray you will hasten the coming of the promised one, the until-now hidden one—His Excellency Imam al-Mahdi, peace be upon him—to reestablish the Caliphate and, at last, bring about the End of Days."

Elena Marie Garcia.

When Marcus awoke in the middle of the night, she was all he could think about.

In his mind's eye, he could go back in time and see her as a rising high school senior, standing on the top of Pikes Peak on a breezy day in early August. Wearing a gray zip-up sweatshirt over a light-blue T-shirt, tan khaki shorts, and well-worn Timberlands, she was holding his hand as she gazed out over the surrounding mountaintops. It was a breathtaking view, but it didn't interest Marcus at all. Only she did. He couldn't take his eyes off her mocha skin or warm brown eyes or her jet-black hair pulled back in a ponytail.

That had been a perfect day—the half-day hike, the picnic they'd packed themselves and enjoyed at the summit, the sunset they'd watched arm in arm, and the hike back down in the dark with headlamps strapped around their foreheads—but it had only been one of so, so many perfect days. Together they had hiked more fourteeners than he could remember. They'd gone skydiving and helicopter skiing together. They'd skied some of the steepest mountains and the biggest moguls. They'd gone white-water rafting through some of the most intense rapids in any river in any state within two hundred miles of their little hometown of Monument. They'd gotten their motorcycle licenses together. They'd even taken flying lessons together, with Marcus going so far as earning his pilot's license for single-engine planes. And Elena had been with him every step of the way.

He loved her zest for life. He could still hear her screaming with delight when he had to practice stalls and restarts at ten thousand feet. He could still feel her arms squeezing him as she sat on the back of his father's old Harley and they raced up and down the Front Range. He could still feel her lips on his the moment their pastor told him he could finally kiss his bride. He could see the tears of joy in her eyes when she'd given birth to Lars. And he could still feel the tears of shock and pain in his when he'd ducked under the crime scene tape and walked across the shattered glass into that 7-Eleven and seen the blood-soaked sheets draped over the bullet-ridden body of the only woman he had ever loved and the only child they'd ever had.

A wave of immense loneliness washed over Marcus. Behind the privacy of the thin curtain, he pulled the blanket over him and curled up in a fetal position. The sadness ran so deep it was physically painful. But Marcus refused to let the dam burst. He genuinely couldn't be certain he could regain control if he let his emotions rise to the surface. Back in Washington, in the seclusion of his own town house, he'd let it happen a few times and been unable to go outside for days. He hadn't told his mom or sisters. He hadn't told his friends. He hadn't even told his pastor. This was not a burden they could bear. It was one he had to bear alone.

And right now it was crushing him.

65

The alarm on his watch startled him.

It was precisely midnight. Marcus turned off the alarm and took a deep breath. Then he pulled back the curtain and slipped out of the coffin-like bunk. It wouldn't be long before they would suit up. But he had made a plan with Vinetti and Hwang to meet in the mess to eat a last meal together, catch up a bit, and give their bodies enough time to process the food before they headed into battle. There was another reason to get up too. It was time for a shift change. Someone else would need the bunk.

Sure enough, as Marcus stepped into the hallway, dozens of men emerged from their bunks and hustled to their posts. Moments later, the men they had replaced—all of them so young, ranging from eighteen to midtwenties and looking spent—piled into their assigned bunks and pulled their curtains shut. It was quite a life. Marcus said a silent prayer of thanks he'd enlisted in the Marines instead.

Ambling down to the mess, he found the place jammed with men arriving for dinner. There were no windows or portholes in the submarine's curved hull. Even if there had been, they were a good six hundred feet below the surface. There would have been no light and thus nothing to see. Only the clocks on the walls—and the food on their metal trays—helped them judge night from day.

Vinetti caught his eye and waved him over. He and Hwang had grabbed a table and gotten their food and a tray for Marcus. Tonight's meal was barbecued chicken, mounds of mashed potatoes, corn on the cob, coleslaw, corn bread, and iced tea—and when they were finished, hot fudge sundaes for dessert. Marcus slapped both men on the back. He hadn't realized how famished he was, but the food actually looked good, and his mouth was watering. "Good to see you gents," he said as he took a seat. "Mind if I say grace?"

Both already had food in their mouths, but they shrugged, stopped chewing, and sat up a bit straighter. Marcus closed his eyes and bowed his head.

"Dear Father, thank you for this food, for this day, for all the ways you've cared for us and protected us, and for bringing the three of us back together," he began. "Lord, we don't know exactly what's ahead of us. But we pray that you would be merciful to us. Give us your wisdom, your strength, and your courage. Give us your favor, Lord, to protect our country from those who would do us harm."

Vinetti and Hwang, assuming he was finished, began chewing again and opened their eyes. But Marcus went on, so they glanced at each other and immediately closed their eyes and clasped their hands again.

"Lord, you alone are our Shepherd, and we shall want for nothing," Marcus prayed. "You make us lie down in green pastures and lead us alongside quiet waters. You restore our souls and guide us in the paths of righteousness for your name's sake. And even though we will walk—and swim and run and drive—through the valley of the shadow of death today, we will fear no evil, for you are with us; your rod and your staff comfort us. You prepare a table before us in the presence of our enemies; you have anointed our heads with oil; our cups overflow. If we give our lives wholly and completely to your Son, the Lord Jesus Christ—holding nothing back—then surely goodness and loving-kindness will follow us all the days of our lives, and we will dwell in your house forever. We pray all these things in the name of Jesus. Amen."

This time Vinetti and Hwang kept their eyes closed, sure there must be more and not wanting to offend their friend. Instead, Marcus dug in like a ravenous wolf.

"Come on, boys, eat up," he chided them. "It's gonna get cold."

Both men finally swallowed and chuckled.

"Sleep well?" Hwang asked. Then he saw Vinetti cross himself and quickly followed suit.

"Well enough," Marcus said, plopping a dollop of butter in the center of his steaming mashed potatoes and sprinkling everything with salt. "You guys good?"

"Sure," Vinetti said. He seemed glad to see Ryker acting so buoyant and relaxed. "So, listen, we've been talking, and we're curious about something."

"Name it," Marcus replied between forkfuls.

"Well, we just can't seem to figure . . ."

When Vinetti hesitated, Hwang finished the thought, though in a whisper so none of the men at the nearby tables could hear. "What you're really doing here. Why you did everything you've done over the past couple of weeks. And why you agreed to join the CIA."

Marcus looked up from his food. "What do you mean?" he asked.

"Come on," Hwang said. "After Elena and Lars died, you quit the Secret Service. You stopped keeping in touch with the guys on your detail. You stopped going back to Colorado to visit family. Except for volunteering at your church, you basically retreated from everyone and everything."

"And?"

"And for all practical purposes you went into seclusion," Hwang continued. "When Annie tried calling you to invite you to join Senator Dayton's delegation to Europe, you wouldn't even answer her calls. When I insisted you get your butt out of the house and come with us, you said you weren't ready."

"I went, didn't I?" Marcus protested.

"Yeah, you did. Eventually. And now here you are at the vortex of the most intense geopolitical firestorm since the Cuban Missile Crisis. You were involved in the assassination of not one but two Russian leaders. You and your Russian mole friend Kracken or Krackow or whatever his name is have been the subjects of an international manhunt that darn near triggered a nuclear showdown between Moscow and Washington. And then, completely out of the blue, you agree to work for the Central Intelligence Agency. Suddenly we're on a nuclear submarine in the Sea of Japan, heading into North Korea with SEAL Team Six. See how this doesn't exactly add up so easily to people who have known you all your adult life?"

Marcus looked at his friends, then down at the half-eaten drumstick on his tray. "Guys, come on, let's talk about something else."

"No," Vinetti said. "This is important."

"Is it? Does it really matter? You guys should eat. The food's really not that bad."

"It matters to us," Hwang said.

Marcus picked the bone clean, then licked his fingers, wiped his hands on his napkin, and looked up again. "Why?" he asked in return. "We've got a mission. We're about to roll out. This isn't the right time to get introspective."

"Dude, I just joined the CIA because of you," Hwang whispered. "We're about to sneak into the world's biggest prison camp because of you. And I don't need to remind you, we might not come back out. So forgive us for being curious about just why you're doing all this."

Just then, Berenger entered the mess and came right over to them. "Finish up quick, gentlemen. I don't want you guys cramping up out there."

"Will do, sir," Marcus said. "You good?"

"All good." Berenger smiled. "Carry on." He then moved off to check in with the men at other tables.

"Look, you want to know why I'm doing this?" Marcus asked.

"Yeah, we do."

"Well, for one thing, the president insisted. You told me that yourself, Nick. Joining the CIA was the only way I could get him to agree to stop hunting me and Oleg and bring us in to deliver the intel that will hopefully stop a nuclear war. But there's another reason I'm doing this. It's because I can."

"What's that supposed to mean?" Hwang asked.

"It means I'm single again," Marcus said. "I wish I wasn't, but I am. No one needs me. No one's depending on me. I can take risks most people can't. Besides, I'm a Christian. I know exactly where I'm going when I die, and frankly, I'm ready to go. The real question is why are *you* guys doing this, and are *you* ready?"

There was a pause as both men stared at the untouched, melting sundaes in front of them. Then Vinetti spoke. "Well, for me, it's pretty simple. Bill McDermott called me. He told me the deal the president had offered you. He told me if you accepted, I was being inducted as well, to be your handler. Then Director Stephens told me we would be heading into North Korea to grab a high-ranking general in charge of the nuclear program based on intel you had provided. I said okay. And here I am."

"I just needed a job," Hwang quipped.

They laughed, but Marcus pressed his point.

"Guys, I'm serious. You know the stakes here, and you know the risks. Let's not kid ourselves. There hasn't been a U.S. Special Operations mission inside North Korea since the end of the Korean War. There's a very real chance one or more of us might not come back out. Now, you know what I believe. You know the Scriptures. I know you do, 'cause I've read them to you before. You know that Jesus said, 'I am the way, the truth, and the life. No one comes to the Father except through Me.' Which means the only way to go to heaven is to receive Jesus Christ as Savior and Lord. We've talked about it over and over again. Yet neither of you have ever said yes. And that worries me. I want you guys to be in heaven with me when the time comes. And I'm just saying, that time might be today."

Two platoons advanced by stealth.

That meant a total of sixteen SEALs—eight per platoon—plus pilots and copilots for two of their underwater vehicles and Commander Berenger. Adding in Ryker, Vinetti, and Hwang, they had a total of twenty-four men. The plan, however, called for them to add three more for a total of twenty-seven on the way back.

They were using two Advanced SEAL Delivery Vehicles—ASDVs— flanked by two standard SDVs. The latter looked like long black torpedoes. They were powered by a single propeller running off lithium polymer batteries and were nearly silent. The highly classified mini submarines had been designed specifically for the U.S. military. Each could transport six of the Navy's best and brightest into enemy territory without being seen or heard. The challenge was that the men were essentially trapped inside a sardine can—windowless, cramped, completely filled with frigid ocean water, and shrouded in pitch-darkness—for the entire journey while they used their oxygen tanks to breathe and state-of-the-art sonar navigational systems to get them precisely to their target. The SDVs were not for the faint of heart, and anyone with even a touch of claustrophobia need not bother.

The advanced versions were significantly larger and more complex. For starters, they could transport as many as sixteen SEALs and all their equipment along with a crew of two pilots to drive and navigate. The key difference, however, was not their size but the fact that their interiors were dry and lit. This not only reduced the stress and cold for the soldiers deployed on already high-risk missions. It also allowed the SEALs to transport civilians who might be wounded, untrained in using scuba gear, or at severe risk of freaking out in tight, dark, cramped conditions.

During the chopper ride to Sado Island, Hwang had asked Berenger why he insisted on using a total of four mini subs—two of the larger ones and two of the smaller—that could carry a combined total of forty-eight men. Why not just use the two larger units? It was a fair question, the commander had replied. He could answer with two words: *"Desert One."*

"Not sure I follow, sir," Hwang said.

"On April 24, 1980, President Jimmy Carter gave the green light to an operation called Eagle Claw," Berenger explained. "U.S. Special Ops—led by Delta—were tasked with rescuing fifty-two Americans who had worked at the U.S. Embassy in Tehran and had been taken hostage by Iranian radicals in November of '79."

Marcus knew Hwang was familiar with the basic plot if not the specifics of the operation.

"In the early hours of the mission," Berenger continued with Marcus and Vinetti listening along with Hwang, "the Delta operators—led by the legendary Colonel Charlie Beckwith and backed up by a force of Rangers—were able to penetrate Iranian airspace without being detected. However, mechanical problems and a sandstorm created a situation in which three of the eight Sea Stallion helicopters they were using were rendered unable to fly. When Beckwith realized there was no longer enough room to bring out all of the hostages on the remaining choppers, he had no choice. He had to order the mission aborted. And then things got worse. No sooner had Beckwith ordered his men to fly back out of Iran than two of the aircraft collided. The accident caused multiple explosions and the deaths of eight Americans. It was a tragic turn of events. The men were brave and well trained. Their cause was noble and their intentions faultless. But they hadn't planned well enough to account for the unexpected. Mechanical problems. Weather problems. And just plain human error."

Berenger wrapped up just as they were preparing to land on the island.

"Now, how does that apply to us?" he asked. "For starters, you shouldn't overcompensate and try to bring in too large a force. North Korea's sonar nets and other coastal defenses are too sophisticated. We'd be spotted immediately, and the whole thing would be over before we really got started. At the same time, however, the better part of wisdom says you'd be foolish not to build some redundancy into the plan. So that's what I did because you never know what's going to transpire."

Now, locked inside one of the smaller SDVs, Marcus did his best to calm his nerves. Holding his breath for a moment, he waited for the bubbles to clear and checked his watch. It was 4:47 a.m. He winced, began breathing again, and closed his eyes. They were only moving at about five knots—about six miles per hour. Any faster and they would be too loud and quickly detected by the enemy. Daybreak was only about ninety minutes away. They needed to be done and gone by the time the sun began to light the tops of the mountains towering over Tanch'ŏn or they might never live to see another day. Still, there was nothing he could do but stay calm, ignore the cold, and pray.

He was certainly praying for the success of the mission. Even more, he was praying for Vinetti and Hwang. He loved these men. There was no one on earth he was closer to—not even his family. They'd been through everything together, and it pained him that after so many conversations over so many years, they still had no interest in a personal relationship with Christ. They still didn't grasp that hell was as real a place as heaven. Nor did they seem the least bit concerned for where their souls would spend eternity. They loved Marcus. And they respected his faith. But they didn't share it. And now they were headed once again into harm's way.

Bill McDermott hated being the bearer of bad news, but it couldn't be helped.

As he entered the Situation Room, he found President Clarke, Defense Secretary Cal Foster, CIA director Richard Stephens, each member of the Joint Chiefs of Staff, including the chairman, and his own boss, General Barry Evans, the national security advisor, monitoring the progress of the mission in Tanch'ŏn in real time. Transfixed as they were, given that this was one of the most sensitive missions any of them had ever participated in, none looked at McDermott as he moved to the podium. So he cleared his throat and apologized for the interruption. "Gentlemen, we have a serious complication," the deputy NSA began.

"What is it?" asked an annoyed President Clarke.

"Sir, I just took an urgent call from Asher Gilad, the head of Mossad. It seems that the Israelis have been tracking a team of Iranian intelligence operatives—all senior members of the Revolutionary Guard Corps—for the past several days. The operatives departed Tehran and have been zigzagging around the globe. At first it wasn't clear to the Mossad where the operatives were heading or what their intentions were. Early indications suggested they were heading to Damascus or Beijing. But then they routed to Moscow, and last night they wound up in Vladivostok."

"So what?" asked the president, growing more irritated. "Get to the point."

"Well, sir, less than thirty minutes ago, the Iranians boarded a military transport flight headed for Pyongyang," McDermott replied. "Gilad said the Israelis were able to identify the leader of the group as Alireza al-Zanjani."

"The deputy commander of the IRGC," said Stephens.

"Exactly," McDermott confirmed. "And given that al-Zanjani has been overseeing Iran's nuclear weapons program, Gilad believes the team was sent to North Korea to help facilitate the transportation of the warheads to the Islamic Republic. If that's true, it probably means they expect to link up with General Yoon, who oversees the DPRK's nuclear weapons program, as soon as they arrive."

At this, Secretary Foster spoke up. "Are the Israelis saying General Yoon is still in Pyongyang right now, rather than Tanch'ŏn?"

"I can't say that for certain, Mr. Secretary," McDermott replied. "We haven't told the Israelis anything about the SEAL operation currently under way. But that is precisely the question. We have confirmation from Yoon, via the Raven, that the general's wife and mother-in-law are in Tanch'ŏn. And the Raven reports that the wife is carrying electronic documents detailing every aspect of the country's nuclear program, including the location of every warhead and every launcher. But it is going to be extremely difficult to make sense of all the data without General Yoon. We absolutely need him—not just the documents. Yet it's becoming increasingly possible that we're sending American forces into grave danger, and General Yoon won't even be there."

67

Tanch'ŏn was a small city.

With a population of only about 360,000 people, it was located in the South Hamgyong province, just a few miles from the coast. But it was a strategic city, the center of North Korean mining operations for valuable minerals and thus the site of a major port that in recent years had been significantly expanded. Marcus had learned in Berenger's briefing that North Korean missile boats and other navy vessels were frequently found near the mouth of the Dongdae River, which flowed down from the mountains, past the city on its southern side, and emptied into the Sea of Japan.

Marcus strained his neck to see the sonar image. On the dashboard monitor in front of Berenger, who was driving the SDV, Marcus could see that they were now well up the river and almost to the location where they would disembark. They had not been spotted yet, and there were no enemy vessels on the digital screen so far as he could see. So far, so good.

Berenger raised his gloved right hand and signaled they had three minutes until they landed. The three Marines all confirmed they'd seen his signal and began doing a final weapons check. From the arsenal back on the base at Yokosuka, Marcus had chosen a Heckler & Koch MP7A1 submachine gun as his main weapon. Equipped with a suppressor and ELCAN scope, the variant on the MP7 was preferred by SEAL Team Six because it was lighter than similar weapons used by other Special Ops units, because its barrel was shorter, and because it could hold either a twenty- or forty-round magazine rather than the more common twelve- or fifteen-round mags. In a holster strapped around his right thigh he had a Sig Sauer P226R pistol that fired 9mm bullets from a fifteen-round mag.

Hwang had chosen an M4 assault rifle variant known as the MK18 CQBR carbine, complete with a night vision laser scope. With a barrel four inches shorter than the standard M4, it was ideal for close-quarters battle conditions, even when fitted with a suppressor. Hwang had used the same weapon often in Afghanistan when tasked with protecting visiting VIPs. Berenger had also insisted that Hwang carry an M79 grenade launcher. It was capable of firing 40mm grenades and was affectionately known among the SEALs as a "pirate gun" because its stumpy barrel and sawn-off stock made it look like an eighteenth-century pistol that Jack Sparrow and Captain Barbossa might have used in the Caribbean.

Trained as a sharpshooter, Vinetti had chosen a McMillan TAC-338 bolt-action sniper rifle. It, too, was fitted with a night vision scope and a suppressor. Vinetti also carried an MK18 on his back with plenty of extra magazines in case he got into a scrape up close and more personal than he was used to.

It was just before five in the morning—less than ninety minutes until daylight—when Berenger brought the craft to a halt and opened the hatch. Vinetti followed the commander out of the SDV. Hwang exited next, and Marcus came after him. They flexed their cramped muscles and prepared to surface.

This was it. Marcus's heart began pounding. The conversation in the crew's mess had not ended the way he might have hoped, and now here they were, heading into the most dangerous mission of their lives.

Berenger had been clear. Whatever happens, he'd said, *"Do. Not. Get. Caught."*

Just a few kilometers from where they were heading, the DPRK had a concentration camp, though they preferred to call it a "reeducation camp." There, some six thousand prisoners were subjected to unimaginable torture, brutally hard labor, and famine-like conditions. Berenger had shown them pictures of the emaciated men and women being held there. They were barely more than skeletons.

"Should I call the mission off?" Clarke asked.

"How solid is the Israelis' intel?" asked the SecDef.

"Director Gilad gave me no reason to think it wasn't 100 percent," the deputy national security advisor replied.

"If I may," Stephens interjected, "Alireza al-Zanjani was the guy responsible for taking out a Mossad team in Athens three or four months ago. The Iranians thought they were negotiating a deal with the Pakistanis to buy nuclear warheads from Islamabad. Turns out it was a Mossad sting operation using a high-ranking Pak nuclear scientist. And when al-Zanjani realized it was an Israeli op, he personally murdered the scientist and ordered the IRGC to kill the Mossad team. Thirteen Israelis died. It was one of the worst attacks in the history of the Mossad. They've been hunting al-Zanjani ever since."

"And now al-Zanjani and his team are heading to Pyongyang?" asked the president.

"Yes, sir."

"To oversee the transportation of the Russian warheads to the Islamic Republic."

"Yes, sir; that's what the Mossad believes."

"By land, sea, or air?" asked Secretary Foster.

"They're not sure," McDermott admitted. "But Yoon would know. That's why we can't call off the mission. It's imperative we grab him and get him out of the country so we can talk to him in depth."

Berenger surfaced first.

A moment later, he signaled his men to follow.

Ryker, Vinetti, and Hwang had been ordered to stay close to the commander, given how long it had been since any of them had been on active duty in the Corps. None of them had ever served as a SEAL. Ryker and Vinetti were still good shots and still in pretty good shape, but they were no match for the younger guys around them, all at the top of their game physically and in terms of their marksmanship.

As Marcus pulled out his regulator and peeked his head above the waterline, he found himself exerting more energy than he'd expected treading water and trying to stay in place against the river's fast-moving current. What he saw first were massive cement embankments, a steel bridge overhead, and train tracks running north and south. They'd been instructed to let their scuba gear drop away. It was tethered to the SDV and would be gathered by a team of four men who would stay behind to guard the vessels, turn them around, and prepare their escape.

Marcus swam behind Berenger to the base of the embankment on the southern side of the river and grabbed hold of a rusty steel ladder. The moment he scrambled onto the train bridge itself, he was tempted to catch his breath and take a survey of his surroundings. But Berenger was already running flat out for the other side. Marcus had to sprint to catch up, with Vinetti, Hwang, and the rest of the men following suit.

Beyond the northern side of the bridge, the tracks began to arc to the right, heading east toward the coast and the port. But a few hundred yards later, Donny Callaghan peeled off the tracks and grabbed a pair of bolt cutters from his backpack. He cut a section out of a chain-link fence topped by razor wire and dropped down onto an asphalt road on the edge of the city.

Working in their favor was that North Korea lacked the electrical power to keep the lights of even small cities on at night. There were streetlamps every few yards, but they were dark. No homes had lights on, nor did commercial enterprises. The moon was full, and that was a problem, but other than that, Tanch'ŏn was—so far—a ghost town.

Once the first platoon—Red Team, led by Callaghan—hunkered down in the shadow of a large warehouse, Marcus and his colleagues among them, Berenger sent Sanchez and the rest of Blue Team to "requisition" some vehicles. Satellite reconnaissance done over the past few days indicated the apartment complex parking lots where Blue Team could find what was needed.

Sure enough, five minutes later, four vehicles pulled up to the Red Team's location, headlights off. The first was a Pyeonghwa Paso 990, a somewhat-new minivan built by a North Korean company. It was hardly attractive but comfortably accommodated six men. The second was marked as a Sungri-58. Essentially a cargo truck with an open, flat bed, it looked like something out of the 1940s or '50s, though one of the men said the owner's manual they'd found in the glove compartment indicated it was actually a 1978 model. It was noisier and looked like a gas guzzler, but it could carry two men in the cab and six on the back, so it was ideal. The third was a Russian-built 4×4 known as a UAZ-469. It was ugly as sin and painted olive drab, but it took care of four men, so it certainly served its purpose. The last was a minibus of some kind, a brand Marcus had never heard of. Still, it appeared to be in decent working order and could comfortably carry up to eight, if need be.

Berenger commandeered the Russian 4×4 and assigned Marcus to be the driver. Berenger would be the navigator, sitting in the front passenger seat. Vinetti and Hwang would sit in the rear seats, weapons at the ready in case a firefight broke out earlier than expected. The rest of the men found spots in the other three vehicles, and as per the plan, they headed off in four different directions.

The problem was it was now 5:19.

68

"Take a left, Ryker," Berenger ordered. "And slow it down."

"Yes, sir."

The apartment complex they were headed to was on the other side of the city, but the streets were as empty as they were dark, and the drive didn't take long. By 5:31, Marcus had parked on a street parallel with the target building, a block away. He put it in park but left the engine running. If all went according to plan, he would not be returning to this vehicle, so it needed to be ready for the men who would drive it back to the river.

Sixty seconds later, two other drivers confirmed their positions over the secure radio link. They had both parked in nearby alleyways, as had been predetermined by Berenger based on his study of the satellite imagery. But there was still one more vehicle on the way.

"Sierra One, this is Charlie Bravo—what's your ETA?" Berenger asked over his whisper mic.

"Sierra One arriving now, Charlie Bravo," came the reply.

The minibus pulled up to the target building and entered the parking garage. There they would turn the vehicle around and leave it by the stairwell on the south end of the building. This would be the getaway vehicle Berenger and his squad would use once they had safely linked up with General Yoon and his wife and mother-in-law and everyone was ready to depart.

A moment later came an update. "Sierra One on scene—ready to move on your command."

"Roger that, Sierra One. Move now," Berenger ordered. "I repeat, move now."

The commander then turned to Vinetti. "You ready?"

Vinetti nodded.

"Time to go."

Berenger ordered the rest of his men to move to their assigned positions.

But just as Marcus was about to slip out the driver's-side door, the commander grabbed his arm. Lights were coming toward them. It was a truck of some kind, apparently not visible to any of the snipers in their perches. Each man in the 4×4 slid down in his seat, feigned sleep, and froze in position after making certain their weapons were not in sight.

The truck turned out to be a street cleaner. It passed without incident, and Marcus began to breathe again.

Vinetti raced up the darkened stairwell using only his night vision goggles.

He was late. He should already be up on the roof. He knew it and wanted to explain his delay, but Berenger had been clear. Radio silence was the name of the game unless someone started shooting at him.

That wasn't the case. But breaking into the back door of the apartment building to which he'd been assigned, he'd nearly been caught by a cleaning crew that was finishing the night shift and preparing to go home.

Now he was taking the stairs two at a time. The teams were counting on him to provide surveillance and overwatch protection in his sector, and he had to deliver.

By the time he reached the twelfth floor, Vinetti was winded. He was discouraged and surprised; he'd thought he was in better shape than this. His shooting skills hadn't atrophied. He'd been going to the shooting range in the basement of the embassy in Moscow two to three times a week. But he wasn't running as much as he used to, and it showed.

Stopping for a moment to catch his breath, Vinetti took off his backpack and removed the first of two booby traps from the pack. He gingerly set the first one and its explosive charge into place on one of the steps leading up to the roof. The second he attached to the roof door itself after he'd already gone through it and locked it shut. These were not large or sophisticated devices. But they just might slow down a platoon of DPRK soldiers if it came to that.

Now out on the roof amid a stiffening wind that was going to make shooting problematic, Vinetti took a moment to get his bearings. He could see Sanchez and the other members of the Blue Team on four nearby roofs. Each man was in position, weapons at his side, using night vision binoculars to look for signs of trouble. Vinetti pulled the rest of his equipment out of his backpack. He quickly sorted through all the ropes, belays, rigging plates, webbing slings, carabiners, a harness, and other gear and scrambled to get everything set up, tied down, triple-checked, and ready to go.

Satisfied he'd done everything he'd been asked, he found a position by the edge of the roof, overlooking the target building. He pulled out his ammo box, opened it, and set it beside him. Then he picked up his sniper rifle and waited for Berenger's call.

Berenger checked his watch.

Marcus checked his own as well.

At precisely 5:35, Berenger radioed his snipers—Sanchez, his Blue Team, and Vinetti—each of whom were positioned on the roofs of the five closest buildings surrounding their target, giving each of them a commanding view of developments and the ability to provide covering fire for their escape if the need arose.

"Angel One, do you have eyes?"

There was a pause, a hiss of static, and then the reply. "Angel One, I have eyes."

"Status?"

"All clear. I repeat, all clear."

"Angel Two?"

"Roger that—I have eyes. All clear."

The last voice to come over the radio was Vinetti's. "Charlie Bravo, this is Angel Five. I have eyes, but we may have company."

"What are you seeing, Angel Five?"

"Three vehicles, headlights on, coming from the southwest."

"Distance?"

"Just over a mile."

"Roger that, Angel Five," Berenger said. "We're going in. Keep us posted."

Marcus glanced in his side mirror.

The street cleaner was gone. The street was empty in both directions.

Berenger finally nodded and gave the go sign, and the three men bolted from the 4×4 and raced down the same alley Vinetti had disappeared into. When they got to the end, Marcus could see their target building ahead and slightly to the left. He pressed close to the wall on the right side of the alley while Berenger hugged the left side and took a quick peek down his side of the street. "Clear," he whispered.

Marcus did the same and saw no people, no moving vehicles, no lights or movement of any kind. "Clear," he whispered back. Hwang was walking backward, weapon up, making sure they were not ambushed from behind.

"Clear," he whispered as he reached his teammates.

Berenger dropped his weapon to his side and walked briskly across the street. The moon was blocked by the buildings, most of them eight to twelve stories high. If anyone was up at this hour and watching from a window, at most they would see a shadowy figure moving across the street, not a face, barely a profile, and certainly not the barrel of a suppressed submachine gun.

69

At Berenger's order, Marcus moved into the empty street.

He mimicked every nuance of the SEAL team commander's pace and gait, but his body was stiff, tense, as if any moment he'd hear the crack of a sniper bullet from a Russian-made rifle. The neighborhood was quiet. Eerily so. Heavy clouds were rolling in. A slight breeze was coming from the east. The early morning air was brisk, and Marcus could see his breath.

Making it to the other side of the street without incident, he took a deep breath, stepped inside the target building, and brought his weapon back up to the ready position. Hwang arrived ten seconds later. Callaghan, the Red Team leader, had positioned two men at the doors to each of the stairwells, one on the north side of the building, the other on the south. Four more men, Marcus knew, had already taken the stairwell to the ninth floor and were holding their positions. That was the entirety of Red Team.

"Angel Five, what's the status of those vehicles?"

"Still coming, Charlie Bravo," Vinetti responded. "Now one klick away."

One kilometer. Six-tenths of a mile. Marcus felt his pulse quicken.

Berenger checked in with the rest of his snipers. They had nothing to report, so the commander told them to maintain radio silence—everyone except Vinetti. Berenger wanted to know the instant those vehicles turned off their current trajectory or when they were within two blocks. Next he asked for a status check from each of the men waiting in the stairwells on the ninth floor. They had nothing to report. The hallway was dark but clear.

With that, Berenger strode through the lobby, bypassing the bank of four elevators—useless in the power outage shrouding the city—and opened the door to the stairwell. He stepped in. Ryker and Hwang followed suit. The door closed behind them.

Marcus paused before beginning his ascent. He could feel the adrenaline surging through his system and began counting to fifty. *All stress is self-induced,* he reminded himself. *It's in your mind. You don't need it. Lay it down. Panic is contagious. But so is calm. Stay calm. Do your work. Slow is smooth. Smooth is smart. Smart is straight. Straight is deadly.*

Oleg Kraskin stood at a window biting his lip and stared without seeing.

In the naval yard three stories below were hundreds of eighteen-, nineteen-, and twenty-year-olds servicing any number of destroyers, battleships, and other surface vessels. They were driving fuel trucks and repainting hulls and firing up blowtorches and shouting to each other over the noise. But none of this registered for the Russian. His thoughts were seven hundred miles away.

Oleg had heard nothing from General Yoon in nearly an hour. Nor had he heard anything from Ryker, Hwang, or Vinetti. The radio silence imposed on the SEAL teams was killing him. He had no idea what was happening. Nor could he help in any way. And his resentment at being left behind—along with his anxiety—was growing by the minute.

Marcus saw Berenger switch on his night vision goggles and did the same.

The SEAL commander had a submachine gun strapped to his back, but he wasn't using it. Instead, he had his silencer-fitted Sig Sauer pistol at the ready as he arrived at the ninth-floor landing. He nodded to the two SEALs waiting there, then motioned the two Marines to follow him into the hallway. Sticking with his H&K MP7A1, Marcus pivoted out the door to the right but saw no one. Simultaneously Hwang did the same, pivoting left, his MK18 at the ready.

Berenger was already heading for apartment 91. Marcus remained at his side, weapon pointed forward. Hwang again brought up the rear, watching their six. When they got close to the door, Berenger held up a fist. Marcus stopped immediately. Hwang backed into them and stopped as well. Berenger then used another hand signal, and two SEALs emerged from the stairwells—one from each end—and quickly, quietly moved to their side. One carried a steel battering ram. Another, a backpack full of explosive charges.

The other two operators emerged from the stairwells and took up positions in the hallway, with direct lines of sight to the door of apartment 91. When everyone was in place, providing cover in every direction, Berenger clicked his microphone twice, signaling they were going in, then strode up to the door and knocked twice.

No one answered.

Berenger knocked again. Still, there was no reply.

Marcus's pulse was pounding. He was once again counting to fifty in his head, but it wasn't working. His heart rate wasn't slowing, nor was his breathing. He was thankful he was wearing gloves. He'd never perspired this much. Not on an operation. Yet his hands were moist, and without the traction the gloves provided, he thought his weapon might very well have slipped out of his hands.

Marcus was tempted to look back but forced himself to maintain discipline and focus on the doors he'd been assigned. The rules of engagement Berenger had set were ironclad. Anyone emerging from any of these doors would be warned once. Any residents who didn't disappear back inside immediately would be shot instantly and without hesitation.

Berenger knocked again. Again there was no response. That's when Marcus heard the battering ram. He heard the door ripping off its frame and Berenger and both of his operators storming into the apartment. That's when the gunfire began.

The sound of the first shot was unmistakable. It came from the Russian sniper rifle, the VSS "thread cutter" known as the Vintorez. Marcus recognized it immediately because he'd used one himself less than two weeks before. There was an almost-imperceptible pause, and then came three more shots in rapid succession. They were all from the Vintorez.

Marcus pressed himself to the left-side wall of the hallway and dropped to one knee. He expected to hear return fire and Berenger's voice barking orders. But the orders never came. What did come, almost immediately but not from the same direction, was the crack of another rifle. An American rifle. A TAC-338 bolt-action sniper rifle.

Vinetti had the approaching vehicles in his sights.

That's when he heard the first shot.

His eyes instinctively came away from his scope. He needed a broader view. He saw successive flashes coming from an open window on the ninth floor of the building directly across from him.

Vinetti cursed. He'd checked and double-checked all those windows not three minutes earlier. They had all been closed. Then he'd gotten distracted by the oncoming vehicles. But there was no time to dwell on it. No one had a clearer view of the sniper's nest than he did, so he redirected his weapon and fired three times into that open window and three times into the closed window two feet to its left.

70

Three vans screeched to a halt in front of the building.

Three more were now approaching at high speeds from the northeast.

Doors flung open. Twelve heavily armed men piled out and began sprinting for the front door. Héctor Sanchez ordered Blue Team to open fire. They did and almost instantly dropped eight men and clipped a ninth. The moment the survivors rushed into the lobby, Callaghan and a colleague cut them down from inside.

Men were shouting updates over the radio.

But Marcus could barely hear them above the cacophony of gunfire in the streets.

Suddenly a door opened. A large man stepped into the hallway. He was holding a gun. Marcus fired two shots to his head and one to the chest, felling him instantly.

When another door opened behind him, Hwang opened fire. Marcus heard the second gunman crash to the floor. For the moment, the hallway was secure. But despite repeated attempts to raise him, there was still nothing from Berenger.

The attack was over in a matter of seconds. Marcus blinked hard and tried to reconstruct the chain of events and picture what had happened. It seemed clear the first shots had come from the adjacent building, not from inside the apartment. Yet an instant later, Marcus had heard multiple rounds from an American rifle. That had to be Vinetti or one of the members of Blue Team. Since then, the only gunfire he'd heard was coming from the ground floor. The North Korean sniper had either been taken out or was in retreat. The fact that neither Berenger nor his colleagues had returned fire, however, could mean only one thing.

Knowing his end of the hallway was covered by other members of Red Team, Marcus turned and stormed into the apartment before anyone could order him not to. He instantly aimed at the window and depressed his trigger, unleashing a long burst of fire through the windows of the facing apartment—just in case—until his magazine was empty. Then, diving right, he moved away from the windows and into the relative safety of the hallway. With a fluidity he could only attribute to the muscle memory he'd obtained in the Secret Service, he ejected the spent mag, replaced it with another, and chambered a round.

Moving down the hallway, he reached the first door on his right, pivoted into the kitchen, and swept the area with his weapon at the ready. It was clear. Moving back into the hallway, Marcus next cleared a bathroom, then carefully stepped into a bedroom. There was no one immediately visible, so he cautiously opened the closet, then checked under the bed. Nothing.

He heard movement in what he assumed was the master bedroom. He quickly glanced into the hallway. It was empty. He waited and heard nothing more but the firefight nine floors below. Abruptly he noticed that his heart was not beating so hard. His pulse was slowing. His breathing was growing steady.

"Clear—coming out," he shouted, then tossed his backpack down the hall.

The moment it crashed to the floor, the door of the master bedroom flew open and a spray of bullets spewed forth. The deception had worked, flushing out the killer lying in wait. Marcus soon heard the distinctive sound of an empty magazine and made his move. Pivoting into the hallway, he unleashed two bursts of return fire—waited a beat—then fired a third. Then he grabbed a grenade from his vest, pulled the pin, and hurled it forward. Ducking back into the bedroom, he braced for impact behind a dresser.

The explosion blew a hole in the wall between the bedrooms. Pieces of Sheetrock rained down on him, but he was fine. The two men who'd been waiting for him were not. Blood and bits of human flesh were everywhere. The stench of gunpowder was unreal.

Only then did Marcus double back and survey the carnage in the living room. Berenger was dead, shot in the head. Both of the SEALs who'd followed their commander into the apartment were dead too. They were lying in large and growing pools of crimson. But that wasn't all.

General Yoon, his pregnant wife, and her elderly mother were all slumped over on the couch. Each had received a single shot to the head, but as Marcus examined them more closely, it was clear they had not been killed by a sniper rifle. The holes were too small. They had come from a smaller caliber—a 9mm—almost certainly a pistol. Their eyes were frozen open in horror. Blood had trickled down their faces from their wounds, but it was not fresh. It was coagulated. The three had been shot at least an hour earlier, and whoever had done it had created a kill box for the SEALs coming to collect them.

Clearly someone had known the general and his family were trying to defect. Moreover, they'd known Americans were coming. Who, Marcus didn't know or care. It wasn't relevant. Only three things were: determining whether there was any useful intelligence in the apartment, removing the bodies of these three brave Americans, and getting the team safely back to the river and back to international waters.

Marcus called for Hwang, who entered and surveyed the grisly scene. Hwang quickly checked the pulse of each man. It was just a formality, tinged perhaps with no small measure of disbelief. Berenger and his two men were gone. Marcus radioed to tell the team their status. No one reacted. They were still fighting for their lives.

As the gun battle raged in the streets, Marcus told Hwang to help him search for any shred of intelligence, starting with the thumb drive the general had sent via his wife. It was unlikely at this point they'd find anything, Marcus knew. Whoever had come to kill them all had to have been known to General Yoon. The man had been sitting on the couch, after all. There were no signs of a struggle. Rather, all signs indicated the general had been blindsided by a friend or colleague. Surely whoever had pulled the trigger had taken whatever intel there was—and Marcus imagined there had been a lot.

The two men carefully checked every inch of clothing worn by both the general's wife and his mother-in-law. They found nothing. Marcus checked Yoon himself, inch by inch. Together, he and Hwang checked the couch, drawers, the refrigerator, behind picture frames, and inside pillowcases but came up dry. Hwang then remembered to pull out a camera from his backpack and take photos of everything.

Marcus checked his watch. It was 5:51. The sun would be up soon. They had to move. Marcus called for help, and more members of Red Team arrived. They put the body of Commander Berenger into a body bag, then zipped the bag up. They did the same for the other two SEALs. Then Marcus, Hwang, and one of the other men each took a bag and slung it over their shoulders in a fireman's carry. They moved to the southern stairwell while their colleagues covered them, front and back.

As they spilled into the parking garage, Donny Callaghan and his colleague were waiting for them. The firefight out in the streets had grown exponentially louder—so loud Marcus was having trouble hearing all the radio traffic in his earpiece. What he was catching, though, was terrifying. Bodies of DPRK soldiers were piling up in the street.

And the power had come back on. Lights were coming on throughout every apartment building for blocks, and headlights of vehicles no doubt bringing reinforcements were visible and approaching from every direction.

They found the minibus parked right where it was supposed to be and loaded the body bags inside. Callaghan ordered the men to smash out every window and do it fast. They were going to get shot out anyway. There was no point getting their faces sliced up with flying shards of glass. Marcus took the butt of his weapon and began knocking out the front windshield. Then he unsheathed his knife and carved away all the jagged shards of glass that remained around the metal frame.

The original plan had been that Berenger would drive them out, but Callaghan now ordered Marcus to take his place. The rest of them would provide covering fire. Marcus opened the driver's door, brushed the seat clean of glass, got in, and turned the ignition. Nothing happened. He turned it again. The third time the diesel engine sputtered and coughed but still would not start.

Marcus said a silent prayer. He could feel the eyes of the men boring into him. He pressed the accelerator a few times to inject some fuel, then turned the ignition a fourth time. Finally the engine roared to life, and Marcus, his face dripping with sweat, put the van in gear and gunned it.

"Blue Team leader, this is Sierra One," Callaghan said into his headset. "Be advised, we're coming out."

71

"All teams, Sierra One is rolling—provide cover, then move to vehicles."

The sun was just coming up behind the buildings when Vinetti heard Sanchez's voice over his headset. Running low on ammunition, he was relieved they were about to evacuate. But then he heard an explosion and felt the roof shake under him.

It was the first booby trap. Someone had triggered it and blown himself to kingdom come. That more were coming, he had no doubt.

Grabbing his submachine gun, Vinetti lay down covering fire as he saw the minibus roar out of the parking garage. He was aghast when Marcus didn't make a left turn and head toward the water, per the plan, but rather sped up the alley and disappeared.

Nevertheless, his work here was done. It was time to link up with Blue Team and get back to the river. Tossing the nearly empty ammo box into his backpack, he threw the pack over his shoulder and raced to the far side of the building. He was putting on the harness when the second booby trap detonated. The force of the explosion nearly knocked him off his feet. Smoke began pouring out of the stairwell. But he wasn't going to take any chances. He took two grenades from his vest, pulled the pin on the first, pitched it through the flaming doorframe, and then did the same with the second.

Each explosion bought him a few more seconds. Vinetti finished strapping himself in, checked the ropes one last time, flung himself over the side of the building, and rappelled twelve stories to the pavement.

There was only one problem. A DPRK sniper was tracking his every movement. The moment Vinetti's feet hit the pavement, the sniper took the shot.

A DPRK soldier in full combat gear rushed into the street.

Marcus saw the blur of the man moving right to left, then the flash of automatic-weapons fire. He pressed the accelerator to the floor and shouted for everyone to get down. At the same moment, Hwang—sitting in the passenger's seat beside him—unleashed a burst of return fire. The soldier dove onto the sidewalk at the last second and the minibus roared past him. Marcus heard a grunt from Hwang and looked over to see his friend's arm covered in blood. He had been hit.

Marcus suddenly heard shouts from the back. An armored personnel carrier had just pulled onto the street behind them. Mounted on top was a .50-caliber machine gun, and its operator opened fire. Marcus could hear rounds pinging off the sides of the vehicle and the engine block. He could hear, too, the SEALs laying down suppressive fire. One of them was hit. Blood sprayed everywhere. The man was shouting in pain. And now Marcus could see in his rearview mirror two more APCs coming toward them. Their gunners, too, began to fire. Marcus had to get off this road and fast.

"*Hold on!*" he shouted as he hit the brakes and swerved left.

He glanced in his side mirror, hoping the APCs hadn't been able to make the turn, but no such luck. Worse, they were in an alley, and now a police car screeched to a halt at the next intersection, cutting off their path. Marcus shouted for everyone to brace for impact. As he did, he drew his Sig Sauer pistol with his right hand while steering with his left. He fired four shots at the two policemen exiting their cruiser, then reholstered the weapon and gripped the steering wheel with both hands. The minibus careened into the police cruiser, forcing it aside, though unfortunately to the right. That made it impossible for Marcus to turn right, toward the river.

He didn't dare maintain a straight line, however. The APC was firing again. Marcus blew through the next intersection and into another alley. He was clipping cars parked on both sides, but he wasn't slowing down. He was now doing almost sixty down the narrowest of passageways. Despite all the chaos he could hear .50-caliber rounds whizzing past the vehicle.

Hwang's left arm was bleeding badly, yet Hwang seemed unfazed. Quietly the physician reached into his backpack, resting on the floor beneath him, pulled out a tourniquet, and began methodically applying it.

Callaghan called for Hwang's grenade launcher. Hwang paused from injecting himself with morphine, grabbed his M79, and tossed it to him. Then he went back to giving himself the shot.

Marcus glanced back just in time to see a 40mm grenade streak down the alley. The resulting explosion not only took out the gunner but caused the driver behind him to lose control. The APC smashed into a parked car and flipped over in a blaze of sparks.

Just before the next intersection, Marcus suddenly braked hard and turned the wheel all the way to the right. Too far. The minibus turned but was also now up on just two wheels. Fearing they were about to tip over, Marcus course-corrected, hopped the curb on the left side of the street, and clipped the side of the building. Then he pulled the wheel hard to the right again as everyone shifted their weight to the right. The other two wheels smashed back down on the pavement, and they kept moving.

In severe pain, Hwang nevertheless scrambled into the backseat and began attending to the wounded SEAL operator. Marcus, meanwhile, strained to hear the updates coming in over his headset. The other three cars were having far more success than they were. They hadn't needed to zigzag through the city nearly as much. They were being chased, but their vehicles had proven faster and more agile. So far none of their men had been hit. Sanchez reported his car was just seconds away from the train yard. They promised to set up a perimeter and hold off the onslaught. Marcus hoped the Blue Team had managed to pick up Vinetti as planned.

Just then, a motorcycle policeman roared in from a side street, rapidly approaching the van. Callaghan saw him first. He pivoted, fired, and sent the man spilling off his bike and through the plate-glass window of a storefront. But now two more police motorcycles were coming up fast. Another APC also swerved onto their boulevard, followed in rapid succession by two more.

The lead APC was less than two hundred yards away. A moment later, its gunner opened fire. Marcus hit the brakes and took a sharp left turn, purposefully glancing off the right side of the alley this time to not flip over. The APCs had just enough warning to make the turn too, but Marcus had gained some ground. They were now two hundred fifty—perhaps even three hundred—yards back.

Though not 100 percent sure, Marcus calculated he was at least a good ten to fifteen blocks away from the train yard. There was no way he was going to be able to make it back. He could see only one APC behind him now. The other two had broken off, their drivers probably hoping to outflank him on his right or at least cut off any option of joining the other three escape vehicles.

He realized there was a growing possibility that they weren't going to make it out of Tanch'ŏn alive. The minibus was running on fumes. He had only just noticed that the gas gauge was close to empty. Were they to stall, they were finished. They wouldn't let themselves be taken alive. They'd fight to the end, no matter how bitter, but there was no point endangering the lives of the rest of the men who could still make it to the SDVs and back to the *Michigan*.

"Don't wait for us," Marcus now radioed to Sanchez. "Get to the SDVs. Start moving downriver."

"We're not leaving without you," Sanchez radioed back.

"You have to," Marcus said. "We're cut off. Can't make it to the rendezvous. Get moving and come to the bridge. We'll try to meet you there. That's our only shot. Sierra One, out."

72

"I think he's stabilized," Hwang shouted. *"What's our ETA?"*

It was a good question. Marcus didn't have a precise answer. But he knew the man's life depended on him now.

After the briefings with Berenger, Marcus had pored over satellite maps of the streets and alleyways of Tanch'ŏn as they'd crossed the Sea of Japan. But it was one thing to study them from above. It was quite another to navigate them at high speeds and while being shot at. Marcus was reasonably confident that unless the DPRK were able to set up enough roadblocks in a very short amount of time—a doubtful task under the circumstances—he could probably get his team to the bridge that crossed the Dongdae River about two kilometers downstream from the train bridge they'd crossed on foot. The issue wasn't so much getting there as having enough time to stop and get all of them and their equipment and the body bags down to the river and into the water before being shot to pieces by the massive army and police forces bearing down on them.

Then came a new wrinkle. Callaghan announced a military helicopter was following them. Marcus could see a second one approaching from the west. He had no idea if there were sharpshooters on board. But even if there weren't, there was no chance he could elude even aging and badly maintained choppers.

Marcus was blowing through intersections at higher and higher speeds. He was still zigzagging, trying to get closer to the river but taking fire from police and military units who were beginning to cut off certain streets. The DPRK had realized all the other vehicles had headed south. They were clearly determined to keep Marcus from following. So far, though, Marcus still had the initiative. His sheer recklessness was something none of the authorities had ever seen before. At times he was driving on sidewalks. At others he was smashing through bus stops, ripping up fire hydrants, and terrifying pedestrians and other drivers as the city awoke and began its day.

Then a new thought came to mind: *What if he could make it to the port?* It was on the other side of the bridge, maybe another kilometer or so. There'd be fairly tight security on the outer perimeter, and he had no idea whether the minibus—being torn to shreds and rapidly running through its last drops of fuel—could break through the front gates and still get them to the water's edge. They'd still be tracked by the choppers, but if he radioed ahead to the SDVs, might they be able to make it there and set up a perimeter to buy them a few more precious minutes?

"*Sierra One, we're under the bridge—how close are you?*" Sanchez asked over the radio.

"Three minutes, maybe four," Marcus replied. "How long would it take you to get to the port?"

"*Why?*"

"The bridge might not work."

"*It has to,*" said Sanchez.

"Why?"

"*We just learned there's a destroyer blocking the harbor. We'll never get in.*"

"Then standby one," Marcus said. "We'll see you at the bridge."

Another idea flashed through his mind. It was crazy actually, yet the more Marcus thought about it, the more he concluded it wasn't just an option; it was their only chance. If it were just him, he'd do it for certain. But the lives of the rest of these men were in his hands. He had to alert Callaghan and the others before he attempted something so reckless. And so he did, ignoring their shocked looks.

About four blocks from the bridge, Marcus tried to turn onto a side street running parallel to a major boulevard. He couldn't read any of the street signs, and even though Hwang could, they were all blurring by too fast for any translation to be actionable. By the grace of God, he didn't roll the van. But they did spin out and come to a full stop facing in the wrong direction. The only break they got was that the lead APC chasing them fared even worse. Not only did the APC not make the turn in time, it smashed headlong through the front of a building and erupted into flames.

That bought them a few more seconds, but not enough to do a K-turn and get pointed in the right direction, Marcus concluded. There was only one choice now. He jammed the van into reverse and hit the gas just as a second APC came screeching around the corner. It, too, spun out but didn't crash. Still, its driver burned a good deal of time making the very three-point turn Marcus had forgone. Police cruisers moved into the gap and began gaining ground. Hwang and the SEALs opened fire.

To the astonishment of every man in the minibus, Marcus never slowed down even though he was still going in reverse. In fact, down the straightaway, he actually sped up. Only when they approached a turn—one of their last two—did he ease his foot off the pedal ever so slightly, making the turn more smoothly than he had when he'd been going forward. A moment later, Marcus made another nearly flawless turn, this one onto the boulevard leading straight to the bridge.

This wasn't something he'd learned in the Corps. This was pure Secret Service training at work—"advanced reverse driving"—something he'd practiced countless times, though in an eight-ton armor-plated presidential limousine, not a crumbling North Korean van.

Sanchez came over the radio, announcing they had suffered a KIA. An operative had been killed in action. The news seemed to suck the air out of everyone's lungs, and then Sanchez transmitted the name: "Nicholas Vinetti. We've got him, but he's gone." Marcus could barely breathe, barely think, yet he knew he had to force himself to stay focused for a few seconds more for the sake of everyone in his care.

The bridge was coming up fast, with a roadblock set up on the far side. Marcus could see not just police and military vehicles waiting for them but giant dump trucks as well. There was no way he was going to blow through those, and he was being pursued and blocked in on the near side as the fleet of police and army vehicles gained ground. At the last moment, he spotted snipers set up at the other end.

"Hold on, gentlemen," Marcus ordered. *"This is it."*

They were roaring up the bridge now. Marcus's foot was pressed completely down to the floor. When they were almost at dead center—directly over the river—Marcus turned the wheel to the left as hard as he could. The back of the minibus smashed through the guardrail and plunged over the side.

Time seemed to stand still. In midair and falling fast, Marcus sucked in a lungful of air, closed his eyes, and held on for dear life. He could almost see the amazement in the eyes of their pursuers. But he would never actually see them again. None of them would. Live or die, they were leaving North Korea.

The van hit the water with such force that Marcus was thrown clear through the missing front windshield. Callaghan's decision to knock out all the windows had just saved Marcus's life.

The water was freezing. The current was fast. The real problem, though, was how muddy it was. Visibility was terrible. Completely submerged, Marcus could see only a few feet ahead of him. He was all turned around and disoriented, unsure which way was north and which was south. He was swimming against the current, fighting not to get swept away from the bridge. But his lungs were straining. His heart was pounding. The more energy he spent trying to stay in one place, the more oxygen he was consuming. He didn't dare go up to the surface. That was a death sentence. Yet if he couldn't breathe . . .

Just then he felt someone grab his shoulder from behind. He whipped around to find Sanchez staring back at him through a scuba mask. Sanchez held him tightly with one hand and gave Marcus his own scuba gear with the other. Marcus took the regulator, shoved it into his mouth, and began sucking oxygen. He gave Sanchez a thumbs-up sign, then donned the mask and flippers Sanchez now gave him and strapped his tank on. As Sanchez guided him closer to the SDV, he could see other SEALs helping the rest of Red Team and taking charge of the body bags.

Finding Hwang already in the SDV, Marcus reached over and grabbed his arm as he got into his own seat. Hwang slowly turned his head and opened his eyes, but his vacant expression would haunt Marcus for the rest of the trip back to the sub.

Sanchez took Berenger's place as pilot. Marcus took his spot behind Sanchez, who quickly closed the hatch, shrouding them in darkness. The engine suddenly purred to life, and Sanchez began to steer them down the Dongdae and back to the *Michigan*.

Marcus shut his eyes. He tried to forget all he had just seen and heard, but it was impossible. Everything he had feared about this mission had just come to pass. Vinetti was dead. So were Berenger and two other SEALs. And they were coming away from the mission empty-handed.

CIA HEADQUARTERS, LANGLEY, VIRGINIA

The first call Richard Stephens made was to Mossad headquarters in Tel Aviv.

"Asher, we have a problem," the CIA director began the moment his Israeli counterpart came on the secure line.

"You just sent a team into North Korea," Gilad said. "Please tell me no one was injured or killed."

Stephens was so caught off guard that the Israelis knew about the mission that he was, for a moment, speechless.

"We're monitoring the North Koreans pretty closely—the coastlines and all phone and radio traffic," Gilad continued. "That said, truth be told, it wasn't actually my guys who picked up on it. It was the Saudis. Abdullah bin Rashid just called me a few minutes ago. He's waiting for your call. We all have been. What did you learn?"

"Nothing, I'm afraid," Stephens admitted. "It was a complete bust. By the time our men got there, our contact was dead. The DPRK ambushed them. Honestly, we're lucky any of them survived."

"How bad was it?"

"Four dead, two wounded."

"I'm sorry."

"It gets worse, I'm afraid."

"The merchant ships."

"Exactly," Stephens said. "They launched everything they had. Very clever. It's a giant shell game now, and we've got too few assets trying to track too many targets."

"We're ready to help you," Gilad said.

"Talk to me."

"At my recommendation, Prime Minister Eitan called the crown prince in Riyadh and the sheikh in Abu Dhabi," said the Mossad chief. "They've all agreed to set up a joint surveillance operation. We've just looped in the Australians and the Indians as well, and my prime minister is on the phone with Manila as we speak. We can work with you to divide up the North Korean commercial fleet. We've already been trying to identify the fifty or sixty ships that strike us as the most likely ones to be carrying the cargo. Next we'll begin dividing up the task among our various assets, limited though they are. Just give us the go-ahead to continue."

The director of Central Intelligence was blown away. "Consider it given—my guys will set up a video conference immediately with all of you, and we'll loop in the SecDef, who is coordinating our efforts out of the NMCC," Stephens said, referring to the National Military Command Center, the joint war room located deep underneath the Pentagon.

In all his years in the intelligence business, Stephens couldn't think of a single time the U.S., Israelis, Saudis, and Emiratis had ever worked jointly on an intelligence operation of such magnitude, much less in Asia or in coordination with so many other nations. The world was changing. It was good to have allies.

Back on the *Michigan*, each man bowed his head in a moment of silence.

But that was it. There was no time at present to mourn the dead properly. They had to get back to business. They had a new mission to plan, and yet again the clock was ticking.

The moment the SDVs had reached and redocked with the submarine, the fifteen officers and 140 crew members had begun coordinating a high-speed run for the Korea Strait. Located between the city of Busan on the southern tip of the Korean Peninsula and the city of Fukuoka near the southern tip of Japan, the strait had become the prime focus of U.S. naval intelligence in the hunt for the Russian nuclear warheads now believed to be on their way to Iran.

"Gentlemen, in the hours following your raid in Tanch'ŏn, the leadership in Pyongyang ordered their entire national fleet of commercial container ships to set sail from North Korean ports and head south," the *Michigan*'s captain explained to Marcus and the SEALs in the crew's mess, in his first briefing since they had reboarded. "Hyong Ja Park's objective here is obvious. By filling the Sea of Japan with every merchant ship he has, he's desperately trying to mask which ship—or ships—are actually carrying the warheads, thus massively complicating our efforts to identify those ships and intercept them."

The captain noted that it was still not clear to analysts back in Washington exactly how General Yoon's superiors had caught wind of his plan to defect and pass along critical intelligence on the nuclear transfer. But he added it was likely that the plan to transfer the warheads to Iran had, from its inception, been predicated on the "flood the zone" concept. It was likely the brainchild of Mahmoud Entezam, the commander of the Iranian Revolutionary Guard Corps, or his deputy, Alireza al-Zanjani, and something upon which Iran's Supreme Leader had insisted.

Whoever's idea it was, thought Marcus, it was a brilliant move, for it added some 240 merchant ships to the more than two hundred container ships that already transited the strait on a daily basis, not counting tankers carrying oil and liquefied natural gas, hundreds of fishing vessels, and untold yachts and other leisure craft. There was simply no way the U.S. could monitor every ship—or even most of them—with satellites, drones, or other surveillance measures. If that weren't bad enough, the captain added that if the warheads were being transported in lead-lined storage cases, which they undoubtedly were, then they'd be almost impossible to detect from the air even by the most sophisticated American-built sensors.

Héctor Sanchez now stood and addressed the men. He explained that he had just received a call from the chief of naval operations in Washington, appointing him as the new acting commander of SEAL Team Six. He urged the men to compartmentalize the deaths of their teammates. They would honor them as soon as they possibly could with full-blown Navy funerals. The best way to honor their memory now, he said, was to complete this mission and not allow these good men to have died in vain.

It was wise counsel, to be sure, but Marcus knew from far too much personal experience how hard it was to stay focused and keep your emotions in check when you'd lost friends as close as these. Indeed, though Sanchez kept talking, Marcus had no idea what he was saying. It was everything he could do not to think about where Vinetti was at that moment. Then he thought of Claire, Nick's wife. Who would tell her the news? How could she possibly bear it? Her world was about to implode around her.

Marcus fought to maintain control. But his eyes were growing moist and his bottom lip was quivering. He didn't dare look around the room. Nor could he maintain eye contact with Sanchez. Instead, he stared at the notepad on the table in front of him and the pen in his hand and tried to tune back into the conversation under way.

"So, Cap, why don't we just wait a week or so and see which container ships proceed all the way to Iran?" one of the SEALs asked. "They can't possibly afford to send them all that far for nothing, right?"

"Probably not," Sanchez replied. "But the thinking back at Naval Intel, Langley, and DIA is that in the end none of the North Korean ships will actually go as far as Iran. Rather, the operating assumption is that in the middle of the night, the DPRK will likely transfer the warheads to ships not owned by North Korea or perhaps offload them at a commercial port someplace, drive them to an airport, and fly them to Iran."

He explained that the North Koreans had developed a tremendous amount of experience in evading international sanctions by transferring foodstuffs and weapons and oil, among other commodities, from ship to ship in the dark of night while thinking that no one was watching.

"Sometimes we catch them," he said. "Our satellites and drones have caught a good number of such transfers over the years. We know they do it. We know how they do it. But they do so much of it that it's impossible to catch it all, much less stop it all. That's why we need to pray the intel guys can pick the needle out of the haystack, give us a target, and let us do our thing—before it's too late."

74

"Sir, I'd like your permission to call Oleg Kraskin," Marcus said after the briefing.

"Not right now, Ryker," Sanchez replied. "We're operating under combat conditions at the moment—only essential communications are being permitted."

"But, sir, he may have sources that could help us identify the right ship or ships."

"Believe me, officers from naval intel are working with him to glean anything they can. He's provided nothing actionable thus far."

That said, there *was* something they needed just now, Sanchez noted—a detailed after-action report on how Berenger and the other two SEALs had died in the apartment in Tanch'ŏn, along with a minute-by-minute account of everything that had happened during the mission from start to finish. "You were there," the SEAL captain said. "You saw everything. I need you to write the report while we plan the next mission."

Marcus assented, of course. But what he really wanted was to talk to Oleg and see if the Russian had any scrap of new information they could use. For the moment, however, it was not to be.

Then Sanchez made another request. He needed Marcus to make a positive ID on Vinetti's body, since no one else on the ship actually knew the man well, aside from Hwang, who was currently undergoing surgery on his injured left arm. Marcus tensed. It was the last thing he wanted to do. But he kept his mouth shut and nodded.

"Will that be all, Captain?" he asked.

"Yes," said Sanchez. "Dismissed."

The walk to the refrigeration unit near the back of the submarine where they were keeping the bodies felt interminable. With every step, Marcus grew more and more angry with the men who'd done this to his friends and more determined to exact some measure of justice. By the time he reached the makeshift morgue, he was ready to explode.

An officer asked to see his ID and had him sign the logbook. Then she took him into the refrigerated vault, found and unlocked the right chamber, unzipped the body bag, and took several steps back.

Marcus stared at Vinetti's pale, stiff body. It was really him. He was really gone.

Marcus finally nodded. "It's him," he said through gritted teeth, then turned and walked out.

He knew he was not going to get a shot at anyone in the DPRK actually responsible for this. But there would be North Koreans on the ship. And there was Alireza al-Zanjani, too. To Marcus, this was the man truly responsible for Vinetti's death and those of the three SEALs. He stood in the hallway, his hands trembling. He was determined to learn everything he could about al-Zanjani and hunt him down, however long it took.

Did this square with his Christian faith? He wasn't sure. And truth be told, at the moment, he didn't care.

It was almost 11 p.m. when Marcus was permitted to enter the operating theater.

Given how little space there was on the sub, the theater was also being used as a recovery room. Marcus found Pete Hwang lying in a bed against the far wall. His head was propped up on pillows. He was covered in thick blankets. He had an IV drip in his left arm, and he was hooked up to a range of monitors that displayed his vital signs.

"Hey, guess who," Marcus whispered.

Hwang slowly opened his eyes. He was too groggy from the general anesthesia to talk, but when Marcus took his good hand, Hwang squeezed his fingers to acknowledge his presence. Hwang's other hand was wrapped in heavy gauze. The surgeon told Marcus everything had gone well. The damage to Hwang's muscles and nerve endings had been extensive, and it was a miracle they'd been able to save his hand. But he expected Hwang to make a full recovery and to regain most if not full use of the hand and arm, though tennis and squash were out for the foreseeable future.

Marcus wondered if his friend remembered much of the operation or even that Vinetti hadn't made it. He hoped not, and he certainly wasn't going to say anything. There were more encouraging matters to discuss.

"We think we've got 'em," Marcus whispered with no small amount of excitement as he crouched next to Hwang while the man fought a losing battle to keep his eyes open. "It's been crazy—you should come up to the CIC and look at the sonar and radar displays. There are literally hundreds of dots—each representing a ship. It's unreal. But about an hour ago, the Japanese navy located two mysterious ships lurking a few kilometers west of the island of Tsushima."

Hwang's eyes were closed, but Marcus kept going.

"Both ships have turned off their satellite transponders—they're not broadcasting their speed, their heading, their location, nothing," he said. "One of the ships is North Korean. The other is registered to a multinational corporation based out of Indonesia—Jakarta, I think. Anyway, Sanchez just briefed us. The theory is that the DPRK is going to transfer the warheads from one ship to the other. We've been tasked with seizing both ships. We move out in twenty minutes. I just wanted to . . ."

Marcus's voice trailed off as his eyes welled with tears. He didn't know if Hwang could even hear him anyway, and he knew if he said much more, he might lose it. So he nodded his thanks to the surgeon and stepped out as quickly as he'd entered.

Just before midnight, Sanchez and his team surfaced in the choppy waters.

The winds were picking up, and a heavy band of clouds blocked the moon, providing an extra measure of cover. Using the SDVs, the SEALs and Marcus had crept up on the two ships from the east. They'd removed their scuba gear and left it all in the SDVs. Now, weapons in hand, they surveyed the scene.

Switching on his night vision goggles, Marcus could see the *Mi Yang 12* to his left, a rusty, aging, 330-foot North Korean container ship badly in need of retirement or at least a serious paint job. To his right was the *Bandur Lampung II*, a rather sleek and far more modern Indonesian vessel with a state-of-the-art navigation and communications system. The lights of both ships were on. Their engines were idling. But they were not moving. Nor did they give any appearance of getting under way anytime soon.

Sanchez signaled his Blue Team to follow him as he resubmerged and swam to the starboard side of the *Bandur Lampung*. Callaghan and his Red Team advanced to the port side. This time, upon the new commander's orders, Marcus was at Sanchez's side.

At the same moment, another forty SEALs arrived from the west, having deployed their SDVs from the USS *Ohio*, another nuclear-powered American submarine that had arrived in the west Pacific with Carrier Strike Group One, headed up by USS *Abraham Lincoln*, a *Nimitz*-class aircraft carrier. Tasked with seizing control of the *Mi Yang*, these additional SEALs split into two squads, twenty men moving to each side of the North Korean ship.

At 11:57 p.m., with everyone in place, Sanchez signaled for Mk1 limpet mines to be attached to the propeller and for his men to scale the sides of the *Bandur Lampung*.

This was it, thought Marcus. He just hoped al-Zanjani was on this ship. And that he got to him first.

75

Precisely three minutes later, they had all reached the main deck.

Just then, the mines detonated. Both ships went dark. Callaghan and Red Team sprinted for the aft stairwells, bounding up the steps two at a time to secure the bridge and prevent anyone from making a distress call. Sanchez, Marcus, and Blue Team, meanwhile, raced down to secure the engine room and the various holds of the ship most likely to be housing the warheads.

Marcus gripped his MP7A1 submachine gun as he moved down the corridor on the ship's port side. The entire team had removed their suppressors. There was no need for stealth, and the chaos created by ear-shattering gunfire could prove useful.

Yet something wasn't right. As they burst into room after room, they weren't finding a single crew member, much less members of the Revolutionary Guard Corps. In less than ten minutes, Blue Team had established full control of the ship's bowels. Yet the only person they'd found was an overweight Indonesian mechanic in his midfifties who had fallen asleep on a bench in the machine shop. They found no guards. No weapons. And after a thorough search with Geiger counters and other devices, they'd found no evidence of radioactivity whatsoever.

Sanchez radioed to the bridge. The skeleton crew on night duty had practically wet their pants when the SEALs burst into the control room. So had many of the Indonesian crew whom the SEALs had found asleep in their bunks. As bewildered as his colleagues, Marcus watched as Sanchez then radioed the SEAL team leader on the North Korean vessel. To his astonishment, the report was the same. No warheads. Minimal weapons. No DPRK or IRGC personnel. The story the *Mi Yang*'s captain told quickly checked out: after experiencing severe electrical problems from fifty-year-old equipment, he had cut his engines and radioed the nearest ship for assistance. The *Bandur Lampung* was closest and readily complied. There was no evidence of sanctions violations, just a group of Good Samaritans trying to be helpful.

Then again, Marcus wondered if there might be another explanation. Could the entire episode have been one elaborate setup designed to consume precious time and manpower while the warheads moved ever closer to their final destination? On the other hand, did it really matter? Either way, they were no closer to finding and seizing the warheads, and the Iranians still had the initiative.

With every hour that ticked by, Oleg Kraskin was growing desperate.

They already had lost an entire day. Now the sun was rising over the Pacific, and they were still no closer to thwarting Pyongyang and Tehran.

Oleg climbed out of bed and stumbled to the restroom of the officer's quarters to which he'd been assigned. Switching on the light, he hardly recognized the face staring back at him in the mirror. The dark circles under his eyes showed clearly that he had slept no more than a few hours a night over the past several days. He was barely eating and thus losing weight, something his already-rail-thin frame could hardly afford. The Navy doctors attending to him were giving him sleeping pills and vitamin supplements and urging him to stop skipping meals, but they were worried about him, and for good reason.

The deaths of the four Americans in Tanch'ŏn—on a mission that for all intents and purposes he had urged and set into motion—weighed on him, and none more so than the loss of Nick Vinetti. It wasn't that Oleg really knew Vinetti or had spent any significant time with him. Yet Marcus had spoken often and well of his Italian friend and fellow Marine from Asbury Park, New Jersey. The two had known each other since boot camp, and even a blind man could see how close the two men were.

But it was not just Marcus's burdens that consumed Oleg's thoughts. He grieved for the deaths of his friend General Yoon and his bride and her mother. Oleg had been so excited about the prospect of bringing them out of the hermit kingdom to finally be safe and free. Of course he had known the risks. Yet Oleg had to admit to himself that he'd never seriously considered the possibility that the general and his family would be found out. Now they were gone and the guilt Oleg felt was unbearable.

Then there was his own family. He did not regret for one moment killing Luganov or that pig Nimkov. They deserved what they had gotten and worse. Yet Oleg missed Marina and Vasily terribly. For all the strains that had pulled them apart, Oleg still deeply loved his wife. They had only been children, university students, when she had bewitched him, heart and soul. How could he not miss the warmth of her touch or the feeling of her breath on his cheek or the sight of her smile and sound of her laugh?

He turned on the faucet and splashed warm water on his face. He forced himself to brush his teeth and run a comb through his hair. He threw on the same wrinkled, unlaundered clothes he had worn since he'd arrived at the American naval base just outside of Tokyo.

He realized he needed to cinch his belt a notch tighter. Then he picked up the phone beside the bed and dialed the operator.

"I'm ready," he said in English.

A few minutes later, there was a knock on his door. Two MPs had arrived to escort him back to the intelligence division. Oleg had proven of little use to his new country so far. He could see no way that today would prove different. But he told himself he had to try.

76

It had taken extensive consultations with the commander of the Pacific Fleet.

Sanchez had even had to talk to the chief of Naval Operations.

But in the end, the new SEAL Team Six commander had convinced his superiors he needed far more tactical flexibility than a submarine could provide and far more men than he currently had with him. A day later, Sanchez and his men had been airlifted to the middle of the East China Sea, where they linked up with Carrier Strike Group One and more than two hundred additional SEAL operators.

The lead ship in the armada was the USS *Abraham Lincoln*, the *Nimitz*-class aircraft carrier based out of the Naval Air Station on Coronado Island near San Diego. Joining her were the USS *Lake Champlain*, a *Ticonderoga*-class Aegis guided missile cruiser, and the USS *Stockdale*, the USS *Gridley*, and the USS *Higgins*—three *Arleigh*

Burke-class guided missile destroyers. Tagging behind them were a logistics ship, a supply ship, and two additional guided missile destroyers from the Japan Maritime Self-Defense Force—the JS *Ashigara* and the JS *Samidare*. Two *Los Angeles*-class attack submarines, the USS *Tucson* and the USS *Santa Fe*, flanked the convoy.

As the sun rose on Saturday morning, Marcus stood on the deck of a supercarrier, sipping black coffee and wrestling with his soul. He'd already scarfed down two plates of eggs, sausages, and hash browns. He'd worked out and showered. Then he'd spent some time reading through the eleventh chapter of Proverbs, it being the eleventh day of the month.

Verse 2 rankled him.

When pride comes, then comes dishonor,
    But with the humble is wisdom.

Verse 19 was even worse.

He who is steadfast in righteousness will attain to life,
And he who pursues evil will bring about his own death.

And then there was verse 23.

The desire of the righteous is only good,
But the expectation of the wicked is wrath.

This wasn't what he wanted to hear. He was in pain. He was seething and consumed with exacting retribution for what had happened to his friends. He'd been telling himself for the past several days that he had every right to be feeling and acting like he was. But he knew better. It wasn't justice he was after. It was pure revenge. It was a desire for evil, not for righteousness. He was consumed with bloodlust. And his conscience was killing him. He hadn't slept well. He'd retreated from the team when not required to be in briefings. When Sanchez had required him to meet with the chief medical officer on board to see if he was suffering from PTSD, he'd given clipped, nonresponsive answers and denied anything was wrong. But he was lying to himself and hardly fooling anyone else.

So, standing alone in the whipping winds, leaning against a railing at the stern of the ship, Marcus finally gave up the fight.

"Forgive me, Father," he said. *"And help me. I want to do your will, not my own."*

That was it. His prayer was as simple as it was direct. Yet almost instantly he could feel the bitterness beginning to drain away.

Once again Marcus requested a meeting with the *Lincoln*'s captain.

He had first made the request the moment he had stepped off a Seahawk helicopter onto the deck of the massive carrier at 6:19 Friday morning. Given the velocity and complexity of the operations the strike group was engaged in, an entire day and a half had passed. It was now 4:41 on Saturday afternoon, and Marcus was finally being escorted by the XO to the Combat Information Center and told he had two minutes with the captain and no more.

Marcus saluted, then asked for permission to use the ship's comms to call McDermott in Washington.

"What for?" the captain asked, not looking up from the sheath of computer printouts he was scanning.

"As you've probably been briefed, I'm not actually with the SEALs," Marcus said. "I work for Langley and have been tasked with helping hunt down these warheads."

"You and about five thousand other people."

"Nevertheless, I'd be grateful for permission to call Mr. McDermott. I've tried to be patient. But this is becoming increasingly time sensitive."

"Don't you have a handler?"

"I did, but that was Nick Vinetti," Marcus said, lowering his voice.

"Now I report directly to the president, which practically speaking means directly to the NSC."

The captain finally looked up at Marcus and then at his XO. "Is this true?"

The XO nodded, offering his boss a folder containing Marcus's orders. The captain neither took it nor read what was in it. Instead, he simply grunted his assent and turned back to the papers already in his hands.

The XO told Marcus to follow him.

Moments later, Marcus found himself parked in a cramped cubicle with a secure ship-to-shore phone and a direct line to the White House Situation Room. There was a hiss of static, and then the voice of a watch officer came on the line. Marcus explained who he was and whom he needed. He did not need to wait long.

"McDermott."

"Bill, it's Marcus."

"Make it quick," said the deputy national security advisor. "General Evans and I are about to brief the president."

His tone was matter-of-fact at best. There was certainly no warmth. He did not ask about Vinetti. That stung, but Marcus didn't have time to worry about it. What he needed was permission to call Oleg, and he wasted no time in asking for it.

"Why?" McDermott asked.

"He might be able to help us find al-Zanjani. I want to work with him on that."

"Forget it. He can't."

"How do you know?"

"Because he's sitting on a base outside of Tokyo twiddling his thumbs. The intel guys have tried to debrief him. He refuses to talk to them."

"That's because he's supposed to be talking to me, Bill," Marcus shot back. "I'm his handler. I'm the one he trusts."

"Let it go, Marcus. We've got plenty of experts working on this. We'll find al-Zanjani and the warheads soon enough."

The patronizing tone infuriated Marcus and he had to fight to stay calm. "Bill, come on—this guy knows the Iranians. He's been to Tehran. He's met personally with the Supreme Leader numerous times—President Afshar, too. He knows their top advisors. He knows how they think. Maybe you're right. Maybe it will do no good at all. But let me at least give it a shot. This is why the president brought us in. All I'm asking is that you let us do our jobs."

"Do your job?" McDermott asked. "Do you know how much danger you've put our country in? Do you get just how much damage you've caused? If it were up to me, you and your Russian friend would be locked up in a supermax prison, not playing James Bond in the East China Sea. The answer is no. Now I've got to go meet with the president. So just keep your mouth shut and your head down and let us clean up the mess you boys have made."

There was another hiss of static, and the line went dead.

Marcus sat in the cubicle in stunned silence.

He'd never been as close to McDermott as to Vinetti and Hwang. But he'd had no idea how angry his onetime Marine sergeant had become with him. Right now there was no time to process, much less fix, the situation. The clock was ticking.

Marcus needed to talk to Oleg, but that was never going to happen without the proper authorization. He ticked through the people who could give it. The list was short.

He could call Stephens. But could the man be trusted? The CIA director had already sold Marcus out to the Russians. Marcus couldn't imagine that Stephens had taken the president's directive to bring him and Oleg into the Agency any better than McDermott had.

There was Cal Foster at the Pentagon. But he had his hands full. And even if he could get through to Foster, what would he say? If the deputy national security advisor had refused to let him talk to the very agent he was assigned to handle, how would he persuade the secretary of defense to countermand McDermott's order to stand down?

Marcus stared at the communications console in front of him for several minutes. But finally he knew what exactly he had to do. It seemed authorization to contact Oleg was not going to happen. But what about unauthorized contact? He'd been given direct orders from the commander in chief of the United States to serve as Oleg's handler and find these warheads. The only way he could obey those orders was to ignore McDermott.

Marcus picked up the headset and spoke to the communications officer in the CIC, just as he had moments before. This time, however, rather than asking for the White House, he asked to be patched through to the watch commander in the intelligence division at the U.S. Fleet Activities Naval Base in Yokosuka. There was no reason for the officer, probably no more than nineteen or twenty years old, to believe he wasn't authorized to make the call. After all, the XO himself had given the officer his personal clearance code to call the White House, and McDermott certainly hadn't had the time to tell anyone of their conversation.

Two minutes later Oleg Kraskin was on the line.

"I can't believe it's you," said the Russian. "Where are you?"

"I can't say," Marcus replied, "but it doesn't matter. We don't have much time and we've got a lot to do. Did they brief you on what happened in Tanch'ŏn?"

"Not in detail, but I got the gist. I'm so sorry about Nick and Commander Berenger and the others."

"Not your fault."

"I feel like it was."

"I know, but don't. Now focus. I need your help."

"Name it."

"Everyone's looking for the warheads," Marcus said. "But that's a mistake. We need to find Alireza al-Zanjani. We find him, we'll find the warheads."

"I agree, but what can I do?" Oleg asked. "They're not giving me access to any current intel. Mostly I'm confined to my barracks, guarded by military police."

"But you're at the intel headquarters now, aren't you?"

"Every morning they bring me over here for a few hours to debrief me on everything I know about my time in Moscow under Luganov."

"And you're not talking?"

"Of course I've been talking," Oleg said. "I'm exhausted from talking. They're recording everything. They have me review memos and notes I wrote when I worked for Luganov, and we go over the details point by point—*Who was in the meeting? What was the point of the meeting? What were the action items that came out of the meeting?* And so on. They've probably recorded twenty-four hours of my recollections so far. Who told you otherwise?"

"Never mind. Maybe I misunderstood. Anyway, are they talking to you about al-Zanjani?"

"No. I mean, his name has come up, but obviously I don't know where he is, so what could I say?"

Marcus quickly brought his Russian friend up to speed on the events of the last twenty-four hours and the thus-far fruitless hunt for the world's now most wanted man. Oleg made clear he sympathized but didn't see what he could possibly add.

"Listen, Oleg, you're the only person employed by U.S. intelligence who has ever met with Iran's Grand Ayatollah, and not once but multiple times. You've been to the home of Hossein Ansari. And you've spent hours with Yadollah Afshar. You know their people. You must have picked up clues about how they operate."

"Of course," Oleg said. "But you have to remember, al-Zanjani was a minor player for most of those years. He only became deputy director of the Revolutionary Guard Corps last spring. I've met him once. He came to Moscow with his boss, General Entezam. But my interaction with him was minimal."

"What did he come to Moscow for?"

"It was an advance trip. They were preparing for a summit that Luganov wanted to hold with the leaders of Iran, Turkey, Sudan, and several Central Asian countries."

"And?"

"And what? It got sidelined."

"Why?"

"What does it matter?"

"Just tell me."

"Well, the summit was supposed to take place in November, but the whole thing got set aside because Luganov was spending more and more time planning for his insane invasion of the Baltics."

"How long did Entezam and al-Zanjani stay in Moscow?"

"I don't know—a day or two, I guess."

"Would you have taken notes from Luganov's meetings with them?"

"Of course."

"Would those notes be included in all the material you gave us on the thumb drive?" Marcus pressed.

"I assume so—but why?" Oleg asked. "How does that help?"

"Can you access those files back at Langley right now?"

"Sure. Should I?"

"Yeah, do it now," Marcus said. "Do a search for everything in your files that mentions al-Zanjani."

Marcus glanced at his watch.

It was now 5:17 p.m. and he was certain the XO or an MP or two would burst in at any moment, cut the satellite link, and rip the headset off him. Yet he pressed on.

Oleg was scrolling through every document he had mentioning al-Zanjani and quoting a section here or there, but they were not hitting pay dirt. Most of the material involved a discussion of talking points for a summit that would never happen. Luganov had wanted to create a formal military and political alliance, a new Warsaw Pact of sorts, for the twenty-first century, incorporating the governments of Tehran, Ankara, Khartoum, and the others. General Entezam loved the idea. Al-Zanjani, so new in his post, hadn't said a thing.

The main elements of the conversation had revolved around how to persuade Turkey's leaders to leave NATO and join a new alliance headed by Moscow. Other points of interest involved whether the Sunni

Arab states—most notably the Saudis—could be lured away from the American camp and into the Russian-Iranian orbit. The notes indicated that Entezam had bristled at the notion of tempting Riyadh away from the West, preferring instead a Russian–Iranian joint military operation to grab the Arabian Peninsula and radically upend the balance of power in the Middle East. According to Oleg's notes, Luganov had actually laughed out loud at this suggestion, then turned the conversation to how to bolster the Palestinians and undermine the Israelis.

All of it was fascinating. None of it was actionable. The more Oleg cited memo titles, the more frustrated Marcus became. One memo included bios for every official Luganov planned to invite to the summit, both principals and their subordinates. Another included contact information for each potential invitee and their administrative staff. Others involved logistical details such as seating arrangements at the summit, hotel requirements for each delegation, vehicle needs, dietary restrictions, media planning, and security protocols.

"Luganov was involved in the planning of such minute details?" Marcus asked, as baffled as he was intrigued.

"Goodness, no," Oleg said. "He cared only about the policy aspects of the summit. After that, he stepped out, and the chief of staff and the chief of protocol took over. But Luganov assigned me to sit in on the meetings and take detailed notes of everything so we could discuss it properly later on."

Marcus glanced at his watch again, then leaned forward and closed his eyes. There was something there, something they were missing, but what was it?

"Pull up the memo on the security requirements," he said.

"All right, I've got it; what am I looking for?" Oleg asked.

"I'm not sure," Marcus admitted. "Look through it again. See if you find anything that could help us."

The line was quiet for over a minute. "I'm sorry," Oleg said finally. "There's really not much of substance here. They hadn't developed a detailed security plan. It's mostly a series of questions that the Iranians had for the FSB and that our chief of staff had for the IRGC and President Afshar's staff. But there aren't many answers, I'm afraid."

Marcus knew they were running out of time, but he refused to give up. Again, he pressed his eyes shut. *Bios. Hotels. Transportation. Dietary restrictions. Media . . .*

"Contacts," he said, his eyes still shut tight and his hands now massaging his temples.

"What?"

"You said there was a memo with some sort of contact information."

"Yeah, so?"

"Open that," Marcus ordered.

"Okay, done. Now what?" Oleg asked.

"What's in there?"

"Not much. It's a bunch of mobile phone numbers, office phone numbers, fax numbers, email addresses, mailing addresses, shipping addresses . . ."

"Is al-Zanjani listed?"

"Of course."

"And what do you have for him?"

Marcus could hear Oleg tapping keys as the Russian searched the document.

"A mobile number, two satellite account numbers, and three office numbers—his direct line, his chief of staff's direct line, and the one for his personal assistant."

"Is there an email address?"

"No."

"Why not?"

"I don't know."

"Does Entezam have an email address?"

"No."

"Do any of the Iranian officials?"

"Yes."

"Who?"

"Everyone who works in the office of the president has one. Those who work in the office of the Supreme Leader as well."

"But no one in the IRGC?"

"No," Oleg said. "What are you getting at?"

Marcus didn't answer the question. He didn't even know why he was asking. He was fishing and coming up empty, but something told him he was on the right track, that he was asking the right questions. Except that now he was stuck.

"Can you pull up a separate document without closing the document you're currently looking at?" he finally asked.

"Of course."

"Good—pull up all of your contact files."

"Okay . . ."

"Pull up al-Zanjani's contact listing."

"Just a second—okay, I've got it."

"Do you have an email address for him?"

"No."

Marcus stood up. He needed to move, but there was barely enough room in the cramped closet-like compartment to stand next to his chair, certainly not enough to stretch or pace.

"How many phone numbers do you have for al-Zanjani?"

"Why?"

"Just tell me," Marcus said, not wanting to be rude but increasingly certain they were going to be cut off at any second.

"Four."

"What are they?" Marcus pressed.

"You want the exact numbers?"

"No—what phones are they for?"

"Three are the direct lines to his office, his assistant, and his chief of staff."

"Are they the same as on the other document?"

Oleg took a moment to check and then confirmed that they were.

"What's the fourth number for?"

"It's his private, secure mobile number."

"And is that number the same as on the other document?"

"Hold on—yes, it is."

"Okay, give me that number," Marcus ordered, jotting it down on a notepad as Oleg dictated it, then reading it back to Oleg, just to be sure. "Now, you said there were two other numbers you had in the memo, right?"

"Right."

"Satellite accounts?"

"Correct."

"And those aren't in your contact file for al-Zanjani?"

"No, they're not."

"Okay," Marcus said. "Give them both to me."

Oleg complied. When he was finished, Marcus again read them back to Oleg to be absolutely certain he'd gotten them right. Oleg confirmed that he had.

"You did good, my friend," Marcus told him. "Now you need to log off that account and go back to your barracks immediately and wait there. Don't talk to anyone, if you can at all help it. And for heaven's sake, don't tell anyone that we spoke. Just sit tight, and I'll get back to you as soon as I can."

79

"Put me through to McDermott in the Sit Room," Marcus told the comms officer.

Thirty seconds later, however, he was informed the deputy NSA was still in the Oval with the president.

"Would you like to leave Colonel McDermott a message?" the watch officer asked.

"No," Marcus replied. "I'll call back later."

The moment the connection was terminated, he contemplated requesting to be patched through directly to the National Military Command Center at the Pentagon. But he knew he'd be denied.

Whom, then, should he call? There was no guarantee his strategy would prove useful. But Marcus was convinced it was worth trying. Should he take it to Sanchez? Marcus quickly ruled that out. The SEAL commander would likely discuss it with the captain and XO before taking it to PACOM, U.S. Pacific Command—or perhaps SOCOM, U.S.

Special Operations Command—and Marcus would likely wind up in trouble anyway for doing an end run around them all.

No, the only way for this to work was to take it to someone above Sanchez and the captain. Or perhaps someone outside the chain of command entirely.

"You're telling me we're nowhere with this?"

President Clarke's face was beet red.

McDermott had never seen him so angry.

"We're not nowhere," said Director Stephens. "I've spoken to my counterparts in two dozen countries stretching from South Korea to Western Europe. Everyone has offered their full cooperation. But unless we're prepared to stop and board all 240 North Korean ships—"

Clarke cut him off and turned to Defense Secretary Foster. "Is that possible?"

"Time-consuming, expensive, politically risky—the list goes on, Mr. President—but yes, it's possible," Foster replied. "Then again, what if the North Koreans have already transferred the warheads to ships flagged by other countries or are unloading them at a port somewhere in Asia and preparing to move them by air? If that's the case, we'll be spending time and political capital for nothing."

"What if we impose a blockade on Iran?" the president asked. "You know, shut everything down by air, sea, and land—inspect every ship, every plane, every truck."

"Well, sir, that would be a logistical nightmare," Foster protested. "But more important, a blockade is an act of war."

"Then call it a quarantine," Clarke said. "Call it whatever you want. Kennedy did it with Cuba in '62. He didn't worry about what he called it. He just made it happen, and it's a good thing he did."

General Evans now stepped in.

"He did, Mr. President, but that was an island—just forty-two thousand square miles and change, and just ninety miles off the coast of

Florida. The Islamic Republic of Iran is, what, about six hundred thousand square miles and half a world away?"

"*Enough excuses,*" the president demanded. "Tell me what we're going to do to stop the Iranians from getting these weapons."

"Sir, we're doing everything we can," Evans said calmly. "We'll brief you again in another few hours, and hopefully we'll have something by then."

McDermott watched Clarke's left hand ball up into a fist. The man was a volcano, roiling and about to blow. McDermott stiffened and braced for impact. And then the president asked two questions McDermott had not expected.

"Where's Ryker? What's he doing to help us?"

The professional staff assigned to the Senate Intelligence Committee worked out of offices located on the second floor of the Hart Building on Capitol Hill.

Normally, the place would be nearly empty and certainly quiet at 4:31 on a Saturday morning. But not today. Every staff member was in his or her office or cubicle, fielding calls from senators spread out all over the country asking for the latest updates. The networks were still running the story of a U.S. Navy raid on North Korean and Indonesian ships in international waters off the southern coast of Japan. The Pentagon wasn't commenting. Nor was the White House. But committee members were demanding answers.

"Miss Stewart, sorry to disturb," said one of the young military officers on the overnight shift after knocking on her door. "You have an urgent call in the SCIF."

Annie Stewart looked up from the piles of classified cables she'd been poring over and the boxes of half-eaten Chinese food taking up the rest of the space on her small desk. She was surprised to see the officer and doubly surprised by the summons to come to the Sensitive Compartmented Information Facility, especially at this hour. She'd already spoken twice to her boss, Senator Robert Dayton, who had called from his home in Des Moines. It couldn't be him, and he wouldn't be calling into the SCIF anyway.

Locking her sensitive papers in her safe and leaving her mobile phone behind since she wasn't permitted to bring it into the SCIF, Stewart followed the officer down the hallway. When they got to the vault-like door, Stewart typed her personal code into the keypad, waited for the LED lights to go green, and then entered the small, drab room as the officer shut and locked the door behind her.

"This is Annie Stewart," she said after putting on the headset and taking the system off mute. "With whom am I speaking?"

"Annie, this is Marcus Ryker."

Stewart was stunned to hear his voice. The last time she'd seen him was when she had accompanied the senator to Marcus's bedside at Walter Reed across the Potomac River in Bethesda. What in the world was he doing calling her and in the most secure fashion imaginable?

"Marcus," she said, her voice trembling slightly. "Are you okay?"

He ignored the question. "I need to tell you something, but it's highly classified and for the moment you can't tell anyone."

"Not even the senator?"

"No," Marcus said. "Let me explain."

Annie Stewart held one of the highest security clearances in the U.S. government and served as a senior foreign policy and intelligence advisor to the ranking member of the Senate Intelligence Committee. She doubted Marcus could tell her anything she didn't already know. She was wrong.

Marcus proceeded to give her a fairly detailed version of the week's events. For starters, he had not actually been ill. That was a cover story to throw off the Russians. He had been forced by the president into working for the Central Intelligence Agency and was currently deployed thirteen time zones ahead of her, in the East China Sea, with a team of Navy SEALs. In the last few minutes, he had come across intelligence that might possibly help locate Alireza al-Zanjani, but he was having trouble getting through to the president and the Joint Chiefs of Staff.

"Annie, I'm calling you because, to be honest, I don't know who else to ask," he said. "And I need a favor."

"Whatever you need," she replied. "You know you can trust me."

"I know, but . . ."

"What?"

"Well, it's . . ."

"It's what?"

"It's a pretty big favor."

"You need to get this intel about al-Zanjani directly to the president," Stewart said.

"Well, yeah."

"And you want me to call the president."

"No. Not exactly."

"You want me to call Senator Dayton, so he'll call the president."

"No, not that either."

"Then what?"

"You speak Russian, right?"

"Yes. What do you need, Marcus? Just tell me. I'll do it."

"All right, Annie, here's the thing—I need you to call Alireza al Zanjani."

80

Annie Stewart took an Uber back to her town house.

This was not a call she could make from a Senate office building.

In fact, the more she thought about it, this was a call that could very well cost her not only her security clearance but her job and perhaps even her government pension. Marcus was asking her to call a man listed first both on the FBI's most wanted list and on the State Department's watch list of foreign terrorists. Could she really do it? Was it worth it? What if she did, and al-Zanjani didn't answer? She would almost certainly still be visited by federal agents. There was even a possibility, though she considered it remote, that she could be convicted of a federal crime and spend time in prison. At the minimum, she could assure herself of weeks of intense interrogations.

As she stepped out of the car, walked up her rain-drenched steps, and unlocked her front door, Stewart made two decisions. The first was that *if* she made the call, she would *not* be doing it for Ryker. Second, *if* she made the call, she would do so only because she believed it was the right thing to do. She would do so because she believed it could help her country stop what was easily the most serious threat to U.S. national security in her lifetime.

She locked her front door behind her, threw her keys on the kitchen counter, switched on some lights, and ran upstairs to open the wall safe she kept in the linen closet in the second-floor hallway. Behind a 9mm Glock, several boxes of ammunition, a stash of cash, her passport, and several folders of important papers was a brand-new satellite phone she had bought a year or so earlier in case of emergency. It was still in its original box, unused. She pulled it out, skimmed the directions, and powered it up. This was it. She was about to cross the point of no return.

She pulled out the piece of notepaper upon which she'd scribbled down the three numbers and dialed. The first call went to al-Zanjani's mobile number. As she'd anticipated, it went directly to voice mail. Not speaking Farsi, she could not understand what the message was and hung up after she heard the beep.

The second number was for the first of the two satellite accounts Marcus had given her. This, too, went to voice mail after a similar message in Farsi.

Annie Stewart's hands trembled as she prepared to dial the last number. There was no reason to hesitate, and yet she did. It was 5:33 in the morning. She figured she had less than fifteen minutes before her entire street was awakened by more sirens and flashing lights than most of her neighbors had ever seen.

The question was whether the NSA and CIA had al-Zanjani's mobile and satellite numbers flagged in their databases. Marcus's operating theory was that there was a chance they didn't. The Kremlin had the numbers because they were allies with Tehran and had been hosting the senior leadership of the IRGC in Moscow. Oleg Kraskin had them because until just recently, he had been a senior advisor to the Russian president. Marcus now had them because he had successfully spirited Oleg Kraskin and all of his computer files out of Russia. Yes, Langley had the same memos that Oleg had read to Marcus over the phone. But had they read them all? Had they processed their significance? If so, alarm bells would already be going off.

Her heart pounding, she dialed the third number.

She had never spoken to a terrorist leader before and wasn't sure if she could do all that Marcus had asked. With each unanswered ring, her anxiety grew. The call was not going to voice mail. She wasn't getting a message, in Farsi or otherwise. Maybe this was really going to happen. After twenty rings, however, still no one had answered.

Stewart ended the call, disappointed. She checked her watch again. It was 5:38 and still no sirens. She peeked out the window of her guest bedroom. The street out front was empty and quiet. She walked over to her safe and closed it immediately. There would be no upside to having a loaded Glock nearby if the FBI really came bursting through her doors, even if she did hold a concealed carry permit from South Carolina and a gun ownership permit from D.C.

Forcing herself to take several deep breaths, she headed down to her kitchen. She set the phone on the table, filled a kettle with water, and turned on a gas burner. Then she took her favorite teacup and saucer off a shelf and set it on the counter, trying to figure out what to do next.

81

The satphone rang.

Having never heard its high-pitched tone before, Stewart was so startled she almost knocked over the teacup. The phone rang again, vibrating on the kitchen table. Stewart just stared at it. When it rang a third time, she finally reached for it. The incoming number was blocked. It might very well be the FBI. But it didn't matter. There was no turning back now.

"Hello?" she said in Russian.

"Who is this?" came the reply.

The language was Russian but the accent was unmistakably Persian. Stewart had to fight to maintain her composure.

"Yes, this is Natasha Kaminsky," she replied in Russian, following the precise script Marcus had laid out for her. "I am an aide to President Petrovsky. I am calling from the Kremlin and trying to reach General Entezam. Is this he?"

"No, I'm afraid you have the wrong number."

"That's impossible," Stewart said curtly. "This is the number the general told us to call in emergencies, if we could not reach him at any of his other numbers. To whom am I speaking?"

There was a lengthy pause, and then the words Stewart had never truly expected to hear.

"This is his deputy, Alireza al-Zanjani. What can I do for His Excellency President Petrovsky?"

"Is the general there?"

"I am very sorry. I regret to say that I am not with the general just now. May I have him call you back the moment he gets back to the office?"

"When do you expect him?"

"I am certain it won't be long."

"Very well," said Stewart, warming to her role. "Tell him His Excellency requests his presence and yours for an emergency meeting here at the Kremlin Monday morning at ten."

"Of course, Ms. . . . ."

"Kaminsky," she sniffed. "Natasha Kaminsky. I am His Excellency's new chief of staff and cannot stress how critical this meeting will be. Have I made myself clear?"

"You have, Ms. Kaminsky. I will inform the general of your call and tell him it is of the highest priority."

"I would expect no less," said Stewart. "And one more thing."

"Yes?"

She could hear the strain in al-Zanjani's voice. She knew he was desperate to get off the line, but Marcus had instructed her to keep him on for as long as possible. "Did you receive the package?"

"Uh . . . I . . . I'm sorry. . . . ."

"The documents we sent by diplomatic courier," Stewart lied. "The package should have arrived yesterday. His Excellency was expecting a reply, and I must say he was disappointed when there was no response."

Al-Zanjani clearly had no idea what to say. Stewart knew he wasn't in Tehran. Thus, he wasn't in the office. Thus, he had no idea whether a package of critical documents had arrived. Yet he was acting as if he were at the IRGC compound and ought to be fully apprised of anything that had just arrived from the Kremlin.

"Forgive me, I just got back to the office this afternoon after meetings outside of Tehran," al-Zanjani said, obviously improvising. "I am not familiar with the package, but I will check on it and make certain the general is prepared to discuss its contents with you when he returns your call and on Monday with President Petrovsky."

"Very well, I—"

Before Stewart could finish, the transmission was cut. She powered down the phone and collapsed in a chair, praying her trust in Marcus Ryker had been worth it.

Events were now set into motion on three continents.

From the moment Stewart had dialed the numbers, the calls—even though they had not been answered—were intercepted by a series of spy satellites operated by the National Security Agency and fed through ECHELON, the agency's monitoring and analysis protocol. ECHELON's supercomputers simultaneously routed high-priority alerts to the two NSA ground stations closest to where the calls had originated and been received. This meant that within two minutes of interception, an analyst at NSA's global headquarters in Fort Meade, Maryland, as well as one at Misawa Air Base in northern Japan, were on the case.

The call to the mobile phone triggered the most attention. The number was, in fact, in the NSA's database and tagged to Alireza al-Zanjani. On a normal day, the thirty-six-year-old senior analyst in Fort Meade might have let the team in Japan figure out the significance of the call while she handled more urgent matters. But this was no normal day.

The analyst quickly informed her counterpart at Misawa that she would take the lead on running this case to ground. Then she speed-dialed her supervisor and informed him that someone in the D.C. area had just used a satphone to call a number connected to one of the world's most notorious terrorists. Though the call had not been answered, the caller had tried two other numbers in rapid succession. The bad news, she explained, was that these two numbers were not known to the NSA. The good news was that the third number had called back, and they had a clear recording of a two-minute-and-twelve-second conversation. It was all in Russian, and though the analyst admitted she didn't speak Russian, she had heard al-Zanjani's name mentioned. She therefore requested permission to forward the recording to the Directorate of Analysis in Langley for an immediate transcription, translation into English, and voiceprint analysis.

"Absolutely—do it now," said the supervisor, who then asked for the precise coordinates of the call's origins and destinations.

The analyst not only sent them by secure server but uploaded the coordinates into a GPS mapping system that allowed them to see on their monitors the two locations displayed in graphic form.

The supervisor was struck by the fact that the final call had origi-nated in the middle of the East China Sea, from a ship located about two hundred kilometers east of Shanghai. It was not proof positive, but the circumstantial evidence that the calls had been made to and from al-Zanjani was growing. But what chilled him to his core was that whoever was trying to reach the Iranian terrorist had made the calls just blocks from the U.S. Capitol.

"Who owns this satellite account?" the supervisor asked.

The analyst entered several commands into her keyboard.

"Let's see," she said. "The phone was purchased almost eighteen months ago by someone named Anne Stewart—she used a Visa card, bought it through Amazon, and—"

She abruptly stopped talking in midsentence.

"What is it?"

"I don't believe this," the analyst said.

"What?"

"She works for the government."

"Which government?"

"*Ours*—she works for a member of the Senate Intelligence Committee."

"I need an address—now."

"Hold on—okay, it's coming up. Got it. Four one seven G Street, Northeast, Unit 3."

The supervisor immediately hung up on her and speed-dialed the Counterintelligence Division of the FBI.

82

CIA HEADQUARTERS, LANGLEY, VIRGINIA

Stephens was speaking with China's defense minister when the call came in.

His executive assistant knocked once, quietly entered the director's seventh-floor corner office, and slipped a hastily scribbled note under his nose that read, *Urgent—line 2.* She knew he hated to be interrupted, but the look on her face told him how serious this had to be, so Stephens excused himself and got off the line, promising to call the minister back in a few minutes. Then he punched the blinking line on his desk console and heard the somber voice of Martha Dell, his deputy director for intelligence.

The DDI quickly explained everything the NSA and FBI and the CIA itself had learned over the past thirty-five minutes—the intercepts, the arrest of Annie Stewart, and her elaborate story of how Marcus Ryker had enlisted her to smoke out al-Zanjani. Stephens was hearing all of it for the first time, and he was stunned.

"Ryker?" he barked. "How would he know al-Zanjani's numbers if we didn't?"

"He says he got the numbers from the Raven."

"You spoke to him?"

"I just got off the phone with him. He's in the comms room on the USS *Abraham Lincoln*."

"Does his story check out?"

"It does," said the DDI. "All of it."

"What about the girl?"

"Stewart?"

"Yeah—do you believe her?"

"I do."

"There's no chance she's working for a foreign intelligence service?"

"Well, sir, I'd suggest our friends at the bureau hold her for a while longer and make absolutely certain. But my guess is she'll come out clean."

"What about the voiceprint analysis?" Stephens asked.

"My guys just finished it."

"And?"

"It's him," the DDI said. "It's al-Zanjani."

"They're positive?"

"The confidence level came in at 92.167 percent—that's as close to certainty as we're going to get."

"And what do we know about the ship the call came from?"

"It's an oil tanker."

"Not a container ship."

"No, sir."

"North Korean?"

"Actually, sir, it's under a Saudi flag."

"That's impossible," said Stephens. "There's no way the Saudis are helping Iran."

"I agree, but you should call Prince Abdullah."

"I will," Stephens said. "But first get me Foster at the NMCC. Then call Evans and McDermott. Let them know what's going on. And set up an emergency meeting of the NSC. We need to brief the president."

No one had said a word.

Not the captain. Not the XO. Not Sanchez or anyone on his team.

Yet as Marcus came up on deck of the USS *Abraham Lincoln* and felt the Pacific breezes in his face and braced himself against the deafening roar of F/A-18 fighter jets streaking off into the morning sky, he didn't need to be told. It was obvious the supercarrier was changing direction. No longer were they heading north. They and the convoy behind them were turning west.

President Clarke entered the Situation Room at precisely 7:30 a.m.

All the members of the National Security Council stood at attention, then took their seats when Clarke sat.

"I understand you guys have good news," the commander in chief began.

"Yes, sir—the last couple of hours have involved several extraordinary breakthroughs," National Security Advisor Barry Evans said as he began the briefing. "The short version is that the CIA and NSA have located Alireza al-Zanjani. Secretary Foster has ordered a carrier strike force to embark on a high-speed race across the East China Sea to intercept him and the warheads we believe are with him. But there are new troubling matters as well."

Evans summarized the events that had precipitated this meeting as McDermott passed out folders containing English translations of the phone call between Stewart and al-Zanjani, a timeline of events, and transcripts of interviews with Stewart and Ryker explaining their roles.

Next, Director Stephens clarified that he had spoken with Prince Abdullah bin Rashid, the Saudi intelligence chief, and confirmed that the oil tanker al-Zanjani was using was not owned or operated by any Saudi company. It was, in fact, a North Korean tanker that had been repainted and reflagged in an attempt to throw the U.S. off the trail. The Saudis had provided additional confirmation that all three phone numbers were in their databases as belonging either to al-Zanjani or to his predecessor in the Revolutionary Guard Corps.

The president was pleased and said so, but Stephens was not finished.

"Sir, I'm afraid I also just got off the phone with Mossad director Asher Gilad," he continued. "They have just learned from a highly trusted source that Grand Ayatollah Hossein Ansari is dying. Apparently he has stage-four pancreatic cancer and is not expected to live more than two to six months."

"They're absolutely certain?" Clarke asked.

"They are, Mr. President. They've even obtained a scan of the ayatollah's medical records, current as of ten days ago. Colonel McDermott is handing out numbered copies, though I will need each of those back when this meeting is over."

Everyone now studied the document with its accompanying English translation.

"Well, good riddance," the president quipped. "Couldn't happen to a nicer guy."

"Sir, the Israelis are quite concerned."

"What for?" Clarke asked. "Now they don't need to take him out themselves."

"Gilad said he'd just come from a meeting with the prime minister and the Security Cabinet. The assessment in Jerusalem is that the ayatollah is ready to gamble big because he has nothing to lose."

"So Gilad thinks that's why the ayatollah has gone all in, buying nukes from Pyongyang."

"Yes, sir. Furthermore, they believe Ansari has ordered the IRGC to improve the range and accuracy of their missiles so that they can reach New York and Washington by the end of this year or early next. As soon as the warheads arrive on Iranian soil, the Israelis believe they will be fitted into the nose cones of the missiles and readied for use in time for the ayatollah to see his handiwork before he passes from this world."

"Are the Israelis right?" Clarke asked, a scowl spreading across his face. "Is that a reasonable assessment of the data?"

"It could certainly explain why Tehran tried to purchase warheads from the Pakistanis earlier this year," Stephens said. "It would also explain why the ayatollah is taking such enormous risks to buy these warheads from the North Koreans right now."

83

The room fell silent.

Everyone was processing the magnitude of what the CIA director had just told them. Finally Evans turned the briefing over to the defense secretary.

"Mr. President, the challenge we're facing right now is one of time," Foster began. "The tanker al-Zanjani and his men are using appears to be headed to the port of Shanghai. Given the distances involved, we estimate it will take our carrier group at least four hours to catch up with him, and by that time it will be too late. Unless he alters course, al-Zanjani will enter Chinese territorial waters in a little over three and a half hours."

"Then we need to take that ship before it gets to China," said the president. "How do we do that?"

The chairman of the Joint Chiefs took that one. "Mr. President, we have more than two hundred Navy SEAL operators pre-positioned on the *Abraham Lincoln*. At your command, we can load them up on a fleet of HH-60H Seahawk helicopters, reach that tanker in thirty minutes, and take it in less than ten."

"Are your men ready, Mr. Chairman?"

"Always, Mr. President."

"What time is it there?" Clarke asked.

"The East China Sea is thirteen hours ahead of Eastern time," the chairman replied. "That means it is coming up on nine o'clock at night. Cloud cover is heavy, so there's no moonlight. There's a storm coming in from the north. But if we go soon, I think we should be okay. We'll have the element of surprise. But there is a complication you need to consider, sir."

"What's that?"

"Two days ago, U.S. military personnel boarded a North Korean vessel in international waters," the chairman noted. "Now we're talking about doing it again, on a much larger scale. Mr. President, as you'll recall, the North Koreans recently formed a new strategic alliance with Moscow. This is a full-blown mutual defense pact. I brought translated copies if any of you would like to read it, but the short version is this: any attack against the Democratic People's Republic of Korea will be regarded as an attack against the Russian Federation and will be met with the full retaliatory force of the Russian military. There's little credibility to the notion that the Dear Leader has ever feared an offensive attack from South Korea, Japan, or any of the regional neighbors. When he signed this treaty with Moscow, he was specifically thinking of how best to protect himself from an offensive assault by the United States military. Boarding one commercial ship with no loss of life on either side is one thing. Dropping two hundred SEALs on a second ship is another, especially when we know al-Zanjani is on board. We won't get away without firing a shot this time."

"What are you saying, Mr. Chairman—that we should not stop a ship carrying nuclear weapons targeted at us?" Clarke demanded, incredulous.

"Sir, I'm simply reminding us all that if and when we take down that oil tanker, we very well could be triggering a circumstance that could lead us into direct military conflict with Russia."

The president leaned back in his seat to take that thought in.

"Given the fact that we just narrowly avoided a war with the Russians," the chairman continued, "I thought it was worth noting."

Clarke looked to Stephens, who said nothing. Nor did Evans or the other officials around the table.

McDermott waited several moments, certain someone would weigh in. When they didn't, he cleared his throat. "Sir, may I?" he asked the president.

Clarke gave him the floor.

"Sir, the chairman is absolutely right to remind us of this new treaty and its potential implications. But let us remember several other facts. First, it's a very new treaty. Unused. Untested. And negotiated by a man who isn't even alive anymore. This treaty was President Luganov's baby, and I'm not sure we can assume President Petrovsky is prepared to honor it, especially if you inform him that the North Koreans were selling Russian weapons to Iran—weapons that I'm not convinced Petrovsky even knew were transferred to Pyongyang in the first place. You'll recall that according to the Raven, Luganov kept Petrovsky completely in the dark about both the treaty and the warhead transfer."

"Good point, Colonel," Clarke said. "Go on."

"My second point is that the North Koreans could hardly invoke their treaty with Russia since they don't even claim this ship as their own."

"Come again?"

"The ship is flagged as a Saudi oil tanker," McDermott noted. "So if we seized it, wouldn't our issue be with Riyadh, not Pyongyang?"

At this, Clarke smiled. "Quite right."

"Third, Mr. President, it's highly unlikely Petrovsky would use our seizure of what is effectively an Iranian-crewed ship transporting Iranian-purchased nuclear warheads to Iranian shores as a pretext to launch World War III," McDermott concluded. "The man just backed down from an imminent invasion of three NATO countries in Europe. He's dealing with the assassinations of three top Russian leaders. He's trying to consolidate his power in the Kremlin. And for the time being, anyway, we seem to have convinced him that Marcus Ryker had nothing to do with the assassinations and that we have no connection whatsoever to Oleg Kraskin. So do we really believe he's going to put all the rest of his chips on this Persian gamble?"

Clarke suddenly stood. Everyone else in the room followed suit.

"Let him try," said the president. "The people of the United States, and our most faithful and trusted allies in the Middle East, are facing an extraordinary and unprecedented threat by the mullahs in Tehran. We are not going to ignore it. We are going to fulfill our constitutional responsibilities and defend ourselves, come what may. Mr. Secretary, Mr. Chairman, by the power vested in me as commander in chief, I hereby authorize you to use all means necessary to intercept this oil tanker, seize however many warheads they have on board, and bring those warheads safely back to the U.S. for inspection and dismantlement. What's more, I want you to capture Alireza al-Zanjani and take him into custody—alive and, if possible, unharmed."

Foster looked as perplexed as McDermott felt. They all did.

"Mr. President?"

"Don't get me wrong," Clarke continued. "I want al-Zanjani treated as an enemy combatant, not a criminal. And believe me, gentlemen, I would love nothing more than to order his execution. Give me that chance. I implore you. But first things first. I want him brought to Gitmo. I want him interrogated using the harshest methods permissible under the Geneva Convention. I want to know everything he knows. What precisely is the state of the ayatollah's health? And what exactly is the ayatollah's plan to rain fire and fury on the people of the United States? After all, what was it that Sun Tzu wrote? 'The art of war teaches us to rely not on the likelihood of the enemy's not coming, but on our own readiness to receive him; not on the chance of his not attacking, but rather on the fact that we have made our position unassailable'?"

McDermott could see the discomfort in the eyes of the SecDef and the chairman. The president had just significantly complicated the mission. But they assured the commander in chief they would do their best to carry out his wishes.

"I know you will," said the president. "Now, let's say a prayer that God will show favor to our forces tonight."

84

"You don't have to do this, Ryker."

Marcus was tying the laces of his maritime assault boots when he looked up to find Sanchez standing in the doorway.

"You've already done enough," said the SEAL Team Six commander. "Why don't you sit this one out? When we get back, I promise to introduce you to your pal al-Zanjani. Then we'll celebrate with a cold beer."

"Forget it, sir," Marcus replied. "I don't want a freebie. I'm going to earn that beer."

"You sure?"

"Oh yeah."

"Fine—finish gearing up and meet us upstairs in two. The choppers are already spooling up for launch. You're in the lead bird, the seat right behind mine."

"Understood, sir."

Sanchez headed off down the corridor and Marcus went over everything one more time. Helmet, protective goggles, and NVGs—*check*. Radio gear and water—*check*. Flak jacket fitted with steel plates front and back—*check*. Extra magazines and fragmentation grenades—*check*. Sig Sauer pistol in its holster, MK-3 Navy knife in its sheath—*check*. Gloves and kneepads—*check*. And his MP7, locked and loaded—*check*.

The first Seahawk lifted off the deck just after 11 p.m. local time.

Flying without lights, Sanchez, Marcus, eight more SEALs, and the crew of four—including two machine gunners, one at each door—banked left and headed east-northeast at maximum power. Nine additional Seahawks carrying ten operators each followed close behind.

No one was talking. It would have been impossible to hear one another over the roar of the two 1,900 horsepower GE engines and the whipping winds from the two open side doors. Marcus closed his eyes and prayed for the success of the operation and the safety of his teammates. He wasn't anxious. He wasn't scared. His anger over the death of Vinetti had tempered, and a counterintuitive sense of calm came over him.

They'd all been well fed, well equipped, and well briefed. They had spent the last hour studying every nook and cranny of the tanker they were about to seize. They had meticulously reviewed what each man would be responsible for when they landed. They'd memorized pictures of al-Zanjani, read his file, and learned about as much as there was to know about him, from the four-inch scar running down the left side of his face and the nine-inch scar down the back of his right leg, to the fact that he was missing the thumb and forefinger on his left hand, the result of a mishap with a grenade more than a decade ago.

The night sky was spectacular. They'd been told there were thick clouds and heavy winds where they were headed, even a rather serious storm descending from the Yellow Sea between China and the Korean Peninsula. But where they were flying just then there were no clouds to be seen, no lights from any ship, just a million dazzling stars spread like diamonds on a black velvet canvas.

The darker the night, the brighter the stars;
The deeper the grief, the closer is God.

The words of the Russian poem, often attributed to Dostoyevsky, bubbled up from his subconscious. How true they had been in his own life, Marcus thought. After the deaths of Elena and Lars, he had hit rock bottom, yet strangely enough—even with all that had happened in recent weeks—he could feel himself resurfacing, and for this he was grateful. Yes, he thought, that was the word. He wasn't happy. Not yet. He wasn't peaceful, not entirely. But he was grateful for his life and the evidence of God's grace, and for now that was enough.

Bill McDermott took his seat in the Situation Room.

He was not there to brief, just to watch, and he stared as a technician made last-minute adjustments to a control panel. A moment later, the lights had dimmed and they were receiving live video, audio, and data feeds straight from the NMCC.

"Two minutes," said the chairman of the Joint Chiefs.

McDermott tensed. His mouth was bone-dry. His hands were clammy. Self-conscious, he wiped them on his trousers and kept them under the conference table. His eyes scanned the incoming data and video feeds. He found himself riveted on one of the small flat screens on the far wall. It displayed a live radar feed coming from the E-2 Hawkeye tactical airborne early warning aircraft operating in the theater far above the Seahawks. He could see the green blips representing the American choppers fanning out in multiple directions. They were preparing for their final assault. But all McDermott could think about was how Marcus Ryker was on the lead bird.

They'd certainly had their differences. McDermott was still not completely convinced Ryker shouldn't have been hauled in and tried for treason, not granted a presidential pardon. But at this point it was impossible not to acknowledge, at least to himself, how much the country owed Ryker. The man had been willing to take enormous risks—first to prevent war in Europe, now to prevent war in the Middle East. Yet McDermott had second-guessed him every step of the way.

The price had been steep. Nick Vinetti was dead. His wife, Claire, was now a widow. Pete Hwang had almost been killed and was out of commission, recovering in a field hospital in Okinawa. Ryker was practically alone in the world. His wife was dead. His son was dead. The man himself had almost died time and time again over the past month. Yet he refused to give up, even when McDermott had given up on him.

McDermott was not a particularly religious man, though he had been an altar boy growing up. Yet right there in the Situation Room, he found himself discreetly crossing himself and saying a prayer for his friend and all the men heading into the night.

85

Twenty miles from their drop zone, a C-17 emerged from the darkness.

The American military transport plane had been dispatched from Okinawa. It now dropped to five thousand feet and opened its massive rear cargo ramp. Marcus switched on his night vision goggles just in time to see two thirty-six-foot RHIBs—rigid-hulled inflatable boats— slip out the back.

The moment their parachutes opened—four per boat—Marcus turned to his left and watched Donny Callaghan and his Red Team jump from a nearby chopper. They pulled their chutes open almost immediately and quickly vanished in the utter darkness. Marcus turned off his night vision goggles. There was no way he'd be able to see anything in these conditions from this altitude. He closed his eyes and imagined the men hitting the waters of the East China Sea. Minutes later, Callaghan radioed back to say they were all on board the speedboats and racing for the target.

Unlike the Indonesian ship they'd boarded, this tanker was not idling. Far from it. The vessel was moving at close to twenty-four knots, almost twenty-seven miles per hour. Marcus continued listening to the radio traffic and pictured Callaghan and his team attaching ladders to the sides of the ship and scaling them with breathtaking rapidity. They would not be able to attach mines to the propeller, of course, as it was churning at full speed. But eventually the call they'd been waiting for finally came. Callaghan confirmed they'd reached and secured the engine room and cut the ship's power, encountering no resistance.

What did that mean? wondered Marcus. No resistance? How was that possible? Did they have the wrong ship again, or were they being lured into a trap?

With the ship now dark and dead in the water, the full assault could begin. Sanchez ordered the pilots to pick up the pace. Soon the Seahawk moved into a hovering position barely fifty feet over a helicopter landing zone painted like a red bull's-eye on the tanker's port bow.

"*Go, go, go,*" Sanchez shouted, slapping his men on the back as they began fast-roping to the deck.

Marcus was the last in line, aside from Sanchez himself. When it was his turn, he moved to the door and heard gunfire erupt and saw tracer rounds streaking through the air. Rounds began hitting the side of the chopper. It was the right ship. There was no doubt about that now.

The gunner behind them returned fire with his .50-caliber mounted machine gun. Sanchez slapped Marcus on the back and screamed at him to get moving.

It had been years since he'd done this in the Corps, but muscle memory and a healthy shot of adrenaline kicked in. Marcus grabbed the rope and dropped through the darkness. The moment his feet hit the deck, he raised his MP7A1 and moved to his right. There was a gap between two massive steel pipes on the starboard side, where he took cover and tried to get his bearings as the deck lurched from side to side in the roiling waves.

The ship's enormous size was daunting. It spanned the length of three football fields from bow to stern and was sixty meters wide. Two sets of large black metal pipelines—elevated by rusty steel columns and girders—ran down the center, nearly the full length of the deck. Toward the front of the ship was a steel mast sprouting all manner of radio antennas and deck lights. Nearby were two windlasses, the mechanisms responsible for raising and lowering the massive anchor chains. Near the ship's center were two steel cranes, port and starboard, capable of lifting the heavy hoses used to load and unload oil, as well as move containers of supplies and other heavy equipment.

Toward the rear of the ship stood a five-story superstructure topped with radar masts and more radio antennas. Behind that was the engine housing with its massive smokestack that had been billowing black acrid filth until the SEALs had arrived and shut the engines down. There were also four lifeboats, two on each side, all once painted orange, though most of that had chipped off or faded with time. Around the edges of the ship were mooring lines, towropes, bollards, winches, and an array of forklifts and other equipment lashed to the decks with chains.

And now it began to rain. Hard. Marcus could see flashes of lightning to the north. The storm they'd been told would hold off for a few more hours had not only arrived, it was gaining strength. A Saudi flag mounted on a steel pole near the bow was whipping something fierce. In such rapidly deteriorating conditions, it was no surprise that there were no guards patrolling the deck. The gunfire, instead, was coming from the now-darkened windows of the superstructure.

As soon as Sanchez dropped to the deck, he made his way to Marcus's side. Then their chopper roared off, disappearing into the night, quickly replaced by another.

"Follow me!" Sanchez shouted, unleashing a burst of covering fire before sprinting for the pipelines running down the center of the ship, heading toward the stern.

Though rounds were pinging all around him, Marcus popped his head around the corner and fired two long bursts—one at the muzzle flashes coming from the second floor of the superstructure, the other at flashes coming from the third floor. Then he raced to catch up with Sanchez.

Just then, a massive explosion shook the giant ship. An enormous fireball lit up the night sky. The force of the blast knocked both Sanchez and Marcus off their feet. Sanchez recovered and scrambled for cover behind one of the steel cranes. Marcus did the same, a tick slower, turning just in time to see one of the choppers falling from the sky and engulfing the deck in flames.

Sanchez was yelling something. Marcus couldn't hear him over the roar of the fire, the .50-caliber machine guns being fired from the remaining choppers, and the screams of the SEALs the burning Seahawk had landed on. He assumed someone had just fired an RPG but could see no contrail. He also assumed Sanchez would head back to the crash to rescue whatever survivors they could find. Yet Sanchez instead furiously motioned Marcus to follow him in the other direction.

Confused, Marcus nevertheless complied. Sanchez was making for the superstructure, and nothing but death was going to stop him. Marcus saw the commander pivot around the left side of the crane. The man fired two long bursts, ejected his spent magazine, reloaded, and then doubled back around the right side and disappeared. Everything in Marcus wanted to go the other direction, to fight his way back to the crash. But that was not his call.

During their briefings, Sanchez had explained Blue Team's mission clearly: secure every level of the superstructure, from the galley and cafeteria to the crew's bunks and radio room to the all-important pilothouse on the bridge. Nothing else mattered until that was done. Others would have to care for the wounded. It was not Marcus's right to second-guess his commander. So he followed suit, firing two more bursts to the left, reloading, and rolling right.

86

Marcus almost tripped over Sanchez's body.

For a split second, he froze, unable and unwilling to comprehend the sight before him. It simply wasn't possible. There was no way Sanchez could have been taken out already. They'd just landed. They'd just—

Marcus saw movement to his right, about thirty yards away. Someone was emerging from a hatch mid-deck. He immediately pivoted and opened fire. The tango's head exploded, and his body snapped back into the hatch and dropped out of sight. Instantly Marcus saw more muzzle flashes, this time from the fourth floor of the superstructure. Fifty-caliber rounds were ripping up the deck all around him. To press forward was suicide, so Marcus beat a hasty retreat behind the crane. It was not much cover, but it would have to do. He tried to make himself as small a target as possible and radioed for help.

As he did, he looked toward the front of the ship. It was an incomprehensible sight. To his left was the raging inferno of the downed

Seahawk. To his right, the deck was strewn with bodies. Some were moving. Most were not. And that's when it occurred to Marcus that he might have been the only person from his chopper who had not been wounded or killed.

Suddenly he heard the hiss of a rocket-propelled grenade streaking across the sky. It came from behind him, then zoomed over his head. Transfixed, he followed its path and watched as one of the pilots turned his bird sharply. Marcus breathed a sigh of relief as the RPG disappeared into the night and fell harmlessly into the sea.

Then came a second rocket and a third. This time the pilot had no chance. Both RPGs hit their target. The Seahawk—not a hundred feet off the deck and in the process of offloading its men—burst into flames. Half of it came crashing onto the front-right section of the ship's bow. The tail section plunged into the sea. Then came additional explosions as the ordnance on board cooked off one by one.

Marcus could feel the searing heat. The repeated booms knocked him off balance. He momentarily dropped his weapon as he instinctively covered his head and face with his arms. When he looked back up, the apocalyptic scene had grown much worse. The rest of the choppers were backing away. They were still firing at the bridge, and not just with .50-caliber machine guns but with air-to-ground Hellfire missiles. But there was no question they were retreating.

Who could blame them? There was no longer any safe place to land. But what exactly did that mean for the rest of the operation?

Marcus was on his stomach now, flattened on the lurching, blazing deck. He reached for his MP7 and pulled it close. Then he turned and saw the flaming wreckage of the bridge. The Hellfire missiles had taken out the fourth and fifth stories. They were gone. Completely gone. The second and third stories were consumed in fire and billowing black smoke. He could barely believe what he was seeing. None of this had been part of the plan. The operating assumption was that al-Zanjani would be on the bridge, likely on the fifth level. Weren't they supposed to take him alive? Hadn't that been the president's explicit order?

His mind reeled. He could tell people were talking over the radio, but it was impossible to hear clearly over the cacophony around him. Then he remembered the warheads. They still had to be secured and safely removed from the tanker. That meant clearing the lower decks of every remaining member of the Revolutionary Guards. But who was going to do it? Looking back, Marcus could see only three SEALs on their feet, pulling their wounded comrades away from the flames.

Still, there was Callaghan and Red Team, Marcus thought. They were already down below, having taken the engine room. He had to link up with them and help them complete the mission before this ship sank to the bottom of the East China Sea. There was no question in Marcus's mind the tanker was going down. That was an absolute certainty. There was no putting out the fires raging in the destroyed superstructure and on the deck. This was an oil tanker. It was only a matter of time before the flames reached some crucial spot and caused a massive explosion that would blow out the hull. The only question was how long they still had.

For the moment, no one was shooting. If he was going to make a break for it, Marcus thought, the time was now. Through the smoke, he could see a steel door on the left side of the first floor of the superstructure. Remembering the briefing and the satellite photos they'd been shown, he was confident that particular hatch led to a stairwell that would take him to the ship's lower levels. This became his new target.

Scrambling to his feet, Marcus decided to use the cover of the pipes running down the center of the deck. He rechecked his weapon to make sure it hadn't jammed, then sprinted forward. He'd made it about fifty yards without getting killed when he saw another hatch open and two tangos climb out. Faster on the draw, they began shooting first, but Marcus immediately returned fire. Two short bursts, then two more. Both men dropped to the rain-swept deck. Marcus kept sprinting and firing until he was convinced they were never going to rise again.

Reloading on the run, Marcus saw movement in one of the blown-out first-floor windows. Whoever it was began firing at him. He couldn't see a face, only the muzzle flashes. But he didn't dare stop. He couldn't. There was no place to hide and precious little time until whatever oil was stored in the tanks below him was going to blow. He raised his MP7 and fired more short bursts. Five rounds. Then another five. Then a third. He didn't expect to kill whoever was in there. He just needed to keep them pinned down for another twenty seconds until he reached his target.

It almost worked.

McDermott sat spellbound by the ghastly images.

The attack was not going as planned. It had become a horror show, and now, as he watched real-time drone coverage, he saw Ryker racing for cover. Just then, he also saw two shadows emerge from the port side door of the bridge. They raised their weapons and McDermott saw two muzzle flashes.

He watched helplessly as Ryker spun around and went sprawling across the deck. He'd been hit. That much was clear. How badly, neither McDermott nor anyone around him could say. But they watched in shock as the two figures moved across their screen from right to left. They were closing in on Ryker, who had dropped his weapon and was crawling to get it back. One of the figures raised his own weapon. He was aiming, about to fire. McDermott couldn't bear to watch yet couldn't turn away.

He saw muzzle flashes from the left side of the screen. One of the tangos dropped, followed in quick succession by the other. They were down but still moving. But after two more flashes they moved no more. McDermott then saw a figure emerge out of the metal door Ryker had been approaching, followed by another figure, and together they pulled Ryker to his feet.

87

"Ryker—you okay?" someone shouted as he grabbed Marcus's hand.

It was Callaghan, flanked by another SEAL, one of the medics. Marcus remembered him being introduced as Warner.

"Yeah, I'm fine," Marcus shouted back over the roar of the flames, still trying to catch his breath. "I was just coming to find you guys."

"Consider us found."

"I owe you," Marcus added, staring at the bullet-riddled bodies beside him.

"No problem. You sure you're good? Looks like you got clipped pretty hard."

"Both rounds hit my flak jacket," Marcus replied. "Knocked the wind out of me, but yeah, I'm good."

"What a mess out here."

"I'll say."

"Where's Sanchez? Can't get him on the radio."

"He's gone."

"What do you mean, gone?"

"Dead."

"How?"

"I think a sniper took him out."

"Where's the rest of Blue Team?"

"Haven't seen any of them. They may all be dead."

"You're the only one who survived?"

"I saw three guys from another squad. They were looking for wounded from the first crashed chopper. I wanted to help them. But they were at least a hundred yards away, and Sanchez insisted we make for the bridge. That's when he got hit. I called in some help against the fifties they were using from the bridge. Can't say I expected them to use Hellfires."

"Me neither," Callaghan said. "The explosions were so massive, Warner and I had to come up and see what in the world was going on, especially when we couldn't get anyone on the radios." He nodded toward the flaming wreckage of the superstructure. "Anyone still in there?"

"Can't say," Marcus said. "I just took out one, but there could be more."

"Clear it, both of you; then meet me back here," Callaghan ordered. "I need to get someone on the horn and let them know exactly what's going on."

Callaghan pulled out a satphone and found a covered position under one of the lifeboats. Marcus hoisted his weapon and moved to a weathertight door a few yards away from the stairway door Callaghan and Warner had emerged from. Warner was right behind him. When they'd both put on their NVGs, Marcus yanked open the heavy steel door just enough for Warner to toss in a grenade, then closed it rapidly and ducked down.

The moment they heard the detonation, Marcus pulled the door open again and sprayed the room with a full magazine. Warner stepped inside, scanning for targets as Marcus reloaded and came in behind him. Warner moved right. Marcus moved to the left, sweeping his MP7A1 from side to side, covering the other half of the spacious but filthy cafeteria.

"Clear!" Warner shouted.

Marcus cautiously entered the galley, checking every crevice where a man could be hiding, including the walk-in refrigerator. *"Clear!"* he finally shouted, reminding himself to keep taking deep breaths.

Warner moved from the cafeteria into the lounge and then the incinerator room. When he had cleared both, they reconvened in a small hallway and went to the stairwell leading to the second floor. As best they could figure, this was where the crew's sleeping quarters were located.

Marcus headed up first. Warner followed but climbed the stairs backward, making certain no one surprised them from behind. Not only was the stairwell pitch-black, it was rapidly filling with smoke. And it was ghastly hot. Quite apart from the driving rains outside, Marcus could feel his whole body now dripping with sweat.

When he reached the landing, Marcus pressed himself flat against the wall, then glanced through the smudged window in the door to see if anyone was waiting for them in the hallway on the other side. Someone was. The shooting began immediately. Marcus pulled back into the safety of the landing as round after round splintered the wooden door. Then he heard something metal rolling down the hall-way toward them.

"Grenade!"

Even as he was yelling this, Marcus realized there was not going to be time to take proper cover. The grenade was going to blow the door to smithereens, and the force of the blast was going to be exponentially magnified inside the steel stairwell. Rather than retreat, Marcus found himself doing the exact opposite. He burst through the door, pressed the trigger of his submachine gun to give himself a bit of covering fire, and kicked the grenade back down the hallway. The moment he did, he saw the eyes of his attacker grow wide. He was crouched in a doorway and clearly had not anticipated Marcus's move. As if in slow motion, both men watched the grenade ricochet off the walls, reach the far end of the hallway, and detonate. The man was dead before his decapitated body hit the floor.

Almost simultaneously, Marcus heard Warner open fire at someone either trying to enter the stairwell or moving through the galley downstairs. Whoever it was returned fire. Tempted though he was to look back, Marcus couldn't assume he was alone. Nor could he wait for Warner to help him clear the crew's quarters. There simply wasn't time. The fires above them were raging. So were the fires on the deck. It couldn't be long before the oil would catch fire and blow. What's more, he knew there must be an unrelenting gun battle under way belowdecks as the remnants of Red Team engaged the Revolutionary Guards. Even if the heat from the fires wasn't yet enough to set off the oil reserves, one stray bullet and they were all goners.

Marcus pivoted into the first room on his left. He found a row of bunk beds on each side of the room and a smoking .50-caliber Gatling-type gun in the center of the room mounted on a tripod facing out of the blown-out window—and hundreds if not thousands of spent shell casings littered across the floor. Someone had been there not minutes before. Perhaps it had been the man he'd just killed. Regardless, the room was empty now and glowed red and orange from the flickering flames of the burning choppers in full view on the deck.

Marcus cautiously reentered the hallway. Seeing it was clear, he crossed into the bunk room across the way. It, too, was clear, though it had no windows and no smoking guns. Again, he entered the hallway and crept forward, his MP7 pointed forward, his finger poised on the trigger. He entered the third bunk room, the last one on the right. The room was empty, but there was blood. Then he saw the severed head of the man who had tried to kill him moments before. It was not only lying on top of one of the bunk beds, but actually resting on the pillow.

88

The vacant eyes stared back at him.

Blood was splattered all over the ceiling. Marcus could only assume that upon the grenade's detonation, the man's head had bounced off the ceiling and landed on the pillow. Yet Marcus forced himself not to look away from the ghoulish sight too quickly. He had to study this face.

The man's hair was jet-black. His beard was thick and full. But there was no four-inch scar. He was too young, barely twenty years old, Marcus reckoned. This was not Alireza al-Zanjani, and that was too bad. He knew President Clarke had ordered them to capture the Iranian alive. Then again, that was the order of a commander in chief who had never been in combat.

Marcus shuddered and turned away, moving back into the hallway, where the heat was unrelenting. There was just one more room to check. He could still hear Warner engaged in a firefight. It occurred to him to simply toss a fragmentation grenade into the last room and sprint back to give Warner a hand. Yet he knew they were also under orders to gather any intelligence that they possibly could. He'd found no papers or computers thus far, but there was always a chance he could stumble on something useful.

Crossing the hallway, he stepped into the last bunk room, this one also bathed in the eerie glow of the flickering flames. Through the blown-out windows, he could see a half-dozen SEALs down on the deck gathering bodies of their fallen brothers along with their weapons and ammo. Just then, Marcus heard someone on the radio saying the deck had been cleared of tangos and asking Callaghan—now effectively the commander of this operation—if the choppers could return from their holding pattern and start picking up the dead and wounded. But Marcus never heard the answer.

For that split second, he'd let himself get distracted by the scene unfolding on the deck. He never saw the man crouched on the top bunk to his right. But suddenly the man leaped at him. Blindsided, Marcus collapsed to the ground. His weapon fell from his grip and skittered across the floor.

Marcus was sprawled out on his stomach. All his attacker needed to do was shoot him in the back of his head or run a blade across his throat.

Instead, the man lunged for the MP7. Marcus realized the man either had no weapon or was out of ammo. He also realized the man— clearly an Iranian commando—had made a terrible mistake. Marcus sprang forward and tackled him, flipping him over. He drove his right fist into the center of the man's face and felt the cartilage of his nose crunch. Marcus's left fist landed the next blow with nearly equal ferocity. Blood flowed down the man's face and beard as Marcus kept raining savage blows down one after the other until the man was able to pull up a knee and with surprising force kick Marcus off him. Marcus was flung across the room and crashed into one of the bunks.

The man sprang for his jugular. Marcus smashed him across the face again before he could get a firm grip. The two men were rolling across the floor, each trying to gain the upper hand until the Iranian again lunged for the gun. This time he got it and began to pull it toward him. Marcus kicked him as hard as he could in the stomach and sent the man reeling. It bought him about half a second. He scrambled to his feet and leaped on the man, trying to pull the gun away but without success. All he could think to do was to chomp down on the man's arm and bite. The man screamed. The gun went off. But Marcus didn't release until the man finally dropped the gun. Marcus kicked it away and then began pummeling the man's face again.

It wasn't going to be enough. Marcus wasn't going to be able to simply knock the Iranian unconscious. He was going to have to kill him. He reached for his Sig Sauer, but the man shifted his weight and maneuvered a stunning reversal that put him on top.

Marcus was on his stomach again, and before he knew it, the man had grabbed a bedsheet, wrapped it around Marcus's throat, and was squeezing it tighter and tighter. Marcus knew he was either going to be strangled to death in the next few seconds or the man was going to snap his neck. Marcus tried to scream for help but couldn't get any air in or out. He felt his face turning purple and his eyes bulging out of their sockets. His lungs were burning. Nothing he did to break free was working. The man was simply too heavy to shake off.

An explosion rocked the room. An instant later the man went limp and slumped to one side. Marcus—his ears ringing—feverishly unwrapped the sheet from his neck and began to suck in as much air as he could while he turned over to see just what had happened.

There in the doorway stood Warner, the barrel of his pistol still smoking. He had saved Marcus's life for a second time.

"Clear," the SEAL said quietly.

Marcus nodded and Warner pulled him to his feet. Together, they rolled the Iranian over. But it wasn't al-Zanjani.

As they exited the first-floor, port side door, Warner broke right and Marcus broke left.

The storm was rapidly worsening. Jagged sticks of lightning flashed all around the tanker, nearly blinding Marcus until he switched off his night vision goggles. Bone-rattling booms of thunder made it almost impossible to hear anything over the radios. Unrelenting sheets of rain completely drenched him. And the deck was now pitching and swaying with growing ferocity.

Marcus checked the stern section of the ship. He found plenty of dead Iranians, though none of them was al-Zanjani. He checked them all for intel but found nothing. Nor did they have any weapons or ammo. All of that must have been cleared earlier by the SEALs he'd seen from the second-floor window. Finding no one alive, he finally came around the engine house and rejoined Warner, who had found Callaghan. Together, they were guarding the starboard door to the ship's lower levels and waiting for him.

"*Anything?*" Callaghan yelled.

"No," Marcus yelled back. "*All clear.*"

"*And upstairs?*"

"*Secure.*"

"*You okay?*"

Marcus shrugged. "*I'll be fine.*"

"*You don't look fine.*"

89

Only then did Marcus realize blood was streaming down his face.

Given the adrenaline pumping through his system and the soaking rain, he hadn't noticed it. Callaghan pulled a first aid kit out of his backpack, but Marcus waved it away. They had far more important matters to deal with.

"What's the plan, Commander?" Warner asked.

"Now that we're secure up here, I've ordered the Seahawks back in," Callaghan shouted back. "The first wave of choppers will load up the wounded and get them back to the carrier. The second will load up the bodies of our dead and take them back as well. They'll come back empty to pick us up—us and the warheads."

"What's the status down below?" asked Marcus.

Callaghan shook his head. "It's bad. I've already lost three men. Another is critically wounded. That's why I need you two. Follow me and pick up those boxes of ammo. We need to finish this thing off, get those nukes, and get off this wreck."

Marcus nodded and followed Callaghan and Warner down the stairs, each man bringing ammo to resupply their brothers down below. They soon passed two members of Red Team guarding the entrance to the second level below deck. But the main firefight was on the third level. There, Marcus found two more SEALs, each exhausted, running dangerously low on grenades and magazines, but maintaining their positions and preventing any IRGC fighters from reinforcing the troops on the main deck. At the same time, though, Iranian fire was making it impossible for the Americans to press forward and reach the warheads.

It was now clear why Red Team had gotten to the engine room without incident. The Iranian fighters hadn't been guarding the engine. They'd concentrated their defensive force here.

"That corridor goes down the starboard side of the ship," Callaghan shouted over the gunfire, ordering Warner to cover it.

"That one runs down the port side," he told Marcus while handing him an M79, the so-called pirate gun.

Marcus took it, moved to his position, and quickly fired a 40mm grenade down the darkened hallway. The explosion was deafening, the sound magnified by the steel walls and close quarters. Little good it did, however. The return fire commenced almost immediately. Marcus had never seen anyone use tracer rounds inside a building, much less a ship, but that's exactly what the Iranians were doing. When one tango paused to reload, another seemed to open fire almost instantly. These guys didn't seem worried about running out of ammo. They clearly had prepared for this eventuality.

But what was their endgame? They'd obviously planned for the possibility of an American assault and figured out the best way to secure the only pathways to the warheads. But how did they expect to win? Were IRGC reinforcements coming? From where? The closest city was Shanghai. Were the Chinese coming to rescue the Iranian Revolutionary Guards? That seemed a stretch. But if it were true, why weren't they here already?

It was far too dangerous to stick his head into the corridor to get a look, even for a moment. So Marcus reloaded the M79, poked it around the corner, and fired without looking. There weren't many grenades left. Maybe a dozen—certainly no more than fifteen. Then what?

Marcus waved Callaghan over. He fired another grenade down the hallway, then pressed close to the commander's right ear. "Are we absolutely certain the warheads are down there?"

"Why else would they be holding their positions so fiercely?" Callaghan replied.

"Right, but are you certain, 100 percent?"

"What are you getting at?"

"Has anyone used a Geiger counter? Have we picked up any radiation?" Marcus fired another grenade, then looked back at Callaghan.

"No," he said. In all the chaos, no one had thought to do it. Callaghan told Marcus and Warner and the other two SEALs to keep firing. He'd be right back. Two minutes later, he returned with a black box about the size of a small suitcase. Inside was a dark-green handheld device. The moment he turned it on, the audio began crackling, and the needle began oscillating wildly. There was no doubt about it now. Radioactive materials had been through there, and recently.

Warner fired a burst of ammunition down his corridor, then borrowed the M79 to launch several grenades in the same direction.

Marcus turned to Callaghan. "Sir, it just occurred to me—I don't think there's oil on this ship. Why would there be? Any oil Pyongyang purchased from the Iranians would have been offloaded in North Korea, right? Why send the ship back to the Gulf unless it was empty? But in this case, it's not empty. I think the warheads are being stored in one of the steel bladders down below. It's possible the bladders have been retrofitted specifically to carry the warheads and that the access hatches to get them out have likely been welded shut."

"Maybe," Callaghan said. "What's your point?"

"Even if we could fight our way down to those hatches, it would take us hours, if not days, to get them open—so why should we? I know the president wants the warheads and al-Zanjani for that matter. But look at our situation. How many men have we lost so far?"

"No idea. Eleven just from Blue Team and my own guys."

"And how many wounded?"

Callaghan grimaced. "Too many."

"How many more Americans are we prepared to give up to fight a losing battle?"

"We're not losing, Ryker," Callaghan snapped.

"We sure ain't winning."

"And what exactly are you suggesting?"

"That we get out of here," Marcus said. "Let's get the dead and wounded off like you're already doing. Then order a full retreat and call in an air strike and blow this tanker to kingdom come."

90

"They want to do what?"

Every eye in the Situation Room was now riveted on the chairman of the Joint Chiefs. "Mr. President, that was Admiral Campbell, head of Pacific Command," the chairman began, trying hard to compose himself. "He reports that the situation on the tanker is deteriorating rapidly. To begin with, we have another SEAL commander KIA."

There were audible gasps around the room.

"Sanchez?" Clarke asked.

"Yes, sir."

They had all watched numerous Americans go down. But given the problem they were having with radio communications—no doubt because of the storm—none of them until that moment had realized that Sanchez had been one of them.

"Sir, the number of SEALs KIA and wounded is rising fast. All the injuries are critical; many are life-threatening. The admiral tells me that just moments ago another chopper went down out at sea during a refueling operation. No word on survivors or casualties yet. Rescue choppers are heading to the crash site as we speak."

McDermott had seen a lot of death during his time in the Corps. But the loss of so many of the bravest and most capable men who had ever worn the uniform in one night made him physically ill.

"Who's currently in command on that ship?" the president asked.

"Donny Callaghan."

"What can you tell me about him?"

"First-rate officer. Was serving as Sanchez's deputy and head of Red Team. Thirty-four years old. Joined the Navy when he was eighteen. Married. Two kids. From the south side of Boston."

"Do his men have control of the warheads yet?"

"No, Mr. President, they do not," the chairman said. "Nor do they have al-Zanjani. Yet they've asked me to bring you an unusual request."

"Which is?"

"That you authorize a full extraction of all our men off that tanker, followed by air strikes."

"Air strikes?"

"Yes, sir."

"To sink the ship?"

"That's affirmative, sir."

At this, CIA director Stephens blew up. "What are you telling us, Mr. Chairman—that your men want to cut and run before the operation is finished, before they get the warheads, before they grab al-Zanjani? *That's* their recommendation?"

"No, Director, it's not *my* men making that recommendation," replied the chairman.

"Then who is?" Stephens demanded.

"*Your* man."

"My man?"

"Ryker."

"You're telling me Marcus Ryker is recommending we sink the tanker?"

"Affirmative."

"What on earth for?"

"We're losing too many men, and we're going to lose more if we keep those choppers out in that storm any longer. He's arguing that if the objective is keeping Iran from getting the warheads, then we could just end this thing in the next two minutes with no further loss of American lives. The water where they are isn't super deep, but it's deep enough to make a recovery operation difficult to impossible—certainly not without a lot of preparation and activity. It couldn't be done in secret. There'd be no chance of an enemy getting the warheads later without us knowing about it and stopping it."

"Is he right?" asked the national security advisor.

"About the depth? Yes, sir. Admiral Campbell confirms they're in waters deeper than six hundred feet. It's not the Okinawa Trough, but it's deep enough."

"And the recovery of the warheads would really be impossible?" Clarke asked.

"Correct," said the chairman. "We've got the most sophisticated recovery equipment in the world. Yet the admiral says he doesn't think we'd be able to do it without surface support vessels and a lot of production. There's no way the Iranians or the Chinese or the Russians could pull it off without us knowing exactly what they were up to."

"Are the warheads in danger of going off, either from the air strikes or from pressure in deep water?" Clarke asked.

"No, sir," said the chairman. "The nukes can't be detonated from explosions alone. And there have been warheads lost at sea since the 1950s by us and the Russians through accidents of one kind or another. Some estimates put the number as high as fifty. But none of them have ever detonated. Nor have any of those been recovered."

"I don't like it," said the president.

"Nor do I," Stephens said.

Evans shook his head. "Me neither. I think we should stick with our game plan, however messy it becomes."

The president then turned to his defense secretary, who had been unusually quiet thus far.

"Cal, what do you think?"

"Mr. President, I don't like it any more than the rest of you," Foster said. "But as much as I'm loath to admit it, Ryker may be right. We're losing a lot of men and choppers at this rate. At this point the SEALs on scene are combat ineffective. The deck is secure. We could certainly order more men in to help them. But the storm is worsening. You've got raging fires at both ends of the ship. I'm not sure how long that tanker is going to stay afloat. This just might be our best option."

"What about al-Zanjani?" the president asked. "I wanted him taken alive."

"I realize that, sir," the SecDef replied. "But honestly, I think that moment has passed. I have to side with Ryker on this. It's time to get our men off that ship and tie this thing off before we lose anyone else."

Under almost any other circumstances, McDermott would have pressed for sending in more men and seizing those warheads. But not tonight. They'd already paid too high a price. And his friend was out there. It was a miracle Ryker wasn't dead already.

"Point taken," the president said. "Get our men off that ship and take it down."

91

They were down to just three grenades for the M79.

For the first time, Marcus wondered whether they were going to be able to contain the Revolutionary Guards at the other end of these two corridors. How many were down there? None of them knew for sure. Nor did they know what other tricks the Iranians had up their sleeves. What if they came charging forward? Could he and Warner and the others hold them off? They were quickly running out of ammo for their best deterrent weapon.

Marcus fired one more grenade, reloaded, and tossed the gun to Warner. He fired, reloaded, and tossed it back. As he did, Callaghan hung up the satphone. "Grab your gear and get your butts up on deck."

"Why?" asked Warner. "What's going on?"

"Washington just green-lit your plan, Ryker. We're bugging out."

Marcus fired the last grenade, then followed Callaghan and Warner up the metal stairs, the other two SEALs right behind him. Along the way, they set up several booby traps, then stepped out into the rain and shut and locked the door behind them.

Callaghan told Warner to take up a sniper's position in one of the bunk rooms on the second floor of the still-burning superstructure and instructed Marcus to take up a position at the base of the nearest crane—just in case.

"Take out anybody who makes it through that door or pops out any of the hatches on this deck," he ordered. "No one comes near those choppers. You got it?"

Both men nodded.

The Seahawks were on scene and onloading the dead and wounded near the bow of the ship, and that's where Callaghan and the remaining two SEALs now headed. Marcus and Warner moved to their positions even as they struggled to maintain their footing. The ship was rocking violently and the deck was not only slick with rain but littered with the bodies of dead Iranians, spent shell casings, and all manner of ropes and chains that had snapped off whatever they once tied down. Thankfully, Marcus made it to one of the cranes without slipping and cracking his head open. Beyond him, he could see a chopper pulling away and disappearing into the storm, heading east.

A moment later, another Seahawk pulled into position. There was too much wreckage to actually land on the deck, so the crew had to lower a winch to bring the men up. But Marcus could see that all the dead and most of the wounded had already been successfully evacuated. They were in the process of removing the last few wounded SEALs. Once everyone else was secure, he, Warner, and Callaghan would be the last to go. That suited Marcus just fine. He was honored to cover the backs of these brave men and was grateful the president had taken his advice.

Callaghan came over to check on him.

"You good?" he asked.

"Good, sir," Marcus replied.

"I've got a present for you," a smiling Callaghan said as he handed Marcus a bright-orange automatic inflatable life preserver. "Don't say I never gave you anything."

"I'll be fine," Marcus laughed.

"No, seriously, put it on," the SEAL commander said.

"You've got to be joking."

"Nope. I just learned the president and the NSC are watching live drone coverage of this extraction and the fireworks to come. I figured it might be nice if your old sergeant could pick you out of the crowd."

Marcus looked up in the sky, tempted to wave.

Callaghan persisted. "Put it on, Ryker—now. That's an order from the new commander of SEAL Team Six."

"Yes, sir," Marcus replied. "And congrats."

"Thanks," Callaghan said as Marcus donned the vest.

Callaghan slapped him on the back and headed over to the hovering chopper. Marcus shook his head and actually started to relax. *This was really it,* he thought. *After all they'd been through, the mission was almost over.*

Still, it was increasingly a challenge to maintain his balance as one massive wave after another pelted the ship. Marcus braced himself against the crane to help him stay upright. But no sooner had he done so than he heard the booby traps explode one by one.

Wiping the fog from his goggles, he gripped his MP7, made sure the safety was off, and aimed at the door to the lower decks. But that's not where the first Iranian emerged. Instead, a hatch about twenty yards behind him suddenly popped open. With the roar of the choppers and the pounding waves, Marcus didn't hear it happen. What he did hear was Warner opening fire from the second-floor window. That caused him to whip around just in time to see one of the Revolutionary Guards collapsing to the deck, his body riddled with bullets.

Marcus heard another explosion. Turning back to the door they'd just come through, he saw it had been blown off its hinges. An instant later, someone came charging through the doorframe, gun blazing.

Marcus reacted instantly, double-tapping him to the forehead. But just then the ship rocked hard to starboard. Marcus fought to stay on his feet as the body of the slain Revolutionary Guard slid across the deck and over the side of the ship, leaving behind a trail of smeared blood, though it was almost entirely washed away by the rains in a few seconds.

An instant later, another Iranian came bolting through the door, this one firing a grenade launcher. Marcus took aim and unleashed two bursts—one into the man's face, the other into his chest—killing him immediately as the grenade went soaring over Marcus's head, though not by much, exploding somewhere behind him.

Warner opened fire again. This time the rounds hit so close that Marcus felt a flash of anger. Warner was going to get him killed if he wasn't more careful.

That's when he saw it out of the corner of his eye. It was a blur at first, and then Marcus realized someone was coming straight for him.

92

WHITE HOUSE SITUATION ROOM, WASHINGTON, D.C.

Via the live drone feed, McDermott could see what Marcus Ryker could not.

Another tango had crawled out an open hatch onto the deck, some twenty yards to Marcus's right. But this Iranian had learned the lesson of the man who had gone before him. No sooner had he popped the hatch than he immediately opened fire at the second-floor window, forcing Warner to duck down. Having momentarily suppressed the SEAL's return fire, the Iranian began charging across the deck toward Marcus, aiming his AK-47 and pulling the trigger.

McDermott tensed, bracing himself for the muzzle flash sure to come, yet it didn't happen. Whether the man was out of ammunition or his gun had jammed, McDermott could not know. But as the Iranian closed the distance on Marcus—who was looking the opposite direction—Warner popped back up and took aim. His first shots went wide, so he fired again. But when these, too, missed their marks, Warner simply stopped, clearly fearing he might hit Marcus rather than the Iranian.

With nothing to stop him now, the man lowered his shoulder and blindsided Marcus, sending him and his weapon hurtling across the pitching deck.

Only later would someone tell McDermott that at that moment he had jumped to his feet and yelled at the monitor in the Situation Room. He would never remember doing it. What he would remember was the knock-down, drag-out fight to the death that ensued.

The first thing Marcus felt was his ribs cracking.

Then he was airborne. Time seemed to slow. He landed squarely on his back. All the breath in his lungs was forced out of him. He was in immense pain and gasping for air. Before he could react, whoever had just tackled him landed on top of him, driving his fist into Marcus's jaw.

The video from the drone feed would later show Revolutionary Guards emerging simultaneously from multiple doors and hatches. It would also show Warner, then Callaghan, opening fire in multiple directions. But at that moment Marcus saw and heard none of it. Rather, he felt his head slam back onto the deck. Had he not been wearing a helmet, he likely would have split his skull open or at least been knocked out cold.

Instead, Marcus instinctively drove his right knee upward, catching his assailant in the solar plexus. He simultaneously threw a right jab. As the deck shifted below him, however, the arc of his fist was altered slightly. The blow did not hit its mark dead-on, glancing instead off the man's left cheek. But the combination was enough to drive the man off him and give Marcus a moment—if only a moment—to suck in some desperately needed air.

Marcus rolled left. He tried to seize the Iranian by his jacket, by his combat vest, by something—anything—but the man slipped away. The two scrambled to their feet. As they did, Marcus found himself empty-handed while the Iranian had grabbed hold of a steel lashing rod and swung it like a baseball bat.

The first blow hit Marcus on the shoulder and sent him crashing back to the deck. Then the Iranian moved in for the kill. He began pummeling Marcus with the rod again and again. Marcus tried to get away, but the deck was so slippery and heaving so much he couldn't get his footing.

Over and over the rod came crashing down on Marcus's chest and back and head and arms. The pain was excruciating. Marcus tried to kick the man's legs out from under him, but to no avail.

He reached for his Sig Sauer, but it was not there. Using his arms to shield his face, Marcus desperately searched for his holster, finally spotting it several yards away. Somehow during their struggle, it had been torn away from him. He tried to move toward it, but the blows kept coming.

Then his eyes went wide. Marcus saw the Iranian pick up his MP7. He saw the man turn and aim the fully loaded submachine gun at his head. Marcus stared down the barrel of his own weapon, paralyzed, unable to think, unable to move. He heard a single shot ring out. The Iranian spun around and dropped to the deck. Marcus looked up and saw Warner in the window, the barrel of his rifle smoking, giving him a thumbs-up.

Lightning flashed. Thunder boomed. Marcus gave Warner a thumbs-up in return and began breathing again. He lay on his back for a moment in the unrelenting rain, staring up at the angry sky. Blood was once again pouring from his nose and mouth. He was certain he'd broken at least one rib and probably several. Still, he was thankful to be alive and ready to go home.

Finally forcing himself to his feet, he scooped up the MP7A1, clicked on the safety, and threw the strap over his shoulder. Then he limped over to the edge of the ship, where his Sig Sauer lay in its holster. He reached down, picked it up, and slid it into a zippered pouch on his combat vest so he couldn't lose it again. With one hand, he took hold of the metal railing. With the other he grabbed a nearby bollard, one of the steel posts used for mooring the ship at port. Steadying himself between the two, he stared down at the tangled web of severed ropes and broken cables and chains all around him, then at the roiling sea, letting himself be drenched again and again by spray from the waves slamming against the side of the ship.

He heard Warner calling to him, making sure he was okay. The SEAL had just descended from his second-floor perch. All enemies were down. Marcus thanked him for saving his life yet again, then responded that he was fine and would be there in a moment. Turning to his left, he realized that everyone, including Callaghan, was now on board the waiting chopper. Only he and Warner remained. The F-22s were no doubt inbound. It was time to go.

Just as he started heading for the bow of the ship, however, Marcus saw in his peripheral vision the Iranian suddenly rising to his feet. Stunned that the man was not dead, Marcus turned to face him and was stunned again. It was the first time Marcus had actually looked at the man's face and into his eyes, and at that moment he realized the figure now advancing upon him was Alireza al-Zanjani.

93

How had he not seen it before?

The beard. The scar. The man's identity was unmistakable. And now Marcus saw vengeance in his eyes.

He reached for the Sig Sauer, but al-Zanjani lunged for him, hitting him directly in the stomach. The two men crashed back to the deck, exchanging blow for blow. Marcus tried to drive his left knee upward, but the wounded Iranian was ready for him this time. He fended off the attack, then grabbed Marcus by the throat with both hands and squeezed.

Marcus tried everything he had ever learned to turn the tables on this guy, without effect. Al-Zanjani was taller, heavier. Marcus could gain no leverage. And there was a wildness in his eyes, the fevered look of a man possessed.

Where was Warner? Where was the chopper? Wasn't there anyone who could finish this guy off?

No one was coming to his rescue. It was all happening too fast. Marcus realized he had to find a way to put this man down or he'd be dead in less than a minute. He tried in vain to move his legs, but they were pinned to the deck. His right arm was as well, though his left arm still had some range of movement. He groped blindly for the lashing rod. All he found was a piece of chain.

Marcus's eyes began to close. He was almost out of oxygen. He was losing consciousness. But suddenly the deck heaved again. Al-Zanjani's weight shifted and he momentarily lost his grip. Marcus's eyes shot open. He sucked in a lungful of air and pivoted to the right. In the same motion, he brought his left hand whipping around. The chain struck the Iranian in the side of the head and opened a large and bloody gash.

Both men scrambled back to their feet, but Marcus seized the initiative. Whirling the chain twice over his head, he built up some momentum and then struck hard, wrapping the chain around the Iranian's neck until it had effectively created a noose. Then, moving behind al-Zanjani, Marcus pulled the two ends of the chain in opposite directions with every ounce of strength he had left. The man's eyes bulged. He choked and flailed and gasped for air. His feet were kicking wildly, but Marcus was careful to stay behind him and kept pulling the chain for all that he was worth. It was working. Unless al-Zanjani could maneuver a reversal, it would now be him who was dead in less than a minute.

Marcus saw Warner running toward him. He had his weapon raised but couldn't take a shot without killing them both. Meanwhile, al-Zanjani continued to thrash wildly, a trapped animal desperate to get free. Marcus kept pulling, kept squeezing, until the Iranian made his final, brazen move. They were stumbling over a bollard, and as they did, al-Zanjani suddenly lifted his right leg and pushed off the bollard, driving all his considerable weight backward and sending them both crashing over the side of the ship.

Marcus had only a split second to fill his lungs with air before he slammed into the swirling waters. Yet despite the searing impact of falling more than twenty feet and hitting the water headfirst, Marcus never lost or loosened his grip. They were sinking fast, but Marcus kept squeezing. Al-Zanjani was going crazy. Though he couldn't possibly have much air left in him, he kept rocking and swiveling from side to side, feverishly trying to turn his body, trying to use his legs to kick Marcus away from him and break for the surface. But Marcus wouldn't let go.

McDermott watched in horror as the two men fell over the ship's side.

He watched them hit the water, then sink below the waves. He stood staring at the monitor, waiting for one of them, either of them, to resurface. But neither did.

The video feed zoomed out a bit, then more, providing a wider view. McDermott continued staring at the heaving, pitching, burning ship and the solitary figure of the lone Navy SEAL operator standing at its edge, looking into the brewing cauldron of the East China Sea.

Thirty seconds passed. Then a minute. Then two. Then three. No one resurfaced.

McDermott staggered back to his chair and watched as Warner hung his head and returned to the waiting, hovering chopper.

Was that it? Was there nothing they could do? Why hadn't Warner jumped in after them? Why hadn't he tried to save Ryker's life?

Down they went.

Marcus's ears popped. His lungs were burning. So were his arms and hands. He could not see the surface. He could no longer make out the lights of the chopper. They were in total darkness now. But finally, *finally*, he felt something in al-Zanjani's neck give way. His body went limp. Marcus pulled the chain even tighter as they kept descending, just to be sure. But at last he let go, and the man drifted away.

Marcus reached for the cord on his life vest and pulled it like the cord of a parachute. It inflated instantly, and Marcus shot back to the surface like a bullet. Moments later, he broke through the waves, coughing and sputtering, then pulled a flare from his combat vest and fired it into the sky.

Soon the last of the helos moved into position over him. Both Callaghan and Warner—now wearing scuba gear—dove into the sea. The crew lowered a rescue basket to them. Marcus insisted he could climb into the basket on his own but quickly discovered this wasn't true. His body was far more broken and battered than he'd realized. He needed all the help the SEALs gave him.

Two minutes later, they were all safely on board the Seahawk and clearing the strike zone. Marcus was wrapped in blankets and given a tank of oxygen and propped against the window that would give him the best view. Callaghan handed him a headset so he could listen to the voices of the F-22 pilots on their final approach. And soon enough, it happened. The pilots launched their Hellfire missiles and each one hit its target. The enormous explosions briefly turned night into day as the tanker disintegrated and slipped beneath the waves.

A medic began treating him, but Marcus paid him little mind. His eyes were heavy. He knew he would be asleep as soon as the adrenaline from the battle with al-Zanjani faded from his bloodstream. But before he drifted away, he found himself wondering about Pete Hwang in Okinawa, about Oleg in Tokyo, about Claire Vinetti and Jenny Morris in Moscow, about Annie Stewart, probably facing charges in D.C. Were they safe? Were they okay? What about his sisters and his mom? What about Elena's parents and sisters back in Colorado and the Emersons in Washington? He missed them all.

Marcus had no idea what his future held. Nor did he care. Not here. Not now. There would be time enough to think about his new position in the CIA and how long he would really stay there. For now, all he cared about was getting home and getting well and reconnecting with the family and friends he had neglected for far too long.

Elena and Lars were gone and there was nothing he could do about it. It saddened him immensely but no longer angered or depressed him. He had finally made his peace. He knew he would see them again one day, and he looked forward to that reunion more than anything else.

For now, though, he had to start living again.

ACKNOWLEDGMENTS

When you write your first novel, you just hope your parents can find it at a bookstore within a hundred miles of their house. Not that it becomes a *New York Times* bestseller. Or garners invitations to speak on radio and television programs. Or opens doors to travel and speak and to write even more books, some of which will be read by kings and presidents and spy chiefs.

Yet miracles can happen. This is now my fourteenth novel, and I must admit, I'm still stunned by the miracle that I get to do this not just for a living but for fun.

Time and space do not permit me to thank everyone who makes this possible. But there are some I want to—and must—publicly thank.

Scott Miller has been my literary agent and my friend since my first novel, *The Last Jihad*, and he and the Trident Media Group remain the best in the business.

The Tyndale House publishing team is stellar—Mark Taylor, Jeff Johnson, Ron Beers, Karen Watson, Jeremy Taylor, Jan Stob, Dean Renninger, Caleb Sjogren, Erin Smith, Danika King, the entire sales force, and all the other remarkable professionals who make Tyndale an industry leader.

Our award-winning PR team—Larry Ross, Kristin Cole, Steve Yount, and Kerri Ridenour and their colleagues—is first-rate and a joy to work with.

June "Bubbe" Meyers and Nancy Pierce work with me at November Communications, Inc. They handle everything from my schedules to flights to finances and so much more with a heart of love and attention to detail.

I'm especially grateful for my parents, Leonard and Mary Jo Rosenberg, and to all my extended family and Lynn's, for their love, wise counsel, and prayers.

Thank you to our four wonderful sons: Caleb, Jacob, Jonah, and Noah—and now to Caleb's lovely wife, Rachel. I cannot imagine life without you five, and I treasure every moment with each of you.

There is no one, however, who compares to my precious Lynn. She has not only been my amazing and wonderful wife for twenty-eight years, she has also been my best friend in the world. I'm so grateful for her love and encouragement and counsel and companionship. I certainly don't deserve her, and I cannot imagine life without her. Her faith inspires me. Her love comforts me. Her creativity knows no bounds. I want to be just like her when I grow up.

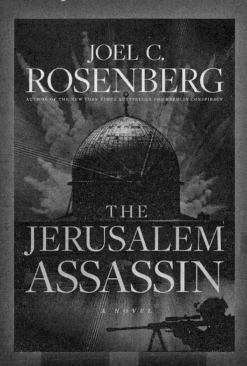

Sign up for Joel's "What's the Story" e-newsletter to receive exciting updates on world news you should know about.

Visit www.joelrosenberg.com to sign up for the semi-monthly newsletter.

CP1456

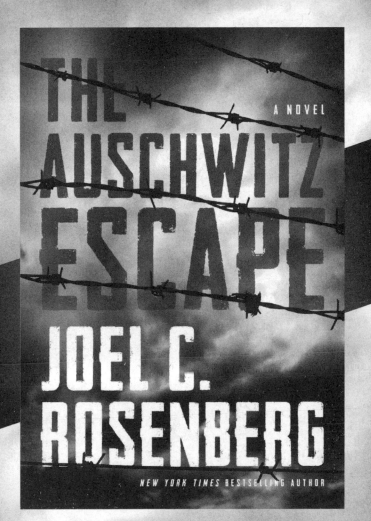

FROM *NEW YORK TIMES* BESTSELLING AUTHOR

JOEL C. ROSENBERG

"IF THERE WERE A *FORBES* 400 LIST OF GREAT CURRENT NOVELISTS, JOEL ROSENBERG WOULD BE AMONG THE TOP TEN. HIS NOVELS ARE UN-PUT-DOWNABLE."

STEVE FORBES, EDITOR IN CHIEF, *FORBES* MAGAZINE

★ ★ ★ ★ ★ ★ ★ ★ ★ ★ ★

FICTION

J. B. COLLINS NOVELS
THE THIRD TARGET
THE FIRST HOSTAGE
WITHOUT WARNING

THE TWELFTH IMAM COLLECTION
THE TWELFTH IMAM
THE TEHRAN INITIATIVE
DAMASCUS COUNTDOWN

THE LAST JIHAD COLLECTION
THE LAST JIHAD
THE LAST DAYS
THE EZEKIEL OPTION
THE COPPER SCROLL
DEAD HEAT

THE AUSCHWITZ ESCAPE

NONFICTION

ISRAEL AT WAR
IMPLOSION
THE INVESTED LIFE
INSIDE THE REVOLUTION
INSIDE THE REVIVAL
EPICENTER

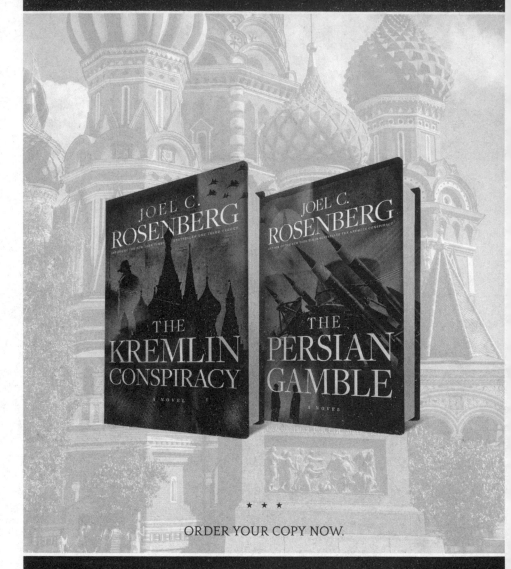